GRANDMA'S BFF DOES COKE

David A. Thyfault

ISBN 978-1-943650-82-8

Library of Congress Control Number 2018910309

Published by BookCrafters, Parker, Colorado.

This book may be ordered from online bookstores.

In Memory of Doris Sourwine

*The author's sweet mother-in-law
spent several years in memory care facilities,
from which many of the lines in this book originated.*

NOTE: These characters were inspired by real people.

Grandma Pauline
Stump
P-Pa
Me-Ma
Michael McFadden
Jared, Yvonne and Tanya
Edna Kline

ACKNOWLEDGEMENTS

Shirley Kelly - Cover Girl (left)
Maggie Mainzer - Cover Girl (right)
Stacie Thyfault - Cover Photographer
Donna MaCauley - Director of
RiverPointe Senior Community
Mark Carbone - Small Aircraft Expert
George Andrews - Law Enforcement
Yvonne Root - Cross Country Trucker
Mark Walker for the way he pronounces the word "exactly"
Dan Rhode - Gun knowledge.
Liz Netzel - Chief Editor
Rickie Fitzsimmons - Volunteer Editor
Nathan Fisher - Cover Designer
BookCrafters

1

*S*enior Identity Theft! Edna Kline scoffed as she observed the title of a pamphlet that she'd just pulled from her P.O. box. As the director of both the Assisted Living and Memory Care wings of Meadowlark Flats, one of southern California's larger senior communities, Edna had seen plenty of similar booklets, but she didn't need a pamphlet to know about crimes against seniors. At 62 and a tad on the petite side, her plastic surgeon had erased her wrinkles and her beauty parlor whisked away the gray from her dark brown hair, lending her a aura of confidence that brought more potential victims to her fingertips than nerve endings.

According to most of the literature on the topic, the majority of vulnerable seniors still lived at home and if they were indeed being ripped off, they needed to look no further than their family members or in-house caregivers to see who was exploiting them.

Out there, in private homes, demented grandma types might have a nice wedding ring or some diamond earrings that could be easily palmed and later pawned off; or a weak-minded and lonely grandpa might be a sap for a sob story about his granddaughter's rising rent. Good ole gramps could easily be duped into covering the expense.

In other cases, unethical piranha-like family members could be added to grandpa's checking account—"for his own good," of course. Not ironically, in most of these situations, the family member's love ran out precisely when the checking account did.

Closer to home, Edna Kline knew of a case in which the son of an elderly woman had more financial woes than the federal government. Whenever the devious offspring needed money, his mother agreed to cover his losses, after which they went to the bank to get the money—in cash. That way Sonny Boy could hide his sins from the IRS, his bill collectors, his wife and his drug dealer.

In another situation, a very ill elderly woman was confined to bed while her hubby and his younger gal-pal played mommy and daddy in the back of the house. They regularly sneaked out with the credit card and dined in nice places before returning home and sleeping together just down the hall from the bedridden woman. Fourteen months later, all of the savings account and the girlfriend disappeared.

Some of the more sophisticated cons against the older folks originated in foreign countries. Heartless callers adopted excited voices and told their victims that he or she had just won the Publishers Clearinghouse Sweepstakes. The elderly person was told that the local TV station was holding the check for millions of dollars and needed to schedule a time to drop off the winnings and film it all. All the winner/victim had to do was verify his or her identity with a Social Security number and some credit card information and that triggered the race to see how much money could be skimmed before the door closed on the con.

Other than the foreign scams, most of bad guys only had one person they could rip off. For them it was like going to a friend's home for dinner. You have to eat whatever is served. But Edna's situation was different. A lot different. She had a buffet full of old peeps with cash stashes just waiting for her to backslide her hands into their pockets - and she'd been doing it for years.

Ironically, regardless of whether the bad types were one-timers or chain scammers they were useful pawns to Edna in her job. It was her duty to share the info in the pamphlets and similar stories with her potential new residents and thereby motivate them to move into Meadowlark Flats where those kinds of things "couldn't happen." Naturally, none of the Meadowlark Flats clients had any way of knowing that most of the garden-variety perps were rank amateurs compared to the upstanding Edna.

One of the ways Edna kept the home office from finding out what she was up to was to keep an extra, off-site P. O. box for her nefarious affairs. With all her bases covered, today was like most other days in that she dropped by the Post Office on her way to work and she'd just picked up several pieces of mail including the aforementioned pamphlet and an envelope from Henrietta Berkwell's bank.

A three-year resident at Meadowlark Flats, Mrs. Berkwell fit one of the profiles Edna Kline looked for. In addition to having failing vision and difficulty getting around without her walker, Mrs. Berkwell's Social Security number and checking account information were part of her original file. It wasn't difficult for Edna to get other pertinent information out of Henrietta when she wanted it. A lot of seniors, including Mrs. Berkwell, were lonely and loved to talk about themselves.

Seemingly innocent friendly chats between Edna and Mrs. Berkwell revealed she had no children, she was from clear across the country in New Orleans, and had been divorced before she married Mr. Berkwell, who owned a small chain of very successful hardware stores. Naturally, he took care of all their financial matters until he passed away nine years ago and the family attorney urged her to sell the business.

Fortunately for Edna, Mrs. Berkwell still had lots of that

money hanging around and never used computers, but she did allow Edna to set up online banking to make things easy for Edna to help her pay her bills. But most importantly, nobody else had reason to check on the woman or pay attention to her finances and that's what Edna liked.

All of that enabled Edna Kline to hop online and apply for a new credit card in Mrs. Berkwell's name. After it was approved and mailed to Edna's P.O. box, the internet usually served as Edna's shopping mall. She had the statements and smaller packages sent to her box and paid the debt online, from Mrs. Berkwell's savings account. The ever-trusting Mrs. Berkwell didn't even know she had a new card in her name, let alone how much pleasure Edna was deriving from it.

Bottom-lining it, Edna Kline's situation enabled her to know which seniors had lots of money and weren't any good at keeping track of it. Henrietta Berkwell was one of her patsies and now Edna had a good reason to go shopping for a new dining room set for her townhome.

After that, she expected to check in on Mr. Cranston's account. He hadn't made a donation to Edna in a while.

She scoffed again. When it came to scamming seniors, it was a lot like dessert time at the buffet: There were plenty of sweet options.

2

Blood. Where the hell was the blood, people? At 19, medium height and build, Stump narrowed his eyes to mere slits as he stomped across the smallish campus. What a friggin' waste of time. A seasoned criminology professor, even in an insignificant town like Carlsbad, California ought to be able to make an *Intro to Forensics* class remotely interesting, but no; that butt-brained instructor made a video of a murder scene duller than a slow-motion rerun of a snail's nap.

Stump rotated the bill of his Nike cap and wiped at his stubby light-brown hair. The limited amount of blood meant the victim was killed somewhere else. He slowed. Maybe he was expecting too much of his classmates. After all, they'd only been out of high school for nine months. Some of them had never been to a real crime scene or sniffed out their own cases.

They hadn't knelt at the foot of a murder victim, let alone one they'd known personally, as Stump had. He removed his cap and wiped the sweat off his forehead. Maybe he should cut them some slack.

Naw. Bullshit. This was second semester. Those bookworms ought to be beyond the basics by now. Instead, they'd wasted the whole hour belaboring the victim's bulleted skull and never discussed the diamond earrings, thereby eliminating robbery-gone-wrong as a motive.

He scowled. His long-time buddy, James, had been correct several months back when he pointed out that they were bored with the basics because they'd already solved some heavy-duty cases. That's why they'd been taking turns cutting classes and updating each other in between.

Stump glanced ahead to the little café on the other side of the street. At least now he could chill for a while with his buds. Suddenly one of his familiar ringtones interrupted. *Warning!* it said. *Your dad is calling, and he sounds pissed. See if you can lie your way out of this one.*

Stump hoped against impossible odds that his adoptive father, Myles, had miraculously decided to cut loose some of Stump's trust money to upgrade his piece-of-crap truck. "Hey, Myles. Wasup?"

"I'm sorry, Stump . . . "

There they were. The three words, as predictable as gravity. Myles was *sorry*. Yeah, right. As if that would land Stump behind the wheel of a chick magnet.

Myles blathered on, through the same routine Stump had been hearing for six long years. Myles would like to help but Stump should save his money for more important things. Someday he'd understand. Yawn. The compromise would be next, followed by the part where Stump should fall to his knees in eternal gratitude—just to get his own damn money.

"You got a hell of a lot of miles out of that truck—"

But . . .

"But, I don't think we need to spend a lot of money right now—"

So . . .

"So, I've wired ten grand to your checking account. You can get another grand or two by trading in the truck."

Stump shook his head. It was more difficult to get a few bucks out of his own trust than it was to get James to bottle up a fart, which he once tried. Disappointed, but not surprised, Stump hung up. It would be two more years before he'd be his own trustee; then he could make his own damn decisions. He hustled across the street, against the red light. At the other side, he reached a former gas station-turned-café. Inside, the familiar whiff of bacon seemed to be saying, welcome back. The permit above the coffee station suggested that Zaklynn Elizabeth Lee was the proprietor of Lee's College Café, but Stump and his pals usually referred to the joint as *Zax Place*.

If forced to tell the truth, Stump would admit that he'd had bedtime fantasies about Zax. Why not? She was attractive, smart and responsible. But he never told her what was on his mind, partly because she was 10 years his senior and might pat him on the head like a puppy and dismiss his advances. But the bigger issue had to do with Zax's 9-year-old daughter, Denise. If Stump were to get into a serious relationship with Zax, he would become something akin to a stepfather to Denise, and that was too bizarre on several levels.

It had been three years since he'd met his first go-all-the-way girlfriend, Maria. At the time, he thought they were "in love" but she proved to be too flirty. After that, he got laid from time to time, including after he got to college, but *here-a-boink-there-a-boink* wasn't meaningful enough. Nearly all of the women he'd dated said they were primarily looking to "have a good time." A good time? Hell, you could do that at a nose-picking contest. It all rang shallow.

Inside the café, Stump scanned the dining area. As expected, James, his old buddy from high school, was butt-parked in their usual booth near the back window. James had always reminded Stump of Clark Kent, but unlike Superman's alter ego, James had a mischievous side. Born in South Africa, James was as white as a bride's dress, but he'd already tweaked countless people by checking the African American box on formal papers such as job applications, medical records and resumes. Now Stump and James were roomies, along with James's *slightly pregnant* girlfriend, Yana, who waited tables at Zax Place and couldn't get enough of the social media sites.

One of the things Stump most liked about James came up whenever they were engaged in something sneaky. The dude had balls the size of coconuts.

"Sup?" James said as Stump slid into the squeaky-clean booth.

Stump smirked. "Myles called about my truck."

"Did you tell him it wobbles all over the road and has over two hundred thousand miles on it?"

"He don't care, bro. He wired me ten grand, but I can't get nothin' decent with chump change like that."

"You want something, Stump?" Yana interrupted. A Russian exchange student, Yana had met James online the previous summer. They'd barely traded first names when she declared that she wore a one-inch lift in her right shoe because that leg was shorter than the other.

As far as Stump was concerned, that was another good thing about James. The dude never cared much about superficial stuff like that, nor her hairy armpits. James was more concerned with how interesting somebody was, and Yana fit that bill perfectly. In addition to coming from another country, and immersing herself in the cyber world, Yana enjoyed sex as much as James did, which was one of the reasons she was in mid-pregnancy with James's baby. Even though it was against the rules for the three of them to live in the same apartment, Stump was all for it. Yana was a clean freak, not a full-blown germaphobe, but a hell of a lot better than Stump and James would have been, combined. What college guys couldn't appreciate a roommate like that?

A minute later, Yana dropped off Stump's drink and limped toward the main entrance where a newcomer had just walked in. "How was class?" James asked Stump. "As bad as the others?"

"True that. Victim's head caught a bullet, but there was

no blood. All those brainiacs got bogged down in irrelevant bullshit like the angle of the bullet so we missed important clues. In the next class, when it's your turn, all you gotta do is check the victim's nails and jewelry, and you'll be ahead of everybody."

James flipped Stump a "thumbs up" just as the new customer reached their booth and looked deep in Stump's eyes. "The waitress said you're Neal Randolph. Is that true?"

Huh? Very few people used Stump's given name. He looked at the stranger. Fortyish, Stump guessed. "Yeah, but most people call me Stump. Who're you?"

"My name's Xander Brooks. I'm your father."

3

Stump looked more closely at the new guy. The jeans and casual buttoned shirt made him resemble a deliveryman. This had to be some kind of gag because the father issue had been a bone of contention ever since first grade when Stump's queries about his missing daddy never garnered a satisfactory answer. When he was 13 he finally learned that he was the byproduct of a stupid thing his mom did at a college fraternity party.

She'd said that she went with a girlfriend, but neither of them knew anybody else at the party. After everybody was good and drunk, they took turns going upstairs in a sex game they called NQA, for "No Questions Asked." When it was Stump's mother's turn, she was paired up with some guy she didn't even know, which was the point. So, she did the same thing everybody else did and staggered off to the bedroom.

Later, when she found out she was pregnant, she couldn't even remember what the guy looked like. Her girlfriend didn't know anything about him either. In fact, there were so many people at that party nobody could have known everybody who was there; so, pregnant or not, it was simply too futile and embarrassing to try and find the guy.

Furthermore, Stump's biological father wouldn't have any way of knowing who Stump's mother was, let alone that he'd knocked her up. All of that meant the nut who'd just claimed to be Stump's dad had to be somebody else.

Stump considered chasing the guy off, but it was the first time anything interesting had happened that morning, so he elected to play along, to see if he could figure out the dude's angle. Stump eyeballed James for some sign of a smartass smirk, which would indicate that James was behind it all, but James held a straight face. "Let him in, bro," Stump said.

James scooted close to the window just as Yana dropped by with a cup of hot water and a teabag for the new dude. The newbie slid next to James and nodded at Yana as if to thank her.

Suspicious, Stump spoke first. "Alright, dude. Let me hear it. What's your angle?"

The guy plopped the teabag in his cup. "It's no angle, Neal. It's the real deal."

"Yeah, right. What did you say your name is?"

"Xander Brooks. I can show you my ID if you'd like."

"Naw. That wouldn't prove anything. So what do you want?"

"I don't really want anything, just to introduce myself and see if we could get to know each other."

"Then what? You going to try and sell me something? I could use a car if you can get me one for wholesale."

"I'm just a retired truck driver. I don't have anything to sell."

"C'mon, dude. You can do better than that. You're too young to be retired."

Xander tilted his head. "Technically, you're correct. More precisely, a few years ago I was driving an 18-wheeler and dropped off a load at the airport in Phoenix. There was an accident. I got racked up pretty good and couldn't drive any more. We settled a lawsuit and I've been on disability ever since. Disability ain't exactly the same as retirement, but I thought it was close enough for now."

"Sounds close enough to me, bro," James said, while sniffing at the air.

Stump snickered. If James was in on the gag, he was playing it pretty straight. "Alright then, so what makes you think we're related?"

"Not merely related, Neal. We're father and son. And to answer your question, your mother told me, of course."

Stump clucked his tongue. "My mother, huh? When was that?"

"A few weeks ago."

Not possible; and something else had become certain. James wasn't in on a gag. James knew all about the house fire that killed Stump's mother and wouldn't have told a prankster to say something that was so obviously incorrect.

"That must have been interesting," Stump said to Xander Brooks.

"She said she'd once seen some mail that suggested you might be in Palmdale. I knew the town and I knew how old you were. I figured you'd be in high school so I asked around and found some guys who knew you. They said you enrolled in this college. From there, I found your landlord who said you hang out here."

Stump tipped his hat skyward. "That's a good one, dude, but you didn't do your homework. My mother died six years ago in a house fire. I was with her. Went to her funeral too. Unless she's come back from the dead, you're going to have to make up something better than that."

James wrinkled his brow and sniffed at the air again.

Meanwhile, Yana had circled back around, tapping at her cell as she frequently did. "Everybody okay here?" she asked.

Xander turned her way. "Would you mind waiting just a minute before moving on?"

Yana nodded as Xander returned his attention to Stump. "I can tell we're not going to get anywhere until you *do your homework,*" he said, making air quotes. "If I were in your situation, I'd probably be skeptical too, but I anticipated this." He mined his shirt pocket and withdrew two tiny test tubes and some cotton swabs. Turning to Yana, "You're Neal's friend, right? I'm trying to convince him that I'm his biological father so I'm going to swab my mouth and ask Stump to do the same."

"I ain't doing no DNA test, dude," Stump said.

"Why not? What have you got to lose? If I'm wrong, nobody loses anything, but if I'm right—"

James nodded, spoke to Stump. "You've always wanted to know, bro."

"I agree with James," Yana said.

Xander swabbed his mouth and slid the little cotton-topped stick in a tube and capped it. He mined his pocket for a preaddressed stamped envelope and spoke to Yana. "Would you mind verifying this address online, just so Neal will know it's legit?"

A few iPhone taps later, Yana lifted her head. "He's right."

Xander slid one of the small test tubes Stump's way and held up a swab. "Okay, Neal, it's up to you."

Stump's eyes darted toward each person in the group. He finally sighed and took the swab. "You guys are all nuts. You'll see." He swished the swab on the roof of his mouth and inserted it in the tube. "This is dumb."

"Give it to Yana," Xander said before looking to her. "Would you mind dropping it all off at the Post Office? I've got a check here for $35 to cover the costs of the test, and here's a twenty-dollar bill for the tea and the postage and a tip for you."

Yana nodded and stuffed both tubes and the check in her apron pocket.

Xander mined his shirt again and pulled out a business card and added it to the mix. "Hang on to this, too. Neal is going to need it." Turning back to Stump, "I hope to hear from you soon . . . Son." Then he walked off and let the door gently close behind him.

"What the F was that?" James asked, while looking toward the kitchen.

Stump shrugged. "Had to be a con man who found out about my trust. Myles has always warned me about guys like that."

"He did look like you," Yana said.

James sniffed the air again. "Does anybody else smell smoke?"

Just then, Zax hustled into the dining area from the kitchen and flailing her arms above her short brown hair.

"FIRE!"

4

"FIRE! I NEED SOME HELP," Zax screamed before rushing back into the kitchen.

Everybody except a small family and Stump followed her. Seconds later and outdoors Stump hurried across the street and called 911.

"911 Dispatch. Is this an emergency?"

"Yes. There's a fire at Lee's College Café. Hurry!"

"Do you have an exact address?"

"It's right across the street from the College of Criminology. Please, get somebody here as quickly as possible."

"Do you see any address numerals on the building?"

"Oh. Uh . . . the numerals are 1818, but I don't know the street name. It's right on the corner."

"Is everybody safe, sir?"

"It's a damn fire," he said, recalling his mother's last few minutes. "Nobody is safe."

"But do you know if anybody needs medical assistance?"

"I dunno. There's a lot of smoke. I ran from the building, but my friends didn't follow me out. You'd better send two ambulances just to be certain—and those fire trucks—hurry."

"What exactly is the problem?"

"I already told you. It's a damn fire."

"I know that, sir, but what exactly is on fire? Do you know if it's a grease fire, electrical fire or something else?"

"No. I don't know any of that."

"What color is the smoke?"

"Color? Are you out of your friggin' mind? By the time you get done grilling me this place is going to burn to the ground and everybody will die."

"I'm trying to determine who to send, sir. Are there any other buildings close by that are in danger?"

"No. It's Lee's College Café. It's an old converted gas station. Don't you people know anything?"

"Gas station? Are there any gas pumps or fuel storage tanks?"

"What? No. It used to be a gas station but it's not any more. You've got to hurry. People will die."

"The fire department is just a few blocks away, sir. They should be there in a minute."

Just then he heard sirens. He slammed his cell in his pocket and rushed into the center of the street to wave them down, while out behind Zax's place, her daughter's dachshund Trixie howled at the high-pitched sirens.

A minute later the first fire truck rounded the corner and headed his way. He jumped up and down waving his arms as an ambulance and a paramedics' truck followed the fire truck. "Over here. Over here."

The first truck reached him as another truck blew around the corner, followed by another ambulance. Finally, two firefighters, a man and a woman, sprang off the first truck. The male grabbed a fire extinguisher and came toward Stump as a few bystanders began to gather. "They're in there," Stump said, pointing to Zax's place.

"Okay," the fighter said as he rushed forward. "You stay back out of the way."

Stump returned to the curb as three additional fighters jumped off the truck. One unrolled a hose in the direction of a fire hydrant that was fifty yards up the street. Another rushed toward the hydrant with a large wrench in hand. Other fighters opened large built-in storage cabinets along the side of the truck and extracted gas masks and fire extinguishers. By that time a dozen bystanders had gathered. The female fighter came in Stump's direction and urged everybody to step back so the other vehicles could get closer. Meanwhile, the paramedics rushed toward the building and the ambulances pulled a gurney onto the street.

Thank God. Things were finally happening. Stump could only hope they'd gotten there in time to avoid another tragedy. He looked back toward the building and saw some action inside through the incredibly thick cloud on the other side of the window. The fighter who'd just gone into the building was already coming back out. He propped open the front door and set his extinguisher down. Why wasn't he back in there putting the fire out?

Then Stump saw James coming out too. And Yana and the other customers who'd stayed behind; but where was Zax? The worst possibility entered Stump's mind. He crossed his fingers behind his back and then saw Zax coming, too. Thank God. It appeared everybody was safe.

A couple other firemen joined the first one and they all went back into the building, while Zax and James and Yana, covered in thousands of white flecks, came across the street to join Stump. "Is the building destroyed?" he asked.

Yana shook her head. "No. It's just a big mess," she said as Stump's cell rang. The 911 operator had called back.

"Hello," he said louder than he needed to. "They're finally here."

"Are you okay, sir?"

"Yes, but you asked too damn many questions. It took fifteen minutes to get any help. My friends could have died."

"I'm sorry it felt like that, sir, but it took six minutes from the time of your call to get the first responders on site."

"No friggin' way. You asked me at least twenty questions."

"It's all logged in, sir. If you're okay, I have to go now."

Huh? He must have been mistaken. "Uh. Yeah. I'm okay. I'm sorry I was such a jerk. It's just that my mom died in a fire a long time ago. I guess I overreacted."

"I understand, sir. Goodbye."

Humbled, Stump observed the emergency crews busily returning their equipment to its proper places. None of them seemed to be upset that they'd basically wasted their time.

Stump looked more closely at the thick layers of whiteness that covered his friends from head to toe. "I called 911," he said hoping they'd appreciate his concern for their safety.

"Yeah. I know," James said, "but we didn't need them."

By that time the lady fighter had joined them and patted Stump on the shoulder. "You did the right thing. It's always better to err on the side of safety."

Stump addressed James. "You guys look like you went through hell."

James scoffed. "It's pancake batter, dude. It was a grease fire."

"It'll take me all night just to get the batter out of my hair," Yana said.

Then Zax came out with Denise's dog on a leash and slumped into one of the patio chairs. She looked like a super thin 30-year-old ghost. "They're doing a final inspection," she said.

"What happened?" Stump asked. "Inside I mean."

"Somehow a miller moth got under the grill. It came flying out with its wings on fire and landed in the grease and I couldn't find the fire extinguisher. Fortunately I'd just got some supplies and had a couple large sacks of pancake batter. Once we threw it on the fire it went out pretty quickly, but the whole place is a mess and I don't have any insurance."

"We'll help you clean it up," Yana said.

"Thanks, but you guys don't understand. The college owns the property. The lease requires me to have insurance. But when they hear I couldn't afford it, they'll think I'm too careless and make me leave. I don't know what I'd do if I didn't have this place, and I don't want to move Denise. School is already hard enough for her." Zax's eyes filled with tears.

"We've got a fan back at our apartment," Stump said. "You can borrow that."

"That would just spread everything around."

James turned to Stump. "You freaked out, dude."

5

Candice Rohrbach, a thin young woman with brown shoulder-length hair had been one of Edna Kline's most reliable caregivers. In her third year at Meadowlark Flats, Candice worked the swing shift in the Assisted Living wing where residents needed minimal physical or mental aid with their meds or getting around or bathing or nearly anything else that didn't require excessive supervision.

Due to their conflicting schedules, Candice and Edna had a late afternoon appointment regarding Charles Dickey, one of the residents.

From behind her desk, Edna saw Candice approach. "Come in, Candice." she said. "Close the door behind you."

Candice sat and began. "I checked on Mr. Dickey a little bit ago to see if he wanted to join us today, but he's with some friends."

"So, what's on your mind?"

"Well, last night I was making my rounds and Mr. Dickey wanted me to look at his checkbook."

"Oh?"

"He showed me the ledger. Most of the entries were in his

penmanship – pretty sloppy – but there was another entry for three thousand dollars in another penmanship."

"Oh, that."

"Yeah. It was made out to somebody called *Specialty Services*. He thought you had something to do with it, but he couldn't remember. I told him I'd look into it and get back to him today, so I'm wondering what I should tell him."

Edna pressed her tongue against the roof of her mouth. She couldn't tell Candice that Specialty Services was her own sham company because that could bring an unwelcome end to one of her activities.

Knowing that certain residents had expendable income, but very little financial savvy, Edna approached selected people with a "simple and safe" way they could make some extra money by investing in a medication delivery company that Edna knew about. The potential new "investors" were assured that other residents were in the group too. That affinity usually lent the new folks the comfort they needed.

If the new investors were to ask for names of other participants in the group, they were told that Edna was obliged by law to preserve their privacy. Most of the investors never asked any additional questions because they believed that their profits were being reinvested, which they were—into Edna's IRA.

"It's an investment club," Edna said to Candice. "There are a few people around here who follow the stock market and so they pool their money and buy a few stocks together. I gave Mr. Dickey a receipt and an information letter. He must have lost it. You know how forgetful he can be."

"That's for sure. Can I take him another set of papers?"

"No. I'll take care of that, but I'm glad you came in early because I have something else I have to share with you."

"What is it?"

"I thought when you set this appointment that you already knew about the other information I heard about you?"

"Information about me? No I haven't heard anything like that."

Edna shook her head. "Well, I hate to have to tell you this, Candice, but I have to let you go."

Candice's eyebrows drew down. "What? You're firing me? But I'm one of your best workers."

"Yes, but I've heard that you're verbally abusive to residents at night when you help them with their baths. My sources tell me that you rush through everything so you don't have to work so hard."

"That's crazy. I love these people. I can't imagine who would say such a thing."

"Well I can't take any chances. I'll get you a couple weeks severance pay, but your termination is effective immediately. I'm sure you'll find some other work."

"But, don't I get a formal notice first?"

"I'm afraid not. I just don't want to take that kind of chance. Don't worry. I'll give you a good reference if you need it. Sorry."

As soon as Candice left, and Edna wouldn't have to worry about her disrupting Edna's applecart, Edna had another self-imposed chore.

She opened up a file of a very sick, cancer-ridden 84-year-old woman named Margareta Thorpe who was about to be transferred from the Assisted Living wing to the Hospice area. Mrs. Thorpe's husband and children had been very active in her care the last few months, but that didn't particularly matter for what Edna had in mind.

Edna called one of several life insurance companies that specialized in low-cost, guaranteed coverage policies for the final expenses of aging people up to age 85. Those expenses could include funeral costs, unpaid debts and medical bills or anything else that might be needed, all for as low as twenty bucks a month. Mrs. Thorpe didn't even have to get an exam.

It wouldn't take Edna long to set up a new policy on Mrs. Thorpe's life. While she was at it Edna declared herself as the beneficiary of the policy. Then when Mrs. Thorpe's final day came, Edna could cash in.

The risk/reward ratio was outstanding. Since Mrs. Thorpe's family was more proactive in her care than some of the other families, Edna would have to keep quiet about the policy and pay the monthly premiums out of her own funds. That way the family would never know about it. The only remaining risk was the policy automatically expired when the insured reached age 85—but based on Margareta Thorpe's health there was virtually no chance of that.

So, a few monthly checks from Edna of $25 each were sure to net her an eight thousand dollar reward, payable upon Mrs. Thorpe's demise. Until then, there was no way anybody else would know of the policy, nor could anybody force Edna to use any of the money for funeral services or anything else.

She placed the call.

6

When Myles Cooper first moved to Palmdale some twelve years ago, the drive to and from LA took forty-five relaxing minutes in which he could think through his job as a detective and his personal matters, such as how he'd overcome his alcoholism. Since that time hundreds of thousands of additional residents moved into the area and transformed the highways into slow-moving parking lots. As far as he was concerned, the term rush hour could be replaced with something akin to *the inch-along*.

It had been six years since Myles's last drink. He met Jean Randolph at an AA meeting and fell in love for the first time in a long while. Before long he'd met her adolescent son, Stump, who had more common sense than most adults. After that, there was a proposal and wedding plans, which went up in flames, literally, when Jean died in a house fire. That night Myles went on a one-night binge for the ages.

Afterwards he and Stump teamed up. It just made sense. The fire left both of them alone and they desperately needed each other. Just thinking about those early days with Stump made Myles grin. Life indeed got better when he adopted Stump. But all that had morphed, too.

Now, Stump was in college and Myles had fallen in love again. That was another reason the ride home seemed to take forever. Myles wanted to get home to see Katherine, whom he thought of as K-Bear. Especially tonight. Scheduled to get another six-years-sober chip from his AA club, he hoped she'd share the experience.

Until then, about all he could do was listen to his favorite country music station. He hit the on-button just in time for a traffic report.

"This is Tall Paul Bullward here in the KRAD studios. We're checking in with Sky-High Sly in Chopper One. It appears there's another dangerous situation on the Palmdale highway. What's going on this time, Sly?"

"You've got it correct, Paul," Sky-High Sly said. *"We're heading west, toward the 14 where we've got word of a pedestrian in the middle of the highway. Seems like we get a fender bender or some other problem in that area nearly every day, Paul. Now I see her, Paul. She appears to be an elderly woman, wearing a bathrobe and tennis shoes. She's trying to cross the highway for some reason. Wait a minute, Paul. Now she's stopped in the middle lane. She appears to be scared. This is not good. Cars are stopping dead. Others are swerving around her on either side. There are no parked cars in the vicinity so she must have walked, headlong, down the exit ramp. No stable person would do anything like that."*

Myles shook his head. He knew what they meant. His own mother, who lived with him and K-Bear, less than a mile from that stretch of highway, had a pretty good case of dementia. Most of the time she was the intellectual equivalent of a four-year-old. A former teacher and an avid reader, she could no longer comprehend books or articulate a three-sentence paragraph. Thank God K-Bear was a professional caregiver.

"In all my years as a traffic reporter, Paul, I've never seen anything like this. This elderly woman is obviously confused, yet people are flipping her off and yelling at her. Our listeners on the 14 are advised to get off the highway and take an alternate route. This area is going to be backed up for at least a couple hours."

Myles thought about several years earlier when his mother had moved in with him and Stump. Katherine was married at the time, but eventually she split the sheets with her ex and Stump went off to college. All of that prompted Myles to invite Katherine to stay in Stump's room.

"What's going on now?" Tall Paul Bullward asked Sky-High Sly.

"Traffic is at a standstill, Paul, and our pedestrian has made her way to the cement barrier that separates the east and west-bound traffic. This is awfully dangerous. I don't know how she can get back across five lanes to the right shoulder, where she'll be safer. We're going to spin back to the tail end of the congestion. Hopefully everybody will see the chopper and figure out something is going on. No matter how it ends, this one is already a big mess."

Myles shook his head and his thoughts returned to Katherine. He should have known that nature would take its course. Before long they began sleeping in the same bed. Thus far, he hadn't told Stump how serious the relationship had become because he wasn't certain how Stump would handle the matter, given that Myles had once loved Stump's mother.

"Wait a minute, Paul. Wait a minute. We've got our first accident, nearly a mile back from where all this started. Oh, no. There's another crash. A pickup truck just got sideswiped. Oh, my God. People in the back of the line are slamming on their brakes and trying to get out of each other's way. You had to know something like this was going to happen."

Myles clucked his tongue. He hated that stretch of road. He and K-Bear had even talked about moving, maybe back east somewhere, but his mother was slowly getting worse and moving could confuse her further. Moreover, he remained the trustee of Stump's Milky Way Trust and it didn't seem right to move before he'd fulfilled that obligation.

"What about injuries, Sky-High Sly? Does it appear that anybody has been hurt?"

"I sure wouldn't be surprised, Paul, but we don't have any

way of knowing that right now. Oh, wait a minute, Paul. This is interesting. We're back to the pedestrian that caused this mess. A tan mini-van has pull onto the median near her. Yes, two dark-haired males, possible Hispanics, are approaching her. Now they're escorting her to their vehicle. It must be her family. We can finally report some good news. Our pedestrian is inside the vehicle and safe."

"Well, that's good to hear."

"Sure is, but none of those people in that van could know about the accidents that they caused a mile back. I don't know if the cops will ever be able to sort it all out."

Myles sighed just as his ringtone interrupted him. It was K-Bear. Good. He was about to call her anyway to tell her he'd be late. "Hi, K-Bear."

"Oh, my God, Myles. Your mother is missing!!!"

7

Myles forced himself not to jump to conclusions. His mother wasn't necessarily the woman on the highway. "How long has she been gone?" he asked Katherine.

"I don't know exactly. She was taking a nap, so I sat back in the recliner and accidently fell asleep, too. When I awoke she was gone. I'm in my car now, looking for her, but—"

A hot, hopeless feeling raced up Myles's neck. "Listen to me, K-Bear. I just heard a traffic report about a woman walking up the middle of the highway. That's probably her."

"Oh, my God."

"The reporter said some guys in a tan van picked her up, but I don't know anybody with a van like that. We have to find her before something bad happens."

"This is all my fault. I shouldn't have—"

"We're not playing the blame game here. But I'm stuck in traffic, so I need you to call 911. Have them call the country radio station and ask them to have that chopper follow that van. You watch for it, too. If you don't see the van or the chopper by the time you get to the highway I need you to head east out of town in case they went that way. I'll be coming from the other direction. I'll watch too but it's going

28

to take me a while to get there. If you do happen to see them, just tail them and call me so we can get some help. If we don't find her pretty soon I'll call the police building and put out an Amber Alert."

"I'm so sorry, Myles, I hope we're not too late."

"Just stay calm, K-Bear. Now I gotta go. Call me if you see that van."

Myles hung up, plopped his portable flashing red light assembly on his roof and turned on his siren. The right shoulder would enable him to make slightly better time.

* * *

In the back seat of the tan van, Myles's mother sat between a young couple. "I haven't been in one of these new school buses yet," she said "It's pretty."

A woman, with a long ponytail and sitting shotgun turned around. "My name's Linda, what's yours?"

"I'm the history teacher."

"But what's your name?"

"I don't know why I'm dressed like this. Do you?"

The man next to her leaned forward. "Does anybody know you're missing?"

"I'm not missing. I'm right here. On the bus."

"I think she has dementia or something," Linda said. "We should get her to a police station."

"Too bad we don't have a cell phone," the driver said, "I told you all we might need one."

"Well, we agreed we could serve the Lord better if we kept things simple—like He would do."

"There's a convenience store up ahead. I'll pull in there. Somebody might know where there's a hospital or a police station."

"We should pray for our guest first," the women in the backseat said.

The driver nodded, dipped the van to the right, parked,

and joined hands with the woman up front. The couple in back took Myles's mother's hands while the driver prayed. "Holy Father, we are gathered here in your name. Hear our prayer. Please guide us, Father, that we might deliver our sister safely to her loved ones, and spare her from any anxiety that this moment may have caused her. These things we ask in Jesus' name. Amen."

"Amen," the others said in unison before the driver got out.

"I had Jesus in my class—and his girlfriend. Her name was Nona or something like that. She had good attendance and pretty teeth."

The woman next to Myles's mom grinned. "We're talking about Jesus Christ, honey. The savior. Do you love Jesus Christ?"

Myles's mother lifted her index finger to her lips. "Shh. We're not supposed to talk about things like that on school property."

"He'll forgive all your sins if you just ask him to."

"Would you get me a fish sandwich? Myles always gets me a fish sandwich and French fries, too."

"Of course, dear. If Jesus could feed the masses with a few fish we can surely follow his example."

After buying Myles's mom a fish sandwich, the devoted Christians pulled into the police station. Inside, a fresh hint of tartar sauce had found its way to Myles's mother's robe.

Satisfied that they'd delivered their sister to safety, they held hands and thanked God for answering their prayers. Next, a mature lady cop led Myles's mother to a back room. "We're going to help you get home," she said. "Would you like something to drink while we figure things out?"

"I guess I'll have a Shirley Temple."

"I'm afraid we don't have anything like that, ma'am. Would a Sprite be okay?"

"No, thank you. Who did you say you are?"

"I'm Officer Greem. I'm trying to get you back to your family. Do you remember your name?"

"I'm Pauline Cooper," she said, looking down to her bathrobe. "Oh, my goodness. I can't teach a class dressed like this."

"So you're a teacher?"

"I think so, but the building looks different. Can you tell me how to get to the History department?"

"No ma'am, I'm new to this school. Do you remember the name of it?" she asked as two additional uniformed officers walked by the window.

"Uh-oh," Myles's mom said. "Is my son in trouble again?"

"Your son?"

"He likes beer, you know, but he's not old enough. My husband will kill him."

"I see. What's your husband's name? Where can I reach him?"

"He's dead."

"But what's his name?"

8

With all his senses on hyper alert, Myles slithered up the shoulder, but it was way too slow for a fellow whose mother may have been abducted. Then he reached an area where the shoulder narrowed and forced him back into the sloth lane and from there onto the striped lines between lanes. One by one, cars slowly parted as if he were Slow Moses parting the Red Tar Sea.

Katherine called back. *"I'm just a couple blocks from the highway, but I haven't seen any tan vans."*

"Did you call 911?"

"Yes. They said they'd try to get that helicopter back out here."

"Good job, K-Bear. I know you feel bad, but this is my fault as much as it is yours."

"No, it's not. I'm the one who fell asleep. I've never done anything like that before."

"But Stump isn't around to help us anymore and I'm the one who keeps you up late at night. And we've all known Mom is getting worse. It was just a matter of time before the two of us got stretched too thin."

"Thank you for saying that, Myles. It makes me feel better."

"For now, we just have to find her. I'm gonna call the

police. They usually won't work missing person cases until the victim has been gone 24 hours, but—"

"*I love you.*"

"You too, K-Bear. Stay in touch." He disconnected and speed-dialed the station.

"*Palmdale Police. Officer Ewing.*"

Myles had met Barrow Ewing about a year earlier. As cops went, the rookie seemed pretty smart. "Barrow, this is Sergeant Myles Cooper, out of LA. I've got a possible 207."

"*Kidnapping. Copy that. Do you need a patrol car? Who's the youngster?*"

"Listen closely. This time the victim is elderly. My mom. She got away from home maybe a half-hour ago. I just heard a radio report about an elderly woman on Highway 14, who got picked up by some guys in a tan van. I'd appreciate it if you'd get a couple black and whites in that area right away and look for that van."

"*I think we can do better than that, Sergeant. Is she wearing a pink bathrobe?*"

"Could be. Why?"

"*She's in one of the conference rooms, telling officer Greem about the 'teacher's lounge.'*"

Myles sighed for the first time in a while. "That's her, alright. What happened? How'd she get there?"

"*Some Jesus fans brought her in.*"

"Thank God. I don't know what I would've done—"

"*You lucked out, Sergeant. They sensed the danger and drove straight here—after a side trip for a fish sandwich.*"

"Are they still there? I want to thank them personally."

"*No, sir, but we got some contact info.*"

"Well done. I'm on my way, but my mother's caregiver is close by. I'll have her come in and hold down the fort until I get there."

"*No problem, Sergeant. We'll make 'em both comfortable.*"

After Myles called Katherine and drove to within a few miles from the station, a tan van, with several young adults in it, came from the other direction. "Thank you," Myles said to both them and God as they passed by.

At the station, Myles sought out Officer Ewing and patted his young ally on the shoulder. "Thanks, Officer. Where are the women?"

Ewing gestured toward the back corner of the office area. "Did you know that the Japanese attach tiny stickers with bar codes on the toenails of people afflicted with dementia so they can easily be found and identified?"

"No, I didn't. That would've been handy. Can you give me the names and contact info for those young people? I'd like to take them to dinner or something."

"There were two couples, just traveling around, staying in campsites and doing God's work. I got an address for one of the women, but it's her parent's place in Indiana."

"Well, I'll send her folks a note and tell them they raised a good kid." A moment later, Myles entered the holding area where Katherine rushed to him and flung her arms around his neck. "You must have been scared to death. I feel so bad."

"This ought to be a good lesson for both of us." He moved toward his mother and hugged her. "You doing okay, Mom?"

"What are you doing?" she said, brushing his hand off her shoulder, "This is no time for lovey-dovey. I'm waiting for my ice cream."

"I love you, Mom. You know that, don't you?"

"What's the matter with you two?" she said. "You both keep kissing me. I'd rather you go get my ice cream."

"She doesn't remember anything," Katherine whispered to Myles. "Only that I said she could have some ice cream."

Myles nodded. "Mom, they ran out of ice cream, but there's another place right up the street. We'll go there and get you as much as you want."

"I like chocolate."

Several hours later, and back at the apartment, reruns of "America's Funniest Home Videos" blasted on TV. While Katherine and Myles held hands on the couch, Myles watched his mother's tired eyelids lazily flutter. "You know something, K-Bear? In some ways, dementia patients have it easier than their caregivers. I put too much responsibility on you. Something bad had to happen sooner or later."

"We have to do something different, Myles."

Myles sighed. "I guess I'll have to call Stump and see if we can work something out with his trust money." He kissed Katherine on the cheek. "I guess it's time to tell him about us, too."

9

"**I**just can't do it anymore, Mrs. Kline," Sandra Peppers said, speaking of her older half-sister, Jessie, who was one of the Memory Care residents at Meadowlark Flats. With the same mother but different fathers and nearly 20 years between the sisters, they were never very close. "I didn't mind looking after Jessie since I live close by," Sandra went on, "but now my husband wants to travel and spend a couple years in Europe if possible. That's why we're hopeful that you can take care of my sister without us."

"Like I told you the other day," Edna Kline said, "we have many other residents in that same situation. In fact, if you were to try and pick them out of the people out in the community room you couldn't tell who they are. They live just as dignified as anybody else."

"I feel so guilty, but she moved out of my parents' home before I was born so she was more like an aunt to me than a sister. We barely stayed in touch."

"I wouldn't worry about it. You've already done a lot more than other people would have done in your situation."

"That's exactly what my husband said."

"He's right. You have to live your own life too."

"She never did have a family, but we raised a house full of kids. Now that the last one has left the nest—"

"Say no more."

"Quite honestly, we didn't think she'd hang on this long."

This was another one of the situations Edna Kline looked for. She already knew that Jessie's father had passed away years earlier and left a great deal of money to Jessie, but none of it to Sandra because Sandra wasn't his blood. But, now that Sandra had to move on, that left a big pot of Jessie money with nobody to keep track of it – and that was something Edna was good at.

"I know you've always had Power of Attorney over your sister's financial and medical matters," Edna said. "How do you want to handle that?"

"To tell you the truth, I don't know much about it, but I think I can assign the role to somebody else. That's why we were hoping you'd take it on. You know her better than anybody else."

"It's no problem. Just review the POA. You'll probably just have to fill out an Assignment and sign it in front of a Notary. We'll have to charge a monthly fee for the extra time it takes. I'm sure you know it takes a couple hours a week to keep on top of everything."

"Some weeks it's a lot more."

"We'll process her Social Security and Medicare needs along with keeping her in nice clothes, well-groomed and making all of her other decisions. We bill a minimum rate of two hours a week at $60 dollars an hour. I will send you monthly reports. You'll see it on your invoice as Specialty Services."

"That sounds very fair. I'm so grateful to you."

"That's one of the reasons we're here; so you can have your own life back and know that your sister is safe and well-cared for."

"As long as she's safe I'm okay with it."

"From what you've said she's got plenty of resources so

we should be in good shape for all the rest of her days. Then I can send whatever is left over to you or the court or wherever you'd like."

"That would be fine. I can't tell you how grateful I am that you can take on this responsibility. I could never hold my husband off for that long."

"Jessie is family to us. She'll never notice any difference."

"Okay then, if you'll get the paperwork ready, I'll get the POA put in your name and we can meet next week for one last time before we begin our new adventure."

"Just make an appointment with the receptionist out in the main corridor."

With all of that over, Edna landed herself a $6,000 annual raise, plus access to the rest of Jessie's money. It wouldn't be difficult to fatten her purse. All she had to do was low-key it until Sandra and her husband were out of the country.

For now Edna could order a few new dresses and sweaters for Jessie. Then she could take half of them back and exchange them for a different set of clothes - a classier set, that would just happen to fit Edna Kline perfectly.

10

On any other Saturday, a small lunch crowd would be trickling in to Lee's College Café. Instead, Zax's volunteers gathered to throw out tainted food and scrub away a gross combination of black smoke and pancake powder that found its way into the tiniest places.

While the others cleaned up the kitchen, Stump swabbed a mop back and forth in the dining area and had a pretty good idea why sailors called the surface of a ship a poop deck. His mop appeared to be as pooped as he was.

But in another way, Stump was invigorated. Having no living relatives, or his very own girlfriend, it was nice to belong somewhere. Of course, he still considered Myles and Grandma Pauline to be family but he didn't see them as much as he used to. Then, while thinking of family, he wondered about that stupid DNA test he took recently. Something like that could change everything.

"Let's take a break, everybody," Zax said, sliding a tray of drinks onto a table. "I just hope all this work makes a difference."

"A difference?" Stump grabbed a Mountain Dew. "Of course it will. It already looks better in here."

"To tell you the truth, this place hasn't been doing all that well. My creditors are getting nervous; if business doesn't pick up—"

Stump nodded, wished he could help his thin but tough buddy.

"We'll still eat here," James said. "We have to eat somewhere."

Stump nodded as his ringtone announced that Myles wanted to talk. "'Sup, Myles?"

After pacing the diner and listening to Myles's story about Grandma Pauline, Stump returned to his pals. "There's some heavy shit going down. My grandma got out and ended up walking on the highway in rush hour. Apparently, a news chopper reported the whole thing. She got picked up by strangers in a van."

"Poor dear," Zax said. "She must've been scared to death."

"That part worked out okay. The van was full of religious people. They took her to the police station, safe as could be."

"Oh. Thank God for that," Yana added. "You had me scared."

"I was, too, but by the time she got to the Police Station, she'd forgotten it all."

James eyed Stump. "Wasn't Katherine there?"

"That's another thing. Myles eventually launched into a lame-ass tale about him and Katherine hooking up. He said they'd kept it a secret because he didn't know how I'd take it, because he and my mom almost got married."

"So, was he right?" Yana asked. "Did it make you angry?"

"Me? Hell, no. I figured out what they were doing a couple months ago, when I called up there one night and he said he was watching a chick-flick on TV. He had to be with a woman and he never spoke of anybody else. I sure as hell wouldn't expect the guy to crawl into a cocoon just because he'd loved my mom six years ago."

"Besides," James said, grinning. "All guys gotta *lust and thrust in the mattress dust* from time to time."

Yana clucked her tongue. "Oh really? And just how long would it take you to lust in the dust if I were to suddenly die? The same night?"

Stump grinned. "Mouth, meet foot."

James chuckled at Yana "I didn't know what real love was until I met you, so if that ever happened, I'd spend the whole time wishing she was you."

"Well. Not me," Yana said with a giant grin of her own. "If you died prematurely, it'd probably be because I killed you myself for making a lame-o comment like that. Then I'd grab the first dude I could find and do him right on top of your grave."

"No prob. I'd make a batch of casket popcorn and watch the show from below."

Zax snickered. "What is Myles going to do, Stump?"

"They want to move my grandmother to someplace nice, where she can stay the rest of her life—and this is where it gets strange again—Myles wants to invest a million dollars of my trust money in a mutual fund and use the income to pay her bills."

James whistled. "No shit, dude? That's a lot of beans."

"Hypocritical too. He never lets me use the money, yet as soon as he needs it—"

"Yeah, but this might open the door for you to get a Ferrari or something."

"No friggin' way. I asked. He said I gotta get by on the ten grand he already sent."

"That doesn't seem fair," Yana said. "He gets to spend it but you don't?"

"What can I say? He's always had this irrational fear about losing money."

"But the money isn't really for him, Stump," Zax said. "It's for your grandma and that's different."

Yana nodded and tapped at her iPhone, while Stump replied.

"I can't say no to Grandma Pauline. It just sucks that Myles won't let me spend a little, too. He thinks I'll become some frizzy-haired, money-crazed wild-child and spend it all before I get out of school."

"You'd look rad with frizzy hair, bro."

"Yeah, right. Myles and Katherine are going to check out some places in the next few days."

"Hey, this is interesting," Yana said, looking at her iPhone. "There's an auction today in the downtown area. '*A dozen vehicles, used furniture, baby items. Everything must go.*' We could use some baby items and some cheap furniture for our apartment."

"What kind of cars?" Stump asked.

"Doesn't say, but it wouldn't take long to check it out. We can clean up and be there in plenty of time."

"I'm in," James said, looking at Stump.

"If they have any decent cars it might be worth it." Stump looked at Zax to see if she was coming too.

"You guys go ahead. Somebody from the administration building is dropping by. They heard about the fire. I think they figured out that I don't have insurance. I just hope they don't void my lease."

"Why are they working on a Saturday?" Yana wondered out loud.

Zax shrugged. "Spring break is coming up. Maybe they're tying up loose ends."

Just then Denise's dachshund darted into the dining area. "Trixie!" Zax yelled. "If the Health Department sees you in here, I'll be in more trouble."

11

With an envelope full of Benjamins tucked safely in his shorts and his bucket-of-rust truck sputtering from one side of his lane to the other, Stump made the final turn toward the oldest commercial area in Carlsbad. They crossed the railroad tracks, which separated million-dollar beach homes from cheaper homes that were too far from the water to command the big bucks.

"I hope we can get some nice furniture or maybe a crib," Yana said. "But with the few dollars James's parents give him for spending money and my tips we just don't have very much."

James bobbed his head. "That be true."

Ahead, a three-block stretch known as Old Main Street belied a previous era when the hundred-year-old, boxy, brick buildings must have been the lifeblood of the area.

"These buildings have character," Stump said as a closer look revealed that all of the buildings consisted of two or three stories and the windows were much bigger on the ground level.

On their right a dingy bar, a tattoo parlor and a vacant building with filthy windows squared off against the other side of the street, which contained a pawnshop and an antique furniture store. Then something else caught Stump's eye. "Did you guys notice the upper floors?"

"What about them?" Yana said.

"Oh, I see it," James said. "Most of them are dark."

"Yeah, dirty windows, no lights, yellow blinds. I wonder why nobody's up there."

Yana shrugged. "I bet most companies want to be in happier buildings."

James smiled. "Happier? How can a building be happy?"

"You know. Newer. Clean. With lawns and flowers and more parking. Happier. That's where I'd rather work."

Stump noticed a couple guys hanging out in a small open area between two buildings. Then up ahead he saw a sandwich sign on the sidewalk. "There it is. *Auction Today.*"

A few minutes later, they squeezed the truck into a small parking spot between a Christian bookstore and a porno bookstore.

They plodded up the sidewalk, crossed the intersection diagonally and continued toward the auction when a man with a long beard and no shirt stepped out of an alley between two buildings. He looked at James. "You guys want some weed?"

"How much?" James asked.

"We can't afford that stuff," Yana said. "We need our money for our baby."

The guy turned to Stump. "I got a pint of sloe gin. Just twenty bucks."

A gentle whiff of urine rose from between the buildings as Stump thought of his mom and Myles and all the pain that alcohol had caused them. "No, thanks."

Two doors down, they reached the auction sign. Stump eyed a parked Lexus. "I'd pay ten-thou for that."

"Dream on, brofriend," James said as they entered the cluttered building, where a registration table served as a gateway to a mass of odds and ends that lent the impression

44

of a gigantic, disorganized garage sale. The entire area smelled as if somebody had watered it down the night before.

At the registration counter, Stump and Yana got bidder numbers and a pamphlet explaining taxes and buyer's fees and a few other procedural rules. Stump pointed to an open garage door on the back wall. "I'm heading outside to see what their cars look like."

After dodging an overabundance of small items of dubious value, Stump eventually made it outside where bigger items such as used lawn mowers, appliances and yard furniture sprawled around half the lot. The other half had a refreshment area and a small stage facing about 60 folding chairs for the bidders. Behind that, an old ambulance and a faded green Popsicle truck bookended a row of eight decent-looking vehicles. Unfortunately, other potential bidders were busy inspecting the cars inside and out. With that much competition, Stump doubted he'd get anything, thereby making the whole trip an exercise in disappointment.

"Good afternoon, ladies and gentlemen," a tall man said from the stage. "I'm Berle Winston, your auctioneer. You have just ten more minutes to examine our inventory. Today's auction is what we call *absolute*. If you're the high bidder you win the item no matter how low your bid is."

Hmm. Stump wandered over to a maroon Caddie that reminded him of Dixon Browne, the sexual predator he had helped to bring down back when he first figured out he had a knack for detective work. He doubted if there was any chance his 10K would snag a vehicle like that or any of the other cars. Mildly disappointed, he bought some buttered popcorn and sat in the bidder's section. After a while Yana and James joined Stump for the auction.

After that, staff members retrieved one lot after the other from inside the building and paraded them outside and past several dozen bidders. Each time, the auctioneer described the item before barking for bids. Stump marveled at how the man maintained an intense pace and a smooth cadence and added made-up words as fillers.

Dozens of lots had passed by when Yana got in a bid of twenty dollars for two lamps with stained glass shades, but the price quickly rocketed out of her price range.

Now it was lot 87's turn. The auctioneer checked his notes. "This lot is for several boxes of adult paperback books and girly magazines that we got from one of the more interesting bookstores on this block."

James nudged Stump. "Porno."

"Yeah, I know," Stump said while discretely scratching his pubic area where his envelope full of cash was causing him to sweat. "I'm waiting for the cars, but you guys ought to bid on it."

"No way," Yana butted in. "We're going for highchairs and a crib and one of those potty chairs."

As with previous lots, the auctioneer scanned the bidders before he tapped his mallet and began the call for bids: "Anawhosagonnaopen wita fittydollabid? Dutta gimmefitty fittydollabid, wouldya wouldya gimme gimmefittydollabid." He paused and returned to his normal voice and cadence. "Look, folks. If you had to buy these priceless items individually it would cost you thousands. We're gonna sell this lot if we only get a single dollar. So let's start over and see who wants to find out what they've been missing." He tapped his mallet again, Then, "Eh makeit twetty, gimme twetty-dollabill. Eh, dutta dutta twettydollabill."

"YO!!!" one of the floormen yelled, while pointing to a 60-year-old bidder with a plaid shirt and bowtie.

"Needa tirdy tirdy," the auctioneer said without missing a beat. "Needa tirdydolla bid. Eh dutta wouldya got tirdy, tirdydollabill?"

"YO!!!" another floorman yelled, pointing to a husband and embarrassed wife combo, in their forties.

"Got tirdy need fordy. Eh fordydollabill wouldya—"

"YO!!!"

James leaned toward Stump. "Don't these idiots know about the internet?"

"YO!!!"

"We gotta fitty," the auctioneer said, pointing back and forth between the two bidders until the bowtie guy wouldn't go any higher. "SOLD! For one hundred and ten dollars to the woman with the red face and a big smile."

"If a few boxes of used books goes for this much," Stump said, "just imagine what a car is going to cost."

After a few more lots, a staff member walked outside with one of the items Yana had been waiting for. "There they are," she said quietly as if she didn't want anybody to know that a pregnant woman would be interested in baby furniture.

"Next up, item one hundred five," the auctioneer said. "We've including several items in one lot. First we've got a freshly painted highchair and crib combination. There's also a car seat and two potty chairs." Stump grinned. One of the potty chairs looked exactly like a real toilet, only smaller.

"Lame." Yana said. "I was hoping they'd split the items up. I doubt we can afford the whole lot."

"You never know," James said. "I haven't seen any other pregos around."

The auctioneer pointed his mallet right at Yana. "We're going to start the bidding at two thousand dollars."

12

S tunned by the auctioneer's statement, Yana paled.

"Just kidding, honey," the auctioneer continued. "I hope you and hubby win this one. Okay, folks. Here we go." He tapped his mallet. "Ehwho's a gonna open wit a fittydollabid, wouldya couldya wouldya make a fittydolla bid?" He looked right at Yana. "Wouldya open for your baby wita fittydolla bid?" Yana relented and raised her bidder's paddle.

"YO!!!" a floorman yelled while pointing right at her.

"Wegotafitty, needasixty, whosagotttasixtydoolabid, eh sixty."

"YO!!!" a different floorman yelped, from the other side of the room.

The auctioneer turned to Yana. "Yorturn ovahere, wouldya go seventy seventydolla bid?"

Yana hesitated, causing the auctioneer to prompt her. "Going once, donletitgetaway fir a seventydolla bid. She sighed and raised her paddle.

"YO!!!"

The call went back to the other bidder for eighty, then back to Yana for ninety, prompting James to elbow Stump. "This is getting fun."

At a hundred, the competing woman hesitated long enough for the auctioneer to prompt her just as he did with Yana: "Going once, going twice—" She squirmed before she slipped her paddle timidly in the air and said something to her partner. Stump sensed that she'd reached her limit.

Stump raised his own paddle, "One twenty-five."

Yana, James, and quite a few others turned Stump's way. "YO!!!"

The auctioneer pointed to Yana. "Wouldya go onefitty? Wouldya, couldya, wouldya?"

Yana shook her head no.

The auctioneer turned to the other lady who was already shaking her head, prompting the auctioneer to wave his mallet over the whole audience as if he were casting a spell. "Alright folks, anybody else at one-fifty? This lot is a bargain at one-fifty. Going once. Going twice. Last chance. Fair warning. He paused a few more seconds, then, "SOLD to the young man who outbid his own friends."

"Rad," Stump said turning to Yana. "Consider it a present."

Yana lifted her hand to her mouth. "Really, Stump. That's so sweet."

While Stump was playing nice with Yana, James leaned over and licked Stump's ear. Stump quickly swiped at his face, "That's gross, dude."

"You deserved a kiss," James said.

Yana laughed. "This is why I like you guys."

Shortly after that, the staff started working the items in the lot. If it weren't for the cars by the fence, Stump would have suggested they blow back to Zax's place for a free burger. Before long it was apparent they were saving the cars for last.

"I'm going to go the restroom," Yana said while James and Stump waited. Finally, the vehicles were the only items left to sell. With all but a couple dozen people heading for the exits, maybe there was room for optimism after all.

The auctioneer stepped off the stage and stood in front

of the Caddie that Stump had inspected earlier. After some typical difficulties getting an opening bid, the prices quickly rose to nearly double the wad of genital-scratching bills in Stump's envelope. Then he heard, "Sold to the man in the Hawaiian shirt for eighteen-six."

After that, an SUV went in the sixteens. Then a nice-looking pickup with extended cab caught a top bid of fourteen-four and Stump noticed the pattern; each vehicle was worth less than the one before it. He only had one more chance: a high-mileage Toyota. His bid of eight thousand had no more chance than a kid's dropped hotdog in a Great Dane parade. "Sold for twelve-two," the auctioneer said.

"I don't know why I wasted my time," Stump said to James, standing up.

With only a few people still paying attention the auctioneer pitched a package of cars. "This lot, friends, is for all three of these clunkers. None of them runs. You can fix them or use 'em for parts. At the very least they ought to be worth a grand each at the salvage yard."

As the auctioneer barked for final bids Yana joined Stump and James. "Any luck?"

Stump shook his head. "I gotta find something else; some other loser car that nobody else wants." Damn Myles.

"SOLD!" the auctioneer said from over Stump's shoulder.

"You guys ready to go?" Yana asked.

"All right, folks," the auctioneer said louder than before. "We saved the best for last. This here Popsicle truck is 16 years old and only has 40 thousand miles on it."

Curious, Stump turned toward the auctioneer.

"We got it from a DEA officer who said it was part of a drug bust and has just been sitting on the back lot pending the outcome of the case. He tells us it's got good road manners and everything works, but it only has one seat. That way you won't have to take your wife with you."

Stump took out the paperwork he'd gotten when they registered, and looked it over.

The auctioneer pointed at the truck. "Now, whosagonnagimme ten—"

Stump held up his bidder paddle. "Eight-thousand, nine-hundred, twenty-seven dollars and sixty-two cents," he yelled before anybody else had a chance to bid.

"YO!!!"

James socked Stump in the arm while Yana lifted her hand to her mouth. "I don't believe this."

"I got—" the auctioneer stopped and pointed his gavel at Stump, "whatever amount that young man just said—under nine thou. Somebody make it ten, wouldyamakeit ten?"

The auctioneer shifted a foot and returned to normal cadence. "You folks ain't gonna let this young fellow outsmart you, are you? Wouldya pay nine? Need nine, dutta wouldya pay nine?"

Yana tapped Stump's arm. "You might get it."

The auctioneer stopped and pointed his mallet at Stump. "Make it nine and it's all yours."

"Can't. It's all I got," he said, taking into consideration the purchase of Yana's baby furniture, taxes and the buyer's premium.

"Alright, folks, you heard him. Last call. Going once. Going twice. We'll take nine. Anybody got nine? Fair warning." He paused for just a few more seconds, then said, "SOLD to the young man who spent his very last dime." He pointed his mallet at Stump. "Best bid of the day, young man."

"Super rad," James said, slapping Stump's back. "That's the coolest set of wheels of anybody I know. Way to go, bro. Maybe you'll find some weed in it."

"If Myles can be ridiculous, so can I."

"I dunno, dude. They said it's only got forty-thousand miles on it. That's a steal for 9K."

Stump turned to Yana. "Can I have one of the potty chairs back?"

"Huh? Really?"

"Yep. They said it needs a seat."

"Cool. Cool. Cool," James said, jumping up and down. "I can't wait to ride in it, bro. This is radtastic!"

"I think I'll call it Pops."

13

After Stump paid for their items, James elbowed him. "Why'd you bid so much, bro? You might have got it cheaper if you'd waited."

"People didn't mind making several little raises, but that usually took them right back to the original asking price or higher. I thought a big weird bid would catch people off-guard. To beat me, they'd have to take a big bite all at once and nobody was willing to do that."

"That's what you did with the baby furniture too, wasn't it?" Yana said.

"Yep. That other lady was willing to raise your bids as long as it was in small increments, but when I bid one-twenty-five she had to go all the way to one-fifty to get the lot. Since her previous bid was one hundred, that was too much for her all at once."

"I do that with donuts," Yana said. "I cut them in half, thinking the whole donut is too much, but I always eat the second half anyway."

"True that," James said.

"Can I ask you guys a favor?" Yana said. "Since I still have the money I brought with me, I'd like to stop in that furniture store on the corner, to look for a dresser or a bassinet for the baby."

As they crossed the street, Stump eyed the back of the furniture building where an alley separated the businesses and a long row of tall, turn-of-the-century Victorian houses. "These old buildings are rad," he said as they reached the entrance to the furniture building.

A chime signaled their entry into the three-story property, where a short balding man approached. "Can I help you?"

"This building is a lot bigger than it looks from the outside," Yana said.

"It used to be a combination grocery store and drug store. It was one of the first places on the west coast to sell Coca-Cola with a scoop of ice cream in it."

"Interesting," Yana said, patting her tummy. "Do you have any baby furniture? Not antiques, though—they're too expensive."

"We don't keep that kind of thing down here. Not enough profit in it. But we've got a few items upstairs," he said pointing to the sidewall. "Just take that staircase. Most of the items have tags on them. If you need me, my name's Jack."

After climbing the squeaky stairs, a tall ceiling in the center hall led to a half-dozen decent-sized offices and a corner restroom. Stump tugged on an overhead string, causing a naked and dusty light bulb to sway as if it were pleased to have something to do.

They stuck their heads in several rooms until James pushed open a door near the back of the building. "Here's the baby stuff."

Inside, a couple cardboard boxes contained small toys and a playpen that housed a child-sized wooden rocking horse, lying on its side. "Poor thing," Yana said setting it upright, "It looks like it's in jail."

"Look at this," James said, holding up another potty chair. "We could start a collection."

Yana clucked her tongue. "Put it down. You don't know if it's been cleaned."

Stump grinned and looked out the dirty back window. "This place is sorta rad. Let's check out the top floor."

"You guys go ahead," Yana said, "I gotta find a bathroom, again."

While Yana trekked downstairs, Stump and James climbed the final flight to find the remains of two large, gutted apartments. Stump looked through a grimy back window and over the rooftops of the old two-story residences. "I bet the manager of the grocery store lived up here with his family."

"Probably, bro. Too bad they don't fix it up and rent it to those guys out in the street."

A couple minutes later, and back on the main floor, Yana rushed to James. "Can you go back upstairs and get that little rocking horse? Jack said I can have it for fifteen dollars."

"What about you fellows?" Jack asked. "You find anything you liked?"

"I liked the building more than anything else," Stump said.

"Oh, yeah? You know anybody who'd like to buy it? I'd make 'em a good deal."

"If I had my trust money, I'd consider it, but I don't know what I'd do with the upper floors."

"People used to live and work in the same area, but it all changed when glass and steel buildings sprang up and everybody could afford an automobile."

"See?" Yana said, tapping James's shoulder. "I told you. People like happy places."

"It's too late now," Jack went on. "The place doesn't meet codes. It'd be too expensive to update it. And the rents in the area are too low to support the investment."

"Have you ever looked for grants?" James asked. "Stump and me helped a whole neighborhood get free fix-up money."

"Not really but sometimes old areas can be classified as Enterprise Zones."

Yana turned her head. "Does anybody else hear that? Somebody must be getting married."

"It's 'Here Comes the Bride' on a harpsichord," Jack said. "An old timer lives across the alley. He plays wedding music all the time."

"Did he lose his wife or something?" Yana asked.

"You wouldn't believe me if I told you. After you get your rocking horse, you ought to wander back there. He'll probably let you participate in one of his rituals."

Yana scrunched her brows down, "Rituals? He's not going to hurt anybody is he?"

"Not that I know of. The guy's eccentric as hell—looks a little spooky too—but he's harmless as a kitty," he said, grinning.

"I'm in," James said.

"You always are," Yana said, withdrawing her checkbook from her purse.

A few minutes later the three of them wandered toward the house across the back alley and to a vine-covered wrought iron fence that encased its back yard. The harpsichord music morphed from a wedding song to a combination of high-pitched but melodic meow-like sounds, and a low-pitched vibration that resembled purrs.

"You guys hear that?" Yana asked.

Stump nodded. "Jack implied this was going to have something to do with kittens."

They walked past an open window with bars on the outside and got a whiff of something like ammonia or formaldehyde. Around the corner they reached a red stone sidewalk that led to a wooden porch, supported by large white-painted pillars that hid behind an unsightly overgrown bush.

High up under the eaves, two ugly basketball-sized gargoyles seemed to be guarding a lone attic window that looked as if it had never been cleaned.

"I'm not sure I want to get any closer," Yana said slowing down and snapping a picture.

"Why not?" James asked. "You heard what Jack said. The guy's harmless."

"It's creepy."

James grabbed her hand and they all walked halfway up the sidewalk, where Stump spotted a goofy-looking bicycle behind the large bush and chained to a pillar. On the handlebars, a large tackle box looked like something Dorothy and Toto might appreciate. Just behind the seat, two foot-long pieces of PVC sewer pipe stood erect. Each housed the butt of a fishing pole that looked stout enough to haul in Moby Dick. Capping it all off, a laughably large triangular shaped fluorescent flag flew high enough over a rider's head to make a group of funeral goers giggle. Naturally, Yana snapped a picture.

When they reached the porch steps, Stump glanced toward the giant front window where two cats sat face to face, one in each corner. The farthest one resembled a small tiger. It leapt to the floor, while the other, apparently a Siamese, must have been blind or unconcerned because it didn't move.

Stump shifted his attention back to the huge door that must have been a hundred years old. A two-foot-wide, round stained-glass window reminded him of a gigantic kaleidoscope. Below that, a tarnished brass knocker with another gargoyle face and a huge ring through its nose seemed to be staring Stump down. When very close, Stump couldn't take his eyes off the door. The aged golden-stain couldn't hide the thousands of tiny bird's eye dots that appeared to be a natural part of the wood.

Before anybody knocked, the harpsichord's cat-sounds morphed into an uneasy collection of agitated meows. The chorus of cats, singing in unison one minute and complaining in unison the next, was too intriguing to ignore. Stump reached for the knocker, just as a shadow from the inside crossed the colorful, round window.

14

The tall, thin man with unusually long ears and a head full of poorly chopped gray hair could have been a character out of a child's storybook. Additional scraggly hair flowed like a waterfall out of his nostrils, and blended with a thick gray mustache. "Yes?" he asked.

"Er. Hi," Stump said, trying to ignore the commanding aroma from within the home. "We were in the furniture store across the alley and heard the music. The manager said something about interesting rituals."

The old-timer's brow furrowed as a pure white cat with long hair and a pug nose wedged between his legs, thereby drawing attention to the man's sky-blue, paper slippers. "*Rituals* are for devil worshipers. We hold positive *ceremonies*, not negative rituals."

"Oh, sorry," Stump said while looking closer at the man's right ear.

James pointed in the direction of the roof. "What's with those carvings by the rafters?"

"Gargoyles," the man said as a plain gray cat joined the white one and both flowed lazily through and around his legs and purred. "They're designed to keep bad spirits away."

Other cats came up behind the old-timer as if they were reinforcements, while still more meowed uneasily from deeper in the home.

"That was interesting music," James said. "Are you having one of your ceremonies now?"

The man dipped his eyes toward their feet and nodded. "Fritz and Ms. Jenkins are getting married."

A wedding ceremony for cats? Stump was beginning to understand why Jack encouraged them to check out the old dude. "Could you use any help?"

The man dipped his head as if checking their feet. "Tell me a little about yourselves."

"My name's Stump. James and I are students at the Criminology College."

"I'm Yana, from Russia. I work in a restaurant."

"She's my girlfriend," James added.

The man glanced at Yana's belly. "We can always use witnesses."

"I'm in," said James.

"Witnesses to what?" Yana asked, setting her rocking horse down.

"Propriety." The man stepped back and afforded them access to the foyer. "I'm Catts McFadden." He turned slightly, thereby allowing Stump to get a good look into the man's right ear, where thick gray hair surrounded a shiny dime.

"I like your nickname," Stump said.

Inside, a tall foyer with a luxurious wooden staircase, replete with plush red carpet, led to the second floor and perhaps to a mysterious attic above that. A handful of bonus cats, two of which were meowing, perched in various places including near a padded bench and a side table.

"Oh, my God," Yana yelped, pointing to two motionless cats on the steps. "They're stuffed."

Stump had noticed that, too, but elected not to say anything. Instead he wondered what was hiding behind the set of mahogany pocket doors that had been drawn from inside the walls and butted up to each other.

Catts pointed to a lectern with an official-looking book. "Before I let you into the ceremony room, you'll have to agree to the pledge and sign the guest book."

Yana's eyes bounced to the lectern and then back to the pocket doors. "What do you do in there?"

"Ms. Jenkins's estrus levels have risen, but we do not allow careless whelping. We must introduce her to an appropriate suitor."

"Mating?" James asked.

The man stared briefly at James. "Mere mating, as you call it, lacks virtue. After a morality ceremony, we'll allow the lovers to do as they must."

Fascinated, Stump reached for the guestbook and read the inscription out loud.

In this place of common decency,
all persons agree to protect those in our charge.

Just below the inscription, a dozen signature lines had but one name: Catts McFadden. Stump grinned and added his own signature then traded glances with Yana and James.

"I'm in."

Yana sighed. "Me, too."

The man pointed toward Stump's feet. "You must remove your shoes before we enter."

One by one Stump and friends sat on the padded bench and replaced shoes with paper booties. Catts then pushed back one of the sliding doors and granted his witnesses access to the original living room. Inside, an eclectic group of cats scurried away from the intruders and protested orally. In the center of the room, a massive, golden chandelier dangled brightly over a long wooden table with a white tablecloth on which a travel cage contained a lone cat, presumably Fritz or Ms. Jenkins.

"How many cats do you have in your group?" Yana asked.

Catts waggled a slow, friendly finger Yana's way. "My precious lady. A group of these priceless creatures prefer to be thought of as a *clowder* or a *family*." He turned in the direction of a large wooden storage cabinet and swung the door outward revealing shelves containing candles, cat toys and a bottle of something.

"We'll need a few things," he said as he placed items in an old milk box and enabled the two-legged types to glance about.

On the left wall, a harpsichord blended into a mammoth wooden wall-to-wall bookcase, consisting of multiple levels and shelves. At least a dozen diverse felines, including live and stuffed examples, used the shelving as perches. To Stump's right a series of litter boxes hid behind a three-piece room divider. Next to that the wall contained framed certificates and licenses including one that declared that C. M. McFadden had passed a course in taxidermy, which explained the smell of formaldehyde.

Stump traded glances with Yana, who stood erect in the center of the room as if she were afraid to touch anything. Unexpectedly, a black cat jumped on a gray one, causing another gray one to jump into the game as if they were members of teams in a pre-game warm-up.

Seconds later, Catts set a collection of can-sized electric candles on the center table. "Flick these on," he said to James, "and spread them in a circle on the floor around the table." As Catts walked toward another set of pocket doors, the white cat with the pug nose rubbed up against Stump's ankles and purred.

Catts slid both doors back, revealing a former dining room causing another dozen cats, all in cages and very much alive, to meow excitedly. In the back corner, under a window, a cot reminded Stump of the nap-couch of his former boss where Stump had made love for the very first time with Maria.

"Not now, gentlemen," Catts said to his furry friends as

he opened one pen and rescued a mostly white cat with both black and fawn blotches.

"Everybody, this is Fritz. After we leave the room he'll be allowed to woo Ms. Jenkins."

"Are all the cats in that room males?" James asked.

"Yes, sir," Catts said, stepping inside the candle circle and waiving a hand around the room, "and these are the ladies. They're the only ones who have good manners at times like this."

While still holding Fritz, Catts reached into the box he'd placed on the table and then Velcroed a bow tie around Fritz's neck. After that he attached a small plastic flower to Ms. Jenkins's collar. By that time Fritz was paying close attention to Ms. Jenkins.

With a chorus of various cat noises as background music, Catts secured an antique-looking Bible from the cabinet and looked at Stump. "Do you believe in morality?"

Stump grinned. He could have confessed a few sins first, but instead opted to play it the way Catts would've wanted. "Yes, I do."

Catts turned to Yana. "And what about you? Do you believe in morality?"

Stump glanced at her belly and wondered how a woman who'd been knocked up might answer the question.

"Um-hm!"

Catts turned to James. "And you sir. Do you believe in morality?"

James paused long enough for Stump to hope that he wasn't thinking up one of his sarcastic Jamesisms.

"Sure I do."

"Then all is right and we are dismissed."

15

Catts McFadden stepped aside as his two-legged guests departed the ceremony room one by one. He turned off the lights and gently butted the doors back together.

"Aside from the obvious, what happens now?" Stump asked.

"Fritz will be neutered tomorrow. If all goes well, Ms. Jenkins will have her litter in ten weeks. A month later, she'll be spayed."

"That's awful," Yana said.

"It says a lot more about people who work all day, play all night and ignore their animals." He leaned slowly down and then raised a tiny gray cat over his head, causing it to hang limply in his hands. "It would do more harm than good to dump additional animals into the laps of people like that, wouldn't it, Pepper?"

Yana held up her cell. "Would you mind if I take pictures of the ones on the stairs? They look so real."

Catts released little Pepper and sat on the padded bench. "I don't think they'd mind." He slowly replaced his paper slippers with sandals.

"How do you decide which ones to stuff?" James asked causing Catts to scowl.

"We do not 'stuff' animals. After their natural demise we 'permanently preserve' them."

"Do you have funerals?"

Stump wondered the same thing.

"*Funerals* is such a glum term," Catts said. "When their final day comes we celebrate how they enriched us. It takes deliberation and laborious effort to preserve them in ways that accurately depict their personalities."

"What about that one?" James asked, pointing to a multi-colored, permanently preserved specimen under Catts's padded bench. "He looks like he's missing a leg."

"First off," Catts said, while reaching down to pat his formerly-alive pet on the head, "all Calicos are ladies. It's not a breed, but the coat colors; and second, Rainbow got her foot trapped in a screen door and nearly bled to death. Her owner was going to put her down, but we nursed her back to health and she had seven more safe years—much of it right under this bench."

"That was nice of you," Yana said, while moving higher up the stairs for a close-up of a permanently preserved feline on one of the upper steps.

"That's Einstein. He's an Abyssinian. They're curious and love climbing. That's why he's high up, where he can see what we're all up to." Catts stuffed his paper slippers into a plastic bin under a table near the door. On top of the table, a wicker collection plate contained a few coins and a handmade sign with the word Donations written with a red Magic Marker.

"Every one of these irreplaceable creatures deserves at least one chance to perpetuate his or her genes," Catts continued. "It's the job of decent people like us to make that lone opportunity special." He rose and yielded the bench to Stump. "Pugsy and Milo liked you. Are you a cat person?"

"I've only known a couple cats. Señorita and Sassy, but I never got to pet Señorita."

"Well, they are usually good judges of character."

Yana quickly scooted down to the bottom step where she

sat and removed her slippers. "How many more have you preserved?"

"I never counted them. That would be too impersonal. I wish we could all be together, but I just don't have enough room."

"What about the attic?" Stump asked, hoping to get a peek in it. "Do you keep them up there?"

Catts shook his head. "Too hot."

"You could put in air conditioning."

"That would take too much power for my circuit box. If a breaker goes off at the wrong time everybody would be in danger. Besides, I don't have the kind of money it would take to make elaborate changes."

"There might be some grant money," James said. "One time, me and Stump helped a whole neighborhood upgrade their homes. We can see if they'd help you."

"Even if I did something like that, the do-gooders around here would raise hell. They already think I'm a coocoo bird, but they're the ones who use drugs and look at dirty magazines."

Stump thought of some of the odd people out on the street.

"Jack's building has its own reputation," Catts volunteered. "A long, long time ago a little girl disappeared over there and then after the big war 'friendly girls' met with Marines in the upstairs rooms."

"That part is nice," Yana said.

James shook his head, while Catts chin pointed toward the door. "I don't mean to run you folks off, but the tide's coming in. That means fish. I gotta get down to the lagoon."

"You know something, Mr. McFadden?" Stump said, dropping two bucks in the collection plate. "I'm glad Yana heard your music. You taught me a lot. Thank you."

Taking Stump's lead, James and Yana each plopped a buck in the plate, after which Catts scooped up all four bills. "This'll buy live anchovies, for bait. I catch sand bass and halibut for the pusses." He held the door open for his guests. "You people may come back if you wish."

Outside, Yana grabbed her rocking horse and Catts climbed on his bike and rode off toward the beach. Stump smiled and recalled a two-wheeled clunker, nicknamed Ol' Ug,' that he had once peddled around for the better part of a year.

"I bet Fritz and Ms. Jenkins are putting on a show," James said.

Yana slapped him on the arm. "You're disgusting."

Stump grinned. "I see what Jack meant. Mr. McFadden was really interesting."

Yana nodded. "Inspirational too. He focuses on nice things. When he remembered that *friendly girls* worked next door, it made me want to develop a reputation like that, too."

James broke into laughter. "Are you kidding me, Yana? He was talking about prostitutes."

Yana slowed and then wagged a finger in James's face. "And once again you've got some explaining to do. Just what do you know about prostitutes?"

"Yeah, dude," Stump said with a mischievous grin. "Tell her about your trip to Tijuana."

She glared at James and plopped her hands to her hips. "Well?"

"No fair. That was before I met you."

"Maybe so, but you shoulda told me about it. That's disgusting."

"It's getting close to dinner time," Stump said, still grinning. "Anybody hungry?"

"I am," James said obviously anxious to discuss something different. "How 'bout you, honey?"

"Either you're taking us somewhere nice for a change or we discuss your trip to Tijuana and the rest of your past. It's up to you."

"Like I said, there's a nice fish restaurant a couple blocks from here by the train station."

Yana nodded. "That'll do." She checked her cell for text messages. "Oh, no. Zax says Denise has to get rid of her dog."

16

In a class of lazy misfits, Edna Kline's 36-year-old son, Franklin Kline, might have made valedictorian. At least that's what Franklin's almost-stepfather, Dr. Richard Rosenberg, and a few other people thought.

Franklin, nicely tanned and thinning hair, never knew how or why his biological father and Edna Kline got together in the first place, but there couldn't have been a worse match. Edna was a college-educated woman, who studied psychology and business. She wanted all the nice things that good money could buy. In contrast, Franklin's father worked in a warehouse. The only real question was why she took so long to file for divorce.

Then Dr. Rosenberg moved in. A Ph.D. and a tenured professor in the Philosophy Department at UCLA, the doctor had prestige and an excellent salary. Over time and without a legitimate marriage, or Franklin having any say in the matter, "Dr. Richard" became Franklin's de facto stepfather. That was 20 years ago.

With the adoration of countless college students, Dr. Richard assumed he could make Franklin into another one of his star students, but Franklin had plans of his own; plans to do nothing, plans not to move out, not to attend college, not to join the military, not to get a regular job. Why should he? Mama always covered for him.

At one point, after Franklin barely made it through high school, Dr. Richard moved out to protest Edna's doting over deadbeat Franklin, but the doc must have gotten horny because he came right back a few weeks later - which amused the hell out of Franklin because it proved that the brilliant doctor was just as dependent on Edna Kline as Franklin was. From that point on Franklin mocked his almost-stepfather by calling him "Little Ricky," and Edna clung to both of them; Dr. Rosenberg because he endowed her with status, and Franklin because he gave her purpose.

Now, thousands of days later, Franklin had been called to his mother's office. He put off a small landscaping job and drove his sky-blue van to Meadowlark Flats, where he signed in and wandered into Edna's private office.

"Close the door," she said before forcing him to hug her.

"Hi mom. You still skimming the grey-haired society?"

"Shh!" she said finger to lips. "Somebody might hear you."

"So what? You're the top dog around here and everybody knows it."

"I don't want to take unnecessary chances."

"Alright, alright. If I promise to be your good little boy can I get you to use one of those secret credit cards of yours and spring for a set of tires for my van?"

"They're at it again," she said, ignoring his question.

"Who?"

"That Coca-Cola woman, Minnie Moore and her sister-in-law."

"Are you still holding a grudge against those old bitches because their doctor wouldn't let you take their Coke away?"

"It's not a grudge. It's a principle. We're not running a delicatessen here. Anyway, I caught them talking about their old farm and that bottle of coins again. This time they sounded more convincing."

Franklin shook his head. "So what?"

"So, one of the guests might believe them and I don't want to create any competition for you."

"For me? What the hell are you talking about, Mom?"

"If that treasure is real, we're talking about old gold coins and they can be priceless. I want you to take a drive out there and see if you can find them."

Franklin sighed. "Did Little Ricky put you up to this, Mom? I thought you said that farm is in Kansas. I don't want to drive out there."

"It has nothing to do with him, but this is the one chance you have of hitting it big on your own. That'll get Dr. Richard off both our backs."

"I know this doesn't surprise you, but I don't give a flying flip about him. I'd just as soon help you skim the brain-dead people around here. We both know that's where the easy money is."

"I have to admit, I just got another POA situation. Could be the best one yet. Mrs. Hennretti's sister wants to do some world traveling."

"Now we're talking. Why don't you just slip me a grand so I can get those tires and we can talk about something else?"

"'Cause I want you to do something special on your own, so that you don't have to mow lawns anymore. That's beneath you, Franklin. You're almost 40."

"I'm a landscaper mom, not just *somebody who mows lawns*."

"Yeah, right, and when was the last time you had a big landscaping job other than the one I got you?"

"There you go again; implying that I'd never be anything without you."

"That's why I want you to find those coins. Rent a metal detector if you have to."

"I ain't doing that."

She clenched her jaw then spoke with forced restraint. "I'll tell you what Mama will do. If you'll make a legitimate effort to find those coins, I'll cover all your expenses. Then when you get back I'll get you those tires and a brand-new computer. That's a lot of money just for going for a drive."

Franklin shook his head and sighed. "Alright, Mom, maybe I can go in a week or so, but I think it's a waste of time, especially if you're just trying to impress Little Ricky."

She pinched his cheek. "That's my boy. Mama likes it when we get along. Maybe after you strike it rich you'll find a woman and make a grandbaby for me."

"That again? The last thing I need is another woman bossing me around."

17

Well past the mid-point of Stump's freshman year, he and Myles had been less close, but Grandma Pauline's near-accident changed a lot of things. For instance, it had been revealed that when Myles had serious financial woes, it was okay to invade Stump's trust; but when Stump needed a car and was too-poor-to-pay-attention, Myles was tighter than a teenybopper's jeans. The double-speak was both maddening and priceless.

Before they could move Grandma Pauline to a safe facility, they had to make monetary arrangements and Myles had found a financial advisor who could transfer some of Stump's trust money to a mutual fund that ought to generate enough income to pay the new expenses. They agreed to meet in the parking lot outside the financial planner's office.

Now in Pops and on the back end of the 90-minute drive, Stump thought about how much his life had changed, including when that Xander Brooks entered the equation.

Logically, Stump knew that the man could not be his creator, but down deep he had always wondered who his real dad was, so in a moment of weakness, he went along with that dumb DNA test.

Since then, he had occasion to fantasize about the possibility that Xander was indeed who he said he was, but it always led to disappointment. Hell, the dude couldn't even make it as a truck driver. That certainly wasn't the kind of thing a son could be proud of. Oh, well, it wasn't true anyway.

Returning his thoughts to the pending meeting with Myles, he'd already decided that he wanted to shame Myles into realizing how ridiculously stubborn he'd been concerning Stump's vehicle situation. That was why he and James had temporarily taped a potty chair to the rider's side floorboard of Pops.

When he arrived at the office building he scanned the lot and parked facing the incoming customers so he could see Myles's first glimpse of the stupid Popsicle truck. He piled out and wished he had a bright-red wig and a bulbous clip-on nose to enhance the basic message: Myles's son had to drive the most ridiculous vehicle in southern California.

Shortly thereafter, Myles's relatively young SUV eased into the lot. He'd brought Katherine with him. With foot on bumper, Stump snickered and sent Myles a well-deserved wave of shame. Katherine grinned and waved back, but Myles drove by and parked a few spaces up. Katherine was still smiling when she and Myles made their way back to Stump and Pops. Myles gave the absurd vehicle a quick glance and tilted his head. "What you got there?"

Duh! The gigantic image of a Popsicle on the side of the truck should have been a sufficient clue. "It used to be a Popsicle truck."

"I see that. Where'd you get it?"

"I bought it at an auction. It was the only thing I could afford."

"I think it's cute," Katherine said.

Myles opened the door, leaned in where he had to see the potty chair. "I thought you wanted a traditional car."

"I did, but—"

"Well, it's unorthodox, but I can see why you did it.

A vehicle like this can come in handy; and, with only 40 thousand miles on it, you can probably get ten years out of it. All you gotta do is buy a rider's seat at a junkyard and you'll be all set. I knew you could find something worthwhile if you put in a little effort. Well done."

WTF? Stump wanted to scream.

"Let's go inside," Myles said, pointing to the office building.

If Stump didn't genuinely love Grandma Pauline he might have stomped off, but he could never turn his back on Grandma Pauline, even to make a point.

Inside, they waited in the lobby. Katherine grabbed a magazine and Stump observed Myles's jittery fingers, which reaffirmed how uneasy Myles was with big-money issues.

"Hello, Myles and Katherine," a friendly female voice said from behind Stump. He turned to see a middle-aged brunette hiding behind two gigantic boobs and a frilly, bright yellow blouse. "This must be Stump," she said. "My name's Olivia de Franken, but you can call me Liv. Let's go to my office. I've got your paperwork ready."

Moments later and sitting at Ms. de Franken's desk, Stump had to fight off his first big grin of the day. He wished James were there because James referred to the large ones as *tig bitties* and Liv had two of the tiggest bitties Stump had ever seen.

"Your father tells me that you're moving some of your trust money to help your grandmother. I'm really impressed."

It was like looking toward two bright suns. Stump didn't dare look right at them. He focused instead on her eyes. "Yes, ma'am," he said, defying nature.

"Mr. Cooper also said that you've solved some murders and are in criminology school. I've never met anybody who has solved a murder."

Stump may have been slightly blinded and slightly flustered but he already liked this woman because she'd bothered to learn a little about him. The people at Sunn Bank, where his three mill had been stagnant for six years, never did anything like that. Stump looked at Myles, who appeared to be oblivious to both the kind words and the glowing twins.

Over the next half-hour Stump played peek-a-boob with Liv de Franken while everybody discussed Grandma Pauline's situation and agreed that Katherine was not to blame for the highway incident.

Finally, they mentioned some of the memory care facilities they'd checked out. "Some of the places were sterile and institutional," Katherine said.

Myles added. "My mom needs a place that feels like somebody's living room."

All of that led to how expensive the better places were, which brought the conversation back to why mutual funds were a good idea.

Liv strongly recommended the Vanguard Group. She put a lot of emphasis on track records, safety and yields, and managed to divert Stump's thoughts away from the hypocrisy of Myles invading the previously *untouchable* trust.

"Nobody at our bank told me those things," Stump finally said.

"Well, they're bankers," Liv explained. "They focus on deposits and making loans, but a Certified Financial Planner has extra training about investing and estate planning."

Katherine spoke next, "The bank always said that CDs were the safest place for Stump's money so that's where Myles put it, but they didn't pay very much."

Liv nodded toward Myles. "The last time we talked, you said you wanted to transfer in a million dollars. If that's still the plan, I can put your money to work within 24 hours after you wire it into our new account."

"Can I just have them give me a cashier's check? I don't like the idea of sending that much money over the internet."

Stump resisted the urge to roll his eyes.

"Sure. People bring us checks all the time. We'd just have to wait for the check to clear before we could invest it for you, but it's definitely doable. I should warn you though, banks don't like giving up that much money. They may try to talk you out of it."

Myles shook his head. "Too bad. They've had their chance. I'm transferring the money tomorrow."

That is, if his fingers quit quivering.

18

"Tell us about yourself, Wilbur," a staff member asked of the elderly African American, whose slacks and button-down shirt afforded him a certain dignity that contradicted the fact that he'd just pulled his dentures from his front pocket.

Stump had never been in a seniors' community, but after his money was transferred to the Vanguard people, Myles and Katherine homed in on Meadowlark Flats in San Juan Capistrano.

"You lived in Jamestown, Virginia, Daddy. Remember?"

After Wilbur's daughter prompted him, his brows scrunched as he thought for a second. Then, "We grew the t'bacci, ya know—smoked it, too." His daughter smiled.

The director of the place, a distinguished woman named Edna Kline, suggested that Myles bring his family around on Saturday morning for a gathering they called *Meet Your Neighbor*, or MYN Day, when selected residents talked to the group about their pasts. Relatives and/or staff members assisted those who needed help, especially those from the Memory Care wing, where Grandma Pauline might be placed.

Now in the audience, Stump and Myles had joined Edna Kline on a couch along with two mature women. Stump sat up as the woman in front took her father's hand.

"Tell them about your mama and papa, Daddy. You loved your mama and papa."

Wilbur's well-established forehead wrinkles indicated he was scanning his memory bank. "We was real poor," he ultimately said. "Mama cooked in Masta's house."

"Don't you mean at Aunt Teeree's house, Daddy?"

"Me and Earl smoked the t'bacci in cob pipes."

The loving woman stroked her father's hand. "Earl was your brother, right, Daddy?"

A slow nod preceded a warm grin. "We was always gettin' in trouble, me and him, for messin' with the horses. Masta had da overseer whip my daddy for what we done."

Stump didn't know a lot about slavery, but he knew it ended during the Civil War era, meaning Wilbur would have to be around 140 years old for his story to be true. Other people must have figured that out too, but it didn't seem to matter to anybody. They'd probably had similar experiences with their loved ones as he and Myles and Katherine had with Grandma Pauline, who regularly conflated times and places and fact and fiction.

That must have been what happened to Wilbur. A person of his background could have easily heard stories from relatives about slavery in generations gone by. Those stories and the people involved would have had a big impact on their heirs and Wilbur might have unknowingly adopted old family yarns as his own. But if he were like Grandma Pauline, it wouldn't do any good to correct him. At times like this it was best to agree with the elderly person or change the subject.

"Tell your friends about when you were a driving instructor, Daddy."

As Wilbur struggled for faint memories, Stump took a cursory glance around the room to see if Meadowlark Flats was worthy of Grandma Pauline. An eclectic collection of padded chairs had been blended among seven long and matching high-backed couches. Around the perimeter, walls of various colors sported interesting pictures, mostly of birds. Big windows welcomed sunlight and bragged of the well-groomed grounds outside.

"Thank your friends, Daddy," Wilbur's daughter said.

The old-timer scanned the audience, which broke into applause. As he and his daughter made their way through smiles-a-plenty Wilbur returned his dentures to his pocket while friendly pats landed on his shoulders.

"Thank you so much, Wilbur," a smiling caregiver said as she took the stage. "We so love your stories." She returned her attention to the audience. "Next up is Bea Douglas. As many of you know, Bea lives in the Hummingbird building. I hope she's going to tell us about her parakeets."

Suddenly, Edna Kline and Myles rose, indicating they were heading to her office to discuss the particulars of Grandma Pauline's potential move. Stump would have preferred to listen to the parakeet woman, but he followed them through a maze of furniture, wheelchairs and walkers before a very short, elderly woman with a cane grabbed his arm. "Do you know who I am?" she asked.

Stump shook his head as Edna Kline took over and smiled at the woman. "You're Ruth, honey. You live here. You're loved and very safe."

Comforted, the confused woman politely sat back down. To Stump, it was living proof that professional caregivers were much better qualified to take care of Grandma Pauline than he and Myles and Katherine were.

Upon reaching Edna Kline's office, she spoke to Stump. "What did you think of our event?"

"I like how well you treat the patients."

"Well, thank you. We refer to them as *residents*, but we think of them as family and try to make our facility feel like home to them."

"I think I'm ready to take that tour we discussed," Myles said.

Katherine nodded. "Me, too."

"Wonderful. I've got the perfect person lined up to show you around." Mrs. Kline pressed a button on her phone. "Tamara. We're ready for you to join us, dear."

Just then Edna got a call from the front desk. Her son was on the line. "I have to get this," she said.

"We'll introduce ourselves to Tamara," Myles whispered before he and Stump left her office and closed the door.

19

"That was sad," Stump said as Tamara brushed some of her shoulder-length hair out of her eyes and led him and Myles and Katherine to the lobby. "I've never seen a hospice before." He'd never seen that many spectacular pictures and paintings of eagles, either.

From an aerial view, Meadowlark Flats resembled a gigantic cross. The Hospice section, which they'd just visited, was the smallest, and made up the top of the cross. The Assisted Living section and the Memory Care wings branched off to either side of the heart of the complex, which included the reception area, main offices, a cafeteria, public restrooms and a gift shop. That left the longest building for the Independent Living residents.

"I have a question, Tamara," Katherine said. "Did the hospice patients live in the other wings before being transferred?"

"Good question. We can accommodate nearly anybody. Sometimes our residents move from one wing to the next as their needs dictate, but we also get referrals and walk-ins." She pointed past the reception area. "After the Hospice, I like to show our guests the Independent Living wing for a contrast. Do any one of you know what we call a group of hummingbirds?"

Stump looked above the entrance to that wing where a gigantic picture of several hummingbirds with frantic wings hovered like helicopters at a feeder. "A swarm?" he ventured.

"Good guess, but a group of hummingbirds is called a 'charm.' It's befitting. We have 118 apartments in the wing, packed with some of the most *charming* people you'll ever meet. There's a two-year waiting list to get in. It's like a seniors' dormitory. The residents can come and go as they please, but we also shuttle them to various places: grocery stores, fancy restaurants and museums, not to mention our own bowling league. There's something for everybody."

"Sounds like *we* ought to move here," Myles said to Katherine.

"I'm afraid you guys don't qualify. You have to be at least 62. Once a year we take a bus to Las Vegas for a weekend. Five years ago, Sandra Burm won over a hundred thousand dollars from a slot machine. Now people sign up for the buses a year in advance."

"My mom would have liked things like that," Myles said, sounding guilty.

"They all do," Tamara said, as they reached the entrance area. "You should see the craziness on Grandparents' day. We've even had a few marriages."

Stump wondered what a honeymoon would be like for old people. Would they go to bed early, and if so, would they do the same things younger newlyweds do? "Can they have pets?" he asked, while observing a silver-haired gentleman coast up to the mailboxes.

"Cats and small dogs," Tamara said while the man scooped up his mail. "Hello, Dr. Ashcroft," she said before turning back to Myles and Stump. "Dr. Ashcroft is one of several retired doctors who live here."

"Hi, Tamara," he said, before addressing Myles. "You folks visiting somebody?"

"We're looking for a place for my mom."

The doctor nodded. "Well, if Tamara here can't help you, nobody can."

"Good to know," Myles said as the doctor moved off and bypassed the elevators in favor of the stairway.

After that they toured the halls of the Hummingbird wing and met a retired dentist who had a collection of false teeth that once belonged to famous celebrities.

From there Tamara showed Stump and Myles the Assisted Living section, or the Canary wing as it was called. Tamara suggested that these people were the toughest group to deal with. Apparently, the bulk of their angst sprang from their lost independence. "They often complain about living around all 'the old people,' while ignoring the individuals in their own mirrors."

"They must get visitors," Katherine said.

"You'd think so but Google has replaced grandparents for many young people, nowadays."

A guilt-chill raced up Stump's back because there had been occasions when communicating with Grandma Pauline was difficult so he reverted to Google and social media, where his world made more sense.

As they made their final trek back to the Memory Care wing, Stump stopped abruptly, spun around and looked more closely at the large pictures of birds that led to the various wings. "You know something," he said to the others. "I think I know why those specific birds were selected for the various wings. Take the canaries, for instance. Canaries are a perfect symbol for people in the Assisted Living section because those people need to be cheered up and canaries are considered to be singers. Get it? Singing cheers people up. It's a perfect match." Both Myles and Tamara smiled.

"The Memory Care wing features peacocks because they have colorful tails. When Grandma Pauline talks to us she mixes up timelines and people and everything else. She has 'colorful tales,'" he said, making air quotes. "Get it? Peacocks have colorful tails too, only we spell it differently."

Myles chuckled and shook his head.

"Hummingbirds symbolize activity," Stump went on. "They're fun, they buzz around and go places in search of adventure. Like Tamara said earlier. It's part of their *charm*."

Katherine smiled. "What about the people in the Hospice?"

"Simple. Eagles fly high and are closer to God. They're also the symbol of freedom. The patients in that wing are like that, too. They must yearn to be set free and to join God."

"That's amazing," Tamara said, nodding. "It all makes sense now."

Myles put his hand on Stump's shoulder. "You never cease to impress me, Stumpster."

Minutes later and back in Mrs. Kline's office everybody agreed that Meadowlark Flats was the correct place for Grandma Pauline. She'd be safe and among experts who had a lot of experience with all senior issues, including dementia.

"You can focus on loving her, while somebody else worries about her basic needs," Mrs. Kline said, "and I've got the perfect suitemate for her. Minnie Moore only has one relative that I know of, so she and Pauline ought to bond real well."

"That's good," Myles said. "Stump and I have agreed to each drop by a couple times a week, but that still doesn't amount to a lot of hours with her."

"I'm sure they'd both enjoy each other. I guess I should warn you that Minnie has to have a Coca-Cola every day. It's like a morning cup of coffee to her."

Stump nodded. He'd seen a woman holding a bottle of Coke while Wilbur was speaking.

"Warn us?" Myles asked. "Why would that bother us?"

"It might not, but your mom might want one too and they're not very healthy."

"Can't you substitute juice or something?" Stump asked.

"Believe me, we've tried, but she threw fits. We also tried diet drinks so she wouldn't get so much sugar but she could tell the difference. Eventually her doctor said it's not much different than drinking a cup of coffee so let her have it, more for her mental health than anything else. I just wanted to make sure you folks are okay with it before we discuss one final item."

Stump glanced at Myles. "I don't see any harm to let them have a few pleasures at this point in their lives."

"I'm okay with it," Myles said. "What's the other topic?"

Edna Kline smiled. "Minnie likes to tell a story about an old family treasure, in a well, at their farm when she was a little girl. It's a cute story really, but it'll get old in a hurry. You'll just have to humor her."

"No problem," Myles said. "We know what that's like. My mom does the same thing. She thinks she's back in her teaching days. We just go along with her."

"Okay, then. Those are the only caveats, so all we have to do is check out the suite where Pauline will live. Do you think she'd prefer the window?"

20

A little over an hour later, while he headed back to campus via I-5, Stump's cell rang out. He flipped his Nike hat around. "Hey, James. Sup?"

"You'll never guess what just came in, brofriend."

"Something for the baby?"

"Nope. We think it's your DNA test results."

Hmm. Part of Stump wondered what it would be like to know his real father, but overall he knew that Xander Brooks was up to something else. "Throw it away, dude. We both know that guy was a phony."

"That's what I think too, but Yana wants to open the package. Is that okay with you?"

"Suit yourself, but I've got more important shit to think about—"

"Go ahead," James said to Yana as Stump continued.

"I think we found a place for Grandma Pauline. She even has her first real friend. We shoulda done this a long time ago."

Suddenly a shrill background scream interrupted the conversation.

"Holy shit, dude!" James bellowed. *"That son-of-bitch really is your old man!"*

"Yeah, right. Nice try, buddy, but you're bullshitting the wrong guy."

"No way, man. Yana just showed me the paper. Switch over to FaceTime if you don't believe me and I'll show you."

"Give it a rest, lame-o. I'm going 60 miles an hour and I'd have to pull over."

"Then go ahead and do that, bro. It'll give you something new to think about on your way home."

"Give it up, James. We both heard the dude say he talked with my mother a while back, but she's been dead for six years. You get that, right?"

"He may have fed you a Burger King-sized whopper, but we both know that DNA tests don't lie. You want to see the results now or not?"

Stump sighed. "If it'll make you feel any better." He flipped his hat bill back to its previous position and pulled over.

* * *

Uh-oh! After seeing key parts of the report, James was correct. It provided Stump with plenty to consider. All his life he'd been led to believe that there was no way to find his bio-dad and vice versa. But all of that had just blown up in Stump's face, which presented another big question: why did Xander Brooks lie about meeting Stump's mom?

Stump made his way to Zax Place and into the dining area, where Zax and James were seated at the usual booth and Yana was wiping down the coffee station.

"What you gonna do, Stump?" Zax asked.

"I dunno. I'm thinking about calling the guy, but I know that he lied to me so I could never trust him. What would you do, Zax?"

"Well, I think you should give the man a chance to explain himself. What's the worst that could happen?"

James grinned. "He could be a crazed serial killer."

"Nobody asked you, smarty pants," Zax, said before

returning to Stump. "This may be your only chance to get your questions answered. He could be a really nice guy. It would be a shame to chase him off after he reached out to you, without really knowing his story."

"You're probably right, but he'd better have a damn good explanation why he lied."

Yana wandered over. "There's only one way to find out," she said, sliding Stump the business card Xander gave her, "and now's as good a time as any."

Stump paused a moment and then placed a call. "The DNA came back," he said the instant Xander Brooks answered.

"This must be Stump. I'm glad you decided to call."

"I guess I owe you an apology."

"Forget it. I admit that I also had some doubts about being your father—until I saw you in person. I'm just glad you checked it out."

"What should I call you?"

"Well, I sure ain't been a father. And Mr. Brooks is too formal. Why don't you just call me Xander, like everybody else does?"

"The first time I met you, you seemed like a conman or something."

"I probably shouldn't have said that part about recently meeting your mother. I could tell that it was like fingernails on a chalk board to you."

"No shit. That wasn't too bright, especially considering she's been dead for six years."

"That's not what I meant."

"At least you admit it. Why'd you lie?"

"I didn't say I lied. I said I shouldn't have brought it up."

"Dude. There's no use trying to wiggle out of it. You're busted. Admit it."

"If you don't mind, I'd rather talk about some other things. Was your mother married?"

"No."

"You got any brothers or sisters?

"No."

"Interesting. Who'd you stay with after your mother's passing? Grandparents? A stepfather?"

"Myles adopted me. He was her fiancé."

"That was big of him. How'd you get your nickname?"

"Aunt Gerry gave it to me when I was learning to walk."

"You got a girlfriend?"

"Not really. You ask a lot of questions."

"You're not going to tell me you're gay, are you?"

"What if I was? Would that make a difference to you?"

"I don't think so, but it might take some getting used to."

"Well that ain't it."

"Then why doesn't an incredibly handsome young fellow, who looks remarkably like his father, and has enough smarts to make it into a criminology college, have a hot co-ed dangling from each arm?"

"I dunno, dude. You tell me. I guess I never found the right one."

A rustling noise came from Xander's side. Then, *"Let's go, Daddy."*

"Give me a minute, Sweetie. Daddy's on an important call." He returned his attention to Stump. *"Sorry."*

"I guess I should ask you about your family."

"Sure. My wife's name is Brianne. We live in Milwaukee and met at a church function. Before long, we had our first son, Danville. He'd be one of your half-brothers. You were born in '95. He was born in '97.

"A half-brother, huh? How many are there?"

"We had three boys in a row. There's Danville, Irvington, and Jett."

"Daddy?"

"Is that one of them? Do you need to go?"

"I can talk a couple more minutes. That's your half-sister. She's the youngest one of the bunch."

"Does she have a strange name, too?"

"Not really, unless you think Barthella Louise-Ann Farnsworth Brooks is strange."

Stump choked back a laugh. "What the hell's the matter with you, dude?"

Xander giggled. *"I was just messin' with ya, Stump. Her real name's Lori Sue. That's not too strange for you, is it?"*

Stump grinned. "You had me there for a moment."

"It's good to hear you chuckle. If you don't mind my saying so, Stump, I think you're taking all of this too seriously. I'm sure we'll like each other if we'll give each other a chance."

"Alright then, when we first met, you said you're a retired truck driver. That right?"

"Pretty much. I drove for 16 years then had an accident. Now I get shooting pains in my legs if I sit for long spells."

"I'd always hoped you did something more important."

"Sorry to disappoint you, but driving trucks is honorable work and it feeds a growing family. That's all I needed."

"I bet you took speed, and spit chewing tobacco out the window, and peed in jugs. That shit's gross."

"You're right about the speed. It helped me to stay awake but it became addictive. I had a rough time giving it up."

"What about chewing tobacco and peeing in a bottle?"

"No and yes, in that order."

"While you were rolling?"

"When it was safe to do so, we peed in mayonnaise jars. Then we'd just pour it out the next time we stopped."

Another exasperated sigh came from Xander's side. *"Come on, Daddy. We're waiting."*

"I'm sorry, Stump," Xander said. *"I really am, but we had to reserve tables at Chuck E. Cheese's for Lori Sue's birthday party and I'm running late. Do you suppose we could finish this tomorrow or the next day? Do you Skype?"*

21

Stump had always been able to read people fairly well, but when it came to the possibility of advancing his relationship with Xander Brooks, he was so confused it was like having somebody else's dream.

When Xander had an opportunity to unravel his lie regarding Stump's mother, he sidestepped the matter. Stump couldn't trust somebody who was both dishonest and too stubborn to admit he'd made a mistake.

At the same time he couldn't overlook how committed Xander was to Lori Sue's birthday party and the love in her voice when she spoke with him.

Then there was that other contradiction. Xander may have been nothing more than an over-the-road truck driver who peed in bottles but he was a good communicator, had a good sense of humor, and was wiser than Stump would have guessed.

Beyond all that, there was something else that made Stump want to give Xander another chance. Stump had always lived within a small family, first with his mom and then with Myles and Grandma Pauline. But all of a sudden he had new relatives, including four half-siblings.

With both his cell and laptop in tow he wandered over to Zax's Place for the Skype call. After getting himself a drink, he plopped into the usual booth, opened his laptop and buzzed Xander.

"I was just thinking of you," Xander said while Stump observed two large beds behind Xander, separated by a nightstand with a couple of beer cans on it. *"I'm sorry I had to cut you off, but a birthday is important to little girls."*

"I know. Zax has a daughter about the same age as Lori Sue. I was at her birthday party a couple months ago."

"Who's Zax?"

"A friend. She owns this café. Are you in a hotel, dude?"

"Yeah. I'm at truckers' convention in Vegas with one of my buddies, Big Rich."

"I thought you retired."

"Did, but once a trucker, always a trucker. I like to see all the new toys in the rigs."

Now that Stump got a closer look at Xander, he could see the resemblance, especially in the eyes and mouth. "Five kids, huh?" Stump said, adding himself to the equation. "You sure like to populate."

Xander smiled. *"Wait until you hear about the rest of the family. Of course, they're your family now, too. I've got a brother and sister. Both are married and have kids. That means aunts and uncles and six more cousins. That's not all; my folks are still alive and healthy. That'd be Grandma and Grandpa to you. Then, there's my wife's family. They're a wild group. They'll all want to meet you."*

Wow! Stump's family was growing faster than the crowds just before Lakers' games.

"Your turn," Xander said. *"How'd you end up in criminology school?"*

"People just said I had a knack for it."

"Hi there." A new head, probably Big Rich, entered the screen from the side. *"I hope you're not as crazy as your old man is."*

Stump grinned. *"Big Rich"* appeared to be about 5 feet tall and no more than 120 lbs. Stump wondered how the dude could reach the pedals in a truck.

"I'm sorry, Stump," Xander said, *"but I have to cut you off again, but I've got a couple open days this weekend. How would you like to come to Wisconsin for a visit? I can cover the airfare."*

Aside from one trip to Houston, Stump had never been out of state. He certainly wouldn't go visit a pack of half-blooded relatives he didn't know. "I don't think so."

"You can bring your buddy if you want to."

"Better not. We've got school and homework."

"Okay, then, I'm pretty wide open next Monday. Why don't I come there for a couple hours? I might even bring one of the boys."

"You gonna come all that way just for a couple hours? You must be rich or stupid."

Xander laughed. *"I'm neither of those things. You got that time open or not?"*

"I dunno, dude. Won't your wife mind if you take off like that?"

Xander scoffed. *"Are you kidding? She's all for it. Big Rich will tell ya. Most cross-country truckers are either single or have independent wives who can run the roost just fine when the old man is on the road."*

Big Rich dipped his head into view. *"My ole lady drove with me for a few years — 'til our first kid could crawl."*

Xander nodded. *"Anyway, Brianne is always in charge of the house — even when I'm there. When I was between hauls it usually just took a couple days before we both felt like I was under her feet. A few days later, I'd be back on the road and we'd miss each other again."*

"It's a trucker's curse," Big Rich said. *"But after a weeklong trip, there's a hell of a lot of bedroom fireworks on that first night back, if you get my drift."*

Stump grinned and tilted his head. "I guess I could see you for a couple hours on Monday."

"Great. If we don't get along, I'll bug you no more. I could meet you in your little hangout."

"Okay, but I'm just telling you, we ain't gonna have a lot to talk about until you apologize for lying to me when we first met."

"I can tell you're very proud of your mother. That's what counts the most."

"You got that right."

"Sorry to cut you off again, Stump, but me and Big Rich are supposed to meet some other guys and check out the new sleepers."

"Okay, then. I guess I'll see you Monday."

"Got it. Lee's College Café. Mid-morning. See you then."

Stump disconnected and remained disappointed because Xander didn't man up about the lie, but Stump was also intrigued by the dual life Xander had lived: one part devoted domestic, one part nomad.

22

On his way to see Grandma Pauline, Stump swerved around a slow-moving truck, causing James to clutch for the dashboard. Stump grinned; the small leathery bucket seat he and James had snagged at a junkyard the previous day looked more out of place than a mink stole at a mid-summer animal rights convention. "That's what you get for making me drive before I could get that seat bolted down."

"I told you, Yana needs our car when she gets off work, and when Yana gets what she wants—"

"I don't need to hear about it."

"I feel sorry for you, dude. I get laid all the time, but you're some damn monk or something. I'm surprised you don't hit on Zax. She might teach you a thing or two. Then you can tell me and I can—"

"She wouldn't do anything like that. She likes guys her own age and wine and expensive restaurants. Let's talk about something else."

"All right. So, what do you want me to do when we get to your grandmother's new place?"

"I don't know yet. Myles and Katherine moved her in yesterday, but I want to make sure she's not too confused."

"That would suck."

"Myles said they have life-sized dolls and stuffed animals and some robotic cats that wiggle around and purr, for people who find those things comforting."

"Dude. Maybe we could make a robot girlfriend that can wiggle around and purr for you."

"You got a one-track gutter, you know that? For now I just hope she likes her suitemate, Minnie Moore. I heard she's addicted to Coke."

"Cocaine?"

"Not cocaine, you dumb-ass. Coca-Cola. She drinks one or two everyday, not Pepsi, not diet Coke. It's got to be the real deal."

"Another wacko, huh?"

"They're not wackos, bro; they're just confused. One woman can't remember her name. Another guy thinks he used to be a slave. But they're nice people with nice families so if you come across somebody like that, bite your tongue."

"We gonna see a bunch of wheelchairs and walkers, cause I feel sorry for people like that."

"Well, you won't see any hover boards, I can guarantee that."

"Good idea, bro. You should invent a hoverchair so old people can get around easier. They could have sky races and everything."

"You're a lame-o. You know that?"

A little later, at Meadowlark Flats they signed in and marched off to the Community room.

"I like MYN day," Stump said. "Mature people are interesting."

"There they are," James said, pointing to Grandma Pauline and another woman on a couch in the center of the room. "They're holding hands."

"She looks happy," Stump said. "Hi, Grandma. Remember me?"

Grandma Pauline studied Stump's face while he glanced

at Minnie Moore, who had a capped, near-full Coke bottle in her lap. "Do you know my sister?" Grandma Pauline asked.

Sister? That was a new one, but Stump knew not to correct her. "Hello," he said to Minnie Moore, "I'm Stump and this is James. May we call you Minnie?"

"Why not? That's my name," she said, sounding more "together" than Grandma Pauline.

An unexplainable ear-to-ear grin jumped onto Grandma Pauline's face while she simultaneously waved her free hand in the air. Curious, Stump turned to see two youngsters on a nearby couch. The youngest one, a 4-year-old girl, waved and smiled just as enthusiastically at Grandma Pauline. Then her 6-year-old brother joined in, which prompted James and Minnie Moore to do likewise. Amused and overwhelmed by group pressure, Stump happily flapped both his hands, too.

After several more minutes of silliness, everybody stopped the hand fluttering except for Grandma Pauline and the girl, all of which reaffirmed that Grandma Pauline belonged among children and happy people.

Turning his attention back to James, Stump gestured across the room. "That's Dr. Ashcroft. He's real popular."

"Maybe you can hit him up for a car loan until you get your trust money."

"I doubt it, but that would teach Myles that I'm old enough to get by without his reins around my neck."

"Good morning, everybody," a new, louder voice came from the stage area. "For those of you who don't know, my name is Josie and this is Meet Your Neighbor day. We have some special people here to share their stories. We're going to start out with Thelma Sullivan, from the Canary wing."

A bit of applause encouraged Mrs. Sullivan, who needed a walker to get to the seat of honor with her daughter. They started off by saying that Thelma was an excellent cook. From there, they mentioned holiday gatherings, a big peach tree and homemade pies for her family.

After two additional residents spoke, a man named Perry

Bernstein told the audience about his career as an engineer on passenger trains, at which point Stump observed that Grandma Pauline and Minnie Moore continued to hold hands, which both saddened and pleased Stump.

After everybody split up, Stump wanted to check out Grandma Pauline's suite. He and James found a doorplate with the names Pauline Cooper and Minnie Moore inscribed. "That's a rad name," James said, "How many more Minnie Moores could there be?"

"Probably many more Minnie Moores," Stump said, enjoying the play on words.

"I bet she has a brother named Lot. He'd be a Lot Moore."

Stump smiled and gently opened the lockless door. Inside, and to the right an invisible line separated two beds with bedside trays and two dressers. The left wall housed two closets, a sitting area and access to a shared bathroom. "It looks like a hospital room, bro."

Stump checked out the bathroom. "I see what's going on. They make the rooms plain so everybody chills in the big room."

After that, Stump and James dropped by Tamara's office. "It's as if they've always known each other," Tamara said, "but Pauline can't keep Minnie's name straight. She keeps saying 'Millie,' as opposed to Minnie."

"Oh I get it," Stump said. "Grandma Pauline had a sister named Mildred, but they called her Millie. Millie sounds a lot like Minnie."

Tamara nodded. "That explains it."

"You must have some bizarre stories in a community like this," James said. "I mean with Viagra and similar pills now days."

What? Boner pills? Why the hell did James ask that?

"At first those medications were mostly just used by the married people," Tamara said, obviously more at ease with the topic than Stump was. "But they quickly became more popular throughout the community."

Now Stump was glad James brought it up. "That isn't going to affect Grandma Pauline, is it?"

"You don't have to worry about that. People in memory care or hospice aren't capable of giving informed consent, and we have an eye on them at all times."

"Whew!" Stump said pretending to wipe sweat off his forehead.

"But we don't have a right to interfere with the hummingbirds or canaries, as long as they know what they're doing. We just try to keep it dignified. No public talking about it. It embarrasses some of the other residents."

Stump knew the feeling.

* * *

In an office just down the hall, Edna Kline took a call. "Hi, honey," she said to her son, Franklin. "Do you have good news for your mother?"

"Not particularly. I wanted to tell you I landed another job, so I won't be able to go on that wild goose chase for another week."

"Don't put if off too long, honey. Mother doesn't want anybody else to beat you to your treasure."

"That's a joke. I know you want me out of here so you and Little Rickey can get it on. I heard you last night. Good God, Mother. You are both over 60. Can't you control yourselves?"

"You just mind your own business."

"Yeah, right. One more thing. I'm going to need those tires you promised me before I go out to that crazy lady's farm. My van will ride more quietly. And when I come back you owe me a nice computer regardless of whether I find anything or not."

"Alright, alright. How much do you need?"

"An even thousand ought to do it."

23

"**H**ere you go," Yana said, placing two menus on the table.

Xander nodded, then spoke to Stump. "I wanted to bring one of the boys but mama said '*no,*' cause it's a school day."

"Before we get started," Stump said, "would you mind telling me how you can come all this way just for a couple hours? That has to be expensive."

"Easy. I fly for free. I already told you that I had a bad accident while offloading cargo at the Phoenix airport. I messed up my hip and back, which is not good for a trucker. I sued the airline, but their insurance company had a herd of attorneys. They could've dragged things out for a lifetime if they'd wanted to, but I had a family to feed. Long story short, I settled the case. After attorney's fees and taxes there was barely enough cash to pull our house out of foreclosure and to set up modest college funds for our kids. I could be on disability the rest of my life."

"That sucks. What about flying for free?"

"It was part of the settlement. At the time, fuel costs were high and the airline had a bunch of empty seats so they gave me a lifetime travel pass and travel vouchers so I could take companions with me. I can only take one person at a time, and we have to fly standby, but we can usually catch a flight."

"That part's wicked."

"Another unexpected problem arose. I have a pilot's license and can fly small planes and small jets, but with a pass to fly for free and a limited income, I barely get enough hours in to keep my license active. I'd trade it all for my job back."

"You guys ready to order?" Yana asked.

Stump turned her way. "I'll have French toast and bacon."

"I'll have a bowl of 'jail food'—with raisins." Xander added with a grin.

"What's that? I've never been in jail."

"It's Danville's term for oatmeal." Yana grinned and made notes on her pad before limping off.

"Danville's the big cheese in our home," Xander said to Stump. "Just got his driver's license. I bet you remember what that was like."

"I drove a pick-up," Stump said, smirking.

"My wife asked me to find out something interesting about you. You got any gossip I can pass along?"

"I solved several murders."

"No kidding? That would impress the hell out of her—"

For the next 15 minutes, Stump filled Xander in on a double murder he'd solved when he was just barely a teenager. Then he spoke of some reward money and the doggie park he'd built with the money. In between topics, Xander asked questions about Myles and Grandma Pauline and Stump's first love, which prompted Stump to mention another solved murder and a serial rapist he'd send to prison.

"No wonder you go to detective school," Xander finally said. "That's damn impressive."

"I guess so. What about you? What's something unusual that you've done?"

"I haven't caught any murderers, that's for sure; but, I'm a distant cousin of Garth Brooks."

"Country music is lame and being somebody's cousin doesn't count. You must have done something important."

"To tell you the truth, cousin Garth wouldn't recognize me if I sat in the front row of one of his concerts." Xander raised a finger. "About five years ago I helped deliver a baby at a truck stop. A young couple was already there when me and my partner pulled in. Since I'd seen my own kids born I knew more about it than any of them so I got the kid out and calmed the mother until some real help arrived. That was fairly interesting."

"I guess that's okay, but there are millions of babies born every day. It's not very unique."

"If you'd seen the grin on that young mother's face when she held her little boy for the very first time, you'd know it was the only baby in the whole world at that moment."

"You're smiling, dude."

"Darn right, I am. It's a good memory. Other than that, I've never really done anything spectacular, except drive a million miles."

"Literally?"

"Yeah. Woulda got two million if it weren't for the accident. But that may not impress you as much as Irvington's claim to fame. When he was in fourth grade he farted so loud in class he had to go to the principal's office."

Stump laughed out loud. "I already like him."

"I'm sure he'd like you too, Stump."

"I guess your wife would be my step-mother. What's her story?"

"Brianne? Gorgeous red hair and the patience of a saint—" For the next half hour, Xander spoke glowingly of his core family and shared a collection of pictures that he'd accumulated in his cell phone. Stump could see the family resemblance but also picked up a pattern of red hair that must have come from Brianne's family.

From the kitchen, Yana and Zax came to the booth with several plates in hand. "I had to meet Stump's dad," Zax said as she slid Stump's breakfast in front of him, "And a bowl of 'jail food' for you, sir. How you guys getting along?"

"Great," Xander said as Yana set the drinks in their rightful spots. "Stump here isn't the big bad wolf after all."

Stump smiled at the implied role reversal.

"We've got so much catching up to do," Xander went on, "we could use a month."

Zax nodded. "Stump and Yana and James are like family to me. A little while back we had a big smoke fire and they busted their butts to get me back in business."

"Glad to hear it, but I'm not surprised. Where's James? Class?"

Yana shook her head. "He was called to the administrator's office. Stump thinks he'll be okay."

"It's the same old story," Stump said. "James was born in South Africa, so technically, he's an African American, but he's not black."

"So what's the problem?"

"When he sent in his application to get into school he checked the African American box and got some financial aid."

"But they figured him out," Yana said. "I'm worried."

"I keep telling you, Yana, they can't throw him out or change anything because he didn't lie."

"I sure hope so," she said before wandering off to her other tables.

"I gotta go too," Zax said. "My smoke-free kitchen beckons."

Twenty minutes later, James arrived and flipped Stump a thumb's up.

Stump nodded. "You remember Xander, don't you?"

"'Course," James said, while shaking Xander's hand. "I knew you were Stump's real-deal dad when you brought that DNA test with you."

Xander pointed toward the campus. "I take it your meeting went well?"

James shrugged. "They can't throw me out just for telling the truth. Did Stump tell you about the time we helped an entire neighborhood upgrade their homes for FREE?"

"No, he didn't."

"Oh, yeah. I forgot about that," Stump said. "A lot of the old homes where Mom and me used to live were dangerous so we found some grant money, told the City Council about it and got the word out."

"We were in the newspaper," James added.

"It sounds like we all have a lot of stories to tell. What would you fellas say to some kind of road trip for a few days? It'd be a great way to get to know each other."

James nodded enthusiastically. "I'm in."

"I have homework and stuff," Stump said. "I better not miss school."

"Spring break is coming up, dude. We could go then."

"I dunno." Stump turned to Xander. "Where would we go?"

"It don't matter much to me," Xander said. "You ever been to the Grand Canyon?"

"What about your wife? Won't she care?"

"I already told ya. After I hang around the house a few days, Brianne is usually as anxious to get rid of me as I am to hit the road. I'll have to check with her, but I doubt she'll mind."

"I'll think about it," Stump said, genuinely torn. Part of him liked Xander's folksy nature, but another part of him couldn't shake the unanswered question that Xander never addressed.

Xander dropped his napkin in his empty jail-food bowl and dug his cell phone out of his pocket. "Before I go, Brianne would never forgive me if I didn't get some pictures. Do you mind?"

"You want one of me licking Stump's face?"

24

A few nights after Pauline Cooper moved to Meadowlark Flats, she awoke in the middle of the night and lifted her head, just as she had done the previous two nights. As before, the room was unfamiliar. She frowned and glanced about the darkness for anything familiar. Then, she saw another bed, with somebody in it. Who was that? She squinted. Stared. It wasn't her husband. She sat up. Where was Raymond, anyway?

Pauline's eyes darted around the modest room while her mind sought answers to its own unclear questions. She must have been in somebody else's bedroom by mistake, but whose? Where? Did she have permission?

A sliver of light under the door might lead her to somebody who knew what was going on. She slowly dropped her thin, vein-stained legs over the edge of the bed and slid to the floor.

Barefooted, she spotted something familiar. Her pink robe rested atop the back of a chair. She clutched at it and wrapped it around her delicate shoulders. She stared again at the person in the other bed. A woman. Elderly. Looked vaguely familiar.

Confused, Pauline pressed past her suitemate, cracked the door slightly and one-eyed a hallway. It appeared to be a hotel.

From down the long corridor a man came her way. "You're not supposed to be out here, Pauline," he said.

How did he know her name? "Where am I?"

"You're in Meadowlark Flats. It's your new home. Now we have to get you back to bed."

* * *

The next morning at Zax's place, Stump's cell issued a warning. *"Your dad is calling . . . "*

Something was amiss. Myles didn't usually call until later in the day. "Hey, Myles."

"I got a call from a woman named Opal Clemens. She's the sister-in-law of Minnie Moore. Something bad happened in Mom's bedroom."

Uh-oh! What if some Viagra-crazed, old dude sneaked into Grandma Pauline's suite and —. "Is Grandma Pauline okay?"

"All I know is after bedtime, one of the caregivers found my mother wandering the halls and put her back in her room."

"Okay. That's why we took her there."

"But after that, at midnight they made a late-night bed check and found her, cuddled up with Minnie Moore in the other bed."

"Really? Why?"

"All I know is Mom's too old for mischief."

Stump assumed the same thing. "Maybe she was lonely and thought she was with her sister."

"Possible. I've heard her say that she used to share a bed with Millie."

"I bet that's it, Myles."

"I hope so, but Edna Kline wants me to drop by before lunchtime to talk about it. You can join us if you want."

Damn right Stump did. He and Myles may have had their differences, but they both wanted what was best for Grandma Pauline.

A few hours later and just 15 minutes away from

Meadowlark Flats, Stump wondered whether he should tell Myles that he'd met his bio-dad. If so, should he mention that blatant lie about Xander meeting his mom? If Stump were to bring it all up, Myles could jump into the mix and screw everything up before Stump had a fair chance to judge Xander for himself.

Furthermore, any mention of Xander would sidetrack Stump from his newest idea: to persuade Myles to authorize another transfer of the trust funds, similar to what they did for Grandma Pauline. Stump could easily live off the profits of a million dollar investment, just as Grandma Pauline was doing. Knowing Myles, it would be a tough sell, but the dam had been cracked and Stump wanted what was on the other side of said dam—his own money.

Stump arrived first. He signed in and felt as if he were going to the principal's office and wondered if a young person had ever grounded his or her grandmother for sleeping around.

"Hello, Neal," Edna Kline said at the first sign of Stump. "Have you examined your grandmother's room?"

"No, ma'am. Not since the other day."

"Go take a look for yourself, and show your father when he gets here. Then we can all visit." Her voice was sterner than the day she wanted their business.

Stump would have preferred to spend some time with Grandma Pauline in the community room before checking out her suite, but Edna Kline's comments had ominous undertones and Stump wanted to make sure Grandma Pauline was safe.

Inside the suite, both beds had been pushed together in the near side of the room. The remaining furniture sat jumbled near the far window. Not sure what to think, Stump took a leak and waited for Myles.

After Myles arrived and inspected the new furniture configuration he and Stump made their way to the "principal's" office. "She got out of her room several times," Edna Kline said. "Each time, we returned her to bed and stayed with her until she fell to sleep, but then last night we found the two of them sleeping in one bed. We couldn't stand for that."

"Nobody got hurt, did they?" Myles asked.

"No, but one of them might fall out. Seniors have brittle bones."

"I've seen them holding hands," Stump added.

"What does Minnie's family think of all this?" Myles asked.

"Her contact person is Opal Clemens. After she heard what happened, she told me she's okay with them sleeping together if you folks are. The way we have it arranged now, nobody should fall out of bed. I gave Opal your number in case she wanted to discuss it with you."

Myles eyed Stump who shrugged. "If it's okay with everybody else, it's okay with me."

"I told you folks in the beginning that I thought Minnie and Pauline would get along real well."

Myles nodded. "You sure did, but I didn't expect anything like this."

"Okay then, if this doesn't work out we might have to give Pauline some meds at bedtime so she doesn't wander the halls and hurt herself."

25

The following Saturday, Yana had to work again so James went with Stump to Meadowlark Flats for Meet Your Neighbor Day. Near the stage area, a slightly pudgy woman in her 70s shared a couch with a smiling Grandma Pauline and her suitemate, Minnie Moore, who had a half-empty Coke bottle in her lap. "Hi, Grandma," Stump said. "It looks like you're having fun today."

"Are you the paperboy? Because we haven't got our newspaper yet."

The third lady smiled.

"No, Grandma. I'm Stump and this is James. If we see the paperboy, we'll get a paper for you."

Grandma Pauline nodded her head a lot more times than she needed to.

"I'm Opal Clemens," the third lady said. "I'm here to help Minnie on MYN day."

Stump grinned. "Oh, really? I didn't know it was her turn. Thanks for letting us push the beds together. Is that working out for Mrs. Moore? 'Cause my grandma sure seems happy."

"Good question." She turned to Minnie Moore. "You

seem to be getting along with your new friend, honey. Why are you so nice to her?"

"Pauline needs me."

"Dude," James said. "She's not as bad off as your grandma."

Stump agreed. If Grandma Pauline had the mental capacity of a four-year-old, Minnie was a notch better.

"Well, Minnie didn't exactly answer the question," Opal said, "but I'm glad she has a purpose."

"My grandma thinks Minnie is her sister."

"Whatever works for them is all right by me."

"Hello, everybody," a staffer named Josie said from the little stage area. "We need you to take your seats so we can meet some wonderful people. Our first neighbor for today is Brent. He lives in the Hummingbird building."

While the buzz died down, Brent approached the stage and spoke of a stint in the Navy and his sons and losing his wife to cancer. As always, Stump enjoyed hearing the things the residents did when they were younger. He sat back and noticed that Tamara and Edna Kline had taken seats at the back of the room and was comforted by Grandma Pauline's new friends.

"I was sad for a long time," Brent eventually said, "until I came here and found other people who've been through it too. I get cookies and casseroles, and bouncy ladies come see me in the evening."

James gently elbowed Stump. "Is he talking about boobies?"

"Shh. I dunno."

"Thank you, Brent. We're all glad you're eating well. Our next neighbor is Minnie Moore. Opal Clemens is here to help her."

Opal Clemens rose and tugged lightly at Minnie's hand, but Minnie quickly realized she couldn't hold Mrs. Clemens's hand and Grandma Pauline's hand and still deal with her Coke. Then, unexpectedly, Grandma

Pauline took charge of the Coke and followed the other two women right up to the stage area as if she were the caboose in the Grey-haired Express, thereby generating plenty of smiles.

"Hello, people," Opal began. "I am Minnie's sister-in-law. My husband Ronnie was Minnie's brother."

"I'm older," Minnie proclaimed.

Grandma Pauline leaned toward a man in the first row and pointed at Minnie. "Did you know we're sisters?"

"In the early years," Opal continued, "Minnie and Ronnie were raised on a farm in Kansas."

"The houses blew down," Minnie injected.

Opal turned back to the audience. "It was near the end of the Depression. They got their water from wells and had to use outhouses."

Minnie nodded. "P-Pa hid a treasure in a big hole."

"Excuse me, ladies." Stump turned to see Edna Kline moving toward the stage. She spoke to Opal Clemens. "Minnie has told us these things before. Why don't you tell us about her life in California instead?"

"Certainly. Minnie's mother and father died in a tornado so she and Ronnie were brought to California, where they stayed with—"

"You want to come up here?" Grandma Pauline asked Stump.

He shook his head and gave her a friendly finger-to-the-lips shush.

"P-Pa had magic cows," Minnie blurted.

Opal smiled toward the audience. "As far as I know, they never actually had any cows, but they heard that steroids made cows grow faster so they considered getting a couple."

Amused, Stump glanced around the room. True or not, this was a cute story.

"Ladies. Please." Edna Kline said, more firmly than before. "I'm sure these people would rather hear about Minnie's life in California."

"Not me," James whispered to Stump.

Opal pursed her lips and tried again. "Minnie and Ronnie lived with their Aunt Clara and Uncle Larsen—"

"Uncle Larsen was a bad man."

"But you were the first one in your family to go to high school. That was important."

Grandma Pauline rose. "Who's next?" she said as she tugged on Minnie Moore's hand.

"Good idea," Edna Kline said. "It's time for somebody else to talk."

As the three women choo-chooed back to their seats, Stump wondered why Edna Kline was so averse to Minnie's tale. It wasn't any more bizarre than the other stories.

After two additional speakers, they broke for lunch, causing Opal Clemens to hug Minnie Moore. "I've got a hair appointment, dearie. I'm going to have to leave now."

Stump couldn't tell whether Minnie Moore knew exactly what was going on, but after that, when he and James were about to return home, Stump stopped by Edna Kline's office for a quick chat.

"Just who I wanted to see," she said. "How would you like to introduce your grandmother to everybody in the next few weeks? I'm sure the people would like to know her."

"I guess that would be okay. She was a good school teacher."

"Okay. Pick a date and let me know. Now, what can I do for you?"

"Well, I was intrigued by Mrs. Moore's story. Has anybody looked for that family treasure?"

"I told you before that she never stops telling us that silly story. But, her family wasn't wealthy, it was at the end of the Depression and they couldn't have had much of anything. Regardless, it would cost way too much to check it out with air fare, a motel room and a rental car, not to mention how far it is."

"When you put it that way, it sounds more like a piggy bank."

She smiled and nodded. "I wouldn't concern myself with it if I were you."

"You're probably right, but I'd still like to verify it just for fun. Do you suppose you could give me Mrs. Clemens's number? She had to leave early and I'd like to talk to her again."

"She wouldn't want to be bothered."

"But she didn't dispute Minnie when Minnie mentioned the treasure. Maybe she thinks it's out there, too."

"I doubt it. You wouldn't have enough time to check it out anyway, with your schooling and all."

"That's true, but it might be fun to look for a buried treasure in the summer. That's just a few months from now. I'd still like to get her number."

"Sorry. I don't think that's a good idea."

"I promise not to make a pest of myself. Do you know the closest town to the coin jar?"

"Why would I know that?"

"You said Minnie talks about it a lot."

"I don't pay that much attention. And you shouldn't either."

Why was Edna Kline being so stubborn? "Well. I'd like to talk with Opal Clemens anyway if you'd give me her number."

"Sorry, but we can't give it out without permission. I have to protect people's privacy from things like this."

Stump tilted his head to the side. While Edna Kline's tone was pleasant enough, her message rang tense. "I don't get it," he said. "The other day when Mrs. Clemens wanted to move the beds together, you gave her Myles's number. Why would you do that, but not the reverse?"

"That was different. This isn't a medical issue. I've made my decision. You should make this easy on everybody and drop the matter."

Hmm. One would think that Edna Kline would want the families of suitemates to have each other's contact info so they could discuss day-to-day trivial matters without bothering the staff. For now it was probably best to stop poking the beehive and call Myles to get Opal's number off his cell.

"Okay, I guess you're right," he said. "Sorry I bothered you. I've got to get back to Carlsbad anyway."

26

The next Tuesday afternoon, Stump trekked 70 minutes northward to meet Opal Clemens. Down deep, he knew there was no significant treasure on a far-away farm, but the saga of lost coins and magic cows offered more intrigue than his classes.

As he drew close, it occurred to him that he liked elderly people and they seemed to like him. In addition to the people at Meadowlark Flats, Catts McFadden was fascinating and told tales of long lost children, lost love and prostitutes; and Grandma Pauline spoke fondly of her career; Minnie Moore's upbringing was intriguing too. Another thing he knew about the mature ones: They appreciated a little respect and that meant using their surnames. "Hello, Mrs. Clemens," he said when Opal Clemens answered her door. "I believe you're expecting me."

"Yes," she said with a cooking mitt on her hand, "but I told you before, you may call me Opal. Do you like peanut butter cookies?"

"Who doesn't?" In that split second, Stump understood why so many widowers liked living in the Hummingbird wing of Meadowlark Flats: *Old dude, meet good cook.* "Thanks for seeing me. I didn't think you would."

"Why not?" she asked, setting a saucer of cookies before him. "You gave me a good excuse to make a batch of my favorite cookies. I got you some milk, too."

"I'm glad that Mrs. Moore is my grandmother's roommate. They get along real well."

"Minnie will be okay unless they take her Cokes away."

"Yeah. Has she always been like that?"

"As long as I can remember. Edna Kline tried to wean Minnie off it, but Minnie went ballistic. Thank God her doctor stepped in. Those people listen to doctors."

"Part of the reason I'm here is because I recently met my biological father. He's a retired truck driver and we're thinking about going on a trip. We didn't have any place in particular in mind so I was wondering if we could go to that farm and snoop around. If we find anything, I'll give it all to you and Mrs. Moore."

She shrugged. "It's okay by me, but I wouldn't get your hopes up."

"No ma'am. I won't. I asked Mrs. Kline about it, but she thinks Mrs. Moore's mind is playing tricks on her. Would you mind if I ask what you think?"

"Minnie was older than Ronnie and the only one who knew about it. She always thought there was a jar with about 25 gold and silver coins and some sort of paper about cows."

"Gold? Mrs. Kline said the coins were silver."

"Quite honestly, I don't think anybody really knows, but we're talking about poor farmers in the Depression. Very few of them had any money, so they couldn't have saved very much."

"What about you? Do you believe there was a jar of coins?"

"I'm ambivalent, but my husband believed it."

"Do you suppose the neighbors might have found that jar?"

Mrs. Clemens grinned and put another cookie on Stump's plate. "I doubt it. The nearest neighbors were more than a mile away and wouldn't have known anything about it. If there was a jar of coins, either it's still out there or somebody got it and never said anything."

"What about that cow story. That isn't real, is it?"

Opal chuckled. "In my opinion, that's the most interesting part of all of this. Do you have time? I can tell you what I know."

Stump let out a relaxed sigh. He always seemed to learn more by talking with people than sitting in boring classrooms. "Yes ma'am, I'd love to hear it."

"Ronnie and Minnie called their mother Me-ma. She was the one who told Minnie about the cows. Both P-Pa and Me-Ma were proud people, not prone to hyperbole, so there could have been a few coins or papers they deemed valuable enough to hide in a bottle."

Stump picked up another cookie.

"Somewhere near the '20s, before they moved to Kansas, they lived in Atlanta. As the story goes, one day, P-Pa saved a boy's life after one of those old-time cars rolled over and pinned the boy underneath it. Apparently, P-Pa had been offered a reward but he didn't want it. After that, the father of the saved boy must have heard that P-Pa and his family moved to a farm because he sent them a paper for a few head of livestock. The messenger said that particular breed of stock was supposed to grow faster than other breeds. My husband assumed it was because of steroids."

"So I take it they never did get their cows?"

"They probably could've used a few cows for milk and meat and breeding, but it would've been too expensive to get them from Atlanta to Kansas, let alone to a farm that was a two-day trip from the nearest train station. Who was going to feed and water the animals along the way?"

Stump nodded. "You said that tornados killed Me-Ma and P-Pa. That must have been hard on Mrs. Moore and your husband."

"Tragic, really. Their first house was blown away, so they built another one. Then, about five years later, a bigger storm hit the second house. Me-Ma had tucked Minnie and Ronnie in the root cellar while P-Pa tried to tie up the plow horse. But the horse spooked, so Me-Ma had to help him. Finally, they gave up and ran for the cellar, but when P-Pa lifted the cellar door, a giant tree—the only one in the area—fell on both of them. P-Pa died instantly and Me-Ma died from internal bleeding."

"Wow, that must have been awful."

"Fortunately, the closest neighbors came by after the storm, like farmers did back then. They found Minnie and Ronnie wandering around. After that, the children were shipped off to California. They never found out where P-Pa and Me-Ma were buried."

"Why didn't Minnie and Ronnie grab the coin jar before they left the farm?"

"Ronnie didn't know about it and Minnie was supposed to keep it a secret. We don't know if she was just keeping her promise or if she forgot about it for a while."

"Do you think the big hole was the well?"

"My husband thought so, but he and a friend checked it out and there was nothing in there."

"They climbed in a deep well?"

"Not exactly. One year he met an army buddy in Kansas City. They drove out there and hooked a rope to their pickup and lowered themselves down the well, but they never found anything. After I-70 went in, it was easier to get to. Several people have checked it out over the years when on their way to or from other places. But nobody ever found anything as far as I know."

"How long would it take us to get there?"

"It's 1,400 miles. It could take two or three days each way, depending on what you do along the way."

Stump's shoulders slumped. "Oh. If it takes three days each way, that'd shoot most of my spring break. I'm having my doubts now, but just in case, do you remember the address?"

Opal Clemens smiled. "I don't think it has one. You just go

to Hays, Kansas, then north 30 miles to the Zurich stop sign and another three miles to the crisscross fence. Minnie's farm will be on your right. There's a big tree stump in the middle of it. If you do find anything, we could split it with you. Either way, I had enough of all this a few years ago and stopped paying the property taxes. From what I can tell, sooner or later the property goes back to the county or the state."

"Like I said. This sounds sorta far. I'd have to check with my dad."

"Of course." She sighed. "It would be nice if there really was a treasure because Minnie won't be staying at Meadowlark Flats much longer."

"What? Why not?"

"Lack of funds. We've spent nearly all her savings and I've already helped more than I should have, but we're going to have to move her to some other facility before too much longer."

Oh! Crap. That meant Grandma Pauline could lose her "sister." Maybe Stump should reconsider. He tapped at his iPhone. There it was. Zurich, Kansas. 35 miles north of nowhere. Population, 99.

27

Stump and Zax's daughter, Denise, pulled up to the curb in front of Catts McFadden's place. "I'm sorry the college wants you to get rid of your doggie," he said, "but I think this place will make you feel better."

"Do you love my mommy?"

"Sure I do, just like you do. That's why I know how you both feel and why I promised to find a nice home for Trixie, so you could both feel good again."

When they walked up the sidewalk, Denise pointed toward the roof. "Why does he have monsters on his house?"

Stump smiled. "They're called gargoyles. They're just carvings. In the old days they used them to scare monsters away."

"Monsters? Are there any monsters around here now?"

"Naw. You don't see any, do you?" At the door, Stump wondered if Catts McFadden might look a little intimidating to Denise. "There's nothing to be afraid of here. Not the carvings and not Mr. McFadden. Anybody who loves pets has to be nice, right?"

"I guess so."

"Okay, then." Stump knocked, and the door swung inward.

"Hi, Mr. McFadden. This is Denise. I told you about her. She still wants to meet some of your cats if it's okay."

"Just the kitties. I only like kitties."

In the foyer, a slow procession of cautious cat-scouts drifted in. Stump pointed to the stairway adorned with both living and preserved cats. "Some of them were alive a long time ago. Mr. McFadden loved them so much he figured out how to keep them around for a long time."

Catts grinned through aged teeth, and spoke teasingly to Denise. "Are you his wife?"

"No. I'm only 9 years old. It smells like a doctor's office in here."

"That means it's clean," Stump said.

Catts turned toward Stump. "How's school going?"

"Okay, but I seem to learn a lot more by interacting with people than I do by reading books."

"Oh, yeah? And just what kind of things have you learned about *the Crazy Cat Man of Carlsbad?*"

"You?" Stump cocked his head. "Well, I only met you once, so I could be wrong, but you're definitely unusual. That was one of the things I liked about you. You also have good morals – that's why you have weddings for cats. I also saw the certificates on your wall for veterinarian school and taxidermy. That means you know a lot about all animals, not just cats."

"Not bad. Anything else?"

"A little bit. The most interesting thing is the upstairs."

"The upstairs? You haven't been up there."

"I know, but the last time I was here you said you have some other preserved animals. I've already seen this level of your home so that means you have to do your taxidermy work somewhere else and you would avoid the basement because you have shaky knees. That suggests the taxidermy area is upstairs, where a bedroom would be. I'm guessing it's messy but interesting."

Catts nodded. "Now, that's astute."

"What's a stoot?" Denise asked.

"It's like being able to solve problems," Stump said.

Denise pointed toward Catts. "You have a penny in your ear."

Catts chuckled. "Actually, it's an old bus token," he said while digging it out with his pinky so she could see it. "I used to put one in my ear in the mornings, before work so I'd be sure to have it when I returned home. Now, I use coins and medals and tokens as *memory coins*. Today, there's an early tide and the pusses would never forgive me if I didn't catch some fresh fish for their dinner."

Denise pointed to a motionless golden-haired tabby on one of the lower stairs. "There's something wrong with his eye. Was he blind?"

"Now, that's *astute*," Catts said. "Her name was Honeysweet, She's a Bengal, like a Bengal tiger only smaller."

"I'm tired of stoot. Can we see the real kitties now?"

"My pleasure." Catts curled a finger and led Denise into the harpsichord room where a tom leapt five feet to a perch on the stack of shelves. Nearly a dozen other fur blobs wandered around lazily or immersed themselves in important activities like licking themselves.

In the corner, a toy mouse hung on a small rope to within two feet of the floor, thereby creating the feline version of tetherball.

"I love them all," Denise said, holding a nearly full-grown kitten while the same white longhaired cat with a pug nose that liked Stump glued itself to her legs.

Stump pointed to a familiar cat on the end of the table. "How are Ms. Jenkins and Fritz doing?"

"Fritz got fixed so he's moving slowly, but Ms. Jenkins is back to her mischief."

"Look at that one," Denise yelped while pointing to a shiny black cat near the corner of the room. "He's walking on his front legs."

"Oh, that's Daredevil. He's the resident showoff."

"That's really funny," Stump said.

"Speaking of *funny*, d'you have time for a true story? I've got a good one for you."

"Sure," Stump said, anxious to hear what a man who kept coins in his ear would consider to be humorous.

"About seven years ago, just before my cross-alley neighbor opened the furniture store, a couple fellows came to my door with a dead black bear that ran in front of their truck in the mountains. They couldn't save it so they brought it to me to mount.

"The next day, after I removed the teeth, claws and hide, I had to do something with the meat. I tried to feed it to the pusses but they weren't interested."

He grinned like he'd not done before. "I knew the trash trucks would come up the alley the next morning so that night I dissected the carcass into manageable pieces of about 30 pounds each. Then, late that night I loaded the chunks in a wheelbarrow and spread them up and down the alley in the trashcans. The front legs were just about the same size as a human's arm, so I put them in the can right behind me. With the claws removed, the paws looked remarkably similar to human hands."

Getting an idea of where the story was headed, Stump mirrored Catts's grin.

"The next morning I watched for the truck. Eventually, while one guy drove the truck the other one, a big guy, popped out to empty the cans. When that guy got one good look at those skinned arms, he jumped back so far I thought he was going to land in my yard."

Both Catts and Stump chuckled.

"Before I knew it, his buddy was out of the truck, took a peek and went pale. They looked like a couple of ghosts. So the driver returned to the cab and called the police. They must have figured out that the rest of the body was missing so they checked the next can. By the time the police arrived, those two guys had seen so much fleshless body parts they buzzed around like a couple of demented bees. Funniest damn thing I ever saw in my life."

Stump beamed.

"The police inspected the cans and were just as befuddled until one of them looked over at me in my window, where I couldn't stand it any longer. I went to tell them what was going on, but when I got there they didn't know what to think so the younger one drew his gun and held it at the ready until I told them what happened. They sure as hell didn't see the same humor in it as I did."

"What did they do?"

"I got a 60 dollar fine for unlawful dumping, but I thanked them for making me laugh so damn hard. That made them even madder, so it was worth every dime."

Stump grinned. "That's funny alright."

"After word got out, the entire neighborhood thought the Cat Man was a complete kook and they've left me alone ever since. It couldn't have worked out any better."

"When you do something like that, do you keep the bones and then fill in around them?"

"Don't need the bones. We just make a temporary frame out of sticks and twine which is used to make a sturdy mold that fits inside the hide."

Stump nodded. "You're an interesting man. You know that?"

"Well, thank you. Do you really want to see what's upstairs?"

28

Presented with the opportunity to observe the taxidermy area of Catts McFadden's home, Stump suspected that such a setting might give innocent girls nightmares. "I don't think I should take Denise with us."

"No problem," Catts said, "I know how to keep everybody down here happy." He spoke to Denise. "Hey, little one, see that blue jar over there on the table? It's catnip. Go pinch a little in your fingers and sit down in the middle of the room. The pusses will love you to pieces."

She looked at the jar and then to Stump.

"Go ahead. Mr. McFadden knows what he's doing."

Both Catts and Stump watched Denise lift the jar lid, causing several anxious cats to purr and move toward her.

"What are they doing?" she asked as some of the animals rolled on the floor and meowed while others rubbed up against her.

"Go ahead." Catts said. "Just pinch a little between your fingers and sprinkle it around you."

A minute later a full score of cats danced around like actors in a musical. Furry acrobats and goofballs caused her to giggle out loud. As the star of the show, she raised her hand high in the air and then brought it down to within sniffing reach of her hairy fans for their overwhelming approval.

"Hey, Denise," Stump said. "Mr. McFadden and I are going upstairs to look at his workbench. We'll be right back."

Catts locked the outer door before they ascended the stairs. On the landing, he pointed to the end of the hall where a tall standing lamp separated two matching, deep-red armchairs. "That's where my wife and I used to read before we went to bed."

A closer examination revealed that the left one looked near-new, while the other had frayed severely from use.

Above the like-new chair, a studio picture of a beautiful young woman, about Stump's age, with blue eyes and long sandy hair sat looking over her left shoulder.

"Is that your wife?"

"1964. She was seven years younger than me. While most young women of that time were engrossed in the hippie movement she wanted to be in movies."

"Did she make it?"

"Bit parts and a couple commercials," he said, before lowering his head, "but then, in '71 she lost her life while giving birth to our daughter. I couldn't handle it. I unloaded the baby on my wife's sister, and left the country to regain my composure, but a broken heart never completely heals."

Stump knew that feeling from the loss of his own mother. He also knew by looking at the chairs, that after Catts returned home, he continued to sit in his reading chair as if his wife were still with him. Clearly the man was a sentimentalist, a quality that contradicted his rough exterior.

Stump and Catts eased past the chairs and into one of the bedrooms. "I think this is the room you wanted to see. It ain't much."

A series of flat doors had been bolted to homemade sawhorses and wedged around the two farthest walls thereby making a long, L-shaped workbench. A large window rested over one side of the bench, offering both a lot of natural light to the work area and a view across "bear-parts" alley to the fabled furniture store with its intriguing tales of a long-lost child and prostitutes of eras gone by. Stump grinned. The whole area was intriguing.

A jar of glass eyeballs, and adhesives and the hide of a skinned gray cat lay beneath an electric-powered magnifying glass, all of which would have been creepy had Stump not known that all of this was part of a man's appreciation of innocent lives.

Stump recalled when Tamara, at Meadowlark Flats, said that Google had replaced grandparents for so many young people. But no Google search could capture the sights and smells and feelings of a person like this.

Finally, while they moved toward the stairway and back to join Denise, "Can I ask you something completely different?" Stump asked.

"Completely different? Like what?"

"Well, I'm trying to make a decision. I wouldn't ask, but you know a lot of things and you'd be impartial."

"I don't see how I can refuse."

When downstairs in the foyer, where they could keep an eye on Denise, Catts sat on the lone chair while Stump sat on the very bottom step of the stairway. "What's on your mind?" Catts asked.

"When I was a kid, I always wanted to know who my dad was, but my mom died when I was 13 and . . . " Stump proceeded to tell Catts about the fire and Xander Brooks and the big lie, and the eventual invitation to go on a cross-country journey. "He's been all over the country," Stump said, "and he has a fascinating family, so I was kinda interested but that lie ruined everything. I can't trust him."

Catts nodded. "Have you asked him about it?"

"Oh, yeah, but he won't come clean."

"I take it you intend to decline?"

Stump bit at his lip. "I was leaning that way and then I went to my grandma's nursing home and heard about a treasure and some magic cows."

Catts grinned. "Magic cows, eh? Now that's a new one."

Stump explained that Minnie Moore had become Grandma Pauline's sister-figure and the discomfort Grandma Pauline faced should they get separated. "I don't think we'll find anything of value, but I'd also be going so I can get to know my father, who I can't trust. What do you think I should do?"

"Intriguing puzzle," Catts said. "I can't really advise you what to do, but I can tell you this. Fifty-eight years ago, when I was in the Marines, I got stationed in a toilet of a place in Korea." He lowered his voice. "War is so damn ugly I don't even like to think about it. I hated it and wanted to die. Then a new batch of men joined our troop. Within days I met PFC Gerald Royals. It must have been fate. We told each other true stories and lies and damn lies and everything in between just to distract each other from all the ugly carnage around us."

"Later, when we got discharged, he introduced me to his sister. That was her picture, upstairs. She was the best thing that ever happened to me. A year later Gerald was our best man. And all of that came out of the gutters of hell."

"Gosh," Stump said, assuming the worst. "What happened to Gerald?"

"Died of cancer about twenty years ago. He was the best friend I ever had."

"So I take it you think I should go with Xander?"

"I can tell you this: If I could erase the ugliness of my stay in Korea but I also had to erase PFC Gerald Royals and the incredible woman he brought into my life, I wouldn't even consider it." He raised a lone finger. "Your trip might not work out, but you can never recapture a lost opportunity."

Catts's words were like a wake-up call from a loud alarm clock and Stump finally knew what he wanted to do about Xander Brooks - give him another chance.

29

After Catts McFadden's comment about lost opportunities, Stump knew he wanted to go to Minnie Moore's farm with Xander Brooks and James. It mattered not if there was a bottle of coins. The point was to find out exactly who his dad was and to do something substantial without Myles telling him what to do.

A couple calls later, Xander agreed to meet Stump and James late Friday afternoon, which was the start of spring break. All of that meant that Stump had one final opportunity to visit Grandma Pauline before his departure. Hence, Thursday, after his last dull class, he made an afternoon trip northward to Meadowlark Flats and high-stepped it to the main bulletin board where he posted a notice.

*"Heartbroken second-grader forced to give up
2-year-old wiener dog. Will you adopt sweet Trixie
and allow Denise occasional visits?"*

Minutes later, the registration book indicated that Myles had been there earlier and checked out. Good. That meant Stump could keep his Kansas trip with Xander under wraps.

He strolled into the community room where a pending wine and ice cream party had attracted dressed-up residents from all the wings except Hospice. He snapped a couple pictures and wandered over to the couch on which Grandma Pauline and Minnie Moore were holding hands. "Hi, Grandma."

She stared at him for a moment, then. "Aren't you my grandson?"

Wow. He hugged her, longer than usual. "That's right, I'm Stump. I came by to see you before I go to Mrs. Moore's farm."

Minnie clutched at the half-empty Coke bottle in her lap. "Me-Ma said I was lucky 'cause I got the shade."

Not sure what that meant, Stump smiled. "I'm glad you like each other."

At that moment, applause broke out near the hallway where staffers wheeled in two carts, one containing a half-dozen bottles of wine and the other mounded with bars of ice cream.

"Some of you can come to the carts," one of the staffers said. "For those of you sitting down, we'll bring your refreshments to your seats. Just be patient."

As the workers handed out goodies, Edna Kline approached Stump. "I need to speak with you in my office for a minute." Once again, she sounded less friendly than the time he first met her.

Curious, Stump followed her until she instructed him to close the door and take a seat. "I hope I didn't hear you say that you're going to Minnie's farm, because that would mean you contacted Opal Clemens after I specifically instructed you not to do that."

"It was okay. She liked me and gave me cookies."

"Not the point. I already told you, you'd be wasting everybody's time. The sun doesn't revolve around you, you know."

"Well, it's not the reason we're going, but I thought we might as well check it out while we're in the area."

"Look," she said, shifting in her seat. "When anybody shows interest in that old farm, Minnie gets excited; then when things don't work out, she gets depressed. You wouldn't want to do that to her, would you?"

Horse manure. Stump had enough experience with Grandma Pauline to know that memory care patients don't think that clearly. He would have liked to tell Edna Kline that his trip was none of her business, but that would probably antagonize her further. "I appreciate your suggestions, but I can't change anything now. We've already made plans."

"Not good enough, Neal. I was hoping it wouldn't get to this, but I'm afraid that if you go on that trip, and make life harder for Minnie or anybody else, there will be severe consequences."

"If it will make you feel any better, I won't talk about it in front of Mrs. Moore. I can report to Opal Clemens, instead."

"I'm warning you, you're treading on very thin ice."

"I don't know why you're threatening me," he said, standing, "but I'm going to spend a little more time with my grandma before I go home."

"Consider yourself warned, Neal. Consider yourself warned."

When in the hall, Stump shook his head and wondered why Edna Kline was so hostile about something she'd previously downplayed.

"Excuse me," a woman's voice came from behind him. "Excuse me. Are you Neal?"

He turned to see a 50ish woman with long red hair. "Yes. Do you need something?"

"Oh, thank goodness. The ladies at the front desk said I could find you here. My mother saw your note on the bulletin board. She's always loved dachshunds and asked me to find out about the little girl's dog."

"Oh, really? That was fast," he said, digging out his cell. "I have some pictures." He handed her his phone and began a brief saga about how Trixie had become available.

"She's adorable," the woman said. "How much does the little girl want?"

"All she wants is the right to visit Trixie occasionally."

"Okay, then, we'll take her. When can we meet her?"

"Well, I'm going out of town for a week, but we could get together when I get back. That would give Denise a little more time to enjoy Trixie."

"Okay," she said, setting his phone down and producing her own. "What's your number? I can call you next weekend."

After giving the woman his contact info, Stump returned to the community room where he kissed Grandma Pauline goodbye and scooted out the back door toward Pops.

Outside, he decided to call Zax about Trixie, but when he reached into his pocket it was empty. Oh yeah. He'd handed his phone to the red-haired woman to see pictures, but she didn't give it back. He turned around and tugged on the door, but as expected it had locked behind him. He groaned and hurried to Pops, then drove around the building to the front entrance and rushed to the area where he'd met the red-haired lady and located his phone right where they left it.

Minutes later and back on track he got a call from James. "Hey, dude. Wa-sup?"

"Sorry, brofriend, but Yana doesn't want me to go on that excursion. When I argued, she offered to go to the nudie beach by Torrey Pines. It's spring break. That beach is going to be packed with hotties. You should stay, too."

Gross. Stump assumed that if he were to go to the nude beach with James and Yana, sooner or later he'd see more of Yana than he wanted to and his idea of a sexy woman didn't include a topless, pregnant woman. "Thanks anyway, dude, but Xander has already made his plans. I don't want to jerk him around."

* * *

After Edna Kline watched Stump drive away she grabbed her camera and wandered into the community room where she spotted Stump's grandmother and Minnie Moore. She tugged gently on Pauline's hand. "Hello, ladies. How would you like to go outside and admire the garden with me?"

"Okay." Both ladies rose and slowly waddled with Edna Kline down the hall, to the back exit and outside.

"You doing okay, dear?" Edna asked Pauline as they cautiously shuffled across a cemented patio.

"I like it outside," Pauline said. "There are birds."

"Yes, there are." Edna led Pauline and Minnie to a large stucco wall with a trashcan near the edge. "Let's stop here. I want to get some pictures. Edna took several pictures of the women together and then had each of them pose separately while she snapped a few more from various angles.

"Perfect," Edna said, as she snapped the last one. "You look so happy together."

"She's my sister," Pauline said.

"I know she is, but have you noticed how hot it is out here? I think we better get back inside where it's cooler and safe."

30

Friday afternoons were always slow at Lee's College Café, but the beginning of spring break made it worse. Some students were going home, more wanted to hit the beaches – but not Stump. He chomped down the last bite of a burger as he waited, alone in his usual booth, for Xander Brooks. Yana wandered his way. "You want anything else, Stump?" She looked more pregnant to him now that James suggested they'd be going to Black's Beach.

Stump focused on her face and shook his head.

Outside, a steady procession of happy students hustled away from the campus as if there were a bomb threat. In a few more hours, the entire student body except Stump would be in party mode. Now he doubted that the three changes of clothes in his half-full backpack would be enough for a whole week.

Inside his head, a mental teeter-totter kept weighing the importance of asserting his independence by leaving the state and finding out who his bio dad really was versus the pure lunacy of traipsing across hundreds of miles of deserts and mountains with a man he barely knew. Especially given that their ultimate objective was nothing more than to find a non-existent piggybank on some dust-pit farm in a crap-hole called Zurich, Kansas.

He considered telling Myles about Xander and the trip, but that would surely trigger a lecture about carelessness and conmen. Besides, Xander said right from the beginning that James could go along. A conman wouldn't do that.

Still debating whether to back out, Stump rose, grabbed his backpack and meandered to the entry area where he could watch out the window for minivans or SUVs. Xander insisted they could save both money and time if they rented a square-back vehicle and took turns driving and sleeping. That was another issue. Just because old-dude couldn't let go of his past didn't mean young-dude wanted to play make-believe truck drivers.

A half-block up and approaching, a dark sports car had a white mini-van on its ass. Stump shook his head in disgust. Truckers were notorious for tailgating and the last thing Stump needed was for his friends to see him climb into a velour-seated mommy-mobile.

A last minute surge of doubt warned him not to go. He'd simply have to level with Xander and let the chips fall where they might. The worst Xander could do was drive off and disappear forever, but that wouldn't be the end of the earth. Stump had already gotten by without the dude for nearly 20 years. He could get by longer if he needed to.

As the sports car and Xander-driven minivan drew closer, Stump wondered if anybody had ever kicked Xander's ass for tailgating. Suddenly, the sports car abruptly veered to the curb. The driver must have been pissed. Stump peeked through the darkened windshield. What the—? Xander! Son-of-a-bitch!

Stunned, Stump rushed outside in time to hear the engine rev. Xander climbed out of the driver's side and looked over the top of the car toward Stump.

"It's a Corvette Stingray," he said, beaming. "How do you like it?"

Nearly laughing, Stump didn't know what was more rad: the extra-long hood, the sleek fastback, the speckled green paint or the bad-ass engine.

Xander shrugged. "I figured since James wasn't going along, the two of us ought to ride in style. Course, you'll have to drive half the time. You okay with that?"

"Are you kidding me?" Stump said, dropping his backpack near the rider's door. "Damn right I am. I've never even sat in a car like this."

"Then it's about time you did—but before we blow out of here, I gotta take a leak. While I do that, you can pop the hood and make sure we have enough turn indicator fluid."

"No prob, dude."

* * *

Inside the café, Xander chuckled and hooked a finger for Yana and Zax. "This is why I called you guys earlier. It should be hilarious."

"What's going to happen?" Yana asked while Stump leaned into the driver's side of the Vette to release the hood latch.

"I told him to check the blinker fluid."

"What's so funny about that?"

"There's no such thing," Zax said, before she turned toward Xander. "He's gonna kill you." She boosted her cell into place.

Seconds later Stump lifted the hood, stared into the massive engine cavity and scanned for a nonexistent reservoir of blinker fluid. He leaned in over the engine compartment and rose to his tiptoes, presumably to see if the elusive reservoir was hiding back by the firewall.

Zax cackled. "You were right. This is funny."

"When I heard that he's only owned one vehicle and didn't know much about mechanics, I thought it might be a fun way to begin our trip." Xander paused a second. "I assume you ladies know that he loves you both like family?"

Zax nodded. "He's very bighearted."

"We love him too," Yana said, now videoing Stump.

For the next five minutes, the XYZ Gang watched and filmed Stump go through all sorts of physical gyrations while he tried to find that darn reservoir. He scratched his head, tongue-poked his cheek, rubbed his neck and blew out deep breaths before he plopped his hands on his hips in frustration.

"Okay. I think we've tortured him enough," Xander said. "One of you should go out and give him the news."

"I will," Zax said before handing Xander her cell. "But keep this going. I want to catch the look on his face when I tell him."

A moment later Zax wandered out to the Vette, gave Stump the news and pointed back to the window where the film crew waved. Stump laughed and flipped the insiders the bird. The only thing left to do was throw his backpack behind the rider's seat and slide in.

31

Anticipating the rocket-like thrust that was sure to follow, Stump waved one last time to his pals and gripped the armrest. Then Xander eased into traffic like an old preacher. "You must expect this treasure you spoke of to pay big dividends," Xander said, "considering you gave up the bulk of your spring break for it."

"Not really. I thought it might be interesting because I've never been out of California, except one trip with Myles to Houston."

"Are you shitting me? That's an insult to Ike."

"Ike?"

"Yes. The 34th president. Dwight Eisenhower. He's responsible for the interstate highway system. Didn't you learn about him in school?"

"I've heard of him, but I don't know much about him."

Xander clucked his tongue and launched into an in-depth and truly fascinating saga of a bald-headed military general who inspired a network of roads which would enable the military to move tanks and equipment to nearly any place in the country should the U.S. ever be attacked. "One mile out of every five," Xander eventually said, "has to be a straightaway so that planes can land in emergencies."

"I never knew all that," Stump said, suspecting that Xander was a one-topic expert about highways because he'd driven a lot.

Xander hit the blinker and changed lanes. "Now that I've taught you something, it's your turn. You said that you solved some crimes when you were still in school. Did Myles teach you how to do that?"

"Not really, but after I solved two murders, when I was 13, he told me I had problem-solving skills. I thought I was just like any other kid, but he'd always been a detective and ought to know."

"How'd you solve two murders?"

Pleased that Xander cared about what he had to say, Stump kicked off his shoes and scooted them up under his seat. He began with a bit about a rad biker and ten minutes later ended up talking about his mother's death in a house fire.

"And then you solved another murder?" Xander asked.

"Yeah. At an apartment building. A maintenance man killed my boss who was like a grandfather to me."

Xander smoothly changed lanes. "What about girlfriends? A smart and incredibly handsome fellow such as yourself must have to chase them away by the dozens."

"Most of them just want to have fun, but I'd rather have a real girlfriend. Most of the ones I meet aren't into that."

"James seemed to find somebody."

"Yeah. He met Yana online. She's from Russia and very nice - but she's got hairy armpits."

Xander snorted. "Well, people from other countries have different customs."

"I guess so. James seems to like it." Stump pointed out the windshield. "See the license plate on that car?"

"Yeah. What of it?"

"When my mom was alive I learned how to switch around

the numbers and letters on license plates and telephone pads to get goofy sayings."

"Oh?"

"If you look at a phone pad, the number two can be converted to an A, B or C. Threes can be a D, E or F and so on. I used that trick to help catch that first killer I told you about. His plate had the word Oreo in it. It was easy to remember."

"That's clever. Truckers see messages too."

"Really, like what?"

"In addition to all the jargon on the CB radios, did you know that many of the exit numbers are based on how far the exit is from the state border?"

"No. I never thought about it."

"If the last exit was number 88 and the next one is five miles away it will be 93, not 89 as you might guess."

"That's sorta rad. Your boys must like knowing things like that."

"Sometimes they're as smart as Einstein. Other times, not so much. One time Irvington convinced Jett that he got his name because he could fly. Gullible 5-year-old Jett donned his mother's bathrobe for a cape, jumped off our roof and broke his wrist. I'll never forget how disappointed he was when he discovered he really got his name because that was the year I got my license to fly jets."

Stump grinned. "I guess we all do dumb things once in a while."

"Another time Irvington nearly burnt the house down when he nuked dry macaroni for ten full minutes. The smoke was so bad the neighbor called the fire department. At the time I was OTR, which means 'on the road.' Brianne had to leave the windows open for two days." Xander pointed out the windshield. "There's a rest area up ahead. This would be a good time to stretch and switch drivers."

Stump's eyes shot to the exit sign and his pulse quickened. He grabbed his cell and sent a text to Yana, James and Zax, boasting that it was his turn to drive. Almost instantly, Yana requested that Xander take a picture of Stump behind the wheel.

Fifteen minutes later, they'd taken a leak, stretched their legs and ducked into the Vette. "Any tricks to this?" Stump asked as he started the engine.

"Just don't give it too much throttle when you're pulling away. You'll think you're in a jet plane."

"Speaking of planes, earlier, you said you can fly jets. That must be cool."

"It is, but it's expensive and it would be crazy to pay to fly while I have unlimited free flights."

Stump nodded. "You know something? I always thought truckers were society's D students—but you know a lot."

"We're like every other profession. Some good. Some bad. Most people don't know that today's truckers are modern-day cowboys."

"How's that?"

"Think about it. The cargo, no matter whether it's mail or goods, is the equivalent of a herd of cattle. It must be delivered on time. There are other examples. Truck stops have replaced campfires. Truckers drink a lot of coffee and carry guns. We watch the sunsets and sleep on the side of asphalt trails. There's nothing like sleeping outdoors, next to a campfire."

"Mom made a sheet-tent for Cousin Willie and me one night, but I waited until Willie went to sleep and crawled into my own bed."

"Don't feel bad. My kids have all climbed into bed with Brianne and me. Anyway, there's a community spirit among drivers. They eat in roadside cafes, warn each other of impending road conditions via CB radios. Half the stops have 'special girls' hanging around to bring business in off the road, just like the saloon girls of the old west."

"I never thought of any of that," Stump said.

"Now you know." Xander pointed a limp finger up the road. "I got us a room at the Bellagio, in Vegas. We can catch a meal and a shower and a few hours of sleep and then get back on the road for a long day tomorrow. If you'd like we can ride a roller coaster around the New York New York or jump off a hundred-story building."

"Wow. I don't know. I've never jumped off a building."

"It's up to you. Did you know that Las Vegas was created by the Mob?"

"Not really."

Once again, Xander shared a fascinating story about a guy named Bugsy Siegel and the Mafia, thereby proving that he had a lot more depth than Stump first thought. Thus far Stump was glad he'd agreed to the trip.

32

Later, after they'd cruised some of the strip and parked, Stump found himself in the Bellagio lobby. "Hi," Xander said to the female registration clerk and handing her his ID. "My son and I have a reservation."

The clerk punched at her keyboard and checked her monitor. "Excuse me a minute, Mr. Brooks," she said before picking up a house phone on a counter behind her.

"What's she doing?" Stump whispered to Xander.

"Checking things out. They're very thorough."

"Okay. Yes sir. I'll take care of it." She hung up and returned to Xander. "Mr. Rion said to comp your room and dinner. Would two double beds be acceptable?"

"Yes, of course," Xander said, raising a finger, "but I want to make it clear that there won't be any gambling this time. My son isn't old enough."

"Yes, sir. I mentioned that to Mr. Rion, but he wants you to know you're always welcome at the Bellagio."

* * *

The late-night Mountain Dew that Stump downed before he and Xander hit the rack had filled his 'gotta-wiz' tank. He tiredly forced a blurry glance at Xander's bed, but the dude was long gone. What the hell? The clock between the beds said 4:04.

Slightly more alert, Stump thought about the night before while he drained his bladder.

Xander had shown Stump a half-dozen touristy sights and topped off the evening by going to a fancy French restaurant downstairs, where the manager recognized Xander and told Stump of million-dollar pots in the poker room and an occasion when men wearing pig masks robbed the Rolex store.

After that Xander admitted that he was a reformed gambler and the bosses were trying to lure him back to the tables. Now Stump hoped that Xander hadn't actually gone gambling after all.

Just then, the doorknob jiggled and Xander slipped in. "You're up!" he said, surprised.

"Yeah. You okay? It's the middle of the night." Stump almost apologized for sounding like a worried mother.

"I'm fine. After I got a few hours of sleep, I went down to the poker room to see some of my old friends."

"Don't you need more sleep?"

"Yeah, but not all at once. I'm a segmented sleeper."

"What's that?"

"Never could sleep a full night so I sleep a couple shorter periods in the day."

"That's weird."

"Not really. Edison, Tesla and da Vinci slept in segments. Anyway, I'm good to go, and if we want to get back in a few days, we should hit the road. It's thirteen hours to our next stop and we lose an hour for the time zones. You can sleep first shift in the car."

Stump reluctantly agreed.

Later, as they approached the Vette, Xander caught Stump off guard. "You can drive again."

"Are you sure? It's your turn."

Xander smiled. "Trust me."

Stump shrugged. Groggy or not, driving a Vette ought to keep him alert for a while. Then, about a half-hour out of Vegas, and nearly alone on the highway Xander said, "You ever driven a hundred miles per hour?"

The hairs on Stump's neck stood at attention. "No way. Not in that old truck of mine. It might explode."

Xander tapped the dashboard. "Top-end in this baby is two hundred, so one hundred will be like a walk in the park."

"Really? You want me to drive that fast?"

"Why not? Everybody else goes 85 in this stretch, so it's not a lot more. It's about 50 miles to the next town and we've got some good open road for a bit. It's up to you."

Stump grinned. Xander actually made it sound safe to race across the desert at triple-digit speeds in the night. "I guess so. I've seen guys drive a lot faster than that."

"There ya go. Give 'er some gas."

Fifteen uneventful miles later, Stump slowed down to 85. "You were right. Now it feels like were crawling along in mud."

"I knew you'd handle it. I bet you aren't sleepy either."

"True that. Wait'll I tell Yana and Zax."

"There's one more good stretch up here. You should be able to take her up to 110."

Stump tried not to let Xander see him smile.

Some 20 minutes later Stump slowed down, drove east through Mesquite like a sane person. "That was wicked."

"The cops are pretty lax back there. From here we're gonna have lots of open space and small towns. This is the kind of stretch that gives a solo driver a chance to think. It's also a good time to switch drivers."

"Good. I could use some more sleep."

A couple hours later the sun had come up and Stump was admiring the scenery in Utah when they came upon a sign indicating I-70 was just ahead.

144

"If you don't mind," Stump said, looking at the dash clock. "I'd like to check in on my grandma."

"Your grandmother? By all means. Go ahead."

Stump speed-dialed Meadowlark Flats and was put through to Tamara Flores. "Your grandma is doing fine," Tamara said when asked, "but has your father called you?"

"No. Why?"

"I'm not real sure, but Edna said she had some bad news for him. I'm not certain if they've talked yet."

"But you said Grandma Pauline is okay?"

"She is. I think something else came up. I probably shouldn't have said anything."

"Alright, thanks for the warning," he said wondering what was up.

"Four short hours to Grand Junction," Xander said just as Stump got a message and a picture from James. Stump swiped the screen to see Yana's naked backside while she stood ankle-deep in the Pacific. "Gross," he said immediately deleting the picture and putting his phone back in his pocket.

"What's gross?"

"James and Yana think nudity is beautiful, but I don't want to see her naked butt. I'm not a prude, but this is too personal."

"I guess that could be pretty awkward," Xander said while pulling over. "I gotta get some shut eye. Can you take the wheel for a couple hours?"

So that's how the segmented sleeping thing worked out. It was probably pretty handy for a pair of truckers. One or the other was usually awake which kept the rig rolling. "Sure I can," Stump said, anxious to do his part.

After trading drivers, Xander reclined the rider's seat and went right to sleep, leaving Stump to wonder why a nice guy like that never did come clean about that outrageous lie about meeting Stump's mom. Oh well. He should have a few more days to find out.

33

"Thanks for coming in, Mr. Cooper," Edna Kline said to Myles. "I know it's not your usual day to visit us, but I'm afraid something concerning came up."

"Did my mother fall out of the bed? Is she okay?"

"I'm afraid she got out the security doors." Edna handed him her cell phone. "As you can see by this picture, she was interested in the trash can by the back patio."

"Oh, my God."

"She's safe now, but there remains a big problem. I didn't really want to say anything, but Neal is the one who was responsible for her getting out and our insurance requires us to call the contact person when something like this happens."

"I understand, but what did Stump do?"

"He was the last person with her. When he left the facility, he left the back door open and she slipped out. She could have been hurt. You know how she wanders."

"Can't you bolt the doors closed?"

Edna shook her head. "Fire Department regulations. The best we can do is label them as fire doors and hook them up to our alarm system. That way only the people who have keys can get out without triggering the alarm. But when they

146

don't lock it back up in a reasonable time, the alarm goes off. That's how I knew somebody got out."

"This is so unlike Stump. He's not usually careless."

"Well, I'm sorry, but I'm going to have to bar him from coming back for a while."

"Of course."

"Gotta be at least two weeks unless he comes in and convinces me he's going to be more responsible and respectful of my duties here."

Myles looked at the picture of his mother standing next to a trashcan. "You can rest assured, you'll get the apology you deserve."

"Well, I hope so because we can't tolerate this kind of carelessness."

* * *

While driving the Vette, Stump got the call that Tamara had mentioned. "'Sup, Myles?" he said into his cell.

"I'm pissed, that's 'sup.' My mother got out. Edna Kline said you were the last one with her and left the back door unlocked."

"She's wrong."

"No, she's not. By the time they found my mother she was half-way across the parking lot, almost digging through the trash. Do you understand how dangerous that is? It's a good thing nobody else got hurt. You and I could've both been sued and you could have lost your trust."

"No way, dude. I remember clicking the door shut behind me. In fact, as soon as I got outside I realized I'd forgotten my cell phone. I couldn't get back in that door so I drove all the way around the building to the main entrance, found my phone and went right back out the front door. If Grandma Pauline got out, it was after I left."

"That's not what Mrs. Kline said. She even has pictures. I've seen one."

"I don't care—"

"You don't care? That's the most callous thing you've ever said. If that's—"

"You interrupted me, Myles. I didn't mean that I don't care about Grandma Pauline. I meant that a picture can't prove that I left the door open. In fact it proves something else."

"Something else? Like what?"

"Think about it, Myles. If you walked outside and saw a vulnerable elderly person, would you help them out or stop to take a picture?"

Myles paused for the first time in the conversation. *"You have a point, there."*

"Darn right I do. When we first met Mrs. Kline, we told her that Grandma Pauline had gotten onto the highway. We said we'd never forgive ourselves if she were to get hurt like that. Yet, miraculously Mrs. Kline has a picture of Grandma Pauline wandering around. It's suspicious."

Myles sighed. *"She's not willing to let you back in until this gets straightened out. Why don't we all have a meeting tomorrow with her or Tamara? You got time in the afternoon?"*

"Uh-oh. "Sorry. I can't."

"How about Tuesday? Or Wednesday. I can meet you then."

"That ain't going to work either. To tell you the truth, Myles, I can't do anything like that for a while. I've met my real father and we're on our way to Kansas in a Corvette."

"Your real father? What the hell are you talking about, Stump?"

"His name is Xander Brooks. We checked DNA and everything. He used to be a truck driver. Since it's spring break, we're going to Kansas to get to know each other."

"What?" Myles said loudly. *"Don't you pay any attention to the things I've told you? You could be in danger. I want you go to the nearest police station and make arrangements to come back to California before something awful happens."*

"Relax, Myles. He's a nice guy and I'm old enough to take care of myself." Stump grinned and decided to tweak Myles. "That's why I only drove faster than a hundred miles an hour a couple of times."

"Are you nuts, Stump? That's the most reckless thing you've ever done."

"It was safer than that piece of crap truck that you made me drive."

"What? That's ludicrous. Why didn't you tell me?"

"'Cause you would have lectured me, just like you're doing right now."

"I want to talk with this guy and check his background."

"No way, Myles."

"You heard me, Stump. Put him on the phone."

"And you heard me. Ain't gonna happen. I'm old enough to make my own decisions."

Myles sighed directly into the phone. *"Look. I know you've always wanted to meet your biological father. I get that, but this is the wrong way to go about it."*

"You don't know that, Myles. You're just afraid to let me off the friggin' leash."

Myles sighed again. *"I guess there's nothing I can do about it right now, but like it or not you aren't getting back in Mom's building without making peace with both Mrs. Kline and me."*

"Alright, but all I know is Minnie Moore might have to move out of Meadowlark Flats and that would break Grandma Pauline's heart."

"Where'd you get that idea?"

"After Mrs. Moore spoke on MYN day, I visited her sister-in-law, that Mrs. Clemens who said we could push the beds together."

Myles groaned. *"What does this road trip have to do with that?"*

"Remember the first time we met Edna Kline? She said Minnie thinks there are some old gold coins on that farm, so me and Xander wanted to check it out."

"Oh my God, I can't believe that all of this is over a few coins in a bottle. This is enough to make me drink again. All I wanted was a safe place for my mother to live."

"Me, too, Myles, but Grandma Pauline is happy now and I want to keep it that way, don't you?"

"I don't like any of this, Stump. You just be super-careful. Remember what I've always told you about conmen."

"No problem, Myles. I gotta go now. I'll call you later. Goodbye."

A shuffle came from the rider's seat. "Wow! That sounded intense," Xander said. "If you need to get back—"

Stump waved him off. "Sorry if I woke you, but Myles treats me like a child and I got accused of something I didn't do."

"I heard you talking about a picture and who took it. Don't places like that have surveillance cameras? That might vindicate you."

"Don't know, but I just wish Myles would realize that I deserve to be in charge of my own life."

"I wouldn't be so hard on him, Stump. All parents want to prevent their kids from making painful mistakes."

"He may have had a point when I was 13, but not now."

"But when you needed Myles the most, he was your rock. He always deserves respect for that."

Stump lightly bit his lower lip.

34

Eventually Stump and Xander made it to the Rockies and then Denver and finally onto an endless carpet of flatlands heading east. Ultimately, near the Kansas state line, it was getting dark when Xander pointed out one of his all-time favorite truck stops. "This is Seifert. We'll spend the night here. They have chili that'll make your teeth melt."

For some reason, melted teeth were supposed to be a good thing.

They wiggled up a service road and ended up in a shopping center-sized parking lot that hosted a couple dozen big rigs, about half of them refueling while the others sat side by side toward the back of the lot. As they drove past the latter group Stump heard and felt the anxious rumble of dozens of huge diesel engines.

"The law requires multi-hour breaks for every rig, every day," Xander said, "so this is a good place for truckers to catch a shower and some TV and shoot the shit in a living room-type lounge. C'mon. I'll show you around."

The second Stump opened the Vette's doors his nostrils were overwhelmed with the stench of diesel fuel and the less-noticeable aroma of greasy burgers. "Whew," he said waving a hand in front of his face.

Xander grinned. "A little 'trucker cologne' won't kill ya."

Inside, a buzz of predominantly male voices came from a packed café on the left, while a large, well-stocked convenience store on the right would have impressed the folks at 7-Eleven. Straight ahead, a hallway led to a spacious lounge with a giant TV and a laundry area and a huge locker room with a half-dozen free showers.

Stump and Xander took a booth next to a half-wall that was topped with a cluttered shelf, on which an interesting taxidermist's project reminded Stump of Catts McFadden.

"What's that?" he asked Xander.

"Those? They're called *jackalopes*—they're a cross between jack rabbits and antelopes."

Stump admired how the taxidermist had posed the animal on it's hind legs as if it were hopping across the prairie. "No kidding. I've never heard of them."

"Oh, yeah. They're indigenous to the plains. The businesses keep them on display to remind the truckers that the antlers are hard on tires."

"Cheeseburgers and chili for you gentlemen," a shapely waitress eventually said, sliding their meal in front of them. Not wanting his teeth to melt, Stump had ordered what the menu referred to as "wimp chili."

With the bullshit bouncing off all the walls Stump soon realized that a truck stop was its own little community, just like Xander had said. No wonder Xander was so at ease.

About halfway through his wimp chili, Stump spotted a couple walk in with a daughter, maybe 10 years old. Given there were no other children and only a few women in the complex, they looked out of place. They walked toward Stump's table and barely passed by when Xander grinned. "I'll be damned," he said loud enough that the newcomers could hear.

All three spun around. "Xander Brooks," the lady said with pleased lips before giving him a hug. "We thought you retired!"

"Did, but this ain't a paying trip. Me and Stump are heading into Kansas—on a treasure hunt."

When he put it that way, it sounded embarrassingly juvenile.

Xander turned to Stump. "I want you to meet some good friends. Jared and Yvonne are drivers. They bring Tanya with them whenever they can."

Xander gestured at Tanya. "And how are you doing, sweetheart? You've grown up quite a bit since I last saw you."

"I'm fine, but I'm running low on books."

Jared snickered. "She drags so many books on these trips it's a wonder we don't get fined at the scales."

Xander smiled at Tanya. "I was just telling Stump about the jackalopes."

The beaming smile on Tanya's face would have won first prize in a clown mask contest.

"You got to be careful," Yvonne said. "Those antlers are hard on tires."

Stump nodded. "Yeah. I know."

"Some of us call 'em 'horny hares,'" Jared added.

Little Tanya looked at Stump and rested her hands on her hips. "Are you retarded?"

Stunned, Stump didn't know what to say. Then Jared touched Tanya's shoulder. "Our little girl has been in 40 different states."

"It's 41, Daddy. You keep forgetting Montana."

"I stand corrected."

Considering this was the first time Stump had voluntarily left California, he respectfully head-bobbed the youngster.

Xander grinned in Jared's direction. "Would you mind if I showed Stump your rig, maybe let him squawk on the box?"

Stump's head spun from Xander to Jared to Yvonne. "Really? Me? Talk on one of those radios?"

"Why not?" Jared said. "Sounds to me like you know English."

"What would I say?"

"You boys go ahead. Tanya and I want to wash up and order dinner."

Jared tapped Stump on the shoulder. "C'mon. Any son of Xander's is a friend of mine. First you gotta have a handle."

Minutes later and outdoors 'the Stumpster' had forgotten all about trucker cologne and enjoyed a private tour of an 18-wheeler. Jared had to reach up to get to the latch of the driver's door. He pointed to a series of steps that led to the cab and an overhead seat. "You can get in right here, I'm going 'round to the other side to join you."

Stump glanced at Xander, who snapped a picture on his cell. "Xander the Great thinks the Stumpster's friends will get a kick out of this."

His chest pumping, Stump grabbed hold of a chrome bar, pulled his way up several built-in steps, a full six feet skyward and slid behind the oversized steering wheel. He dragged his hand across a smooth leather seat while he admired the instruments. Behind him in a little bedroom area at least forty books had been packed on a bookshelf.

While Jared climbed into the other side of the cab, a crackle came from the dash. *"Anybody in Seifert got your ears on? This is Boy Toy. C'mon back."*

Jared grabbed a corded microphone and handed it to Stump. "Push the button and answer him."

Stump grinned and squeezed. "Yes sir. We're here."

"Sir? Ain't nobody called me sir for years. That you, horsing around, Big Brawler? Come on."

Xander grinned. "Tell him your handle and ask how you can help him.

"Er. I'm the Stumpster, can I help you?"

"The Stumpster, huh? You new on this route, Stumpster?"

"I'm in a friend's rig." Stump said, using the only trucker lingo he knew. He slapped his spare hand over the mic. "Should I tell him who you are?"

"Sure. They call me Mama's Honey. And you don't have to cover the mic. Just release the trigger."

Stump nodded. "I'm hangin' with Mama's Honey."

"Don't believe I know him. Are there any hot cats up there tonight, Stumpster? Come on."

Both Jared and Xander snickered while Stump looked around the parking lot and doubted if cats could survive amidst all those gigantic tires.

"Boy Toy is looking for a long-legged cat. Any good ones on the prowl, Stumpster?"

"I don't see any," Stump said. "Mostly just other drivers and a couple ladies."

Jared shook his head, causing Stump to suspect something. He looked at the ladies again, released the mic trigger and spoke to Xander. "Is he talking about prostitutes?"

Xander grinned and nodded. "Tell him they're by the bulldog."

"Boy Toy likes 'em with short jeans and long legs."

"Good news, Boy Toy. There are a couple cats working the back row, near the bulldog."

"Copy that. Much obliged, Stumpster. 10-4."

Stump smiled and rested the mic back in its holder. "I feel like a pimp."

35

This time, when Stump awoke and Xander was missing Stump had a pretty good idea where his bio-dad was - a couple hundred yards away in the truck stop.

He checked his phone while he strolled to the porcelain stool. Yana had replied to the jackalope picture Stump had sent the previous evening. *"LOL. James says look up Jackalope."*

Stump did and snorted through a wide grin when he discovered that jackalopes were actually the product of mischievous taxidermists who blended two species together, and that had to be why a wise little girl asked him if he was retarded. Stump replied to Yana. "ROFLOL!!!"

Before taking a shower, he sent a brief message to Myles. "In Kansas. Xander's rad." Maybe Myles would finally get the hint that Stump was capable of making important decisions, such as running his own trust.

Then he made another call and was put through to voice mail. "Hello, Mrs. Kline. This is Stump. My dad said that Grandma Pauline got out and you think I left the doors open, but there's some mistake. I definitely pulled on the handle after I left. Please call me back, or I'll call you later so we can straighten this out. Thanks."

Later, while Stump brushed his teeth, Xander returned and flipped Stump a new red hat. "I thought you might like this."

Stump spun it around to see "Jackalope Killer" on the front. He plopped it on his head. "Rad, even though they're a gag."

"Oh. How'd you figure it out?"

"What you talking about, old dude? I knew it all along."

"Well, if that's true, you sure fooled me."

"Naw. You guys got me, but I owe you one."

"We can take it back when we go for some breakfast."

"No way. I like it," he said popping it on his head and turning it backwards. "It's my new lid. But I wouldn't mind doing my laundry while we're over there. I didn't bring enough clean clothes."

While they walked to the café, Stump had an idea. Maybe if he confessed something to Xander, Xander would feel compelled to do the same thing and clear up how he really learned about Stump's existence. "You know something, Xander? I seriously owe you an apology."

"Oh? For what?"

"I get it now. I understand why you liked your career, and that sense of community thing you talked about, and being like cowboys. That stuff is pretty rad. I'm sorry for doubting you and your peers."

"Well, thank you, Stump. It's not for everybody, but I'm glad you've learned something."

"I just thought I owed you an apology, cause we shouldn't keep secrets from each other, right?"

Xander flipped Stump a two-finger salute. "Darn right. Let me ask you something, Stumpster. What's your attitude about guns?"

Hmm. Guns, huh? Another sidestep. Why the hell was Xander so evasive? Since neither the subtle approach nor the direct approach worked out, Stump would have to think of some other way to drag out the information. "I generally don't like guns, except for the police and soldiers."

"What about hunters?"

"Barbaric. I don't see how people can kill innocent animals."

"If it weren't for hunters the herds would grow so big that there wouldn't be enough natural food to sustain them through the winter. Would you rather see a few animals taken out humanely and used for meat, or the entire herd die of starvation?"

A cool chill visited Stump's spine. "That's a good point," he said as a call came in.

"Yo, Zax, 'sup?"

"Oh, Stump, this is awful. I need your help."

"Why? What's wrong?"

"I went to see my accountant. If I don't make some serious changes I'm going to have to file for bankruptcy. Now, I have to let Yana go."

Stump's gut tightened. "That's awful. I'm sorry for both of you."

"I haven't said anything to her yet. I worry about her and the baby. I don't want to break her heart and lose all three of you as friends."

"That's not going to happen, Zax."

She sniffled. *"I have to hire a cook and do everything else myself. Hostess. Waitress. Janitor. Denise will have to help, but she's already struggling, especially since she's only got a few more days with her dog. I don't want to say anything to Yana until you get back, but maybe you can help me make her understand."*

"Of course, but I'm sure she'll be okay. There are other jobs for waitresses."

"Not within walking distance. She's going to hate me."

"Nobody's going to hate you, Zax. You're a good person and a good friend. She knows that."

"I gotta go now."

Stump turned to Xander. "Looks like Zax has got to fire Yana."

"They're both lucky to have a loyal friend like you. If you'd like to head back we could drive straight through and be there about this time tomorrow?"

"I dunno. If we do that there's no chance of finding the

coin–treasure and it's only a couple hours away. If we're this close, we might as well keep going. Anyway, a couple more days won't make a difference. If it's okay with you, I think we should stick with the plan."

"Makes sense to me."

An hour later, they reached Hays, Kansas, slid off the highway and headed north for Minnie's family farm. Stump was astonished by how much Xander knew about the area's long history. His enthusiasm was something Google could never have matched, proving yet again that Stump learned the most through direct contact with people.

With less than an hour to go on an oft-rutted dirt road, they saw a few farms, including one with a couple horses and a donkey. They imagined how much more primitive the area must have been some 80 years earlier, when Minnie's family lived out there.

Some 15 minutes later they finally saw another vehicle coming toward them – a funky sky-blue van with a dent in the fender. The driver and Xander traded friendly waves. Then, just before one of the very few clumps of trees, Xander reached under the driver's seat and pulled out a revolver. "You ever shoot a .38?"

Stump nearly freaked out. "I've seen Myles's guns and been shooting a few times, but overall guns make me nervous."

"You don't have to worry about guns, it's the people you gotta worry about." Xander let off the gas and pulled over and parked in the shade of the only stand of trees in sight. "Get out. I want to show you something in the trunk."

The trunk? Stump had been on the road for several days and never had a need to see inside the trunk. Now they were in a remote place talking about guns. The whole experience had an eerie feeling. He slid out of the Vette and quickly scanned his iPhone. No signal. He thought about all of Myles's warnings over the years and resisted the suspicious thoughts that crept into his mind.

What if . . .

36

Apprehensive for no rational reason, Stump held his breath while Xander opened the trunk. Inside, a half-dozen suitcases hid beneath a frying pan, a bowling ball bag and an old folded and taped–up baby swing. It didn't make sense.

Xander had flown from Wisconsin to San Diego where he rented the Vette. He either brought all these things with him or picked them up along the way, perhaps when Stump was asleep. Suddenly, Stump's mind flashed to a TV show he'd seen, in which a bad guy killed an old man and cut the corpse into pieces and . . . "What's going on?" he asked, trying not to complete his own morbid thought.

"Here, take this," Xander said, scooping up the frying pan, "and set it on the ground over there." As they removed the odds and ends Stump got a better look. Thankfully, the suitcases were way too small for body parts.

"Here we go," Xander said, opening a gun case that contained a Smith and Wesson Shield pistol. "I thought we might enjoy a little target practice. Go ahead; check this one out."

Stump had been shooting with Myles several times but had never actually "admired" guns in any sense of the word. He eyed the weapon, while Xander opened several additional cases, each with ammo and a gun of various types including a Glock, a Ruger, a Magnum Desert Eagle, and a Colt .45 revolver. Every weapon came with a glowing synopsis of its virtues. "Which one would you like to try first?"

Feeling both relieved and guilty for his previous suspicions, Stump shuffled his feet. "How'd you get these on the plane?"

"No problem. You just have to empty them, use the right case and declare them. Done it many times. I own about thirty of them, but only brought five with me. So which one catches your interest?"

"I don't really know. I guess the Ruger would be okay."

"Good choice. Bad guys like to turn the Ruger vertically to show off."

"Yeah. I've seen that on TV. They look rad."

"Yeah, but the show-off stuff sacrifices accuracy."

"They still look rad. How'd you learn so much about guns?"

"Grew up with them. My father, your grandfather, was a prison guard when he was young. Took me hunting when I was old enough."

Stump paused to savor the thought of having a prison guard for a grandfather.

Xander pointed at the baby swing. "Help me remove the tape from the swing and I'll show you something—that is, if you want to do a little target practice."

No grandson of a prison guard could turn down an offer like that. "I guess we got a little extra time."

When all the tape was removed, Xander proceeded to unfold the light-weight legs and set up a pint-sized version of a back-yard swing set. "Now I need you to get the bowling ball and set it in the seat where the baby would ride."

While Stump went for the ball, Xander cranked a handle on the swing's crossbar, which tightened a built-in spring. A moment later Stump placed the ball in the canvas seat and hoped Xander didn't plan on shooting some imaginary kid.

"Now, the frying pan," Xander said pointing.

Having no idea what was up, all Stump could do was go along with the plan. "Here ya go." He watched with child-like amusement as Xander tied 30 feet of strong fishing line to the front of the baby's seat before tying the other end to a hole in the handle of the pan.

He stretched out the line and dangled the frying pan over a branch of a nearby tree so that the pan hovered a few feet above the ground. "That should do it," he said as he returned to Stump's side and the swing.

Finally, Xander pushed the bowling-ball-in-a-seat backwards, which caused the frying pan on the end of the line to rise up at least a foot. Then Xander let go of the ball causing the swing's seat to go forward and the frying pan to drop back to its previous point. "There we go," he said, as the swing clicked back and forth and the frying pan rose up and down. "A moving target. Now all we need is to get our weapons."

Stump literally laughed out loud. "That's really funny, dude. You're warped. You know that?"

"It'll be twenty minutes or so before we have to crank her up again."

Xander grabbed the Magnum Desert Eagle. "You go first." Stump nodded, double-handed the Ruger and stood some thirty feet back from the target. Sixteen rounds later, several with the weapon held sideways he got his first frying pan ping. Then Xander took a turn and hit the pan nearly every time.

After that they passed the weapons back and forth. Most of the time Stump missed the target, but he did slightly better with the .38 that Xander originally pulled from under the Vette's seat.

"No wonder," Xander said. "That one belonged to my dad. It's been in the family for years." Stump smiled. It was extra rad to shoot a gun that his granddad, a former prison guard, had also shot.

While trying to decide which weapon to try next, several planes flew overhead. Xander paused to look them over. "Three Cessnas," he said. "Probably going to Kansas City."

Stump nodded and snagged the Colt .45 from its case. Shortly thereafter he imagined the moving pan-target was a criminal, trying to get away out of a window. The imaginary bad guy usually won the contest, but on the few occasions when he hit the pan, it pinged just like on TV. "Take that, you bastard," he said each time.

On one of Stump's stray shots, he actually hit the fishing line, causing the pan to fall like a limp dead man. Xander laughed and retied the line. "There ya go, Dead Eye," he said with maximum sarcasm.

Finally, after hundreds of rounds, they had to get back to their major objective: finding Minnie's farm and a potential secret treasure. Repacking the trunk, Stump handed Xander each of the guns. When he got to the .38 Xander smiled, "My dad told me to give that one to you—the case too and a very old holster—that is, if you want them."

Stump's knees went limp. "Impossible. That's impossible."

"No, it isn't. My dad's like that. It's all yours, Stumpster, compliments of Grandpa Brooks."

"Of course, I want it," he said cradling it in his palms and staring. "Aside from my truck, this is the best gift I've ever gotten."

"Good. He'll be glad to hear that—and to meet you someday."

Stump nodded enthusiastically. Darn right he wanted to meet the man who'd raised his bio-dad, but first he stuck one gun in his belt and held two other guns in his hands and posed by the pan for Xander to catch a couple pictures.

Moments later. "Hi, Myles. Just thought I'd let you know I got in a gunfight with the Frying Pan Bandit and killed the bastard—all without hurting anybody."

37

Several more miles slipped by before Stump and Xander came upon a sign indicating they'd reached Zurich, population 99. Roughly a dozen weathered and bedraggled structures straddled an alligatored road. Fresh paint and groomed yards were as scarce as a toothbrush at a Hell's Angels rally. "Three more miles," Stump said.

After the town, an abundance of road ruts established that the Vette was out of its element. They took it easy until they reached the crisscross fence and an old shack that Opal Clemens had mentioned. Stump pointed off to the right where he saw some remnants of a former building. "This has got to be Minnie Moore's property."

"Not exactly the Bellagio, is it?" Xander said.

"What do you think we should do?"

"Well, these people probably watch out for each other, so we might be better off to introduce ourselves to the nearest neighbor first."

Stump glanced at the cabin behind the crisscross fence. This time he noticed a barn or garage, a faded pickup truck and several mid-sized animals. "I guess you're right."

They inched toward the neighbor's driveway where a pair

of longhaired, barking mutts ran toward them. "I hope they don't kill us," Stump said.

"I don't think so. They're barking, not snarling. They're telling their owner he's got visitors. The one on the left is the leader. Just wait for the owner to tell them its okay."

A moment later an unshaven man about Xander's age complete with coveralls and a greasy gangster-like hat, pushed open a screen door and slowly headed their way.

"Just so we're on the same page," Stump said to Xander, "I don't think we should say anything about a potential treasure."

"I suspect this is the kind of thing a young detective likes," Xander said before touching his lips. "Mum's the word."

The farmer moved in their direction and waved a hand at his dogs. "Bomber. Daisy. Shut yer yaps." He walked up to Xander's side. "Wooeee! That's some fancy car you got there. What can I do for you gentlemen?"

As Xander dealt with the man, Stump caught an unpleasant whiff of sewage and wrinkled his nose.

"We were interested in looking at that land over there," Xander said pointing. "You know anything about it?"

"Maybe. You thinkin' 'bout buying the place?"

"No. No. Nothing like that. We know the people who own it and they asked us to check on it while we were in the area. I saw some debris in the field. Is that the old house? We heard it got hit by a tornado."

"Ain't much to know, but I could probably show ya round."

"That'd be great. My name's Xander. This is Stump."

"I'm Herbert. Herbert Happy. People says I'm happy 'cause I ain't never been married. "If I show you folks around," Herbert continued, "you suppose you could do me a favor?"

"If we can," Xander said. "What is it?"

"Ya'll come 'round the back and I'll show ya."

Seconds later the trio walked their way toward the back of the cabin where the sewage stench picked up.

"It don't smell too good 'round here." Stump said, thinking he sounded too much like Herbert.

"That's what we're a-fixin'," Herbert said, pointing some 40 feet back to an outhouse and a big mound of dirt that neighbored a deep hole in the ground. "My little urination station is all fulled-up," Herbert said bending down to pick up a rope. "We're gonna slide the whole shebang on top a the new hole."

What the hell? Stump looked at Xander, who appeared to be enjoying the moment.

"When we's done," Herbert said. "You can try a bottle of my home brew 'fore we check out that land for ya."

"A good beer would be great," Xander said, grinning. "What would you like us to do?"

Herbert wrapped his rope around the base of the outhouse and tied a couple knots at the end of the rope. "Two of us would tug the rope while the other guy pushes. That way, the whole kit and caboodle should jist scoot right where we want it-over the new hole."

"Okay by me," Xander said, looking at Stump. "You want to pull or push?"

Stump may not have been the smartest farmer in the dell, but he sure as hell didn't want to be any closer than necessary to the stink-hole of death. "Couldn't we just tie the rope to your truck?"

Herbert grinned. "What's a matter, city boy? You 'fraid of bathroom leavin's?"

"It's not that. I was just thinking it would be easier to let the truck do the hard part."

"Well, I don't want to trample my flowers."

Stump looked around. All he could see were weeds and more weeds and some grass that had been nibbled to the ground by the farm animals.

"It won't be too heavy," Herbert said. "It's jist a one-seater."

Stump shook his head.

"Let's get this done," Xander said, smiling. "You guys pull. I'll guide the back-end."

Whew! Now Stump had another reason to like Xander.

A few minutes later, the cozy little outhouse on the prairie creaked in protest as the three-man crew tugged it off the most disgusting poop pit in the entire history of mankind. "There we go," Herbert said a couple minutes later when the wooden porta-potty settled in its new home. "That wasn't very hard, now was it, city boy?"

Stump couldn't help himself. He glanced at the abandoned cesspool to see if it were as disgusting as he'd suspected and instantly wished he hadn't looked.

Xander turned to Herbert. "I think we can assume that Stump here has never changed a diaper or done any plumbing."

Herbert nodded. "You boys is alright. Come on inside now 'n have that brew I promised ya."

"I'd like that," Xander said, while Stump hoped a breeze would blow in a friendlier direction.

As they moved toward the front of the cabin, Bomber and Daisy, tails wagging, took turns stealing crotch sniffs from Xander and Stump. Stump tried to push Bomber away and caught a glob of dog spit on the back of his hand. He patted the dog on the head and returned the DNA to its rightful owner.

Inside, the place had just two windows. A potbelly stove resided in the back corner. To the right a gun rack contained a long rifle, a shotgun and a musket. "Is that a family heirloom?" Stump asked.

"Egg-sack-ly," Herbert said, uttering yet another mispronounced word. He moved to the side of the stove, knelt and lifted a trap door. "I'll be right back with those beers."

Stump and Xander traded glances then watched Herbert descend a ladder. "Why do you have a donkey out here?" Stump asked.

"'Cause they're mean suns-a-bitches," Herbert said as he climbed out of the cellar with three dark amber bottles. "Donkeys keep the coyotes from messing with my goats.

When ya got goats, ya gotta have at least two of 'em or they get real lonely and nasty."

Xander nodded. "You learn something new every day."

Beers in hand, Herbert scooted over to the sink and pumped some water over the bottles.

"Do you have a well?" Stump asked.

"You betcha. Ain't no city water out this far, but most of my neighbors have 'lectric pumps."

Herbert opened the beers and handed two to Xander, who passed one along to Stump. The bottle was a lot cooler than Stump expected. He watched Xander take a glug before he too took a careful sip. It had a much stronger flavor than the few commercial brands Stump had sampled. Xander pointed his bottle toward Herbert. "This stuff is good."

"Thankee." A few swallows later, Herbert rose. "You fellows ready for that tour?"

Not wanting to be rude, Stump took a couple more big slugs and detected some sediment in the last one. He carefully wiped his tongue on the back of his hand and looked for Bomber, but no luck.

38

"Where ya'll want to begin?" Herbert asked as he and Xander and Stump stepped off the gravel road and onto a mound of tall grass. "This land is about twenty acres."

A bit light-headed from the homebrew, Stump suspected that any treasure would be buried somewhere near the center of the lot where stubborn leftovers of a fallen-down farmhouse hid in the weeds. "Could we walk the perimeter first, so I can see just how big 20 acres is?" Stump asked, thereby concealing his true interest.

Herbert nodded. "Okay. This way."

As Stump crunched through the grasses and weeds, he wished he could trade his sandals for a pair of boots. "Is this Tornado Alley?" he asked remembering something Xander said on the way in.

"I'd say so. We get small ones pert-near every year but ain't had no real bad ones for quite a while."

Stump glanced toward the debris pile again. "When did our friend's house blow over?"

"Don't know, egg-sack-ly."

"She said they had two houses blown down. Do you know where the other one was?"

"I 'spect they woulda built them in the same spot. That way they could use the same well and reuse materials."

Made sense.

After they plodded through a couple hundred yards of weeds and stickers, Herbert stopped and removed his sweat-stained hat, releasing several trickles of perspiration. "Too bad there ain't no trees no more."

From there they made a left turn and walked more or less parallel to the road. A couple dozen steps along that route Stump accidently tripped over an unexpected grapefruit-sized stone and nearly went down. "Damn! What the—"

"You okay?" Xander asked.

"Dinged my big toe," Stump said, looking back at the rock. "Hey, what's that?"

"What you got there?" Herbert asked.

Stump squatted. "Right there, in between two rocks—it looks like an eggshell."

Herbert leaned in, took a look. "That's a quail egg. Them speckles make it hard fer the snakes to see 'em."

"Looks like the snake won this time," Xander said.

Stump picked up the shell. "It's a lot smaller than a chicken egg."

"You can eat 'em, but it takes a lot to make a meal. We got pheasants and geese 'round here too. A couple years ago we had a wild turkey up by my place fer a while. It musta been lost though, cause they like to be 'round trees."

Xander raised his brows. "You obviously know a lot about birds."

"Jest the ones I can eat."

They resumed their walk, which enabled Stump to glance furtively toward the debris area for a likely hiding place for a bottle of coins. "I'm surprised we don't see any cinderblocks." Stump said. "They would have resisted tornados better."

"Ah. The story of the Three Little Pigs," Xander said grinning.

"Cinderblocks was fairly new when this place got blowed over," Herbert said.

Almost halfway up the sideline, Herbert pointed forward. "There's a big ole stump up ahead."

"I see it," Stump said rubbing his sun-warmed neck. "It's flat on top. Somebody must have taken a saw to it."

"No use wastin' firewood," Herbert said.

Stump jumped onto the flattened area and spun toward Xander and Herbert. "Look, I'm a Stump on a stump."

"You mean a bump on a log," Xander said, grinning.

"That tree blowed over," Herbert said pointing north. "The jet stream brings wicked wind down from Canada what meets up with the hot air we got and it all spins round like a bunch a drunk square dancers."

Stump smiled. "A big tree like that would need a lot of water. Did they have a well?"

"It's over here," Herbert said, leading them closer to the debris area. A small shot of adrenalin perked Stump up. This was the moment he'd been waiting for. If he were careful and lucky, he might find the bottle of rare coins. If he were even luckier, those coins would be valuable enough to allow Minnie Moore to remain in Meadowlark Flats as Grandma Pauline's needed almost-sister.

He followed Herbert to a short, circular wall of bricks.

"How deep is it?" Xander asked, obviously thinking the same thing Stump was.

"Don't rightly know."

Stump stepped forward and got his first look into a well. The upper bricks were in decent shape considering the years and countless storms. More optimistic, he looked down the shaft only to get a completely different impression-and a deeper message.

He wasn't exactly sure how deep the well was but enough of the bricks had been removed to make it obvious that if there ever had been a secret treasure down there, somebody found it.

"That's about it," Herbert said, wiping his head for the third or fourth time. "I could use another beer. How 'bout you fellas?"

As interesting as Herbert was, Stump had had just about enough of this place. "I don't know about Xander, but I've got some things I need to do," He checked his cell again but still no bars. "I'm thinking we ought to be heading back."

Xander nodded. "We gotta take it easy. Our car wasn't meant for country roads."

After a casual walk back to the Vette, Xander reached for Herbert's hand. "Thanks for the tour, Mr. Happy. It's been a real pleasure meeting you."

"You boys is always welcome 'round here."

"Thank you," Stump said, catching a handshake of his own. "You're a very interesting man." As older people always were.

A few minutes later and down the road a bit, Xander spoke first. "It looks like that treasure was a farce."

"Either that or somebody found it already." Stump didn't say so but secretly looking for a treasure, and meeting a man who still used an outhouse, justified the whole trip, not to mention all the fun things he and Xander did before that. He couldn't imagine a better spring break or a better bio-dad.

About halfway back to the highway, and with the sun dropping, Stump checked the time. "I'm getting a little nervous. It took us four days to get here. We'll need to really haul ass to get back in time."

Xander raised a finger. "Or I can get us there by tomorrow night."

"How you going to do that?"

"Easy. I fly for free and I have a few vouchers. You can use one of those. It's just a few hours to the Kansas City airport. We can fly out tomorrow. You'll be home by dinner time."

"What about the car?"

"No problem. They'll take it at the airport."

"You sure you don't mind using your vouchers?"

"Hell, no. You're my son. That's what they're for. I'll get home a little earlier too. It's all good."

"Okay, let's do that. That'll give me a chance to solve a couple of my problems too."

"All we gotta do is check flight times."

Stump's cell showed two bars—good enough. "Looks like the best flight time is just after noon."

"Perfect."

A cathartic calm washed over Stump. They could make the drive, sleep in and then have plenty of time to get to the airport in the morning.

Mere minutes later, Xander made an unexpected stop at a well-kept farmhouse that they'd passed on the way in. Near the small barn, two fenced-in horses and a donkey didn't even acknowledge them. "Wa-sup?"

"I want to check on something," Xander said, sliding out of the Vette. "I'll be right back."

Before Stump could ask any more questions, Xander marched up to the front door where a middle-aged man answered. A few minutes later, after pointing toward the animals, Xander returned. "I thought so."

Stump looked at the house and then the animals. "Thought what?"

"That brown and white mare is about to have her foal and we're going to help."

39

"Her name is Lulu," Xander said, referring to the mare. "She's leaking milk and they think tonight's the night. We're bunking down in the barn."

"What the hell you talking about, dude? I ain't sleeping in no barn."

"It'll be interesting. Lulu will tell us if the time is right and all we have to do is pass the message along to our host."

"Is this another one of your jokes, 'cause—"

"'Cause nothing, Stump. On the way in I told you that I'd slept beside rivers and campfires and you smiled. Now this is your chance to make a memory."

"But what about our flight tomorrow?"

"All we gotta do is get out of here by 7:30."

"Hi there," Stump turned to see a man a bit younger than Xander with a paper sack in hand. "I'm Roy Bloodale. My wife put some sandwiches and a couple apples in this bag for you. Go ahead and gather your belongings while I bring Lulu into the stable."

The dude was friendly enough but Stump would have preferred to meet a grumpy manager of a comfortable motel. "I've never done anything like this before," he said.

"No problem. Most of it is natural, but it's nice to have the help should we need it."

A few minutes later while Stump tried to ignore the marijuana-like stench of the stable, Mr. Bloodale gingerly led a now noticeably fat and mildly agitated horse with big eyelashes into the stable. "The mama-to-be gets the area with the hay on the floor. You fellas will bunk down over there against the wall."

Stump swung around to see a single cot piled with a couple of blankets, and a couple dozen hay bales.

"The stallion's name is *Stub*, for stubborn. I'm going to leave him outside for the night. All you gotta do is come get us if Lulu tells ya she's ready. Until then, we're grateful for some much-needed sleep."

Stump looked closer at his overgrown four-legged bunkmate. She stood taller than he and looked woefully uncomfortable. She nose-farted. Stump felt the same way.

"I can use some z's too," Xander said. I'll take the first shift on the cot. Just wake me up if Lulu starts acting differently."

Stump sighed. "You're a strange dude, you know that?"

A big grin filled Xander's face. "It runs in the family."

As Xander removed his shoes, Stump paused for a moment, and then decided the time was right to clear the air. "Speaking of family, can I ask you something and get an honest answer?"

"'Course."

Stump sat on a hay bale. "It has to do with the first time we met. You seemed like a conman, but you're actually a straight shooter. It just doesn't wash. You lied about how you found me but every time I bring it up you wiggle out of the conversation. Why don't you just tell me the truth and then we can move forward?"

Xander shot a hand behind his neck and sighed. "I'd hoped you'd let this go."

"It's important, dude."

"Are you really, really sure you want to talk about this,

Stump? It's probably going to shake up your world in ways you may not like."

"You're the one who doesn't get it, dude. My mom died in a fire but you tried to feed me some bullshit about meeting her. That ain't possible."

Xander stared at Stump. "Let me ask you this. When you were a kid, did you believe in Santa Claus?"

"What the—"

"I'm guessing your Santa fantasy was going along fine until somebody busted your bubble. At first you didn't want to believe that your mother was actually Santa. But then, when you came to grips with it, you were glad you were one of the enlightened ones and probably snickered at younger kids. Is that about right?"

"Dude! What the hell are you getting at?"

"The point is things aren't always as we believe."

"You're not telling me I'm a knuckle baby, are you?"

"Knuckle baby? I'm not familiar with that term."

"You know. You needed some money so you choked your chicken and sold the sperm."

Xander grinned. "I wish it were that simple. Are you certain you can handle an alternate reality?"

Stump leaned back against a bale of hay and locked his hands behind his head. "Go ahead. I'm all ears."

"Alright. About all I know about the woman who raised you is her name was Jean and she died in a fire; but she wasn't your biological mother. Another woman was. That's the one I know. Your biological mother's name is Debra Kirk."

Stump threw his hands in the air. "I call b.s. That's the most ridicu—"

"You're the guy who believed in Santa Claus. Remember? Now are you going to listen to your father or do I have to take away your phone privileges or something?"

Stump smirked. "Okay. I guess I'm up for a fairytale."

"Alright then. Before you were born your biological mother, Debra, lived next door to Jean in an apartment building in Wisconsin. I didn't know either of them, but one of my buddies, named Rod, knew that Debra liked to 'party' with various men. In fact, she already had a young son by that time."

Hmm. Stump remembered his mom speaking of Wisconsin so this story had a small hint of credibility. "Yeah? So?"

"I'm ashamed to admit it, but Rod and Debra and me spent a wild weekend getting drunk and everything else you might imagine. We were just a bunch of careless young people, inspired by animal urges, with no concern for the potential consequences. After that, we all went our own ways. Then before long, I met somebody else and eventually met Brianne and got married."

"So, you're saying I was Debra's baby? I don't think so."

"I know this is difficult for you to believe, Stump, but hear me out. After that weekend we all lost touch. That is, until Rod saw Debra waiting tables in a restaurant a few months ago. He went back to see her a few more times and she eventually mentioned that she'd gotten pregnant from that weekend. The father had to be either him or me, but Rod was sterile due to an accident when he was a kid, which meant that I was the father. I told you earlier that I still had some doubts of my own after I heard all this. After all, Debra had *a reputation*, so I too wanted to get that DNA test, but as soon as I saw you—"

"You knew it was true." Not sure what to say next, Stump sat motionless.

"When Debra figured out she was pregnant, that left her with a big problem. She couldn't afford another baby and wasn't a great mother to her first kid, so she and Jean waited until you were born so Debra could get a bigger welfare check. Once that was set up, Jean took you away and they both had reasons to keep their secret. If the government had figured out what happened, they both could've been charged with welfare fraud, and Jean would've been forced to give you up. She obviously loved you too much to take that risk."

A sinking feeling filled Stump. He could've said that his

mother wasn't the diabolical type, but in actuality, Xander's story had entirely too much believability. Like Debra, Stump's mother had a propensity for drama. She became a struggling alcoholic who slept around, lost her driver's license and had been in both the hospital and the county jail because of her drinking problems. Stump looked deep into Xander eyes for any hint that he might have been kidding around, but it wasn't there. "Why didn't you say so earlier?" he asked timidly.

Xander rose and sat next to Stump. "Simple. I could tell that you loved Jean, and a dad doesn't want to take something like that away from the people he loves."

Stump lowered his head.

"Look at it this way," Xander said, resting a hand on Stump's knee. "Your mother risked everything for you. There are millions of kids who never experienced so much motherly love. You were incredibly fortunate."

"Now I wish I'd appreciated her more. I owe you an apology."

"Well, if you'll let me get some sleep now, I'll forget all about it."

"Thanks for leveling with me. I'm really glad you're my dad."

"Me, too. And there's one more thing."

"What's that?"

"Ho. Ho. Ho. Now give your dad a hug."

Stump grabbed hold of the man he'd always wanted to meet and hugged him like he'd never hugged anybody before. "Can I start calling you Dad?"

"Damn right you can . . . son."

40

"**S**tump! Wake up. Lulu needs us."

Huh? Oh, yeah. The horse. But he'd had so little sleep. He pushed aside a heavy blanket that Xander must have laid on him.

"Lulu's water broke," Xander added. "I gotta get Roy. I'll be right back."

Stump looked around. Lulu had lain down. She lifted her head, looked over her rear quarters toward Stump and let her head rest. Unsure what to do, Stump rose to his feet. "Take it easy, Lulu. Help will be here in a minute."

Lulu snorted, sending dust into the air. Suddenly, a slimy, softball-size sack emerged under her tail. Stump turned his head away and then back. It was both gross and intriguing.

"We're coming, Lulu," Mr. Bloodale said, as he and Xander returned.

Stump pointed at her vagina. "She's blowing a bubble."

Roy chuckled. "You ain't seen nothing yet. Everybody stay back so she doesn't feel threatened."

"I've seen all my kids born," Xander said, before catching himself. "Well, except for the oldest one. But I've never seen a horse give birth. How long does it take?"

"Like humans. Sometimes an hour, sometimes longer."

Lulu lifted her head again and looked over her shoulder right at Stump. "I think she wants us to keep quiet so she can concentrate."

This time Xander chuckled.

"Naw," Mr. Bloodale said while Lulu squirmed and the bubble ballooned. "As long as we stay away, she ain't thinking about us. My wife will be here as soon as she gets the kids up."

"Kids? You're not going to make them watch this, are you?"

"They'll be all right. They've seen videos."

After Stump asked a couple additional dumb questions, Roy's wife arrived. "Hi, everybody. I'm Gretchen. This is Johnnie and Emma." Johnnie appeared to be about eight and Emma a few years older. "I put on some coffee in case we're in for a long night."

"Do you want a boy horsey or a girl horsey?" Stump asked Emma.

She clucked her tongue. "They're called 'foals,' not 'horseys.'"

"Oh, sorry."

"When they're older you can call them colts or fillies," little Johnnie added.

"It takes eleven months for the dame to have her foal after mating, huh, Mommy?" Emma asked.

Mating? Did these kids really know about mating? Stump looked to Gretchen for confirmation of Emma's question.

"That's right, honey."

How embarrassing. Stump was deep into his first year of college, yet these grade-schoolers knew more "horsey" facts than he did. Not willing to display any more ignorance, he nodded, as if he agreed with Gretchen.

Suddenly something in the bubble moved. "Here comes the front hooves," Roy said, gently patting Lulu on the hind side. "That-a girl."

"Are the feet facing down, Daddy?"

"Yep. That's good."

Then the little hooves kicked as if they were waving at Stump. He considered waving back like he did with Grandma Pauline and the youngsters back at Meadowlark Flats, but he couldn't withstand any additional humiliation.

"The nose will be next," Gretchen said.

As expected, the fluid-soaked sack inched its way out until the foal's nose looked as if it were attached to its knees. Lulu paused long enough to gather more strength and then the foal's head inched forward.

"That-a girl, Lulu," Mr. Bloodale said.

Breathing hard, Lulu laid her head on the floor for a moment, then her offspring's head slithered out and rested on the floor like a tired fish.

"Doesn't that hurt?" Stump asked nobody in particular.

"Why don't you try it?" Emma said.

Gretchen lifted a finger to her lips. "Now honey, that's not nice."

Stump felt like sticking his tongue out at his younger foe, but the truth was she had a better handle on the moment than he did.

"The shoulders are the tricky part," Mr. Bloodale said.

After another breather Lulu pushed and squirmed but the shoulders wouldn't come. Another try also failed. "If she can't swing it next time, we'll have to help her."

Help her? What could that mean?

Roy and Xander petted Lulu until she made another attempt but couldn't quite do it.

"Okay, everybody," Roy said, "the next time she pushes, I'll pull." He looked at Xander. "I'll need you to squat between her haunches and the birth canal so she won't kick me or her foal. Stump, I need you to kneel up near the tail for now. You might have to help me guide the little guy out."

WHAT? Stump couldn't believe his ears. How the heck was he going to help? He was having a tough enough time just avoiding ridicule.

"Kneel or squat right here," Roy said, pointing to the correct location. "We have to be ready the next time she pushes. Be careful, now."

Stump swallowed and inched his way toward his station, but just as he squatted, his feet shot out in front of him due to the birth water underneath the hay. He landed on his butt and fell backwards, soaking his pants, shirt and hands in the liquid. He cringed and wanted to get away, but Lulu swatted him with her tail as if to tell him to stay put. He maneuvered himself into position.

"Okay, this is it," Roy said, while quickly sliding his fingers inside the mother's vagina and around the foal's neck. "I've got her lubed. Stump, you cradle the foal's head. Don't squeeze or twist its neck. Just glide it out when Lulu signals us."

For a split second, Stump wished he had some gloves but he nodded and reached out just as the foal's head glided into his hands. The birth canal contracted and then Lulu pushed.

"Easy, everybody," Roy said tugging just enough while Stump gently cradled the foal's head and aimed it in the perfect direction.

"Good job, Stump," Gretchen said from over his shoulder.

"It's coming. It's coming. Just a little more."

Stump gently held the little guy's head while the mare's opening stretched farther and farther, causing Stump to want to do more.

"C'mon. C'mon, baby," he cheered.

Back behind him, Emma and Little Johnnie applauded. "You can do it, Stump," Emma shouted.

All of a sudden, the foal squirmed, the mama pushed, Xander stiffened, Roy pulled and Stump felt the foal's entire body slip forth onto the floor, causing him to lose his footing and to fall into the fluid yet again. This time he didn't give a damn. He bolted to his feet, jumped up and yelled, "That is the coolest thing I've ever done in my entire life."

Gretchen patted him on his dry shoulder. "Your mama would be proud."

He jumped again. She sure would.

On the floor, both horses, still joined by an umbilical cord, shifted and rested on their sides for a moment.

"It's a filly," Roy said, as he pulled away the torn sack from the foal's nose and lifted its head so its nostrils could drain. Stump watched in stunned awe as the filly took her first real breath. Then he realized he hadn't filmed any of it. He hustled for his iPhone.

"Do we cut the cord or something?" Xander asked.

"Not usually," Roy said. "It takes a few minutes for the placental blood to transfer. Then we'll let the cord break away naturally."

"It heals quicker," Gretchen said.

Little Johnnie poked Stump's arm. "You need a bath."

"He'll have time for that in a little while, honey. He wants to get some pictures now. Emma and I will get some drinks."

Sticky, damp, exhausted and as excited as a mother, Stump wiped his saliva-drenched lips on his cleanest shirtsleeve and snapped pictures as if he had to catch up.

After a little more resting, Lulu rose to her feet and licked her baby clean. For some reason, it didn't seem gross. "They're bonding," Roy said, as they all sat on hay bales and watched the affection.

A half-hour later, when Stump was completely drained, the foal struggled to her feet and took her first milk. Stump looked in Lulu's eyes and once more felt overwhelmed by the instinctive love that mothers of all types have for their offspring.

As usual, he missed his mom.

41

"**W**hew. That was a night for the ages," Xander said when he and Stump first hit the highway later that morning.

"Yeah. You were correct about making a memory, but I had to throw my clothes away and only got three hours of sleep."

"Welcome to the club. You can get some rest now if you want to. I can drive for a couple hours."

That sounded great, but now that he and Xander had cleared the air about Stump's mom, and Stump was certain Xander wasn't a conman, it seemed appropriate to mention his trust; after all, it was an impressive reward for his solving a murder. Who wouldn't want to share such an accomplishment like that with his parent? "Can I ask you something first? I was wondering what you'd do with the money if you hit one of those huge jackpots in Vegas?"

"Ah, yes. Everybody ponders questions like that from time to time. Just how big is this particular fantasy jackpot?"

"I dunno. Let's say three million."

"That's a nice sum all right."

"Would you still work?"

"I don't know. What about you?"

"I'm not sure what I'd do, but I wouldn't take on some lame-ass job either. I guess I'd like to be an entrepreneur or investor. Would you invest some of it?"

"I'd probably follow your grandpa's advice: *Invest a little and spend a little.*"

"Invest in what?"

"There's a lot a guy could do with that kind of money, but if I had to make that decision right now, I'd partner up with a buddy of mine in west Texas. They're getting into fracking."

"I heard that's bad for the environment."

"Who told you that?"

"One of my professors."

"There are people who think like that. Most of them don't like nuclear energy either, but these forms of power are safer than wind or solar. You can look it up. T Boone Pickens, an environmentalist billionaire, converted all his oil stocks into natural gas investments because it's abundant and cleaner."

"But what about fracking? Aren't they pumping dirty water into the ground?"

"The water gets dirty while it moves around underground. Ultimately, it replaces the oil that's taken out. Ordinarily, there's no net difference. Anyway, my buddy owns drilling rights on a few sections of west Texas land, that's almost 2,000 acres. They've already taken all the easy oil out, but now people want to buy him out, especially for the natural gas."

"Why doesn't he sell it to them?"

"Good question. He'd rather put together a group of smaller investors who should split up 10 to 20 million."

"Sounds interesting. I'd do something like that, but Myles is too conservative."

"It sounds like we've moved from a theoretical jackpot in Vegas to a real-life situation. Are you trying to tell me that Myles is rich?"

"Not exactly. We're talking about me."

Xander grinned. "You? You can't even afford a complete set of clothes."

"Well, there's something I wasn't sure I should tell you, but it goes back to when I was thirteen, the year my mother died."

"Did she have a big insurance policy or something?"

"No. This all has to do with what happened after that, when I solved those murders. I already told you about my assistant principal, Ms. Johnson."

"Yeah. I believe you said she got pushed off a platform and into a canyon, and that you figured out who did it."

"Yes, and her grandmother gave me a reward for figuring out that it wasn't suicide."

"I remember. You said you used the reward money to build the dog park that you named after your mother and Ms. Johnson."

"That's all true, but something else happened after that. Granny was super rich and Ms. Johnson was her only relative, so after I had the dog park built she put ten percent of her estate into a trust for me. We didn't even know about it until she passed away and me and Myles got a call from her attorney."

"Really? That's quite a story. I assume it was three million?"

Stump nodded. "Myles is the trustee. I don't get any of the money until I'm 21, unless Myles authorizes it, which he won't do, except for school and a little spending money."

"That's pretty conservative all right."

"When my truck wore out, he'd only let me have 10 thousand dollars for a better car, but you can't get anything decent for that. But that's not all that bothers me. He never does anything with any of the money. I tried to get him to buy stock in Apple or Microsoft, but he says that's just gambling. What good is it to have money if you never get to spend it or even invest it?"

"I see your dilemma, but I also understand why Myles does it like that."

186

"I know that he's just trying to make sure he doesn't lose any of it, and I appreciate that, but when you miss opportunities that's just another way to lose money. If Myles would just invest half of it, I wouldn't need to work or go to boring college."

Xander tilted his head to the side. "I guess school would seem pretty boring to a fellow who'd already solved some real crimes."

"See. You get it. It's going to be two more years before I get my money and then I'll be set for life. But I might miss some profits and die of boredom before all that happens."

Xander suddenly pointed skyward. "See that little jet up there, coming this way? It looks like a Lear."

"Yeah, I see it," Stump said. "What of it?"

"Nothing really. It's the kind I love to fly. I think it's equivalent to your license plate trick. You and I just automatically see these things when they come into view. Sorry, but I wanted to point that Lear out before it blew past us."

"No problem. I get it."

"As I was about to say regarding your schooling, it's not about need; it's about the gratification that comes from maximizing your potential, opening doors, and making a difference in people's lives."

Stump shook his head. "I shoulda known that you'd be on his side."

"Now I get to call b.s. Schooling and nearly every job you'll ever get will be boring from time to time, but I've been watching you and you gain the most pleasure when you help others. Think about that granny who gave you all that money. You did something spectacularly unselfish with it then she gave you even more. It's almost like she was urging you to do it again. You're the kind of person who makes a difference in other people's lives. Think about your grandma and Minnie Moore and Zax. School is the vehicle to get you the smarts that can do the most good. That's why I think you should stick it out, even if it is boring from time to time."

Stump turned his head. "Nobody ever put it like that."

"I meant every word of it. You don't even know how much potential you have."

"Well, thanks. I just thought that I should level with you since you leveled with me about my mom."

"I'm glad you did, and now I want to level with you again. You should get some sleep so you can drive the Vette one more time before we turn it in."

42

After returning the Vette to the rental place, Stump and Xander rode the shuttle to the airport. "I just thought of something," Stump said en route. "It would be dumb for you to fly all the way to San Diego and then have to take another flight back to Wisconsin, especially with all your 'special cargo.'"

"I thought about that, too. It would save me a lot of time, but I'd have to pay cash for your ticket."

"I can reimburse you when I sell my truck. It's the least I can do since you've paid for everything else."

"It's okay with me, if you're okay with it."

At the airport Xander found a flight that would work for him and they both checked in. "You know something," Stump said while they walked together to his terminal, "After James backed out, I almost didn't go on this trip, but now I'm super glad I did."

"Me, too, Stump. Before we run off in our separate ways, I was wondering what you would think if I called Myles?"

"Why?'

"A couple things. I'd like to give him the credit he deserves for the person you've become. That's remarkable parenting under any conditions, but especially from a single parent who didn't have to do that."

Stump paused a moment then nodded. "I guess that'd be okay."

"If he's open to it, I might also talk to him about the trustee role. While I think he's handled it very well, you seem ready for a little more responsibility to me. Maybe it's a forest and trees thing to him. He might appreciate somebody else's perspective."

"You'd do that for me?"

"Sure. You're my son too. No promises though."

"Wow. I'd appreciate that. I can give you his number."

"If you don't mind, I'd rather you call him and ask him if it's okay for me to call. Now, I'm gonna stop in the restroom. I'll meet you at your gate in a few minutes."

Stump reached the seating area near his gate where he sat down, and placed his fourth call in three days to Edna Kline. He assumed she'd ignore this call too, but surprisingly, the receptionist said she could put him right through. While he waited, Stump strongly suspected that she knew more than she was saying about the open-door episode, and Grandma Pauline's theoretical vulnerability, but he didn't want to antagonize her further.

He heard the click. "This is Mrs. Kline, Neal. I presume you're ready to apologize for defying me?"

"I don't know what makes you think I left that door open, Mrs. Kline, but I swear I locked it up."

"These kind of things don't happen in a vacuum, Neal and you were the last person seen in the area."

"Well, I'm coming back from Mrs. Moore's farm now. There were no coins, so—"

"So you got everybody excited for nothing, just like I said you would."

"I'm sorry, but I just want to get back into Meadowlark Flats so I can be with my grandmother."

"You should have thought of that before, Neal when you had

a fair warning. Quite frankly, your defiance is unbecoming. You're not getting back in until you sit down before me and agree to stop encouraging Minnie and pestering her family. You'll have to stop talking about that stupid coin story and then tell your father that this was all your fault. You want an appointment or not?"

This didn't make sense because Opal Clemens liked Stump and Minnie wasn't capable of understanding Stump's positions. However, since Stump already knew there were no coins on the farm, he didn't need to discuss it further. The only remaining issue was whether or not he wanted to kiss Mrs. Kline's butt, and admit to something he didn't do. "Yes, please. I'll make an appointment with your receptionist."

Just then, his iPhone announced an incoming call. "Jackson Tresher?" He didn't recognize the name, but he could get back to the receptionist a little later. He switched over to the caller. "This is Stump."

"Hi, Stump. I'm Jack. We met at the furniture store."

"Oh, yeah. How'd you get my number?"

"Yana's number was on her check so I called her and asked how I could reach you. Can you talk for a couple minutes?"

"I guess so. What's up?"

"When last we spoke, I believe you said something about fixing up some older properties."

"James mentioned that, not me."

"Well, I got to talking with my tax man and he tells me this would be a good year for me to lease or sell my building, so I can give you one hell of a buy on this place if you're interested."

Stump's eyebrows drew down. "I don't know why Yana gave you my number, dude. I don't have any money right now and even if I did, I don't know what I'd do with a place like that."

"Yana said something about a friend's struggling restaurant. They might have to close down."

"That's Zax Place, but there's nothing I can do about it. I might have some money some day, but not right now."

"All I know is I'm very motivated and thought I'd give you first shot at it. If you change your mind or know anybody else who'd be interested, look me up. Like I said. I'm very, very motivated."

"I'll keep your number, but I don't know anybody who'd be interested. Thanks anyway."

"You solving the world's problems again?" Xander said, rejoining Stump.

"Oh, I just got a chance to buy a rad commercial building in downtown Carlsbad. It's got some intriguing history, concerning prostitutes and a missing kid. Too bad I don't have my trust money. I even have a potential tenant."

"The College Café?" Xander asked.

"Yeah. Zax would do better if she had a fresh start. She could pay rent, but Myles is always holding me back."

"If Myles is tired of managing the trust, you might be able to get a bank officer or attorney to replace him. I doubt if a banker would let you buy an old building but he might loosen the reins a little bit."

"Oh, yeah? I didn't know I could do that."

"I'm no expert, but those kinds of legal arrangements usually have a back-up plan in case the person in charge wants out or loses capacity. Why don't you ask Myles what he thinks of the idea?"

Stump nodded just as a crackle came from overhead. "Last call for boarding to San Diego Flight 325. Please make your way to the boarding gate so we can depart on time."

Stump turned to Xander. The dude may have been nothing more than a retired truck driver, but he was one of the most interesting and wisest people Stump had ever encountered. "Do we hug or what?"

Xander smiled. "Damn right we do." He wrapped his arms around Stump. "Remember, I'm just a phone call away. Next time I'll try to bring one of the kids."

"Or maybe I can come see you all when school is out."

"That would be even better. Then everybody can meet you. Let me know how things work out with Myles."

Stump nodded, handed his papers to the boarding agent and proceeded to his seat.

* * *

A half-hour later, after Stump's plane climbed and leveled off, a flight attendant made some announcements. Finally, she said, "The skies are calm. We should be in San Diego egg-sack-ly on time."

Stump grinned. There it was again. That goofy word that so many people, including Herbert the farmer, mispronounced.

With the announcements out of the way, Stump reclined his seat and laid his head back and wondered about that fracking deal Xander talked about. It sounded pretty interesting. But Myles would never go for it. As he faded closer to the nap he sorely needed, his head rolled to the side where a vague dream delivered him to a small wooden building and an unknown farmer who undid his coveralls and sat over a hole. Although there was no noticeable odor, snoozing Stump scrunched his nose. Deeper in the dream, the shack door opened. *"I came to join ya, Pa,"* a farm woman said and sat down next to the man. Sleeping Stump smirked at the thought of a two-seater.

"Mama, can I come in? I gotta go stinky, too."

"Sure, honey bee. Daddy and Mommy always got room for the young 'uns."

"We should get a three-seater."

"Egg-sack-ly."

Egg-sack-ly? What a goofy word.

Suddenly, an incredible idea interrupted Stump's dream. He opened his eyes and sat up. Why didn't he think of it before? Birds and eggs had been flying into his head for weeks.

In addition to the peacocks and eagles and canaries and hummingbirds at Meadowlark Flats, he'd seen quail eggs and Herbert mentioned pheasants and turkeys. It all made sense now.

He grabbed his iPhone and began taking notes. Lots and lots of notes. He could hardly wait to tell Zax and James and Yana about his revelation. Egg-sack-ly.

43

"*Sergeant Cooper, here,*" Myles said to his caller.

"Hi Myles. This is Xander Brooks. I just got a call from Stump. He said you agreed to speak with me. You got a moment?"

Myles hesitated, then, "*I guess so.*"

"Thanks. As you probably know, Stump and I just got back from Kansas. I wrongly assumed he told you of the trip beforehand, but it wasn't until you called about your mother that I knew he'd left you out of the loop."

"*Um-hm.*"

"I'm just hoping you won't hold that against him because he was deeply aware of your advice about trusting strangers. You know how young people are. One minute they're ready to fly away; the next minute they need your support. That's how he is. He thinks a lot of you, brags you up all the time."

"*Sometimes I wonder.*"

"I wanted to let you know you've done a remarkable job of raising him. He's got a big heart, great character, and a lot of common sense. Even loves his grandmother and solved a bunch of crimes. You and Jean get all the credit for that."

"*Thanks. It wasn't easy for either of us.*"

"I'd guess not. I should have been the one who raised him, but I didn't know he existed until recently."

"So I hear."

"I don't know if he told you but I'm a retired truck driver. One thing I learned as a trucker and as a pilot is that trips give a guy time to think things through. In this case, I realized I owe you an apology."

"Oh? About what?"

"I just assumed he knew about the arrangement between Jean and her neighbor."

"Oh, you know about that, huh?"

"Yeah, but when I realize he didn't know about it, I tried to keep the secret, but he pinned me down. I couldn't lie to him."

"No I guess not. How'd he take it?"

"He seemed okay. I'm not sure really, I went to sleep after that and first thing in the morning we gave birth to a foal."

"A colt?"

"Yeah, I'm sure he'll want to tell you all about it."

"Sounds interesting."

"Thanks for taking my call, Myles. I just wanted to make certain there are no hard feelings between us, because I know how tough it can be raising kids and Stump is an incredible young man thanks to you and his mother."

"No hard feelings. He's always wondered who his dad was and there's plenty of room for everybody here."

"Before I let you go, there's something else I should tell you. In the full disclosure realm, years back I used to have a gambling problem. It took me a while to beat it. I'd rather you hear it from me now than catch a rumor sometime later that makes you wonder if I'm after Stump's trust, cause that ain't happening."

"Oh he told you about the trust, too?"

"Eventually. He kept it to himself for quite a while, but he asked me about trustees. I think he was wondering if I'd replace you, but I want to assure you that I'm in no position to do that and I think you've done a great job. However, I did tell him that if you're tired of the job there are lawyers and bankers who'll do it. I just wanted to let you know all this so you wouldn't think I was trying to undermine you."

"Okay, thanks. I suppose he told you I'm a recovering alcoholic?"

"No. He never mentioned it."

"Well, that was nice of him."

"I think he respects you a lot more than you know. One more thing. I get to fly for free, so next time I come to California, I hope we can get together for lunch or something."

"It's possible. You said something about flying. Do you fly cargo or passengers or what?"

"Small planes and small jets. Just for recreation. It's been a hobby for years."

"The reason I ask is I stay in touch with people in various law enforcement departments. Last year one of our jurisdictions was involved in a case in which the perps were flying drugs into the country from Mexico. Long story short, they confiscated the jet—a small one—and want to sell it now. You wouldn't be interested in it, would you?"

"To buy? Not me. I don't have that kind of money, but I do know a few people. What is it? A Lear?"

"I didn't pay that much attention, but I think they said it was a 2006 Hawk. I could probably get more info if you'd like."

"Sounds like a Hawker Beech Jet. "That's a nice little single-pilot jet."

"It has a loan on it. I was told they'd take less than it's worth for a quick sale."

"Well, those babies are worth a couple mill."

"I think they're at half that."

"Sounds like a great deal. I'll check with a couple guys. You never know. Some of these things work out."

"That's why I mentioned it. I'm glad you called, Xander. And thank you for the support you've shown me. I look forward to meeting you."

44

The next morning, after another lackluster breakfast cycle at Lee's College Café, Zax and Stump - wearing his Jackalope hat - were on their way to Downtown Carlsbad. "I don't know why you want me to look at that furniture building, Stump. Neither of us can afford it."

"I got a great idea on the plane, Zax. I just want you to hear me out."

"Did you get your trust money? 'Cause you know damn well I don't have any money."

"Not yet, but Xander is going to talk to Myles. If Myles doesn't want to loosen up, I might get a lawyer or bank officer to be the trustee."

"Well it better be cheaper than what I'm doing now, or we're wasting—"

"Yesterday, I told James and Yana some of it. They think it's a great idea."

"What's there to talk about? Bacon and eggs are the same everywhere."

"That's the problem. You serve the same things everybody else does, so there's no reason for anybody, other than the students, to eat at your place. You need to do something different to draw people in. Did you know you can put duck gravy on an omelet?"

"Sure I do, but that kind of thing means I'd have to charge more money."

"So what? When you go on dates, I bet you prefer interesting meals to a boring hamburger, even if it costs more."

"A date? Now I know you've lost your mind! Nobody wants to date a hash slinger with no future."

"Maybe that's another reason to get away from the campus, Zax. You'll meet new people, older people. It would also mean bigger tips for your workers."

"Well, that would make it easier to keep good people."

"When I was out at that farm we talked about wild quail eggs and pheasants and turkeys. This morning I went online and found a place that sells odd eggs. We could come up with some fun things. James suggested a Dr. Seuss omelet."

"Let me guess. Green eggs and ham."

"You got it. We found somebody online who serves 'blood hash' made from potatoes and beets. That would catch people's attention. So would the Unlawful Waffle. 'It's so big it should be illegal.' There can be weird omelets too. People will come just to read the menu. Most of them will still order the basics but who cares? As long as they drop by, have a good time and spend money, you don't care what they eventually buy."

"I guess that's true. You're really stoked about this, aren't you?"

"Sure I am, Zax. Nobody else is doing anything like this." He grinned right at her. "We have to have a really fun name too."

"Let me guess. You've got that figured out already?"

"Egg-sack-ly," he said, barely able to contain a grin.

"Okay, then, what is it?"

"I just told you."

"No, you didn't. I said you probably already have a name figured out and you said —"

"Egg-sack-ly."

"Right. So what is it?"

Stump laughed. "This is better than I thought. It's a combination of a goofy way people say the word exactly, like I just did, and your legal name, Zaklynn Lee. It's *Egg*, then *Zak*, then *Lee*. Put it all together and you get Egg-Zaklee's."

She paused a moment, then chuckled. "Oh my God, Stump. That's so cute I can hardly believe it. Egg-Zacklee's, huh?"

"Egg-Zaklee, and nobody will forget it."

"Egg-Zaklee's?" she said nearly begging him to say it back to her.

"Egg-Zaklee."

"Egg-Zaklee's. I love it!!!"

Stump grinned wide and turned onto Main Street. "See that used furniture store up there on the corner? That's it."

Zax scanned the buildings, where dirty windows and faded signs provided backdrop to a half-dozen unkempt loiterers. "I don't know, Stump. I knew this area was run down but some of these people look downright scary."

"It's a 'character area.' Haven't you seen the sidewalks in San Francisco? Everybody just ignores them." He pulled to the curb across the street from the furniture store. "It's got cool wood and colored windows."

"It might have been nice once-upon-forever-ago but there are bars on the windows and cobwebs and this building right next to us is vacant."

"But bars make it safer—as long as they have safety latches on them."

"I don't know, Stump. Off-beat items. Ancient buildings. Homeless people. I'd feel like I need a gun."

"If you want certainty, Zax, you can stay where you are, and get certain failure. The only people who have absolute certainty are prisoners. That's what you are."

"I can tell this is important to you so I'm willing to take a look but don't get your hopes up."

They already were.

"Hello, Mr. Tresher," Stump said minutes later. "This is Zax. She owns a restaurant and might be looking to relocate."

Jack Tresher shook Zax's hand. "This place would be perfect for a restaurant. It used to be a grocery store and has a big walk-in cooler."

Zax looked toward the stairway. "Stump said there are two more stories above this one. I could never use that much space."

"You could rent that space to other businesses or make it into offices or apartments. Are you two going to be partners?"

Stump shook his head. "I might be able to use my trust money. I'd buy your building and Zax would rent the main floor from me. I met a commercial real estate man one time, so I guess you have one of those. How much is he asking?"

"Excuse me," Zax said. "I don't need to hear the money-talk. If you guys don't mind I'd like to look around so we can get out of here sooner?"

"In the old days," Jack said to Stump a moment later, "the stairs were on the outside of the building. You'd probably want to do something like that again so the upstairs people have their own entrance."

"Good idea."

"You didn't see the basement last time. There's not much down there - just the electrical system and an old boiler that isn't necessary. Would you like to take a look?"

"Sure I would."

From a creaky wooden staircase lit by a bare, dusty light bulb, Stump and Jack entered a garage-sized, musty basement. Overhead, and attached to the beams, a galvanized pipe had grown a thick rust-colored crust on its joints. "That's sorta gross," Stump said.

"You'd likely have to replace some of the pipes to accommodate a restaurant. The same goes for the electrical system, but any improvements would add value to your building."

Stump pointed to a heavy metal door about the size of his laptop, near the boiler on the outside wall. "What's that?"

"A coal chute. That's how they got coal into the boiler room."

Intrigued, Stump moved in that direction until his face ran into a thick spider web. He cringed and clawed the silken net away from his face and wiped it on the wall. "Yecch! That's disgusting!"

"Sorry about that." Jack said. "Nobody's looked back there for a long time."

"I'm ready, Stump," Zax said from upstairs.

After a little more chitchat Stump and Zax made their exit. Outside and excited, he asked for her impression.

"Do you really have to ask?" she replied. "That place is a dump. You do what you want, but count me out. Now I gotta get back to work."

"What if we made some apartments upstairs? James and Yana could live in one, I could live in one and you and Denise could live in one. Then you could have baby sitters close by plus low rent on both the restaurant and the apartment."

She shook her head wildly. "I can't let Denise live in an area like this. There are no other children, the people on the street are scary and the whole thing gives me the creeps. I'd rather just stay where I am. Things might get better."

"I call b.s. Your accountant said you have to make some big-time changes."

Zax went silent for a moment, then sighed. "I just don't know about this area, Stump, or this building. Did you know there's only one functioning bathroom upstairs and the bathtub has mouse poop in it?"

"What would you expect? Nobody goes up there. You've seen those fix and flip shows on TV. This building is like those. It can be real nice."

"You may be able to fix the building, but you can't erase the ugliness on the street."

Not willing to give up, he had another idea. "I'll tell you

what, why don't we go have a talk with Mr. McFadden? He's right across the alley. He's lived in the area for a long time. Maybe he'll make you feel better."

"The cat man? I doubt it. Based on what Denise said, that guy's spooky, too."

"Because he's a taxidermist? He just does that because he likes the animals and it gives him a way to remember them. That's a good thing, not something spooky."

She looked down the side street to Catts McFadden's home. "All right. He's so close, I guess it wouldn't hurt to have a talk with him, but if I think he'd hurt Denise or me or anybody else, there's no way I'm going along with any of this. You understand me?"

"Okay, but don't be surprised if you see something in his ear."

"Denise already told me," Zax said while lifting her finger to her temple and spinning it in little circles. "Coo coo."

45

"At least it smells clean," Zax said when she and Stump reached Catts McFadden's porch and knocked. "That would be hard to do with so many cats."

Seconds later, Catts came to the door, holding a homely gray cat with splotchy long hair. "Ah yes. Stump, I see you brought somebody else to meet the crazy Cat Man."

"I don't think you're crazy, Mr. McFadden. This is Zax. She's Denise's mother."

"The *'stoot'* girl? I can see the resemblance. Did you know that most male cats are left-pawed?"

"No I didn't," Zax said.

"This is Gracie. At first I just called her Grey Cat. Poor puss doesn't have many more days." He raised Gracie over his head and spoke in a high-pitched voice. "The Cat Man won't forget his precious Gracie, will he? No, he won't."

Zax nudged Stump. "Tell him why we're here."

"Oh, yeah. Sorry. To tell you the truth, Mr. McFadden, we're thinking about becoming your neighbors. Several things would have to fall into place, but if I can get to my trust money, we might buy the furniture store behind you and open a really neat breakfast place. Zax and I were wondering what you think of the idea."

"Why don't you ask the other business on that block?"

"Well, I bet you know more about the area than they do, like that story about the bear parts. There must be some reason you never moved away."

"Well, you've been nice to the Cat Man, and the pusses like you, so I can do you one better. You know that vacant building across the street from the furniture store?"

"Yes, sir. We parked right in front of it."

"I happen to own that property."

"Really? It doesn't even have a For Rent sign in the window."

"That's 'cause I don't like cleaning up after tenants. If you've got some spare time I gotta go over there. I could show you my collections."

"Rad. I got time. How 'bout you, Zax?"

"I just want to know if it's safe to work around here."

"It's as safe as anywhere else," Catts said as they stepped outside. "Did Jack tell you about the missing girl?"

"No sir. I think you mentioned it one time but I never heard the details."

"When was that?" Zax asked Catts, obviously thinking of her own daughter.

"Before my time, when it was a grocery store. When I bought my place a young couple owned the store. The husband and I got along pretty well, but his wife wanted to start a family and when she heard that a little girl had disappeared from that place in the late '40s, early '50s, she insisted that they move. After that a few other people tried to run a store in there, but eventually Jack got it."

"What about that little girl?" Stump asked while eyeing a couple guys leaning up against the corner of Catts's building. "Did she ever come home?"

"As I heard it, she was around four or five. They couldn't find her. Eventually her folks gave up and just skipped out in the middle of the night. It all sounds a little spooky, but all of those places have been around for nearly a hundred years and had multiple owners. Some legends were bound to emerge."

"Interesting," Stump said as they crossed the street and into the path of a couple street people.

"You got an extra smoke?" one of them asked Zax.

Mr. McFadden reached in his pocket. "You guys know you're not supposed to bother people on the street. Here's a quarter. Please leave the nice lady alone."

"Sure, old man. No prob," the beggar said before heading off.

"Thanks," Zax said to Catts.

"The liquor store sells single cigarettes for a quarter. That's illegal, too, but some of these folks don't have much going for them so I try not to judge." He stepped forward and inserted his key in the door.

The inside of Catts's building resembled the furniture store, except that there was only one story above the main level, which resembled a large barren box, with enough dust to make mud-pies. Catts pointed off to a stairway. "If my ankles will hold up, I got some things to show you, upstairs."

After a slow climb, they reached the upper floor where a lone large room contained several full clothing racks. In addition a handful of long tables, each covered with blue plastic sheets hid other collections of various types.

Catts limped toward one of the clothing racks and removed a drape that he used as a cover. "When my wife's studio auctioned off some of their wardrobes we bought these racks because she had worn some of these pieces."

"That's a lovely wedding gown," Zax said, "But it's yellowed quite a bit."

"She wore that in a commercial. It's over seventy years old."

After that they examined a collection of early editions of 19th century fiction books. Catts's favorite was a first edition of *Huckleberry Finn*, by Mark Twain. On other tables, collections included European stamps, a stack of Do Not Disturb placards from hotels all around the world and records from the '40s called 78s. Each collection had stories and each collection had to be well-covered before they examined the next.

Eventually, Catts led them down to the basement where he had a half dozen autos of various ages backed up side-by-side to a wall. "What's with the cars?" Stump asked.

"Bought them one at a time over the years and kept them as reminders—right up until the county made me fill in the back driveway in '92."

Stump spun around and realized there were no longer any garage doors. He glanced at Zax who did her finger circles to the temple trick and mouthed, "Let's go."

Stump nodded. "Thanks for showing us around. Mr. McFadden, but Zax has to get to work."

"You bet. Thanks for indulging an old man. I don't get to show my things to many people."

Minutes later and walking toward Pops, Stump couldn't help noticing Zax shaking her head. Apparently, she wasn't as big a fan of Mr. McFadden as he was.

46

"What kind of man keeps a rack full of hundred-year-old women's clothes in a vacant building just so he doesn't have to deal with renters?" Zax wondered out loud.

"I dunno, but it would be a lot of fun to move down here."

"Fun? That would wear off in a hurry. We're talking about work, not entertainment."

"I know. But lots of people like goofy things, especially college kids and tourists. When I went on my trip with Xander I saw that jackalope and I'll never forget it. People remember things like that and they'll remember your place especially if we name it Egg-Zaklee's."

"I repeat—for the benefit of the young man who refuses to hear—neither of us has any money."

"But I might get some money. Xander is going to talk to Myles and if Myles is tired of managing the trust, I can get somebody else."

"Even if you could get your money, I wouldn't want you to do all of that for me. If I flopped, we'd both be screwed."

"I wouldn't rely exclusively on you, Zax. After seeing Catts's collections, I'm thinking people might like storage rooms."

"But nobody wants to live in this area."

"Catts does. So do his neighbors and blocks of houses after that. I know you don't want to live here, but everybody else is always complaining about high rents. I can just charge less than the other places do."

"Well, I guess there are people who can't afford very much."

"Yana and James might like to live here. That would make it easy for her to get to work."

"I still love the name but would rather go somewhere else. Someplace safer."

"C'mon, Zax, you're thinking like the masses, but this area is better because of the very things you don't like. Plus, the price is better. You know. Buy low, sell high. That means lower rent, too."

"I dunno, Stump. How much would my rent be?"

"First, we'll charge the same as you're paying now. Then when you make more money you can pay a percentage of the profits."

"And what if there are no profits?"

"Then you don't owe me a dime. I'll rent the place to somebody else or sell the property and take a small loss. I can afford it. But I think it'll work."

"Really? You'd do that? Really?"

"Sure I would. You're good at what you do. You're just a little too biased to see things a new way."

"Well, I guess if you'd pay for everything I wouldn't have much to lose."

"We might even be able to make a dormitory-type place and rent out bedrooms. Those people could be your customers."

"Yeah, right. Be sure to get me some prostitutes, too, and call me madam."

Stump smiled. "Okay, then. I'll talk to Myles. Now I need to ask you for a favor. I want to see my grandmother but Edna Kline is ignoring my calls and giving me a bunch of crap. I need you to help me get back into Meadowlark Flats."

"How in the world do I do that?"

"Simple. You're going to pretend to be my attorney."

"What? I'm no attorney. And I surely don't like misleading people."

"I don't either, Zax, but Edna Kline lied about my leaving a door open. If I have to beg her to let me back in everybody will believe her, and arguing will only make me look like a juvenile. There's only one way to neutralize her."

She sighed and raised her index finger. "If you hadn't been so nice to me lately, I wouldn't do anything like that. Just don't use my real name. Okay?"

"Sure. Thanks. This is all for my grandma. But Edna doesn't like me and I don't want her to think she can push me around, especially since I didn't do anything wrong."

"I guess that makes sense. What did Myles say about his misleading you?"

"Misleading me? How has he misled me?"

"When you were on your trip, you sent Yana and me a text indicating that your mother wasn't actually a biological mother."

"Yeah. That was sure strange."

"But Myles was about to marry your mother and she probably leveled with him. If that's true, Myles has always let you think that Jean was your mother when he knew otherwise. That seemed like *'misleading'* to Yana and me."

Caught off guard, Stump went silent. Zax had a good point —Myles had to be fully aware of Stump's other mother and never elected to say so. Any beginning detective knows that's deception by omission.

It was time to take a stand—a real one this time. When they reached Zax's place, he searched the internet for a site where he could speak with an attorney for free. A short time later, he picked a site and registered as The Stumpster.

ATT26: *Hi, Stumpster. I'm Kelly. What's on your mind?*

The Stumpster: *Hello. I'm 19, in Criminology College and want to ask an estate question.*

ATT26: *Okay. Whose estate are we talking about?*

The Stumpster: *Mine. My father is the trustee. I'd like to know how difficult it is to change trustees.*

ATT26: *It would depend on the details of the trust itself. Have you spoken with an attorney before now?*

The Stumpster: *Not yet. I just want to drive a decent car and invest some of the money, maybe in stocks or real estate, as opposed to just leaving it stagnant in a bank. What do I have to do to replace him?*

ATTY26: *Sometimes it's real easy, but if there are conflicting interests, a court might have to approve it. Have you read the trust?*

The Stumpster: *Not really. Nobody ever gave me a copy.*

ATTY26: *I'd suggest you ask for a copy and read it. Then try the easiest route, first: Ask your father if he'd allow somebody else to take over. But if he won't give you a copy or let you replace him, you could contact an estate attorney. We can refer somebody if you'd like.*

The Stumpster: *Okay. That sounds good. Thanks. I'll check it out and get back to you. Out.*

ATTY26: *Good luck!*

47

"I don't know about this, Stump," Zax said as she and Stump reached the front door of Meadowlark Flats. "I wish you would have brought James for this job, instead of me. He's better at bullshitting people."

"Couldn't. Everybody knows him up here. Plus you're older. You look more like an attorney."

She sighed. "What did you find out about Myles and your mother?"

"Nothing yet. I wanted to see his face when we talk about it so I just told him I want to meet him at Meadowlark Flats while I'm up here."

"I'm glad that's not my problem."

At the sign-in desk, Stump acted on something Xander had said when on their trip to Kansas. "Can I ask you something?" he said to the elderly receptionist, "We're thinking about moving my grandmother to a community that has outside surveillance cameras. Do you guys have those?"

"Oh yeah," the woman said. "We just got a new system last year. The cameras are small and hidden."

"Have they ever broken down? What happens if the electricity goes out?"

She glanced to a row of books on her desk. "I think they have a back-up battery system."

"That's good to know. I guess we won't have to move my grandma after all. Thank you."

From there, they walked to Edna Kline's office. She invited them in and closed the door. "Thanks for meeting me, Mrs. Kline. This is Denise Stevens," Stump fibbed. "She's an attorney."

"Pleased to meet you," Zax said to Edna Kline. "I admire your work."

"An attorney?" Edna said to Stump. "Why would you think you need an attorney?"

"I probably don't, but she's a family friend who knows about this type of thing."

"And I had the day off," Zax added, while opening her sham briefcase and gathering a small leather case. "Do you mind if I use a recorder?"

"I guess not."

"Thank you. Stump tells me he wants to keep this friendly, so I'm going to let him speak for himself."

"How was your trip?" Mrs. Kline asked, glaring at Stump.

"My trip?"

"Yeah, your trip. You didn't fool anybody. You were anxious to get Opal Clemens's number from me, and then you disappeared for a while. It only took one phone call to confirm that you called her in spite of my request to the contrary. I don't like people stirring up trouble with our residents and their families. I want it to stop."

It didn't take a detective to know that Mrs. Kline had no right to tell Stump whom he could call, but it wouldn't do any good to poke that beehive right now. "It would have been easier if you would have given me her number when I asked for it."

She glared at him for a moment. Then, "This might surprise you, Neal, but we're not running this place for your benefit. Sometimes other people matter too. Minnie is psychologically frustrated by that jar story and I want her to think about other things. Your interference is counterproductive to that objective and I don't have time to unravel the damage you cause."

Hmm. That made a little sense. There were occasions when Stump and Myles and Katherine had a difficult time getting Grandma Pauline off of a topic that tormented her. He'd have to think about that a little more.

"Just as badly," Edna continued, "you didn't pull that back door closed. Then your grandmother got out. We can't have that, either. Somebody could get hurt. Your father could get sued."

And there it was: the blatant lie. "I don't want to be disrespectful, Mrs. Kline, but I didn't leave that door unlocked. If it was open, somebody else—"

"It was you alright. I have pictures and a witness."

She might have pictures of Grandma Pauline outdoors, but that didn't prove how she got out; nevertheless a blunt "you're-full-of-crap" rebuttal would be akin to falling for a queen sacrifice in chess—he'd win the move but lose the game. "Do you mind telling me who said they saw me, so I can speak with that person?"

"Sorry, but I don't want to drag anybody else into this. It strains relationships and we have enough of that already."

Yeah, right. It was time to call her bluff. "Well, I know you have surveillance cameras with battery backups. The video should show that I didn't leave that door open. Can we look at them?"

"I don't think the home office would want me to do that."

"You must know their number. We can call them and get permission."

Zax unexpectedly leaned toward Edna Kline. "Don't you use Avery Alarm Systems? I'm familiar with those people. I could get somebody over here in an hour or so. They could show us the video and we could end all this very quickly."

Where the hell did Zax get that information? Stump waited for Edna Kline's response.

A couple seconds later, "I don't see any benefit in bothering anybody else. I think we've all learned our lessons here, and that's all I really wanted. I'm going to go ahead and reinstate Neal's privileges, effective immediately. And, just to show there are no hard feelings I'd like you to feature your grandma tomorrow at MYN day."

Checkmate. Hopefully, this would put an end to their dissention. "Thank you, Mrs. Kline. That's all I wanted too. If you don't mind, I want to go visit with my grandma now."

After Edna dismissed Stump and Zax, they headed for the community room. "How'd you know who the security company is?" Stump asked.

"When we spoke with the receptionist she glanced at the back of a notebook that had Avery Alarm's logo on it."

Stump grinned. "Well played."

"You too. You're pretty smart."

* * *

After some enjoyable time with Grandma Pauline and Minnie Moore, Stump left Zax in the community room and wandered into the main cafeteria for his appointment with Myles.

While there, he thought about how he and Myles had grown apart, and about the secrets Myles had kept from him.

"Hey, Stumpster. How's it going?"

Huh? Stump turned. "Oh. I didn't see you coming. Things sorta blow. That's why I wanted to meet with you."

"Sounds serious. What's up?"

"I'm pissed, Myles. That's what's up. On top of all your tight-fisted handling of my trust you've been keeping a big secret from me. That's the same as lying and I don't appreciate it."

"What big secret? Where's this come from?"

"My mom always told me there was no way to figure

out who my biological father was and I believed her. Then Xander's DNA proved he was the real deal so I forced him to tell me who the hell I really am."

"You're somebody who was lucky enough to have a mother who loved him."

"Cut the crap, Myles. Xander didn't even know my mom; that's because she isn't really my blood mother. Somebody else is. That's who Xander slept with."

"The important thing—"

"The important thing now, Myles, is you knew the truth all along and let me believe a crock of deception."

"I'm sorry you think that way, Stumpster, but your mother felt it would be better if you thought she was promiscuous rather than a kidnapper. She made me promise not to say anything, for your own good."

"I'm not talking about her, Myles; I'm talking about you. After Mom died, you should've leveled with me."

"I couldn't. I made a promise and I saw no reason to burst your bubble."

"Yeah, right. It makes me wonder if you've been keeping other secrets. With my trust, for example."

"That's ridiculous. I've always been real careful with your money. You've got a decent vehicle and schooling. That's all you need right now."

"I don't need school, Myles. I can invest the money on fracking and stocks and real estate, and live on the profits. I'm probably going to drop out."

"No. No. No, Stump. That would be a big mistake. I hope Xander didn't put you up to all this, because I've always warned you about outsiders."

"No way, dude. As a matter of fact, he supported nearly everything you've done."

"Okay, then, so what's the beef?"

"The deception, Myles. That's a big effing deal. I want a copy of my trust. I want my money or for you to turn it over to somebody else."

"You know I can't do that."

"The hell you can't, Myles. I've talked to an attorney and verified it. You're just afraid I'll do better with my money than you have."

"You're overreacting, Stump. Why don't we—"

"I'm not going to listen to your excuses, Myles. You've pissed me off. I want an apology and a copy of the trust. Or are you hiding something?"

Myles paused, looked Stump in the eye and shrugged. "Okay. I'll send you a pdf version of the trust, but I'm not resigning so get used to it." He rose and walked away.

48

"**I** saw the cook kill a man with a frying pan," Conrad Keats said softly. "Somebody should call the police."

Stump sat up. At meet Your Neighbor day, he knew from first-hand experience that there was usually some element of truth to the words of memory care patients and trying to figure out where the truth and the confusion parted ways resembled solving a who-done-it on late-night TV.

A few minutes earlier, when he first arrived at Meadowlark Flats, he passed Edna Kline in the hall. His polite "good morning" was returned but he wasn't a hundred percent certain that they were at peace.

If some other conflict were to arise and Stump were to challenge her, he could easily imagine her saying something similar to, *"if you don't like how I do things, you can take your grandmother elsewhere."* After all, Edna knew that Stump didn't want to do anything that might jeopardize his grandma's mental well-being. Extreme wariness was in order, but in the meantime there was a more pressing problem at hand – did the cook really kill a man?

"That was a movie, honey," Conrad's wife said to him. "You don't have to worry about that."

"I saw it," Conrad insisted. "He was a bad man. The cook killed him."

"'*Fried Green Tomatoes*,'" Conrad's wife said to the others in the room. "It's his favorite movie." Several heads bobbed as the woman spoke lovingly to her husband. "The police will handle it, honey. Why don't you tell your friends about Yapper?"

"Is Yapper here?"

"No, honey. He's home waiting to bark at the mailman."

Conrad put his finger to his lips. "Yapper don't like the mailman."

Over the next minutes Conrad's wife coaxed a handful of Yapper memories out of her husband. Then she leaned in, wrapped her arms around his neck and kissed him right on the lips. "I love you, honey. You know that, don't you?"

"Are we going to screw now?"

"No, honey," she said, red-faced and emphatically, while staffers and visitors, including Stump, chuckled. "We don't do that anymore. Now we have to go back to our seats and let somebody else talk."

Among those still smiling, Tamara Flores moved toward the stage area. "Well, some of our best memories stick with us like glue. Now I'd like to introduce one of our newer residents, Pauline Cooper, and her grandson, Stump. Let's all welcome them."

A peppering of polite applause, mostly from staff members and guests, confirmed yet again that this program lent a certain familial status to all those in attendance. Stump rose and tugged lightly on his grandmother's hand. "Come with me, Grandma."

She glanced at Minnie Moore. "Where we going? I don't want to leave my sister," she said.

"I can sit with Minnie," Tamara said, slipping over and substituting.

After they settled into two chairs, Stump began. "My grandma was a great teacher in Oklahoma."

"I like assemblies."

Stump smiled at the audience. "You may not believe this, but my grandma and I actually solved a murder together."

"We did?"

"We sure did, Grandma, after you told me about Jack Ruby."

"That sounds familiar. Who was he again?"

"He was just somebody you knew about when you were a teacher." Stump returned his attention to the group. "A few years ago my boss had cancer and was about to die when somebody killed him. Nobody could figure out why somebody would kill a man who was going to die anyway. Then I remembered the story that my grandma told me about Jack Ruby. Some people believed Ruby was sacrificed for another cause. I wondered if something similar had happened to my boss and it did. I might not have solved that murder or gone to criminology college if my grandma hadn't told me about Ruby."

"Ruby? Are you talking about Ruby Boyles?"

As he'd done a skamillion times, Stump overlooked Grandma Pauline's insignificant mistake and spent the next 10 minutes employing the trigger phrases that tended to draw out some of her oft-repeated comments about the old days. Eventually, he said, "Aside from my mother, I've never loved a woman more than I love my grandma," and with that he escorted her to the sofa, where she enthusiastically reached for Minnie Moore.

After the meeting, a bunch of people complimented Stump on his presentation and said nice things to Grandma Pauline. Finally, after a meager lunch with Grandma Pauline and her friends, Stump had to return to his other life. En route, he sent another text to the legal hot line.

ATTY14: Hello, Stumpster. *I'm Josh. Can I help you?*

The Stumpster: *Yesterday I spoke with Kelly. Is she in?*

220

ATTY14: *No. We're all volunteers. Today is my turn. What's on your mind?*

The Stumpster: *I'm a college student with a trust. I want a new trustee as soon as possible. Can I pick anybody I want?*

ATTY14: *It would depend on the terms of the trust and the people involved. What's your rush? Do you suspect foul play?*

The Stumpster: *I don't know. My father is the trustee and he took a million dollars out for his mother. Is that okay?*

ATTY14: *That's a lot of money. Did you know about it? What did he do with the money?*

The Stumpster: *We both took it to a mutual fund manager and planned to use the profits to pay for my grandma's housing expenses. She's in an old people's home.*

ATTY14: *Took it? Did you actually get a check and open a new account with that check?*

The Stumpster: *Yes. We got it out of the bank and then went to meet somebody at a different company.*

ATTY14: *What about the taxes? How are you handling that?*

The Stumpster: *What taxes?*

ATTY14: *When you took that money out, you may have triggered federal and state income taxes on unearned income. Have you spoken with a tax expert?*

The Stumpster: *No. How much taxes?*

ATTY14: *I'm not saying that's what happened but counting the feds and the state, it could be 50%. You should definitely talk to a CPA or tax attorney ASAP!*

The Stumpster:

ATTY14: *You still there, Stumpster?*

ATTY14: *Call us if you need us. Out.*

49

Fifty percent in taxes? That was a half-million dollars. Stunned, Stump could hear his breaths swishing through his teeth. Not knowing what else to do, he called Xander.

"Hey, Stump. How's it going?"

"Awful! I just found out Myles screwed me out of a half-million dollars and I want a divorce, or what ever they call it, even if I have to lose all the rest of my money. I don't care anymore."

"What happened?"

"I got tired of Myles ignoring me so I spoke with some online attorneys. They said I owe income tax because Myles made me take money out of my trust for Grandma Pauline. What the hell am I gonna do? I don't have no money, except in the trust and if I take more out to pay the tax I'll owe even more. All my money will go to the government. I gotta get a new trustee, and—"

"Slow down, Stump. Take a breath. One issue at a time. The first thing we need to do is talk to a tax expert. It might not be all that bad."

"I can't afford an attorney."

"What about a CPA?"

"I don't know any but Zax might know one."

"Start there. That person should be able to give you a better idea of what you're up against. Many of these things aren't as bad as they first seem."

"Those attorneys I talked to aren't stupid."

"But they didn't know any of the particulars, either."

"Myles just wanted to impress that lady with the big boobies."

"I don't know who you're talking about, but Myles plays it safe."

"He should've at least known about the taxes."

"Maybe not. Does he do his own tax returns?"

"Yeah. So what?"

"If he prepares his own tax returns, I'm betting he approached the trust in the same way as his own taxes. He reported the income and expenses and thought that was all there was to it. I think he deserves the benefit of the doubt."

"But we're talking really big money here."

"That's for sure, but don't attribute an honest mistake to bad motives. They're two entirely different things."

"It's still a huge loss, and when I think of all the other crap he's been doing lately, I want to make a change."

"What other crap?"

"Lying to me about my mom. And I asked him for a copy of my trust but he hasn't sent it yet. Now I owe a half-million dollars. I want to replace him."

"But we don't know that yet, and your mother probably asked him to keep her secret."

"Even if all of that is true, he treats me like a damn toddler. I want a new trustee—and not a banker or attorney. They'd approach it just like he has. I want you to do it—that is, if you'd be willing. You can help me invest my money in fracking and real estate and stocks."

"Whoa. Whoa. Whoa, amigo. Hold on there. I don't want to come between you two."

"He deserves it. We can sue him if we have to."

"No. No. No. I don't want any part of something like that."

"But playing nice hasn't worked. Would you talk to him about me getting another trustee? He might listen to you."

"Before we do anything rash, you should talk to Zax's tax expert to get a better handle on the tax matter."

"I will, but I think those attorneys were right."

* * *

A few days later at the office of Roberta Diver, CPA, Stump moved toward the seat across from her desk. "Thanks for seeing me. Did you figure out how much I owe?"

"Well, I can't be certain without the documents, but based on what you told me, it's not quite as much as you thought but it's still around $380,000."

Stump should have felt better for owing a lot less than he thought, but how could he smile inside when he owed the government twenty times more money than he'd made in his entire life? "Are you telling me if I buy anything, like a car or computer, I have to pay taxes on that, too? That isn't fair."

"Actually, it's the opposite. Think about a fleet of Fed/Ex trucks. The company buys them, but employees drive them. Those employees don't have to pay estate taxes on those trucks and neither do you if the trust owns the car you drive."

"But I still owe a lot of money and I don't have it."

"You can have the trust 'lend' you the money, as opposed to *transferring* it into an account with your given name on it. That's what triggers the tax."

"Lend myself money? That's dumb."

"Maybe so, but the trust is like another individual. It would act on its own behalf, so if it distributes funds, it would want them back. The point is to buy things in the name of the trust as opposed to moving the money into some other account with your personal name on it. Of course the trust will have to charge you interest and you'll have to make monthly payments just like you would for any other loan."

"Yeah, but I can't afford to make payments of any type."

"Some people borrow extra money from their trust and make the payments that way."

"Then I'd owe more. That's even dumber."

"It seems like that, Neal. As things stand now, you might want to shift things around. Pay your grandmother's bills out of the trust, and pay the tax that you owe out of the money you already set aside for her. Then you could use whatever is left over however you'd like."

Stump sighed. "I can't do that. That would be like stealing from her."

"I hate to sound like a nag, but you should always consult experts before you make any major financial decisions."

"Yeah. No joke," he said as a text came in from Xander.

"Spoke with Myles. Not much luck."

50

"It's dumb, dumber, dumbest, bro," Stump said to James in their favorite booth at Zax Place. "I'm supposed to borrow 380 grand from my own damn trust—and pay myself back with interest."

"Maybe that's why Myles never did much of anything with the trust. It's too complicated."

"They tell me I should invest the money that's in the trust and then use the profits to pay everything, but Myles never allows any investing. This blows and sucks at the same time."

"There's got to be reasons rich people use trusts, dude."

Your dad is calling . . . a voice said from inside Stump's pocket. "Speak of the devil. I asked Xander to call Myles. Now, I probably gotta listen to Myles's excuses." Stump pushed the button. "You calling to lecture me about wasting money, Myles?"

"Hi, Stumpster. Xander called me and told me what happened. I double-checked it with somebody else. Looks like I screwed up big time. I'm really sorry."

"No shit, Myles. You lied about my mom, too. And said you were going to send me a pdf version of my trust, but you've never given me one. I'm pissed about the secrecy and how you've handled the money and how you ignore me. What are you going to do about it?"

"I understand your anger, but I've always wanted to downplay the trust so you could live a normal life."

"I'm driving a friggin' Popsicle truck, and owe the government a bazillion dollars, Myles. Does that sound normal to you?"

"Nevertheless, I'm deeply embarrassed and ashamed about that. I should have spent some of the trust's money on legal fees and tax experts."

"Well, duh. But those people would have told you to invest the money and you think that's too risky. Now I'm screwed because of you. I want you to let me be my own trustee, before you lose it all."

"You know I'm not going to do that, Stump, but I will check around and get some better advice — from real experts this time."

"That won't recover the half-million you already lost or fix the big problem, Myles. You're overly cautious. I want to be my own trustee."

"I'm not doing that, Stump. I'm supposed to watch over the trust until you're 21 and I intend to finish the job. That's all."

"If you won't let me do it, then let Xander take over. I've called some attorneys. They said we can do that. Xander knows about investments."

"We don't need a new trustee, Stump. We just need to figure out how to protect the money a little better."

"I call b.s. You need a lot more than a little help, Myles. You don't know how to protect the money or invest it. Do you realize if you'd made a lousy three percent on that money for the period we've had it, I'd have an extra half-million dollars now. But instead of making that much money you found a way to lose that much money. That's a million-dollar swing, Myles. I can't afford to be your science project. Don't you get that?"

"I deserve that, Stump, but I'm not turning the trust over to you or Xander. You're both amateurs too."

"Xander isn't. He's got some stocks and has money invested for his kids' college and knows about fracking. And I knew about tech stocks and a real estate investment."

"Xander's a nice enough guy, Stump, but I'm not turning all that money over to him or anybody else."

"Then let's get a banker or a trust attorney. We need somebody who knows how to make money and how to keep it and that it's okay for the beneficiary - me - to drive a decent car and that somebody with millions of dollars doesn't need school."

"Now you're being ridiculous."

"No I'm not. I haven't been going to very many classes lately and I don't even miss it."

"That would break your mother's heart, Stump. She'd want you to stay in school and I agree with her."

"If you don't let me change trustees, Myles, I'm going to go see an attorney."

"Ain't going to happen, Stump—"

"Oh, yes, it is. Bye, Myles."

51

"**H**ello Xander, this is Myles."

"Your ears must have been burning. I was just about to call you. What's on your mind?"

"It has to do with the tax debacle. We all know I screwed up. Understandably, Stump is pissed and wants to get a new trustee. He mentioned you, but I have the obligation to see this through."

"I don't blame you. It was a job you didn't ask for, but you want to do it right. I get that."

"Thanks. You've become a middleman of sorts so I was hoping you could calm him down. I don't want him to be angry with me or affect how he deals with my mother."

"I've already talked with him. He's angry right now, but he's a smart fellow. If we can give him a little time, he'll probably come around. Along those lines and on that other topic we discussed, my fracking friend is very interested in that jet. I think there might be a way we can use that transaction to smooth over some of your problems with Stump."

"I need all the help I can get. That's for sure."

"It sounds like your people are willing to give the buyer a good deal and are working off of a 'net price.' If I can get my guy to pay

your people a little more than their minimum price, we might be able to steer the difference into Stump's trust and recover a good chunk of the lost tax dollars."

"I don't know. Isn't that sort of sneaky?"

"Not really. It's basically just a brokerage fee or a commission. Happens all the time with heavy construction equipment, motor homes and real estate. Only we don't have a license, so we'll have to do it another way."

"This is the kind of thing that makes me nervous."

"It's not all that complicated. I've bought a few big rigs this way. First we'd need to get an option to buy the merchandise. That usually takes something like 50K, but let's set that aside for a moment."

"We both know that Stump's the only one who has that kind of money and I can't risk losing it."

"You might not have to. You just need the 'right' to get in the middle of the deal. Once we verify that my guy has the funds and your people have the title to the jet, we'll need to negotiate the price. You and I will stay in the middle of it so nobody tries to cut us out."

"Okay, that all makes sense."

"After we hammer out the numbers, the buyer gets to inspect the merchandise. If he doesn't like the deal, the deal dies. Everybody goes their separate ways. No harm. No Foul. However, if the jet passes inspection, we've got a deal and the money and title go back and forth — all of it under the eyes of attorneys. Like buying a house or farm equipment or a big boat. But we definitely want attorneys looking over every step."

"Good, cause I wouldn't do it any other way. How do we get paid?"

"That part is fairly easy. The buyer wires funds to the attorneys who split it up and send us our share."

"That's all very interesting. And you're willing to do all of this and give our share to Stump?"

"Sure. Let's call it back payments for raising him."

"Well, if we have the right supervision, and can't lose anything, I'm okay with it, but you know me. I'd have to double check with the other cops before I commit to anything."

"Of course. Like I said. It happens all the time with other big-ticket items. The tricky part is the option. Ordinarily, we'd have to put up some big money, but sellers will sometimes give a short option period for free if they're comfortable with the parties. With your reputation, I bet you could get them to give you a free look for a week or so."

"I don't mind telling you this kind of thing makes me diarrhea-level nervous. What do we do next?"

"You should probably check with whoever is handling the sale. See if you can register our buyer's name and get past putting up any option money. If that works out, all we gotta do is exchange money for title and deliver the jet to the buyer, and I can do that."

"Well, if there's no risk I guess it's worth a try. I admit I'd feel a lot better if I could get him some of his money back."

"It's certainly possible."

"Alright, I'll make my calls."

"Great. If all of this works out, maybe we can calm Stump down."

"I hope so, but while I've got your ear, did you tell him he doesn't need school, 'cause I don't think that's a good message."

"That was part of what I said. I acknowledged that a smart person with that kind of money could probably live off his profits, but I also said that he'd gain more from school than most other students because he can learn new ways to help people, both in a career and his private life."

Myles snickered. "It appears he forgot to tell me that part."

"He may have just heard what he wanted to hear at that moment, but I'm guessing that he knows the value of a good education."

"I hope so, but one thing at a time. If you don't mind, I think we should keep this jet deal from Stump until we know more. I don't want to get his hopes up and then let him down again. Neither he nor I could take that."

"Fine with me, Myles. If the deal does work out, I think I know a way we can smooth things out between you two but, like you said, one thing at a time."

52

Drive. Drive. Drive. It seemed as if that was all Stump ever did. This time he was supposed to meet Myles at the Wal-Mart near the John Wayne airport 35 miles outside Los Angeles. Still upset with Myles for the tax matter, Stump almost didn't go, but Myles said it had something to do with Stump's trust and Grandma Pauline. He more or less had to go. Somewhat curious, Stump pulled into the parking lot where he spotted Myles's SUV near the back of the lot. Myles rolled down his window. "Go ahead and park and then get in."

"Did you have any trouble finding the place?" Myles asked Stump a minute later.

"Forget the niceties, Myles. What's so important you couldn't tell me on the phone?"

"You'll see." Several quiet minutes later, Myles pulled into the parking lot at the smallish airport. "Did Xander ever say anything to you about his interest in flying?"

"Yeah, so?"

"If I've got my directions correct, we'll find Xander around that small Hawker Jet with the blue stripe down the side."

"Huh? How do you know that? What's going on?"

"Trust me," Myles said while pulling close to the Hawker. "How would you like to go for a ride?"

Stump looked at the jet just as its door swung downward, exposing a set of stairs and Xander standing in the doorway.

"We thought you might like to take a ride before we sell it," Myles added with a grin.

Stunned and confused, Stump glanced back and forth between smiling Xander and bigger smiling Myles. Then, he spoke more or less to Xander. "What the hell's going on?"

"Well, that's a little complicated."

"We both played a role," Myles said.

"A role in what?"

Xander hooked a finger. "Come inside the cabin for a moment. We've got a little time before we take off."

Still confused, Stump sighed and followed his two dads into the four-seater jet and splatted himself in one of the seats. Xander thumb-pointed to Myles. "You've got him to thank for this. He's the one who found this aircraft."

Stump looked at Myles for more information.

"The feds confiscated it. But it had a loan against it and the bank wanted to get their money back."

"Yeah, so?"

"Xander knew a buyer."

"My fracking friend," Xander said. "We got an option to buy the plane at the seller's price—"

"A million-one," Myles said.

Xander nodded. "But it's worth quite a bit more than that. My friend was willing to buy our option for a nice profit and that leaves a little profit to distribute."

"Including to you," Myles said.

"To me? Have you two been tipping a bottle, cause—"

"After all the expenses," Myles went on, "there's a profit of almost three hundred thou. We decided to give that to you."

"Partly to recoup some of the tax money," Xander said, "and partly to cover some of the costs I should have paid to raise you."

234

Stump tilted his head to the side, looked back and forth between Myles and Xander then grinned with all his face. "No bull? You guys did this together? You too, Myles?"

"Yeah. I was diarrhea-level nervous but Xander knew what to do."

"Wow. I don't know what to say."

Xander nodded. "We kept it a secret until the deal was finalized. But we still have to deliver it to the buyer."

"Before you get too excited, Stumpster," Myles said, "this time I checked in advance. You're going to have to pay taxes on the profit, but you still get a nice chunk."

"We're just sorry it couldn't be more."

"Really?" Stump said, shaking his head. "You guys did all that for me? Now I feel guilty for the way I've been acting."

"Are you ready to go to Texas?" Xander asked. "After that, we'll fly back commercial."

"Xander's going home, Stump. You and I will head back to LA, but you gotta reimburse me for our tickets out of your profits."

"I dunno, dudes. That's a lot to ask," Stump said through a stretched-out happy face. "I can't believe you guys. I wish James were here to see this."

Xander nodded. "We'll also have time to ask a few questions about that fracking deal while we're in Texas."

"I know that I'm always the wet blanket," Myles said, "but I don't think I'd be willing to spend any of the trust money on something like that right now."

"Whatever you gentlemen think," Xander added.

"I owe you both an apology," Myles said. "I didn't trust either one of you at different times. I'm genuinely sorry for that."

Xander shrugged. "I wouldn't be so hard on yourself, Myles. Your goal was to preserve Stump's trust and you did that."

"Until I needed money for my mom, then I went right to Stump's funds and lost a lot of it in taxes."

"Well, it all worked out," Stump said. "Grandma Pauline is safe and I still have almost as much as I had before."

Xander's head bobbed. "That's what families do for each other. Speaking of families, what would you fellas say to me bringing my entire family out here for a little summer vacation? They want to meet you guys."

"Grandma and Grandpa too? I've never had a grandpa."

Xander nodded. "I bet I could arrange that."

"Man hug," Stump said, without realizing he was going to say such a stupid thing.

"Alright," Xander said. "Now that we're done with the mushy stuff, as your captain I'd like all passengers to buckle up while I take my place in the flight deck."

He grabbed his mic. "Ground November-311-Alfa-Victor ready to taxi."

"Yes, November-311-Alfa-Victor, taxi to runway 21, via taxiway Charlie."

After a revved-up engine and the release of a brake, the Hawker inched out to the runway and Stump couldn't wipe the grin off his face.

53

After delivering the jet to Xander's friend in Texas, Stump and Myles and Xander went to a restaurant to ogle Stump's check, which was just south of 300K. "This is awesome," Stump said with a toothy smile. "It'll pay almost all of the taxes."

Myles raised his eyebrows. "I think it would be okay to get the rest from the money we gave to Liv de Franken's company. You'll still have close to a million with them and you'll have plenty more in your trust if you need it."

"That way," Xander added, "you won't have to borrow additional money from the trust and then borrow even more to make payments."

"Yeah, that was stupid. I don't like using the money I set aside from Grandma Pauline, but I gotta admit, this makes more sense."

"Besides," Myles added, "if we're lucky, that mutual fund might generate more money than we need for my mom anyway."

"Speaking of your mother," Xander said. "How's she getting along after that episode where she lives?"

"So far, so good. Edna Kline let Stump back into the facilities and said it was all a misunderstanding."

Stump scoffed. "It was more than that. She lied about me leaving that door open and we both knew it. She doesn't like me because I wanted to look at Minnie Moore's land, even after Edna told me there was nothing out there."

"I think she had a point," Xander said. "That land had been turned upside down. If there ever were any coins, somebody surely got them, so why stoke Minnie's fire?"

Stump rubbed his neck and shrugged. "Maybe you're right. Mrs. Kline, too. I just wish that Mrs. Moore won't have to move."

Myles nodded. "I have something else I'd like to discuss with you gentlemen. It's good news for Stump. Now that we know how well the plane deal worked out, it's obvious that we make a good team. I've been thinking about loosening up *a little* on the trust money."

"Really?" Stump said, stunned. "That's great. I can think of all kinds of things I'd like to—"

"Hold on, Stump. That's the kind of wild enthusiasm that makes me want to change my mind."

Stump pretended to withdraw his head into an imaginary turtle shell. "Oops. Sorry."

Xander grinned, then addressed Myles. "That's a big step, Myles. What did you have in mind?"

"First off, let me make it clear that I'm still going to be the one and only trustee."

Stump sighed, "Then nothing has changed."

"Hear me out, Stumpster. I might be willing to let you invest some of your money, but there are three conditions.

"That figures."

"But let me be clear; this is strictly on a trial basis and I can revoke it at any time for any reason. You understand that?"

"Yeah. It's clear all right. If I want some of my money, you'll say no, and if I don't like it we go back to me having no voice at all. Whoopee!"

"That's not fair, Stump," Xander said. "You haven't heard everything yet."

"Issue one," Myles began, "I'm willing to give each of you an equal vote on what we do with the money. All three of us get to vote and we'll employ a majority rules arrangement on a *trial basis*. So if Stump wants to buy a car or buy some stock and Xander agrees, you've got two votes and I'll go along with it, as long as it's not too radical. But if you two get too weird or careless, I'm going to exercise my right to end it all."

Stump sat up. "Really? That's better than nothing."

"What's the second issue, Myles?"

"You are, Xander. I admit that my mother's health has been stressful for me, and that I've had a tendency to brush aside other matters such as the trust. But meanwhile you've convinced me that you're a level-headed straight shooter with lots of street smarts. Neither Stump nor I have asked you if you would even want to be involved in this arrangement, so what do you think?"

Stump mentally crossed his fingers while his head spun in Xander's direction.

"I wouldn't say that '*I want to*,' but as I understand it, we're talking about two years. Is that correct?"

"That's when I get full control," Stump said.

"Well given that it's only for two years, it's the least I can do. You can count me in."

"Yahoo!" That made two issues down, one issue to go. If Myles didn't have some bizarre third issue, there was a good chance Stump could get a car and make some investments and live on the profits, thereby eliminating any need for more dumb school and any kind of traditional job.

"And the third issue," Myles said, looking right at Stump, "is you have to stay in school. Xander and I have agreed that you don't technically need school to get by, but we also agree that you will have lots more options in life if you stick it out."

Stump felt as if he'd just found a worm in the bottom of his banana split. He would have liked to renegotiate, but his two dads had essentially already outvoted him, and this was too great an accomplishment to hand Myles a reason to change his mind. Maybe he could rearrange his schedule and take fewer classes for the next two years. Then he could do whatever he wants.

"Stump has accomplished a lot of good things over the years," Myles added. "He and Katherine have been kinder to my mother than anybody. I've decided that he deserves some say in the trust matter - after all he's correct when he says that it's his money."

"Thanks, Myles. Now that I have some say in the matter, let me put a few ideas on the table and see if either of you guys will salute them."

"Don't you think you could wait a while?" Myles asked.

"Are you kidding me, Myles? I've been thinking of these things for a long time."

"Alright then, let's hear it. What would you like to do?"

"Easy. Get a car, and some technology stocks like Tesla and Apple and Facebook; and invest in Xander's fracking project and buy the furniture building in downtown."

Myles rolled his eyes. "I just made a new rule. You can't do everything at once."

Xander grinned. "Myles is right, Stump. That's too much, too fast. Setting the car aside for a moment, which one of those other things appeals to you the most?"

Stump paused a moment. "If I could only do one thing, I'd want to be proactive. That means fixing up the furniture store and renting out one floor to Zax and putting in apartments upstairs."

Myles cringed. "Are you sure you couldn't be happy just buying a better car for now?"

"That's what I thought you'd say, Myles. Of course I want a better car, but I have to make some investments too. That's how I get some income. Remember?"

Myles sighed. "What do you think, Xander?"

"Well, I like the idea that he wants to be proactive. He'll learn a lot more that way than sitting back and watching others move his money around. I don't see a lot of risk. A building always has an intrinsic value so he could sell it if he needs to. If we can get a decent deal on it, I'd go along with it."

"Really. That's rad." Stump turned to Myles. "That makes two of us."

"There's one other thing," Xander said to Stump. "If you would settle for a nice 'near-new' car, I know how to get one for six thousand dollars or so."

Myles turned Xander's way. "How you going to do that?"

"Simple. Take over somebody else's lease. There are a lot of people who lease cars for five to seven years and then get in financial trouble and can't get out. We can step in and take over payments for a couple years and then turn the car in."

"That makes two of us," Stump said, smiling at Myles.

54

"Are you sure you about this, Stump?" Myles asked as they and Xander rode the last few blocks to the furniture store. "We could look at some other places."

"We've been talking about it for weeks, Myles, and we all agreed I need to get my money working. I even took Zax over there again and verified that she'd be willing to move. We both think we can make a lot of money. And I can get those upper floors converted into apartments. That way, if Egg-Zaklee's should fail, I'll still have income or free rent until I can get another tenant for the main level."

"You said the asking price is four-eighty?" Xander said from the rider's side. "That seems awfully stiff."

Stump nodded. "That's what Jack said he'd take. And it's not much more than lesser places, yet it has a lot more charm and potential."

"Do you know how he determined that price?"

"I didn't ask," Stump said as the store came into view and they picked a parking spot.

Forty-five minutes later, Jack had taken Team Stump on a fairly thorough tour of the old building, after which he locked the front door and they shifted a few pieces of furniture around so they could talk in private. "So, what did you think?" Jack asked Xander and Myles.

Xander shrugged. "There are things to like about it, but it's pretty rough and the neighborhood isn't great."

Jack nodded. "That's why it's not a million bucks or more."

Xander glanced at Myles and Stump then back to Jack. "Stump said you want four-eighty for it. Is that correct?"

"I think it's worth all of that and more, being this close to the ocean and all."

"I wasn't sure, so I called a commercial broker who's familiar with the area. He said this property has been on the market, on and off, for several years."

Myles folded his arms while Xander continued. "The broker said he wouldn't pay more than three-hundred-thousand for it."

If that were true, Stump thought, they were way too far apart to put a deal together. He'd essentially already lost the deal.

Jack raised a hand slightly. "Brokers say lots of things, but this place is worth a lot more than that, and sooner or later the whole area will get refurbished. Then it'll be worth a fortune."

"Maybe so, but right now, it's a tired old building that needs work and resources. Do you have a current appraisal?"

"Not really."

"I'm told an appraisal costs several thousand dollars for a property like this. Are you willing to pay for an appraisal and then sell the property for the appraised price?"

Appraisals? Where did that come from? Stump and his two dads had pretty much planned on paying cash and buying the building in the trust's name. No appraisal would be necessary. He glanced at Myles whose arms were wrapped so tightly around his torso it appeared he was hugging himself.

"I was hoping to find a cash buyer," Jack said, "and thereby avoid the appraisal process."

"We wouldn't want to pay for an appraisal either, Jack - unless we knew you'd accept the appraised price."

"Well, I don't know what kind of loan a particular person might get, but I need the four-eighty."

Xander shook his head slightly. "I don't mean to be difficult, but that's not going to work for us. I already told you what the broker said. On the other hand, Stump here likes this property so I'm willing to discuss it further before we go look at other buildings, but you're going to have to get reasonable."

"Well, I might have a little wiggle room, but not much."

Xander reached in his back pocket pulled out a folded sheet of paper and handed it to Jack. "I got this information from the broker. It shows you've given this building plenty of time to sell for an even four-hundred thou, which is eighty less than you're telling us you want."

That, too, was news to Stump.

"In all that time, nobody has taken it for four hundred," Xander went on. "That means four hundred is too high. As I said, the broker told me he wouldn't pay more than three hundred and we know it hasn't sold for four hundred. So the value is somewhere in between and probably closer to the low end."

Sweat beads had risen on Myles's forehead.

"As Stump's trustees," Xander said next, "neither Myles nor I can justify any more than three-fifty. Since you won't have to pay commissions, it's like selling it for three-seventy and that's damn close to what you've really been trying to get. And we'll pay with cash. No loans. No appraisals. No lender requirements. That's the best we can do, Jack. If you don't want that, we'll just have to look elsewhere."

Myles nodded and Jack went silent. So did Xander. Stump followed Xander's lead.

Finally, Jack broke a long silence. "How soon could you close escrow?"

"As soon as you move your things out," Xander said, looking at Myles, who nodded timidly.

"How about two weeks?"

244

"Okay, then," Xander said. "Three-fifty it is, and we'll close escrow in two weeks."

"You got it," Jack said, extending his hand to Xander, who'd just saved Stump a heart-pounding one hundred and thirty-thousand dollars.

Jack then shook Stump's hand and finally Myles extended his quivering fingers to make it unanimous.

After discussing a few loose ends, Jack agreed to have his attorney draft the contract.

Outside, Myles spoke to Xander as they returned to Myles's vehicle. "That was very impressive, Xander."

"Thanks, but it's no big deal. I've bought a half-dozen big rigs and a few houses."

"And a plane," Stump said. "You both did that."

Xander slid his papers in his pocket. "A guy learns to do some homework, especially on big-ticket items. I'll send the commercial agent to dinner for his help."

"Simply, spectacular," Myles said, shaking his head.

"Well, thanks, but it's the least I can do. But I still have one more obligation before I fly back home. To get Stump that car I promised."

55

"Awesome wheels, brofriend," James said, smiling and wide-eyed when Stump pulled to the curb at Lee's College Café in his sporty, near-new Fiat Spider.

"Xander was right," Stump said. "We found several people who would let us take over their lease payments. The owner of this one lost his job, couldn't make payments and couldn't sell it because he owed more for it than it was worth. By me taking it over, we saved his credit and I'm only obligated for 26 months. By then, I'll be in charge of my trust and can do whatever I want. Win/win."

"Dude. I should totally do that."

"You probably could—if Yana would let you take on the payments."

James paused. "Nope. She'd never go for that."

"The beauty of it is I can pay for it all out of my trust, like a company car. I wish I'd known this shit a long time ago. Are the ladies here?"

"Yeah. It's pretty slow inside."

"I'm stoked," Stump said as he and James gathered with Yana and Zax around their usual booth.

"Congratulations, Stump," Zax said. "What are you going to do with Pops? Sell it?"

"Myles suggested I keep it because it's got low miles and it's handy. I think he's correct."

"You could have 'Egg-Zaklee's' painted on the side."

"Good idea, Zax. I might do that," he shifted his attention to the group. "The reason I asked you guys to join me today is to discuss what Egg-Zaklee's should be like. Since I'm funding everything out of my trust, I'd like everybody to have a voice, but as soon as it's up and running, Zax will own the restaurant and I'll own the building. Who wants to take notes?"

"I will, bro."

"This is fun," Yana said, "I think we need to have real nice restrooms."

Nobody argued so James wrote it down.

"I was thinking about the menu," Stump said. "If it's the same as everybody else's, potential customers won't have an incentive to drive past other places to get here; but at the same time, if we don't have the old reliables like plain old bacon and eggs, the less adventuresome customers won't want to eat here, so we should discuss the menu first. That way we can set the mood of what we're trying to do. James and I already got a good start on it, so let's go over our ideas and then add anything that we think would draw people in, even if they want traditional items."

"I think we should have two different menus, Stump." Zax said. "One plain one for the normies and a colorful version with the odd items."

James nodded and made a note.

Then, Yana raised a finger. "Xander referred to oatmeal as 'jail food.' That was cute."

For the next hour, they discussed potential weird but interesting menu items such as banana omelets and French toast with a side dish of lime pudding.

After the creative juices slowed, Stump said, "James and

I have come up with some ideas for posters which we can frame and hang on the walls. And James knows a contractor who can make the repairs."

Zax said she'd use her current suppliers and Yana offered to set up a webpage and run want ads on CraigsList for cooks and waitresses.

"I'm hoping we can get the menus printed and open our doors in a month," Stump said. "That way, I can start getting a return on my investment."

Zax scoffed. "That's a laugh. It takes that long for smaller projects. You're going to have to get permits and inspections. Once all the plumbing and electrical items are up to code, it'll take that month just to get a kitchen and bathrooms put together. I just hope that the stigma of prostitutes and missing children doesn't chase all our customers away before we get started."

"Don't forget the street people, and that crazy Catts McFadden," Yana added. "They can be creepy, too."

"I think it's the opposite," Stump said. "Those kinds of things compliment the kooky mood we're trying to capture."

* * *

After the brainstorming meeting, Stump and James went to the furniture store for another conference, this time with Jack. Stump easily slipped his Spider into a tight parking spot. "Let me ask you something, Jack," Stump soon said. "Do you keep a gun on the premises?"

"Have to. With a bar up the block and dope heads on the streets you never know who might wander in or what they're up to. I keep a Beretta behind the counter. Only had to get it out a couple of times, but it chased them away."

"Why'd you ask that, bro?"

"I was just curious," Stump said, just before a ping indicated somebody had breached the main door.

"That's Nicholas," James said. "Over here, dude."

After the intros, Nicholas spoke to Stump. "James tells me you want to set up the restaurant first and phase into making apartments on the upper two floors. That right?"

"Pretty much. We've already got a manager and some great ideas for the main level, but we haven't made any final decisions about the upper floors."

"The reason I ask is when running pipes and electricity it's better to think ahead. What are you doing about appliances in the restaurant?"

"This place used to be a grocery store so there's a large walk-in cooler but nobody knows what it'll take to get it running again. We'll also need an oversized gas range and an oven and a couple microwaves."

"You'll need a lot of hot water too, and a refrigeration expert for that cooler. There will also be permits and inspections."

"Whatever it takes," Stump said. "All of that will raise the value of the property."

"You might have to make the place ADA compliant, too. Ramps. Wide aisles. Parking spot on the street. Things like that."

"No prob. How much we talking about?" Stump asked.

"I still gotta crunch the numbers, but we'd be lucky if we got the main floor done for a hundred bucks a square foot."

Stump tried not to look surprised. "That's a couple hundred thousand dollars."

"At least. Where are the mechanical systems? I need to see those before I can give you an accurate bid." They paraded downstairs, where Nicholas scanned the dimness and examined an inadequate electrical box. "Alright then," he said. "I'll get you a bid in a couple days, but it ain't going to be cheap."

Somehow Stump had already figured that out.

56

With dozens of well-to-do, mentally challenged seniors under the stretched-out roof of Meadowlark Flats, Edna Kline had the means, motive and opportunity to scam them at will. The problem was, her son Franklin, who also liked the easy pickings, wasn't the least bit cautious.

"Why not?" he asked from across her desk after having just been chewed out. "It's a candy dish. I reached into the account, grabbed a few goodies and nobody knows."

"Shh. I don't like it when you're indiscreet."

"Indiscreet? Who the hell are you to talk, mother? This morning, I found a large bottle of sex jelly in the silverware drawer, and I sure as hell didn't put it there."

Her eyes widened as she drew in a deep breath and then released it. "I thought Ricky put that away."

Franklin shook his head. "It was the friggin' kitchen, mother. The figgin' kitchen. I ought to turn you and Little Rickey over to Child Protective Services for humiliating me."

"Oh, stop pretending to be so naïve."

"Good. Then we're right back where we started. I needed

a little spending money and hit the old-timer's ATM for a couple-hundred bucks again. You oversee his account so it's no big deal."

Edna banged a clenched fist on her desk. "Damn it, Franklin. It is too a big deal. Mr. Winston came to me in confidence. He was ashamed to say he didn't know why he was bouncing checks. If his sons look at his account, they'll ask questions."

"That ain't going to happen. His kids already took his driver's license and car keys away. He's afraid of them. That's why he came to you. He doesn't want them to know that he can't handle his accounts. He's not going to say anything to them."

"Goddamn it, Franklin," she said, louder than before. "We can't take that kind of chance. I already told you we don't want to do things like that to residents who are capable of figuring out what's going on. One careless slipup could end everything."

"You don't got to worry. I parked my van out of the eye of surveillance cameras and wore a wig. Nobody knows it was me and the cops don't have time to investigate petty banking errors."

"Listen to me, Franklin. If you need money that badly, I'd rather you go out to that farm again and look for those coins. They could be worth thousands, maybe tens of thousands, or more."

"You're boring me, Mother. It's a long drive and there's no guarantee there ever were any coins."

"I wouldn't be so dismissive if I were you. Some of these Memory Care residents have vivid recollections of certain moments and Minnie Moore has been touting those hidden coins since she first got here. She could be right. Do you understand that?"

"Would it do any good if I said no?"

"Before we make any decisions, I want to have one of the staff members bring Minnie in here. Maybe we can get some new information out of her."

"Suit yourself, mother, but I ain't going out there again unless she knows exactly where the coins are."

"Okay. That's my boy," Edna said, picking up an internal line. "Tamara, dear. I need you to go out in the community room and bring Minnie Moore back to my office."

Edna turned back to Franklin, "When Minnie gets here, you let me do the talking."

"I'd rather just stay here and hit old man Winston's ATM."

"You'll do no such thing," she said, shaking her head. "You understand me?"

Franklin put his fingers to his lips. "Shh. Somebody will hear you."

* * *

Having arrived at the parking lot of Meadowlark Flats, Stump felt busier than a centipede on a hotplate. Between the chaos of schooling and trying to convert an old run-down furniture store into a unique, up-and-coming breakfast restaurant, he barely had time for the one thing that lent him serenity: visiting with Grandma Pauline.

After signing in, he expected to see his grandmother in the community room, but she wasn't there. Neither was Minnie Moore. He quick-paced to their suite, which proved to be dark and peopleless. A quick glance at the closets revealed that Minnie Moore hadn't been taken to some other facility.

He scurried back to the community room and across it to a similar hallway on the other side where there were additional rooms.

"Do you know where my sister is?" a familiar voice asked just as he looked up the corridor.

A worried look filled Grandma Pauline's eyes. Stump sighed. At least she was safe. "Hi, Grandma. Are you okay?"

"I lost my sister."

"Here, take my hand. I think I can find out where she is."

Hand in hand, Stump and Grandma Pauline slowly made

their way back toward the center hall and then to Tamara's office. "Hi, Tamara," he said. "Have you seem Minnie Moore? My grandma misses her."

"She's in Mrs. Kline's office."

"Oh? Is Opal Clemens here too? Maybe they're talking about Minnie's options."

"She might be, but I haven't seen her."

Stump glanced at Grandma Pauline before turning to Tamara. "Would you take my grandma into the community room while I make a phone call? I'll only be a few minutes."

As Tamara and Grandma Pauline walked off, Stump checked the registration book in the center hall but saw no indication Mrs. Clemens was on the premises. He snagged his cell and placed a call. Then, "Hello. Mrs. Clemens, this is Stump. Do you have a couple minutes? There's something odd going on with Minnie Moore."

"Is she okay?"

"As far as I know. She's in a private meeting with Edna Kline. Does that make any sense to you?"

"Not really. But I can tell you Mrs. Kline has agreed to let Minnie stay there for a while longer for free, even though Minnie no longer has the financial capabilities to afford the facilities."

"Really? I'm glad to hear that. That means my Grandma and Mrs. Moore won't get split up for a while."

"I don't think it'll be for more than a few weeks."

"It's better than nothing," he said while wondering if he'd misjudged Edna Kline.

57

The next morning, tired as hell from classes and working long days at his building, Stump drove to the San Diego airport and spotted Xander at the Passenger Pickup curb. He darted over and opened his trunk. "It's nice of Brianne to let you come down here again."

"No prob," Xander said, flopping his bag in the trunk and closing the lid. "Her days can get rather hectic with four kids and a nosy hubby hanging 'round. My free flying pass is a blessing to her. How's the auto running?"

"Double rad. You want to drive it?"

"Maybe later. I take it the renovations at your building are coming along?"

Stump sighed. "It's a lot slower than I thought, even with a general contractor. The place got uglier and uglier as they tore out the old fixtures and everything, but now they're putting it back together. New walls and windows, electrical system, that sort of thing."

"What about Myles? Is he still planning to meet us?"

"Yeah, the general contractor and Zax should be there too. She's been stressed out a lot, too—between taking care of her daughter and moving her old business and all."

After more discussions they made it to Stump's building. Inside, a musty smell prevailed. "I see what you mean," Xander said. "This place has been gutted."

"Yeah, but the contractor says we won't recognize the place when it's done."

"There they are," Zax said with a push broom in hand. "Hi, Xander. I hope you're here to help out?"

"I guess I could. How you doing, Zax? How's the walk-in cooler coming?"

She shook her head. "Not good. There are strict environmental restrictions because of the Freon. We're damned if we tear it out and double-damned if we upgrade it. Either way it's expensive."

"Just like everything else around here," Myles said from behind Zax. "It's one problem after another."

Myles and Xander traded handshakes just as a well-dressed, middle-aged fellow came in the door and walked right up to Myles.

"Are you part of the Milky Way Trust?"

"Not really."

"My name's Brock Thorndale, commercial real estate broker. You folks looking for any additional properties?"

Zax walked off and Xander pointed at Stump. "Ask him. He's the big cheese."

Thorndale turned toward Stump. "Really? You bought this place? But you're so young."

"Some people have trusts, you know."

"Well, in that case, congratulations. My records show you paid three-fifty for this place. Is that right?"

"That's personal."

"You'd think so, but all sales are reported to the county for property tax purposes. That's a lot of money for this area." He looked around at the gutted walls. "What you gonna do with it?"

"Open a unique breakfast restaurant."

"A restaurant? Down here? Sounds risky."

Myles nodded.

"Any chance you're looking for another property?" Thorndale asked. "I could get you something in a better area that doesn't have a tainted history."

"All old buildings would have a history."

"Not like this one. I'm talking about a missing kid and prostitutes. Some of those girls were awfully young."

That again? "I don't know why everybody is so focused on those things. That was a long time ago."

"Reputations matter to some people. That's all. What about buying another property on this street? Several of the other owners would like to sell, too. You might be able to flip a building and make some big bucks."

"No, thanks," Stump said as a young woman, about his age, walked in and approached Thorndale. "Do you guys have any openings for a waitress or greeter?"

"Back there," Stump said, pointing in Zax's direction and then returning his attention to Thorndale. "I'll keep your card in case anything changes, but we gotta get back to work." As Thorndale walked off, Stump turned to Xander. "This is exciting. I'd like to buy more property some day or get into fracking. You mentioned that before."

"I think you've got your hands full right here. You'd better get this place under control first."

Once again, skittish Myles nodded.

Then a building inspector and the contractor came down the stairs and meandered into the main room. The inspector headed for the exit while Nicholas approached Stump. "That guy is driving me nuts. He wants everything brought to today's codes. I hate to tell you this, Stump, but your project is going to cost you a lot more than I thought."

Myles's jaw visibly tightened.

"Bummer," Xander said before tuning to Stump. "What do you want to do?"

"Keep going, of course. I want to get Egg-Zaklee's done so we can focus on making apartments on the upper floors and generate some income. If I can do that, I'll never have to pay rent or work for anybody else."

"Well then I gotta get back to work," Nicholas said before marching off.

Myles lifted a slightly shivering finger. "If I didn't know about Stump building a doggie park and upgrading those homes in his mother's old neighborhood, I'd urge him to stop right here and cut his losses."

"Quite honestly," Xander said, "I think they have a good chance. Zax really knows her stuff about the business and Stump has good instincts."

Stump nodded. "We've ordered menus and are making some framed posters for decorations. When the time is right, James and I plan to deliver brochures door to door announcing our grand opening."

Myles chuckled before speaking to Xander. "He and James and I did something like that a few years ago."

Stump nodded. "That was fun and productive. I want to throw some parties too, both before and after we're open - to get more attention."

"I guess that fits too," Xander said. "Young folks and parties go together like bacon and eggs."

"Thanks a lot, bitch." For some reason the lady who'd just come in was pissed at Zax and headed right back out the door.

"I'm sorry," Zax said to the woman's back, "but this isn't the right kind of work for you."

"She was cute," Stump said to Zax. "What set her off?"

"She once turned in a substitute teacher for saying she looked nice in her jeans. I told her if she's that easily offended she won't last a month in the restaurant business."

DAREDEVIL MENU

At Egg-Zaklee's, we "toast" all our breakfast guests.
Your choice: wheat, white, sourdough, 9-grain or swirled rye
with any of the following items

These Dishes Cost Egg-Zaklee 9 Bucks

The Pancake Pillar Filler

All you can eat. Blueberry, wheat or buttermilk pancakes.
We'll start you off with six. Go ahead, we dare you!

The Pope's Six-Pack

Six near-holy donut holes, dipped in clouds
of powdered sugar and then drizzled in a variety
of heavenly syrups. Great to go!

The Mon Ami

You'll love our French toast with any one
of our gourmet syrup flavors.

The Unlawful Waffle

This delicious waffle is so big our competitors think
it should be illegal.

The Good Girl

Your choice of hot or cold cereal topped with
plump raisins, plus two slices of turkey bacon and
a glass of wholesome juice of your choice.

These Dishes Cost Egg-Zaklee 10 Bucks

Monkey Omelet

This fun one is filled with bananas
(or pineapple, apples, or blueberries).
You decide. House spuds or two 5-inch pancakes.

Stranger Danger

Three-egg omelet packed with spicy sausage,
diced onions and three kinds of peppers.
House spuds or two 5-inch pancakes.

Corned Beef, Blood Hash and Eggs

Recommended. Top-quality corned beef.
Chopped beets added to the hash for color and
two large eggs cooked Egg-Zaklee as you like 'em.

Roll, Roll, Roll Your Boat

Three ultra-thick slices of homemade cinnamon roll
French toast served in a bowl, with gourmet syrup.
Plus a side of two eggs, cooked Egg-Zaklee how you like them.

Meat Your Jail Food

Sausage, ham, and bacon, plus a large bowl of
gourmet oatmeal topped with plump raisins.

These Dishes Cost Egg-Zaklee 11 Bucks

Jalapeno Bread French Toast

Two extra-thick slices, served with two eggs cooked
your way plus bacon or sausage.

The Quackle Doodle Do

Three-egg duck omelet
(yes, it's made with real duck eggs).
Surprisingly good.
Topped with duck gravy.
House spuds or two 5-inch pancakes.

The Mexican Mother Clucker

So many jalapeno peppers piled on two chili rellenos,
you'll beg for a fire truck. Served with a cup of green chili
and a tortilla.

Stumpster's Dumpster

Chef's choice. If you're a gambler (or too baked to think),
let our chef decide what you'll eat. Huge portions.

ZAX'S REMINDER:

For more traditional breakfast choices,
See our standard menu.
They're all tasty too.

Which came first:
Chicken-Zaklee's or Egg-Zaklee's?
Nobody knows

. . . so I told that ostrich
to pull his head out
of the sand
and take me
to Egg-Zaklee's, man

Egg-Zaklee's:
A place where all good
eggs get a fair break

Egg-Zaklee's:
where egg-sperts
serve egg-citing dishes
to egg-stra special guests

To get fed up,
eat at Egg-Zaklee's

Did you know?
A group of chickens
is called a peep.

Got egg on your face?
Come to Egg-Zaklee's.
You'll fit right in.

Humpty Dumpty sat on a wall
Humpty Dumpty had a great fall
Brought to Egg-Zaklee's
by all the king's men
They scrambled him up,
ate him and grinned

58

After a couple more long days of brainstorming and problem solving, Stump had returned Xander to the airport. It being Sunday, he was alone in Egg-Zaklee's. He gazed at the numerous half-finished projects that never seemed to get finished before wandering upstairs. He dragged a makeshift table to one of the windows and dared to hope that Egg-Zaklee's would be up and running in mere weeks.

"There you are," an annoyed voice said from behind his back.

What the—he'd been so immersed in the moment he hadn't heard anybody coming. He spun around to see Zax leading Yana and James right to him.

"You sound angry, Zax. What's going on?"

"You got that right, bro."

Zax pointed a finger in Stump's face. "I'll tell you what's going on. Earlier today Denise started talking about that cat man kook. Something about it bothered me, so I did a criminal search. That creep is a sex offender, Stump. Did you ever bother to check on that?"

"No. Why would I?"

"It's true, Stump," Yana added. "I saw it, too."

Stunned, Stump shook his head. "You guys must be mistaken."

"So help me, Stump," Zax said, her face red, "If you knew about this and kept if from me, I could never forgive you."

"No way. I don't even know what you're talking about."

"His actual name is Michael McFadden."

Stump hesitated a moment. Then, "I don't think that's the same guy, Zax. When we signed the witness book, I saw a piece of his mail. It was addressed to *C. McFadden*."

"That doesn't change anything. You probably get mail addressed to Stump, but that's not your given name. Besides, the address checks out. It has to be him. I can't let my daughter be around a sicko like that."

"I can't believe this, you guys. Maybe he has a son or brother named Michael, but Mr. McFadden is a nice man. He wouldn't do anything like that."

"What difference does it make if it's him or any other perverted relative? Whoever it is lives right behind this place. I'm sure as hell not going to dangle my daughter in front of a deviant like a piece of bait. Yana and I are out. James, too."

"That's right, Stump," Yana said. "I agree with Zax. Now I could never recommend that anybody come here."

Stump's eyes shot to his loyal friend James for some last-ditch support.

"They have a good point, brofriend. I think we should go kick that old man's ass."

Stump clucked his tongue. "I ain't doing anything like that." He looked at Zax. "What did he do, anyway?"

"What difference does it make, Stump? He's on a sex-offender list. That's all I need to know. One pervert is as bad as another. Now I gotta get back home. My daughter needs me."

"We gotta go too, Stump. I gotta find another job."

"A fellow has to support his girlfriend, bro."

Zax grabbed the sides of her head. "I should never have

closed down my other place. I knew it," she said before leading the threesome downstairs.

Alone again, Stump leaned against the wall and slumped to the floor. How the hell was he to know to check sex offender lists? If all of his best buds were out, it wouldn't be any fun to continue. Worse, no other safety-conscious tenant would want to operate a business in an area like that. Same with the potential apartments upstairs. Nobody in their right mind, especially girls, would want to live in a place with a known sexual deviant nearby.

He considered asking Jack for his money back but immediately scoffed at the idea. This wasn't Wal-Mart where you could take things back for refunds. He had no business venturing into commercial real estate. He flopped his arms and head on his knees. "You fucked up, big time, Stumpster," he said out loud. "You've only had your money a couple months and all you have to show for it is an expensive, run-down building in a crappy area that nobody wants. That's as bad as what Myles did."

Desperate, he pulled a card from his wallet and called Brock Thorndale. Thankfully, the broker answered.

"Thorndale. Who's this?"

"Mr. Thorndale, you were in my building the other day in downtown Carlsbad. My name's Neal. Do you remember me?"

"Sure, I do. You looking to buy another building?"

"No, sir. It's the opposite. My friends backed out. They don't want to operate a restaurant anymore. I was wondering if you could sell the property to somebody else and get my money back?"

"I doubt it, especially when it's all torn apart."

"But we've already done a lot of the work. I should get more than I paid for it."

"The building itself has some charm, but everybody knows that the area is dead. With all those homeless people in the streets, there simply isn't much demand for property down there."

"But if I like it, somebody else should like it, too, or else all the buildings down here would be vacant."

"They darn near are. Most of the upper floors are useless or dingy, and a couple of the buildings are completely vacant. Apparently, you didn't know that your property has been on the market for several years. Nobody wanted to take on that area, especially in this economy."

Stump clenched his fist. "Well, it should be worth at least what I paid for it."

"I'm sorry, but most buyers won't see it that way. That property is suited to an owner-user, like Jack was, but any new owner wouldn't want the same upgrades you've made. They'd see a money pit. I probably couldn't sell it unless you'd take a big discount and you'd have to pay broker fees. You'd be lucky to get half your money back."

"What if we finish up those apartments? That should make somebody want it."

"Not really. Nobody wants to live in that area, unless the rent is cheap and investors won't pay much for a low rent situation. We live in southern California. People want nice neighborhoods, not rundown areas."

Stump sighed. "What do you think I should do?"

"For now, I think you're stuck, at least until the market changes."

"When will that be?"

"Could be years. About all you can do is finish it off and bide your time or sell it at a deep discount or pray."

Stump hung up and took a deep breath. How could he have misjudged Catts so badly? "Think, Stumpster. Think," he said out loud. Everything was going along well until Zax stumbled upon the sexual predator site.

Come to think of it, she never did say precisely what crime was committed. Desperate, Stump tapped at his cell phone and found the county records for sex offenders but was unable to find whatever it was that Zax was talking about. Still, he knew that she wouldn't make up something like that.

Forced to pick between several bad options, his best hope

was to persuade Zax to change her mind. After all, her café was doomed and she had to do something different. For now, about all he could do was confront Catts. If there was a good explanation, maybe Zax would reconsider.

A short, slow walk later, Stump stepped up to Catts's door and banged on the knocker.

"Hi, Stump," a perky Catts soon said. "I wasn't expecting you. Come on in."

Inside, Stump plopped on the bottom stair in the foyer. "To tell you the truth, Mr. McFadden, I heard something disturbing about you. If it's true, none of my friends want to work in my building. I could lose all my money."

"Well, we wouldn't want that. What did you hear?"

"It's about Zax, Denise's mom. She was wondering if it was safe for them down here, so she checked the sex offender site for the county."

Catts held up a hand. "Say no more. This is about Michael, right?"

"Yes, sir. Zax thought you might be Michael."

Catts smiled. "I can assure you, I'm not Michael."

"Does he live here, cause I've never seen anybody else—"

"I can see that you're troubled. It might help if you'd meet Michael. I suggest you go back to your property and then up the block and cross the street to Nick's saloon. Michael is working there right now."

Hmm. A saloon. Stump had seen that place. It had a sign in the window touting cold beer, burgers and fries. "I guess I could."

"Then, you'd better get going. Let me know how it works out."

"Okay. Thanks."

Head down and on his way to Nick's saloon, it occurred to Stump that it might be a good idea to have a little back-up.

59

"Thanks for coming," Stump said to James, outside Stump's building. "After what you guys said before, I wasn't sure you'd help me."

"I got your text, but didn't tell Yana where I was going. What's hangin'?"

"I haven't given up on Zax yet. She never did say what crime was committed, so I confronted Mr. McFadden and verified that he and Michael are two different people. Not only that, but Michael doesn't live at Mr. McFadden's house."

"But if this Michael creep still comes around, Zax won't change her mind. Neither will Yana."

"That's why we need to go meet him. Catts told me that Michael's working right now at the saloon up the street. I just want to find out if he's scary."

They crossed the street and headed toward the saloon when a shoeless surfer, who'd been sitting on the sidewalk, held out his hand toward Stump. "Hey, buddy, you got a cigarette or a spare quarter?"

"Not now, dude. I got bigger problems."

Moments later, inside Nick's saloon, a half-dozen stick-holding male customers encircled two pool tables, while a tall, not-thin waitress with brown hair wiggled her way through the herd. "It smells like puked beer in here," James said.

"That's the least of our worries. Don't start any fights, okay?"

"If you fellas ain't 21," the curly-haired bartender said, "you gotta go into the back room away from the bar."

"I bet that's your boy," James said.

Stump agreed and waggled down the hall, past the restrooms and into a small room with four tables, all with tablecloths. "It's going to be difficult to learn anything from back here," he said.

Then the waitress entered the hallway and spoke over her shoulder toward the pool tables. "I've turned down better men than you," she said teasingly to one of her customers before approaching James and Stump. "What can I get you gentlemen?"

A closer look revealed a shapely 30ish woman with a nice chain necklace and several large rings. 'Em' on her nametag probably stood for Emily.

"Is Michael in?" Stump asked.

Em looked over her shoulder as if to see if Michael was within earshot. "Who wants to know?"

"I'm Stump. I'm a friend of Catts McFadden. He said I could find Michael here."

"Stump, huh? How 'bout a cheeseburger and fries? We got good malts too."

"I'm in," James said. "I'll take chocolate."

"And what about Stump?"

"I'm sorry, but I'd rather talk with Michael."

"Trust me. You'd better order something first. Then I'll see if Michael wants to talk with you gents."

Stump sighed, "Okay, same thing as James, only I'd rather have a vanilla malt."

"I'll sprinkle some fresh ground cinnamon on it. You'll love it." She turned around and bolted off before Stump had much time to argue.

"I think she likes you," James said.

"No way, dude. She's older than us and flirts with all her customers. But I was impressed because she didn't need an order pad."

Minutes later, Em retuned with the malts. "Your burgers are on the grill. What do you want with Michael? You gotta give me a hint."

"We're sorta doing a favor for a friend of ours. She's scared to work down here and we need some information."

"Oh, yeah, what's your friend's name? Does she know Michael?"

"Her name's Zax. Nobody here would know her."

"You're gonna have to give me a little more information or Michael will just say no."

Stump glanced down the hall, then said, "Okay, but we have to keep this quiet. We were told that Michael has a criminal record and that scares my friend. I just wanted to find out if it's as bad as it sounds."

"Oh, I see."

"Zax wants to run our breakfast restaurant across the street, but she's scared for her daughter and all the other women customers."

"I don't blame her. That's pretty serious all right. You wait right here. I'll get Michael."

"I still might want to kick this guy's ass, dude," James said as Em walked off.

"That'd be pretty dumb, even for you. Did you see all those pool sticks? Those guys could put enough dents in your head to make you look like an ugly golf ball."

After a few minutes, Em slipped back into the little room and pulled one of the chairs from under James and Stump's table and sat in it. "Hi," she said, with a toothy grin. "I'm Michael. I understand you want to talk with me?"

James spit some of his malt into his glass. "You're Michael? Oh, I get it, Em stands for Michael."

Still smiling, Michael nodded. "It gives me some anonymity and avoids explaining why I've got a boy's name."

"That's a good one," Stump said. "So how do you know Mr. McFadden?"

"He's my grandfather, but I call him Daddy because it makes him feel younger. My mom dropped me off at his place when I was a newborn. We ain't seen her since. Did he tell you his bear story?"

Stump nodded, "That was pretty funny."

"He can be colorful at times. Did he tell you that he's a Marine?"

"Yes he did. I was surprised that a man who cares about kittens would be a Marine."

"Why not? We have hearts too, you know."

Stump cocked his head. "We? Are you saying you're a Marine, too?"

"Military Police."

Stump wondered what kind of sex crime Michael or any woman might commit, unless it was against another woman.

"Daddy didn't want me to join, but it all worked out okay."

"Have you arrested other Marines?" James asked.

"Had to. That was my job. Look, I gotta get back to my other customers. What did you guys want?"

"Would you mind if I ask you something personal?" Stump asked.

"As long as you're not going to propose to me. I get a marriage proposal just about every day around here."

"It's not that. I hope you won't get mad at me, but my friend, Zax, said she saw your name on a site for sex offenders. That's why she doesn't want to work down here. What did you do that was so bad?"

Michael grinned, "If I told ya, I'd have to kill ya."

"Did you rape some dude?" James asked.

"You're a sick-o." Michael said, before turning to Stump. "Since you want to keep this private, I'll whisper what I did in your ear." She leaned in and spoke through cupped hands, taunting James.

"Pissing in public? Are you kidding me?" James said after he and Stump left the bar and Stump exposed Michael's big crime, which fell under the broader heading of Indecent Exposure. "I've done that a hundred times."

"Me too," Stump said. "Not a hundred times, but whenever it became an emergency."

"Yana's done it, too. I bet all women wiz outdoors in an emergency—like pregnancy."

"I was surprised she gave me her number."

"I'm not. I told you she had the hots for you."

"No way. She was just being nice—in case Zax wants to call her."

"Either way, I had a feeling that Zax and Yana were blowing everything out of proportion."

Stump thumped James on the arm. "I call b.s. You were ready to hang both Catts and Michael. You're a dweeb."

"I'm just flexible. That's all. You gonna rub Zax's face in it?"

"No. I got another idea but do me a favor. Don't say anything about any of this to Yana yet."

"You got it, dude." James said as the same guy they'd seen earlier approached them. "You guys sure you can't spare a quarter so I can get me a smoke?"

Stump nodded reached in his pocket and snagged a small group of bills before he peeled off a buck. "Here ya go. I'm sorry I didn't help you out the last time, but I had something on my mind."

The guy pointed to Stump's remaining wad. "I saw a five-spot in there. I could sure use something to eat."

Stump sighed and peeled off the five.

James pointed at the fiver. "That's from both of us."

60

"**I** don't believe I'm doing this," Zax said.

Perhaps Stump should have come right out and told Zax about Michael's "crime," but it would take more than a few flowery words to get Zax back on board. She had to meet Michael face-to-face in a natural way, like Stump and James had done. And sometimes the most "natural" way was to lie.

After finding out Michael's schedule, Stump told Zax that he wanted her to go with him to get a couple of "the best cheeseburgers in town," but when she found out that those burgers were in Nick's saloon in the downtown area, she reminded Stump that she'd had enough of that neighborhood, which forced Stump to employ the guilt card. He reminded Zax about the smoke fire and that he'd found a good home for Denise's dog when they needed him. It wouldn't be fair to deny him a favor in exchange. She had no choice.

Stump swung his Fiat into a parking spot in front of Catts McFadden's building. Almost instantly, a scraggly fellow with a long-legged swimsuit and sandals asked them for spare change.

This time Stump pulled out a single buck.

"I've never liked this area," Zax said as they neared the last half-block of businesses.

"Like I said. They got great cheeseburgers and a fun waitress. Don't you think it's about time you had a little fun?"

"I gotta find another job, not have fun in bars. Next thing I know you'll be telling me to let somebody pick me up."

"Just trust me."

Zax sighed. "All this for a friggin' burger."

Inside, Michael was behind the bar. "If you ain't 21," she said, "you gotta eat in the back, away from the bar. I'll be with you in a minute."

Stump smiled. "That's the fun waitress," he whispered as Zax scanned the place.

"Smells like the inside of a beer keg in here."

In the same room as before, a cardboard box and a dozen napkin holders had been crowded onto one of the tables. Zax sat with her back to the far wall.

A few minutes later, Michael hustled down the hall and slid menus in front of them. "Sorry. I had to fill in while the bartender unloaded a beer truck. I'm Em. I'll be your server today."

Stump smiled. "We're Stump and Zax. We'll be your customers."

Michael shook her head. "The first time I heard that stale line, I threw my Cabbage Patch doll out of my crib."

Zax grinned.

"We got good burgers and chili today. Everything else sucks."

Zax grinned again. "I was told to try your cheeseburger."

"Let me guess. I bet you want bottled water to drink?"

"That'd be nice. Thank you."

"What about you?" Michael said to Stump. "You want a burger too, or what?"

"And a vanilla malt with cinnamon."

"Of course." Michael looked at Zax. "It's not fair. The hunks never have to worry about their figures."

As Michael walked off, Zax smiled for the third time in a couple minutes. "I see what you mean. She's very likeable."

A few minutes later, Michael retuned with their drinks. She included a clean glass, one wedge of lemon and another wedge of lime for Zax's water. She pointed to the cluttered table off to the side. "You guys mind if I hang around a bit and fill these napkin holders?"

"I can help you," Zax said, rising.

Now that Zax had grown comfortable with Michael, Stump had his chance to show that the infamous bad-boy Michael was actually a fabulous good-girl Em.

"That's something you guys have in common," Stump said. "You both serve people."

Michael looked at Zax. "You got a store or something? Maybe I've been there."

"Just a small café by the criminology college. That's how I met Stump. How long have you been working in this place? Do you like it?"

"A couple years, now. It pays the bills."

"We were thinking of opening a breakfast place close by," Stump said, "but a couple things have bothered Zax."

"Oh, yeah," Michael said, turning to Zax, "like what?"

"Well, there are a lot of street people around here. I have a daughter to think of. Are they a problem?"

"Well they can be a little irritating on occasion, but most of them are harmless."

"What about the prostitutes?" Zax asked.

"Prostitutes? Those rumors are from the old days. You probably know about the Marine base up the street. When those guys got discharged, they could either have a bus ticket back to their hometown or stay here, in the beach towns. That meant tattoo parlors, nudie bars, and—"

"Prostitutes," Stump said.

Michael nodded. "It was before my time, but I heard there were enough cheap beds in the area to accommodate everybody."

276

"I'm ashamed to say you know a lot more about the history of the area than I do."

"You hear a bunch of things when you work in a bar. Anyway, I can tell you that it's better for young guys like that to have an outlet for their needs, and if it helps a few women get by, I don't see any harm." Michael smiled in Stump's direction. "What about you? I bet you're all for prostitution."

"This time you're wrong," Stump said. "I had a chance to go with some of my pals down to the Adelita bar—"

"Ah yes. The best-known brothel in Tijuana," Michael said to Zax.

"It sounds like desperation for everybody," Stump continued. "If I want to have that kind of fun there are older high school girls and hot coeds all around the campus and down on the beach. But I don't go for much of that either. I'd rather be with one woman many times than many women one time."

"Refreshing," Michael said.

"Maybe all that prostitution stuff is overblown," Zax said, "but I hear there are bad guys living down here too, criminal types, perverts. Aren't you afraid of people like that?"

"Me? Hell, no. I'm a former MP. The guys around here are more afraid of me than I am of them."

"An MP? I can see how that would work for you, but I don't know much about self-defense and I can't expose my daughter to people like that."

"You could get a gun, just in case," Stump said.

"Ain't happening. Guns scare me. If I were held up I'd rather give away the money than get out a gun."

Michael pushed a bunch of napkins into a holder. "You're right. The worst thing to do is provoke a nervous person. They might go crazy. It's not worth it. It's better to have surveillance cameras. That's usually enough to prevent the crime in the first place."

"I never could afford anything like that."

"If nothing else, you should put up some fake cameras.

The perps won't know if they're real or not. Either way it's better to focus on the perp. Study their face. Is it round, egg-shaped? Look for eye-color and tats. How tall? Stuff like that. What's the name of your place? I'll stop by there sometime."

"It's Lee's College Café."

"Who's Lee? Your hubby?"

"My last name."

Stump grinned. "That's something else you guys have in common. You both use male names."

Zax glanced across the table. "Em isn't a male name."

"Stump's referring to my first name. When I ain't hanging around here, people call me Michael."

"Michael McFadden," Stump said.

Zax raised her brows, looked at Stump and then back to Michael. "You?"

61

"Tell Zax what your crime was," Stump said to Michael.

"Sure. You'll get a kick out of this. It was at an outdoor concert. The bastards only had three Porta-potties, all with ridiculously long lines. I don't know who screwed that up but my bladder was about to explode. I couldn't wait fifteen minutes so I slithered between a couple parked cars and took care of business - just as a cop and a couple kids with their mommy came by. Mommy insisted on pressing charges, so I got arrested for lewd behavior, which is considered a sex crime. Screwy, huh?"

Zax's hands shot to her mouth. "Oh, my God. I know exactly what that's like."

"Would never have happened if the organizers had provided enough potty houses."

"I know what you mean. They load us up with beer and then don't have enough restrooms. I've had to do that too. One time . . ."

Stump grinned and sat back while Zax and Michael began trading bathroom woes like two sorority sisters at a reunion.

"So what happened in your case?" Zax eventually asked while wiping down a napkin holder.

"Not much. The judge liked my military record and ruled if I had no similar charges for six months, the records would be expunged. I'm surprised you found out about it, because it wasn't supposed to be in the court records."

"Well, it wasn't really in the official records. I just saw an article that said you'd been arrested."

"Oh, that. That's a tiny local paper. You're the only person I know of who read that little article."

"I'm so sorry, Michael. This area is a little more colorful than near the college. I got nervous and then—"

"I introduced her to your 'father,'" Stump said, making air quotes.

"Say no more," Michael said, raising a hand. "Daddy doesn't always make a good first impression, or a second one for that matter."

"Regardless, this isn't his fault. It's mine. I'm the one who jumped to conclusions. When my daughter told me how much fun she had playing with the kitties . . . well, I started wondering why a man would do all those things just for cats. I don't even want to tell you some of the thoughts that popped into my sick head."

"Actually, he's really Michael's grandfather," Stump said.

Michael nodded before turning to Zax. "I don't blame you for worrying, but I can assure you Daddy is as harmless as one of his kittens."

"See? I told you," Stump said.

Zax turned her hands palms up. "I had to butt my nose into something that was none of my business. Then your name came up. Naturally, I assumed you were a man and jumped to more unfair conclusions. Can you forgive me?"

"Of course. Any mother would have done the same thing."

"Can we start over? You're obviously a very interesting person. What was it like growing up with a big-hearted grandfather who likes cats?"

"In a way, I was one of his strays. Apparently, my mother was a wild child and ran off before finishing high school.

Naturally, she got pregnant, but she didn't have time for a baby. She dropped me off with Daddy. From that time on it was just him and me."

"I can relate," Stump said. "My biological mother did something like that and somebody else ended up raising me, too."

"Daddy runs ads on Craigslist and tells people he'll give their unwanted cats a home, no questions asked."

"He has to go fishing, just to get enough food for the cats," Stump said.

Michael clucked her tongue and shook her head. "No, he doesn't. He pretends to be poor, but he's got more money than he'll ever need. Did you know he owns the vacant building just down the block?"

"Yeah. He even took us on a tour of it. Showed us some rad things."

"He leaves it vacant because he doesn't need the rent and doesn't want to deal with most people. You could say he's a misanthrope."

Stump scrunched his eyebrows. "What's that?"

"The opposite of a party-goer. He's basically disappointed in most people so he stays to himself."

Zax sighed. "And to think I—"

"At least you gave him a second chance. That's more than other people do."

"Did you always have lots of cats around?" Zax asked.

"Hardly. We only had two when I joined the Marines, but he got carried away after that. I guess he needed a way to fill the hole in his heart."

"See, Zax? I told you he's a nice man."

Zax puffed out her lower lip.

"By the time I was discharged, Daddy had accumulated about 30 of them and had begun his taxidermy endeavors."

"And preserving them isn't as weird as people think," Stump said. "It's just his way of keeping them from leaving him, too."

"I've tried to get him to throw them out but it's as if he's betraying a child. He just can't do it."

"I get that," Zax said. "We've had to get rid of my daughter's little dog. It was painful."

"Some of the neighbors don't like what he does, but on balance he does a lot more good than harm so the authorities cut him as much slack as they can. I just wish he would slow down a little. He's had a few problems with this heart and doesn't seem to want to relax."

"Do you think a breakfast place could work down here?" Zax finally asked.

"I don't see why not. There's nothing like that close by."

Zax sighed. "You've made me feel so much better, Michael. I just wish you'd join us."

Stump's eyes shot from Zax to Michael. Aside from the fact that Zax had just established that she was back on board with Egg-Zaklee's, he also liked the idea of adding Michael to the mix.

"And leave all this?" Michael said sarcastically.

"When we first came in, you were behind the bar and handling a cash register. You also wait tables and do prep-work. You can do it all."

"It's all part of the job. I fill in wherever I'm needed."

"You've got good people skills, too. There's no doubt about that. Would you have any interest in managing the front-end of our place? I'd handle the kitchen and take care of the books, and you'd run everything the public sees."

Michael's head pinged from Zax to Stump. "What about you? How do you fit in all of this?"

"My trust owns the building. Zax owns the restaurant. So you'd be working for her."

"Well, depending on the paycheck, it might be nice to have my evenings off and deal with some sober people for a change. Let me think about it a little bit and I'll get back to you."

62

"**I** still think we should have made six separate single-stool bathrooms," Stump said to Zax, "and say they're for either the hens or the cocks, whoever needs them."

"You don't get it. Most women don't want to use the same bathroom a man has just used. Men splatter and dribble, and I'm not putting that vulgar name on the doors because of its sexual connotations."

"Yeah, but—"

"Is that offer still open?" a woman asked from behind them.

"Oh, hi, Michael," Zax said, holding up crossed fingers, "I hope that mean you've decided to join us?"

"Yeah. Nights off and fewer drunks sounds pretty good—but I have to give my boss two weeks' notice."

"Wonderful. That works better for us too. It's going to take a month or so to get this place operating, so you can take three weeks if you want to."

"Whatever works. Until then, I can drop by for a couple hours each day before my shifts at the bar. This might give me a little more time to see Daddy, too."

"We're taking resumes and applications. Would you like to talk with the ones you'd supervise?"

"Yeah, especially the ones who say they have experience. I can ask them one question and find out how seasoned they really are."

"What question?" Stump asked.

"Simple. *Where's the most dangerous place in a restaurant?*"

"I'd guess it's the stove," Stump said. "How 'bout you, Zax?"

"The cash register."

Michael's head bobbed. "That's right. When bad guys rob a place, they're usually packing heat and wave it in the cashier's face. On top of everything else they can be hyped-up on drugs. That's why whenever I go to a restaurant or bar I like to sit where I can keep an eye on the register."

"Has it ever paid off?" Stump asked.

"A couple times. One day I was eating lunch and observed a man and woman casing the place. Then a pregnant woman stepped up to pay her bill, prompting Bonnie and Clyde to snatch her purse. Unfortunately, the victim ran after the perps and fell. That evening, she lost her baby."

"That's awful," said Zax.

"I was able to give the cops rock-solid descriptions of the perps and days later picked them out of line-ups. When asked how confident I was, I said 'one-hundred percent.'"

"What happened to those people?" Stump asked.

"Prison. Juries don't like it when people flash guns around and innocent babies become victims." Michael addressed Zax. "I don't know if you're interested, but I know a couple homeless hammer-slingers who'd like to help with the remodeling if they could get paid in cash and catch a shower upstairs from time to time."

"We don't have a shower yet," Stump said, "but we can rig something up on a temporary basis."

"These guys are talented, but they don't want long-term gigs and may have some 'issues,' like nightmares."

"My dad has sleep issues too. He sleeps in spurts."

"Are you going to scavenge the booths and kitchen items from your old place, Zax? My buds could help with that."

"Not yet. About all I need for now is my heavy file cabinet."

"I have an idea," Stump said. "Michael and I could take Pops to the old place and get the cabinet." He turned toward Michael. "That is, if you'd like to go."

She shrugged. "Only if we can play the Popsicle truck jingle."

"Done."

In the truck and sitting in a small bucket seat that Stump and James had gotten from a junk yard, Michael grinned as if she were a youngster who'd just been told she was tall enough to go on the big-kid's ride at the amusement park. "This is fun, Daddy. Now play the jingle song."

Already taking a liking to Michael, Stump laughed, turned on the slow-paced tinkle song and pulled slowly away from the curb like a popsicle truck would do. "I'm really glad you decided to join us."

"No big deal. If it doesn't work out, I can always get my old job back."

"Or one just like it."

"Yeah. People around here like vets. I know it's none of my business, but I was wondering how you wrangled up enough money to buy your very own building."

Stump tilted his head to the side. This was a chance to impress her. "Well, I got a trust after I solved a couple murders."

"No kidding? How'd you do that?"

Glad to fill her in, Stump began a short version of how he came upon his money and that he was using some of it to take care of Grandma Pauline, which also earned him an approving nod. He went on to explain Meadowlark Flats and how he'd met Xander. "He spit in a test tube for DNA purposes, then we went on a super rad, five-day trip to Kansas to look for a treasure."

"A treasure hunt? Don't tell me. It came off a pirate ship and nobody could figure out how it got there?"

"It wasn't quite that silly, but if there had been some money there, it might have guaranteed that my grandmother wouldn't lose her best friend."

"Are you telling me you went all the way out there, just for a couple old ladies?"

"That was part of it, but it was also to get to know Xander. He brought some guns and put together a homemade moving target that we shot at. And he gave me a .38 that used to belong to my grandpa."

"I'm more impressed about the nice thing you did for your grandma and her friend."

"Who else was going to do it? Have you ever been to a shooting range?" Stump asked.

She chuckled. "You ever hear of Iraq?"

"Yeah. That was dumb. I could use some shooting practice and coaching if you'd be interested."

"Yeah. I haven't been to a range for a while. I guess I could do that."

"Great," he said before turning off the jingle and speeding up.

63

With the grand opening of Egg-Zaklee's still a few weeks off, Stump and Michael were more or less in the way until the construction was complete. That lent Stump an opportunity to find out if the most alluring woman he'd ever met could ever be seriously attracted to him. The problem was, nearly everybody Stump had ever cared about, romantically or otherwise, eventually left him. Grandma Pauline was even slipping away.

If all of his relationships were doomed to end in painful voids, it would be juvenile folly to imagine that a well-traveled women, eight years his senior, could be interested in a first-year college student who'd only been out of his home state one time.

But regardless of all that, Michael was interesting and fun to be with and he couldn't stop thinking about her. The best way to find out if he could ever grow their relationship was to share a common interest. Fortunately, the Marine in her welcomed a trip to an outdoor shooting range.

After signing in and fussing with their gear, Stump wondered if he'd put too much mousse in his hair. "I have to admit I'm a little nervous," he said. "I've shot Myles's guns a few times and Xander taught me some additional things about shooting, but I'm still a novice."

Michael snatched a large black handgun and some ammo from a stout aluminum case. "At least you're smart enough to acknowledge your shortcomings. That's the best way to stay alive."

"Wow. That's a big gun. What is it? An assault rifle?"

Michael tilted the weapon so he could get a good look. "First off, that would make it a machine gun and those were outlawed thirty years ago. This is a Browning Hi-Power 9mm semi-auto. One of my faves."

"It looks heavy."

She pretended to weigh it in her palm. "Two pounds. Thirteen rounds. Pretty, walnut grips that hide at my sexy hips." She playfully thrust her right hip in his direction.

Amused and mildly aroused by her flirty poem, Stump admired her confidence. "All I brought was the .38 that Xander gave me. My grandpa used it when he was a prison guard."

"A reliable piece," she said, extending her hand. "Let me take a look."

At least Stump knew to release the cylinder and check the chambers. She examined the bore. "Do you have a cleaning kit? This thing is filthy."

"Xander said I should do that, but I didn't know how."

She sighed. "That's no excuse, Stump. I hate to be a nag, but you have to clean it every time you use it. You wouldn't want it to jam when you need it most."

"Can you show me how to clean it?"

"I can tell you this. I won't go shooting with you again if you don't respect your weapons—and that would make me sad."

Rad! Michael had essentially implied that she'd go target shooting with him again. "No problem. I'll even take a shower with it if you want me to."

"TMI. Before we get started, I'll explain a few basics. Then we can watch some of the other guys shoot for a while. You got a holster?"

Stump sighed. "No. Xander gave me one, but it fell apart."

"You can't be setting your weapon on the ground when it's not in use. You'll need a better carrying case, too. For ammunition and supplies."

"Yes, ma'am," he said, with only a hint of sarcasm.

"Speaking of ammo, nothing screams amateur more than somebody who refers to a loaded cartridge as a bullet. The bullet is the projectile that leaves the gun, not the casing."

"Okay. I'll try to remember that."

"Next, we'll talk about loading," she said spinning the cylinder and examining the chambers. "If you're in battle or defending yourself or just developing your reflexes, you'll have to reload on the fly. That's one of the bennies to the 9mm. I can shoot 13 rounds in three seconds, reload in three seconds and shoot 13 more rounds in three seconds, all without losing sight of my target. This one exercise could save your life."

"Neither Myles or Xander told me anything like that."

"There's a difference between target practice and emergencies."

Next, she spoke about gripping the gun and said one good shot was better than two bad ones. She shared great pointers about the positioning of the legs, shoulders and the head when shooting. "This isn't cartoons or the movies," she said, "so use two hands. The better shooters use their thumbs as effective sights. It's quicker too.

"After the shot, bring the gun back to the exact same point so you don't have to move your head and eyes to find your sight or target. Lots of shooters like the draw stroke. Keep your elbows bent until you get the weapon to shoulder height and then 'stick it' toward the target or threat before you shoot."

"Wow. That's a lot to remember."

"We're talking life and death here," she said, tapping him on the chin with her free hand, "and your life is worth the time."

A little while later and finally on the range and facing a

paper target, Stump tried to implement her lessons. In spite of his multiple errors, Michael remained supportive and used both "show" and "tell" to cement the lessons deep into his head. After a while they practiced shooting while on one knee and then lying down. As far as Stump was concerned, her confidence and well-fitting slacks were sexier than naked women on the beach.

Finally, it seemed to Stump as if two hours had melted into minutes and they called it a day. "So what did you think?" Michael asked as they brushed the dust off their clothes. "Did I badger you too much?"

"If I'm being honest, this wasn't as fun as shooting a frying pan with Xander," except for watching her brush off her backside, "but I learned a lot more."

"Both situations have their place, but a good cop or detective needs to know how to be effective. Some day a partner might have to depend on you. Next time we'll stand behind covers and pretend we're in a gunfight."

Next time? There was some sweet music.

On their way home, in his Spider, Stump knew that he wanted to return to the range and practice what he'd learned, especially if Michael would go with him. But more importantly, he'd never met a woman who was both as graceful as a cat and tough as a hammer. She could kick his ass one minute, be playful the next, and out think Solomon's smarter sister after that.

He couldn't help wondering if their eight-year age difference would prevent her from taking him more seriously some day. At least he had one thing going for him. As a wannabe detective, he'd learned that people like to talk about themselves.

"Why'd you become a Marine?" he asked.

"Me?" she said rolling down the window. "I was always a tomboy. Liked sports and motorcycles and other guy things."

"Trucks, too? I know a few things about truckers."

"Yeah. I like trucks and tanks. Planes and trains, too. All

290

of them. Anyway, when I was 18, I dated a Marine, a lance corporal from Camp Pendleton. He was the first one who said I'd make a good MP so I looked into it. Worked my way up to sergeant."

"What did you do?"

"You mean duty? I mostly patrolled grounds and facilities. Kept the peace and enforced the rules."

"Did those guys listen to a lady cop?"

She shrugged. "They pretty much had to. I was no wimp, but most of them could have put the hurt on me if it would've gotten to that. Even so, the other guys wouldn't have put up with that." She looked directly at him. "Before you drop me off, I want to thank you for the way you've treated Daddy. He's told me that you've got a big heart. I've noticed that too. I'm just glad you distract him from his neighbors. They get under his skin. It's not good for his heart."

Wow. That kind of respect could be promising. "Thanks. Has he ever considered living in a seniors' community? I could show you Meadowlark Flats, where my grandma lives."

She scoffed. "Daddy is way too independent to live by anybody else's rules."

"I woulda thought that too, but there are all sorts of people there, not just the Memory Care people like my grandma. A lot of them have pets. I even know a doctor."

"Thanks anyway," she said as Stump pulled up in front of Nick's saloon for one of her final shifts. "I just don't think he'd go for it."

"Maybe I can take Denise over again to see him and the kitties. Zax is so busy now, she'll appreciate it."

Michael looked him in the eye and nodded. "Would you like me to show you how to clean your weapon?"

64

"**I**'d like to go with you guys next time," James said, while Stump got ready to meet Michael at Egg-Zaklee's.

"How you going to do that? Yana made you get rid of your revolver."

"I can borrow yours until she softens up and I get another gun."

"I dunno, dude. Michael might think you're too amateurish."

"I call b.s. I've shot more handguns than you have—and I was a better shot when you and I went trap shooting with Myles. I just want to practice a little so I don't get rusty."

"It would be better if you and I go together some other time, bro, after Egg-Zaklee's opens and Michael is busy."

James paused for a moment. "Oh, I get it. This isn't about shooting. You ain't *been with* anybody for quite a while and you want to hook up with her."

Stump waved a hand. "That ain't it. I can get laid anytime I want."

"Yeah, but you don't do much about it. Yana and I were beginning to think you're asexual or gay."

"That ain't it either. I just don't like casual sex as much as most guys. It's too shallow."

"Admit it. She's worldly. You like her and you want to see how it plays out. And good ole fun-loving James would be in your way. Why didn't you just say so, brofriend? It's no problem. You and I can go some other time."

"Good. Thanks."

"In the meantime you've been cutting classes again. You going to drop out?"

"I don't know. I agreed to stay in school, but most classes bore the hell out of me. And I have better things to do."

"Everybody should be that lucky."

"I'll probably cram at the end of the semester and take the finals just to keep my promise to Myles and Xander. Now I have to go meet Michael. She's going to show me the right way to clean our guns."

"'Clean your guns,' huh? That's a good term for what you really want her to do. Clean the gun in your pants."

* * *

At Egg-Zaklee's, the aroma of fresh-brewed coffee emanated from the soon-to-be restaurant. Off toward the back of the building, a couple electricians were connecting wall outlets to newly-run wires. Stump dragged a couple makeshift tables to the front corner of the dining area, where he could sit with his back to one window and watch for Michael through the other.

He plopped down his brand-new cleaning kit and a shiny new stainless steel gun case, replete with the .38 that Xander had given him, plus a brand new 9mm that resembled Michael's. Both of his weapons wore new and expensive carved-leather holsters that now looked pretentious. He shrugged, then laid out his supplies and rearranged them several times so they would look just right when she arrived.

Then he saw her across the street, briskly heading his way

with a rolled-up towel in her hand. Her neatly pressed clothes and bouncing hair projected a mesmerizing confidence.

He watched closely as she abruptly stopped and faced the front wheel of a parked car. She smiled, tucked the towel under one arm and reached into her back pocket as a masculine hand rose up to meet hers. Stump nodded. She'd probably slipped one of the homeless guys a buck or two that she'd gotten as a tip from somebody else.

A minute later she reached the end of the block and crossed over toward Egg-Zaklee's. He would have liked to open the door for her, but instead focused on his .38 so neither he nor she would think he'd been watching her.

"Hi, Stump," she said, a minute later and laying down her rolled-up towel. She scanned his newly purchased booty. "Did I miss your birthday or something?"

"These things? Nah. I saw a sale at Cabela's."

She tapped the 9mm. "You'll like this one. It'll hide well against your body—that is, if you use a smaller holster." Now that Stump got another look at his overly decorated holsters, they reminded him of a gaudy prop that a comedian might use. He wondered if the store would take them back.

Michael smartly flipped her rolled towel toward her feet and an apron emerged from the inside. She'd seemed to think of everything.

"You told me you've never cleaned a weapon," she said as she sat across from him, "so stop me if I sound too bossy."

"I'm sure, you'll be more interesting than my professors."

"Okay then. You asked for it. There are lots of ways to clean weapons. Some guys will only use certain supplies or methods, but most of the certified armorers will tell you that the important thing is to get the burnt powder or carbon off. How you do that is up to you. Let's take a look at your .38."

Enjoying the experience on multiple levels, Stump pulled his grandfather's pistol from its now-ridiculous holster, released the cylinder, checked the chambers and handed it her way.

She grabbed a rag and some cleaning solvent. "These items will work fine, but I know hobbyists who use their girlfriends' underwear and fancy lubricants. Other guys simply use toothbrushes and paper towels, but like I said, it all works."

Stump liked the underwear talk. "Doesn't the barrel get scratched?"

"Naw. These weapons are made of hardened steel. If you keep them clean and don't bang them around they're good for thousands of rounds."

Over the next half-hour Michael spoke of brass brushes, long Q-Tips and patches of cotton material on a thick wire. She taught Stump to push the jags and brushes completely through the bore before backing them out. "Here, you try it," she eventually said.

Stump slowly reamed a couple chambers before he switched topics to something that might impress her. "Did I tell you that Denise and I stopped by to see Catts yesterday?"

"Daddy? No, you didn't. I appreciate how nice you are to him and how you humor him."

"I wouldn't call it humoring him. I just get his point."

"What point?"

"He once said something about all the lonely pets. I assumed that he meant people are like that, too. Some of them don't have anybody who loves them either. It's sad."

"That's true. Some of the people out on the sidewalk are like that."

"I just think your dad deserves more respect than most people would think."

Michael rose, stepped around to Stump's side of the table and kissed him on the forehead. "Thank you for noticing. Nobody else seems to get that."

A peck on the head was okay, something a mother might do. "Thank you," he said, hoping that someday a more affectionate kiss would be appropriate.

Just then, Zax came in the front door and marched toward

Michael and Stump. "Guns? You guys have guns in my restaurant? I don't like that."

Stump wrinkled his forehead. "Sorry, Zax, but—"

"When you leased this place to me, it became my domain. I get to make the rules and I don't like guns in my place of business. If you want to play cowboys, you can go upstairs. That's still your turf."

Stump might have reminded Zax that she had not yet paid any rent if Michael hadn't butted in. "I'm sorry, Zax. This was my fault. I practically forced Stump to do this. You can blame me."

Stump scoffed. "No way. Xander told me to keep my guns cleaned but I couldn't be bothered. When Michael saw—"

"Look, you two, we're going to open in a few weeks and I don't need distractions," Zax said. "If you want to get together, I'd appreciate it if you'd do it on one of the upper floors where I don't even have to think about it."

"Sure thing, Zax," Stump said, "we were just about ready to clean up anyway."

After he and Michael put their stuff away, they strolled toward the restrooms to clean up. Still unsure if Michael could be interested in him due to their age difference, Stump was already looking forward to any other opportunities to be alone with her and he already had something sexy in mind. "I have an idea," he said. "Would you like to get together for a professional full-body massage sometime?"

65

In the weeks that followed the gun cleaning, Stump looked for additional opportunities to be alone with Michael, but she always had other things to do. Eventually he assumed that their age difference must have mattered to her more than he hoped.

In the meantime, the night before Egg-Zaklee's grand opening rolled around and Stump wasn't the only one who was on edge.

"Screw you, Stump," Zax said as Michael joined them, her back to the raindrop-riddled window. "I've been busting my butt around here more than anybody. I don't need you lecturing me."

Stump looked over Michael's shoulders and into black skies with sporadic lightning bolts. "Screw you back, Zax. If we'd opened weeks ago, like I wanted, we wouldn't be in this mess. Now, because of the rain, we're not going to have very many customers."

"I can't help that," she said as thunder rumbled from the clouds. "Besides, we couldn't have passed inspections back then. Remember?"

"Yeah, I remember. But, I've got a ton of money tied up in this place—your place, remember? I can't afford to keep putting it off."

Zax folded her arms across her chest. "Too friggin' bad for you. I can't help it if it you didn't listen to everybody who told you it would take longer. I would have preferred some other place. Something newer."

"And then you'd be doomed again because you'd be like all the other places and you don't have the buying power of the chain restaurants. You couldn't compete. How would that help Denise?"

The muscles in Zax's neck visibly tightened. "Who the hell do you think you are, lecturing me about my daughter? You're just a 19-year-old college kid with a trust. That doesn't make you an authority on much of anything, especially raising my child."

"Hold it, you two," Michael said, making a time-out sign. "I know that this is none of my business, but I've seen plenty of conflicts in my life, some of them life-and-death, and this is usually not the way to settle them. You guys both want the same thing. You're on the same team."

"That's beside the point. Michael. We're nowhere near ready. On top of that, this storm is supposed to be a monster. We're not going to do that much business the next few days and we could've used that time to get more of the work done. I still think we should take another month."

Stump cringed. "No way. We've already put this off once and sent out a second set of marketing brochures. We can't postpone again. We'd look like a bunch of fools."

"Duh!" Zax screamed.

Somewhere in Stump's brain, where logic and common sense usually prevailed, he knew that Zax was correct. Whenever they came across something major to do, they needed permits and inspections. All of that took time. He wished he had listened to people who knew more about these things. He also wished that Xander or Myles had fought harder to discourage him from taking on the project in the first place.

"I'm sorry for being so difficult, Zax. I realize that you know a lot more about restaurants than all the rest of us put together, but I can't put this off again. Xander is bringing his family into town just for this occasion. Besides, the county gave us the go-ahead."

"Maybe so, but the county doesn't care that some of our tables haven't arrived, or whether we have finished decorating, or the fact that customers can see the mess upstairs. We still need to put up some plastic sheeting to hide that mass of ugliness."

"Well," Michael said more or less to Zax, "if this storm is as bad as they're saying, we might not have all that many customers anyway."

"If I wanted a low turnout, all I had to do was stay at my old place."

Stump glanced out the window where the corner parking spot was available. "I gotta move Pops into that parking space so it'll be like a big sign in the morning."

Zax shook her head. "What good is a sign, if nobody is here to see it?"

Outside, there were fewer cars than usual. Stump covered his head with a towel and rushed across the street toward Pops. Before he could open the door, he saw a couple familiar homeless guys huddled up in the doorway of Catts's building. They almost seemed to enjoy beating the odds. Stump scooted their way. "If you guys want to get out of the rain, you can stay in our building over night. You'll have to sleep upstairs and on the floor but it's better than drowning."

"Thanks a lot, dude. You suppose we could get a cup of hot chocolate, too?"

"Sure. Just tell my friends that Stump said it's okay." While the street fellows hustled toward Egg-Zaklee's, Stump slid into Pops, executed a U-turn and took the corner parking spot.

Back inside, on the other side of the dining area, the two wet, homeless guys, each with a cup of hot chocolate in hand, thanked everybody before they climbed the stairs. "No problem," wet Stump said. "Maybe when you guys dry off you can hang a sheet of plastic across the top of the stairway so none of our customers will see the mess up there."

"That was nice of you, Stump," Michael said, "to give those guys a dry place to stay."

"No big deal. Now, where were we?"

Zax sighed. "Losing credibility, that's where."

Stump noticed Michael's eyes dart in the direction of the entry door. "Somebody else wants in," she said.

Stump looked in time to see Xander hold the door for a slightly pudgy woman and young girl about Denise's age, all of them dripping wet. The long red hair meant the woman could only be one person. Stump rose. "Brianne and Lori Sue. Over here, you guys."

"You must be Stump," Brianne said, hustling toward Stump with her arms out. The heavy-duty hug caught Stump off-guard. After all, he was Xander's bastard child and had taken Xander away from her and their kids at least a half-dozen times. But that didn't appear to matter. "I'm so glad to meet you," she said, grinning through full lips.

"These are my friends, Michael and Zax," Stump said.

Brianne hugged both of them.

"Come meet your oldest brother," Xander said to his daughter and then turning Stump's direction. "This is Lori Sue."

Wow. Until that moment, the idea of having his very own sister was just that—an idea. But there she was. Flesh and blood - about nine, with a pageboy, and the same oval-shaped head as he and Xander.

"I thought Danville was the oldest," Lori Sue said.

Xander shook his head. "That was before we knew about Stump."

"Mama, why didn't you say you had another baby?"

Stump grinned. "Can I have a hug?"

Lori Sue looked to her mother for approval, then said, "I guess so."

Stump embraced her and would have liked to hold the hug for a while longer but he wasn't sure what was appropriate.

"You people are going to have to excuse me," Zax said. "I have a lot of work to do if I'm going to be ready for a grand opening in the morning."

"Don't go because of us," Brianne said. "We just wanted to stop by for a few minutes before we check in at the B&B."

"It's not just that. I'll see you all tomorrow, just don't expect much, with this weather and all."

"I'm sorry that I yelled at you, Zax," Stump said.

Zax didn't reply.

66

"**W**hew. I'm not used to this early shift, let alone all the rain," Michael said, brushing some rain water off her shoulder and restraining a yawn. "I only slept a few hours last night."

"Welcome to the club," Zax replied before addressing the others. "Alright everybody, listen up. Like it or not, today is our grand opening and none of us really knows what to expect. We've only got 15 minutes until 6:00 o'clock when we'll open our doors. I've got a list here of everybody's duties. For starters, Michael and Yana need to police the dining area. I'd like you to double-check all the table settings and make sure the tables and utensils are spotless." She turned to James. "You're going to help me in the kitchen."

"Rad. I can cook up a batch of omelets and put them in the frig. That way when somebody wants one, we can just toss it in the nuker."

"Not happening. That would be like serving leftovers. You're going to shred cheese, make toast and mix batter for omelets and pancakes."

Stump raised his hand slightly. "What about me?"

"You're going to stand outside in the rain as the official greeter."

"What?" he said wide-eyed. "You've got to be—"

Zax grinned. "Relax, Stump. I was just pulling your chain. We'll need you to serve the food and be our busboy. Keep an eye out for anything we might have overlooked, like fingerprints on the windows or bathroom issues. Check TP, hand towels, trash. That sort of thing."

Stump nodded and checked the clock. Ten to six. The customers ought to start showing up any minute.

"One final thing, everybody. Since we haven't received our last six tables, we need to serve at least two parties on each table by 10:00. So, serve them quickly. Now, if there are no questions, I'm going to get the grill ready. James, you can come with me."

When everybody split up Stump circled the seating area. Next to the outside wall a plate-sized puddle indicated that somebody had dropped an ice cube. He went for a towel, came back and wiped it up just as a familiar dripping wet person entered the front door.

"Okay," Xander said. "It's six o'clock. I'm ready to work."

"Dude," Stump said, "You don't have to help. You should spend the day with your family."

"You guys are family, too. I've been up for hours. Couldn't wait to get over here. Now whatcha got for me to do?"

"That's nice of you. You probably ought to report to Zax. She and James are doing some prep work in the kitchen."

"No prob. Brianne and Lori Sue will be by later. They might lend a hand too, but I gotta warn ya, Lori Sue expects to do something fun today."

Michael chimed in. "On clear days there are all sorts of things to do, but considering the rain, you might try one of the dozen museums at Balboa Park in San Diego. You could probably get there in an hour and have the place to yourselves."

"What's the weather supposed to be like tomorrow?"

Thousands of raindrops pelted the windows while Stump checked his iPhone. "Rain should be letting up in a few hours and gone by tomorrow."

At ten after six there were no customers. Stump paced the floor again, looking for chores he could do. Then finally at seven, he approached Michael near the entry area. "I didn't expect this," he said. "We've been open an hour and not one paying customer."

"I know. I just spoke with Zax. If we don't get some business in the next hour or so, she wants to lock the doors."

A deathly quiet half-hour later, Myles called to see how the grand opening was going. Stump gave him the bad news and said he was thinking about taking a drive north to be with Grandma Pauline but, considering the fact that Minnie Moore was about to be ripped away, that was just as depressing.

Then the first real paying customers, a man and woman, came in. Michael seated the guests near the corner windows, where Yana took their drink order and left them to scan the menus. With a hint of renewed hope Stump and Xander sat at a dining table along the back wall. Stump watched the customers scan the menus and happily discuss their options. A few minutes later, Yana answered some of their questions and took their order.

When Yana walked away, Stump hooked a finger and asked what they ordered. "They work down the street at the bookstore. Unlawful Waffle for her. The man went for the jalapeno bread French toast."

Stump nodded. "At least that proves that people like the unusual things."

"I wouldn't get too excited," Xander said. "You'll need a lot more customers than that to declare a trend."

By late morning, only a few additional waterlogged customers managed to drop by. "That's it everybody," Zax said coming from the kitchen. "That was *the big rush*. Nine paying customers. We might as well lock the doors right now."

Stump detected a crackling in her voice. "I guess I was wrong, Zax. If things don't pick up, I'm not sure we should even finish off the place. That would at least cut the losses." This time he saw her red eyes.

"We might as well stick it out for a few more days," Zax said, "then you and Michael will be free to frolic off to the shooting range again or wherever it is that you guys sneak off to."

"What?" Michael said loudly. "I put plenty of free time in this place before I left my other job. Now when things aren't peachy, you climb up my back. If you don't want me here just say so 'cause I can—"

Uh-oh. Stump sure as heck didn't want to see Michael go anywhere.

Then Zax blew out a deep breath, "No. No, Michael. I didn't mean that. I don't want you to go. I'm just so disappointed."

"Okay, then. We're all disappointed, but let's not snipe at each other."

Yana stuffed her order book in her apron. "That first couple said they expect business to pick up when the rainstorm blows over."

Zax nodded. "Why don't we pick up our messes and try again tomorrow? If we get the same response for a few days after the rain goes away—"

"I can mop up the floor," Xander said. "There's a puddle over there by the wall I've been meaning to get at."

Stump looked toward the area. "Yeah. I saw that earlier."

"Me too," Yana said. "I soaked it up twice."

"There's no table in that spot," James added. "There must be a leak behind the wall or something."

"Great. That's all I need," Stump said. "Another thousand million-dollar problem."

"That could be dangerous," Xander said. "You'd better hope that water doesn't run into some electricity somewhere."

"But there aren't any outlets over there," Stump said.

Xander shook his head. "Doesn't matter. The actual leak

could be nearly anywhere. Water can run across joists or subflooring. I've seen water drip from light fixtures before."

Stump moaned. "Okay, I guess we should buzz up to the top floor and see if we can determine what's going on."

67

The guys climbed the stairs and quickly found the problem. "There's the leak, right there," James said, pointing to a steady oozing trickle in the corner.

"That's just where it's coming through the ceiling," Xander said. "The actual leak could originate somewhere else."

"This pisses me off," Stump said. "We inspected that roof and didn't see anything suspicious. Jack had to know there was a leak, but he lied to us."

"Not necessarily, Stump. Roofs are tricky and there haven't been a lot of rainstorms in California for a while."

James pointed off to the side. "When we were downstairs, the puddle was ten feet over that way."

"That's what I meant," Xander replied. "Water can run along rafters or floor joists to a lower spot before seeping through the ceiling or running down the wall."

"I hope we can fix it ourselves," Stump said. "I can't afford to hire anybody else."

"You might just need some flashing or tar around a vent pipe. For now I'd check the basement. That water has to be going somewhere."

"You might have an indoor swimming pool down there, dude."

Stump's eyes widened. "I can't believe this crap."

Xander laid a hand on Stump's shoulder. "We might as well grab a mop and bucket on the way down."

Stump had barely opened the door to the basement when he got his first glimpse at a half-inch of standing water. "Son-of-a-bitch," he said loudly before looking at everybody's feet. "I'm the only one with tennis shoes. I'll mop up. You guys stay back just in case Xander's right about that electric problem."

"We could rent a pump," James said, handing the mop and bucket to Stump.

Xander shook his head. "I don't think it's deep enough for that. Besides, the rain is letting up. We might not need it."

Twenty minutes later, the rain had slowed to a heavy drizzle and they'd taken dozens of buckets of water up the stairs and flushed them down the toilet. Stump wiped his forehead and opened the small window. "We're making progress, but it's still seeping in. I gotta air this place out ASAP."

Xander ventured down to the formerly soaking cement floor. "If we were going to have an electrical problem down here it would have already happened. I can take the mop for a while. You deserve a break."

Stump squatted down and pointed to where one of the walls met the floor. "That's where the trickle's coming from. It's slowing down though." He looked again. "That's strange."

"What is?" James asked sliding next to Stump.

"Tiny green specks."

"I see them. What about them?"

"Do you see any green paint around here? It doesn't make sense."

"Maybe it came from the roof or something?"

"Naw. The roof is black tar. Besides, if the particles are coming from the roof, why didn't we see any of them in the puddle in the dining room?"

"I dunno. What do you think it is?"

Suddenly, Stump recalled a rumor that Catts McFadden and others had mentioned. He looked out the basement window toward Pops, which was still parked in the street. Then he looked back at the wall and the specks one more time. Either of you guys got a quarter?"

"Why?" James said drawing closer.

"Yeah, I got one," Xander said, handing it over. Stump promptly bent down and used the edge of the coin to scrape at the bottom of the wall just above the leak.

"You know what he's doing?" Xander asked James.

"No, but I've seen that intense look on his face before."

Stump leaned close to the floor and looked thoroughly at the scraped area. "I thought so."

"Thought what, dude? What you got?"

"Look at this. There's a little groove at the bottom of this wall, like you'd expect to see between bricks."

"Mortar joints," Xander said.

"Yeah, but why don't we see signs of mortar joints on the rest of the wall?"

"Somebody must have plastered over them," James said.

"That's what I was thinking, too."

"Meaning what?" Xander quizzed.

"I'm not sure yet. Can one of you guys go get me a coat hanger or something I can slide under this wall?"

Obviously intrigued, James bolted up the stairs, while Stump used the quarter to chip along the bottom of the wall for another foot. "Here's another joint."

"I got one," James said hustling back down the stairs with a hanger.

"Thanks, dude." Stump untwisted the hanger and made it into a large L-shape. "This ought to do it." He squatted and slid one end of the wire under the wall and pushed it inward causing Xander to bend forward and place both hands on his knees. "If this was an original foundation wall,' Stump said, "we couldn't do that. Foundation walls are solid cement."

"Not exactly," Xander said. "Floors are poured separately, but you're correct on your main point. That wire couldn't go underneath a foundation wall like it went under that wall."

"This wall is made of cinderblocks," Stump said, rising up. "Remember when we were in Kansas? Herbert said that cinderblocks weren't used much until the '30s or '40s."

"Yeah, I remember that."

"This building was constructed before anybody used cinderblocks."

"So, we have a cinderblock wall inside the original foundation wall," Xander said.

"And whoever built this wall went out of their way to cover up all the mortar joints and the coarse surface and smoothed it all out, and then painted all the walls so they'd all look the same."

"What's wrong with that?" James asked. "I bet lots of people paint their basement walls."

"Maybe if they use the area as living space, but this place is like a dungeon. Nobody comes down here, except for maintenance reasons."

"I see what you mean," Xander said. "There wouldn't be much justification for painting walls down here."

"That's right, and there are no doors in this wall and this building didn't need any extra support. I can only think of one person who'd want to put in a wall like that."

"Who, dude?"

"A little girl's father. If I had to bet, I'd say there's a body behind this wall."

"No shit? A dead one?"

"What kind of stupid question is that, bro?" Stump went quiet for ten full seconds, then smiled. "You know something, you guys? I think I know a way to scare up more business for Egg-Zaklee's than Zax can handle. But first I need a tape measure."

To confirm his theory, Stump soon measured the distance between the window and the block wall. After that he and

James and Xander went outside, where the drizzle had subsided, and measured the distance from the same window to the outside corner of the building. "I thought so," Stump said, with a toothy grin. "There's plenty enough space behind the block wall for a narrow room. Now I gotta call an old friend."

James smiled. "The TV guy?"

"Yep. Irv Wedlock."

Xander put his hands on his hips. "Will somebody please fill me in?"

68

An hour and a half later, Irv Wedlock of KLAC TV, whom Stump had met twice before, arrived with a cameraman in tow. Stump led them downstairs while the rest of the anxious Egg-Zaklee's crew gathered on the steps to see if Stump's suspicions would play out.

After the introductions, Irv spoke to Xander. "I wouldn't have dropped everything for just anybody, but Stump and I have a symbiotic history."

"So I hear. He gives you scoops. You give him publicity."

Irv nodded. "If there really is a body back there, I'll broadcast the story on the five-o'clock news. By tomorrow morning everybody will be clamoring for more."

"Okay," Stump said with his back to the block wall. "Let's do this."

"The cameraman flicked on both a bright light and his camera and zoomed in on Stump's face. "Go for it."

"Hello everybody," Stump said to the camera. "My name's Neal Randolph, but I go by Stump. We're in the basement of a new and really rad restaurant known as Egg-Zaklee's in downtown Carlsbad. A while back, a special friend told me that almost seventy years ago a little girl had disappeared in this area and we think we've found her right behind this wall. Earlier today, some of us were cleaning up rainwater around the bottom of this wall and saw some weird specks that looked out of place. We eventually figured out that this is a cinderblock wall that somebody plastered over to make it look flat. We wondered why anybody would do that for a useless basement.

"Now we're going to remove a few blocks to see if we're correct. We've already chipped away the mortar and loosened the blocks, so it shouldn't take long."

Both Stump and the cameraman knelt as Stump inserted his fingers around one of the lower blocks where the mortar had been removed. He slowly dragged it toward him until a new void in the wall revealed total darkness behind it.

After pushing the block aside, Stump looked into the camera again. "Irv Wedlock of this TV station, and the people who operate Egg-Zaklee's upstairs, where they have a radtastic breakfast menu, have urged me to preserve as much evidence as possible so the Carlsbad Police Department and their forensic team can do their work. Therefore, we're only going to remove enough blocks to verify our suspicions, and this one is next."

Once again, Stump jiggled a block until it too broke free from the wall and he could look again. "It's still too dark back there," he said, "but I think one more block will be enough for the cameraman to get a good angle for you."

Stump squatted and jiggled the block that had sat on top of the other two for generations until it too broke loose. He let it fall to the floor and pushed it away. "Now if my friend James will hand me a flashlight, I'll check it out."

Prepared for the moment, James moved into the camera's view and grinned before handing Stump the light. Stump shone it through the new opening and leaned down to get the very first view. "Oh my God," he said, pulling back and blowing out a deep breath for the camera. "It's gross, people. Don't look if you get sick easily." He rose and spoke once more to the camera. "There are two skeletons in there. One could be that little girl I mentioned before. By the time you see this, we will have called the police. It'll probably be a very long night around Egg-Zaklee's in downtown Carlsbad. If you want to find out how all this plays out, they're open for breakfast at six a.m. tomorrow."

Irv Wedlock moved toward Stump as the cameraman scanned the dark cavern and the bodies. "I'm going to have to edit your sales pitch quite a bit, Stump, but we'll make sure our viewers know where this went down. Now we gotta hustle. I'm gonna make this the lead story on the 5:00 news."

* * *

Less than an hour later, the TV crew had left and the cops had been called. "There they are," Michael said, going for the door where several shirts and ties showed up.

"Hello, detectives. I'm Michael McFadden, she said upon opening the outer door. She looked at the older investigator with the salt and pepper hair. "The victims are downstairs. I can show you the way and fill you in regarding how we found the bodies."

"I'm Sergeant Frelton," he said while head nodding to his African American associate. "He's Detective Cassidy. We heard there are two skeletons. Is that correct?"

"Yes. Our guys got a good look-see. They think two females have been entombed in a small room for 65 to 70 years."

"If that's true, whoever put them there has likely been dead for a long time."

"Anybody know who they are?" Cassidy asked.

"No names, but a grocer's daughter came up missing a long time ago. We think the younger one was that little girl. Based on the clothes, the other one is an adult woman."

"We'll still have to treat it as any other crime scene, but if all that checks out, I doubt we'll put many resources into the case, except to notify the next of kin—if we can find them."

"If that'll be all," Michael said, "I'll let you guys do your work and keep all the staff upstairs in case you want to ask any questions."

"Thank you, ma'am. We might do that. If we don't have any surprises we can wrap this up today."

"If you'd like a cup of coffee or anything, let us know."

"I'll take you up on that coffee right now," Frelton said. "It's been a long day."

While Frelton waited for his brew, the forensics team dragged everything from hazmat masks to sledgehammers downstairs. After some preliminary shuffling, Detective Cassidy came up from the basement and approached Stump and James and Xander. "Who took those blocks from that wall?"

Stump raised his hand.

"You shouldn't have done that. It's called tampering with evidence."

"We didn't tamper with anything."

"Yes, you did. That wall should have been disassembled from the top down. You weakened it. You'd better hope it doesn't collapse on the forensic guys and make the investigation more difficult."

James shook his head. "If we did that, dude, we would have had to take out even more blocks and stir up more dust and stand on rickety ladders to find out what was back there."

"That's why you should leave the work to the pros."

"Get real, dude. Your people had 70 years to solve the case but we figured it out in less than an hour. Do we have to show you how to disassemble a wall too?"

Sergeant Frelton smiled. "I'm sure everything will be okay, Detective."

"Hey, everybody," Zax loudly said from the back room where Denise kept a small TV. "Irv is coming on right now."

The Egg-Zaklee's gang hustled over just as Irv began his report. "This afternoon this reporter observed the discovery of two skeletons in the basement of a downtown Carlsbad restaurant, known as Egg-Zaklee's. Apparently two females had been encased in a makeshift tomb for over seven decades. Our sources tell us that the building was originally a grocery store. Back in the late '40s the daughter of the store manager disappeared. Nobody ever did find her, until now. We still don't know who the other person is, but she could be a mother or sister.

"Interestingly, Neal Randolph and James Nagle, the young men who found the bodies, have previously solved other big-time crimes. I wouldn't be surprised if they can figure out who killed these victims and add two more solved murders to their quivers. Not surprisingly, they're both students at the nearby college of criminology and they operate the most unique breakfast restaurant I've seen in years. I can personally recommend the banana omelet. Back to you, Karen."

"Fantabulous dude," James said to Stump, "We've almost solved two more murders—"

From a few feet away, one of the hazmat guys had returned. "We're in," he said to Sergeant Frelton. "We got two females—a young child and her mother. We also have this suicide note. It says the daughter was infected by the poliovirus and they didn't want to subject her to the 'gruesome' iron lung, as they called it. They also quote the sixth commandment—"

"Thou shalt not kill?"

"Right. Apparently the parents couldn't bring themselves to subject the little girl to a lifetime of torture in the iron lung, nor come right out and kill her—"

"So they chose to starve her to death. That's not much of a choice."

"Path of least resistance, I guess. If the coroner agrees with our conclusions, we can have the bodies removed tonight."

"Good plan."

It sure was. Now Stump could call Irv Wedlock with some new information and guarantee that Egg-Zaklee's would get another shout-out, this time on the 9:00 news.

69

While the rest of the Egg-Zaklee's staff waited to be interviewed, Stump and James hustled over to Catts McFadden's home to see if he knew the last name of the grocery store owner, which he didn't, but Catts recommended they check with the Carlsbad Historical Society. A little research revealed that the grocers' last name was Theisen. After turning over the name to the detectives, they had essentially solved the crime.

A little later the detectives interviewed the staff with most of the attention focused on Stump, James and Xander.

As expected, the coroner's office removed the skeletons an hour after sundown. By that time a small crowd of spectators had gathered on the sidewalk and another reporter dropped by.

Finally, at about midnight when Stump got back to his apartment, he had a rough time erasing the image of the two skeletons from his mind. Too tired to sleep, he checked Google for information regarding polio and discovered that some victims spent years on their backs in a barrel-like tube while the so-called "lung" moved air in and out just so they could breath—all of it with no hope of getting better. He felt genuine sadness for the grocer and his family.

At 4:00 a.m. and unable to get back to sleep, Stump thought of Xander's sleeping habits. Too bad everybody couldn't get by on just a few hours' sleep at a time. He threw off his covers and grabbed a shower.

After chomping down a couple crackers, he jumped in his Spider and drove to Egg-Zaklee's where he descended to the basement. It appeared as if the cops had blown off several frag grenades. Since the cops weren't going to clean up their mess, the debris was essentially Stump's problem. He sighed. It would take countless hours just to get to the point where he could sweep the floor. For lack of a better plan he carried multiple sets of broken cinderblocks up the stairs and out to the trash dumpsters.

Then, at a little past 5:00 a.m., Zax made her entrance with a very sleepy Denise tucked under her arm. "Another day, another dollar in the hole," she said.

"I hope not, Zax, for all of our sakes."

"After I take Denise back to her sleeping cot, I'll put on a pot of coffee."

A couple more trips up the stairs preceded the arrival of Michael, James and Yana. Stump closed off the basement and joined them in a lively rehashing of the events of the previous day and speculation on what effect the publicity might have on business. "Couldn't get much worse," James said, belaboring the obvious.

Zax chin-pointed to Yana. "The tables have gotten dusty. Can you wipe them down?"

As Yana began her tasks, a hint of daylight invaded the lower eastern sky.

"Everybody has the same responsibilities as yesterday," Zax said, "but if you see any obvious problems like dust on the glasses, or puddles on the floor, either take care of it yourself or tell me about it."

When they split up, two gentlemen knocked on the main

door. It may not have been six yet, but Stump sure as hell wasn't going to let any paying customers get away. He hustled over and let them in.

The taller guy's face lit up. "Hey, You're the fellow who found those bodies."

The other guy chimed in. "You reminded us of Geraldo Rivera when he thought he'd discovered Al Capone's vault, only you actually found something."

"Thanks, but it was more horrible than I expected."

"What do you recommend for breakfast?"

Really? Ears, meet music. "Everything is good. We have a great cook and two menus. If you're really hungry, you might try Stumpster's Dumpster from the creative menu. It's named after me. If you're traditional, there's a standard menu with all the typical items."

"I'll seat them," Yana said from behind Stump. She rushed to a pouch on the wall by the door where they kept menus. "Where would you gentlemen like to sit?"

Stump grinned as Yana took them into the dining area.

"You folks open yet?"

What the—? Stump turned to see a man and woman in the doorway. "Oh, yeah. We're open."

"We saw you on TV."

"I'm back, Stump," Michael said from near the kitchen. "I was helping Zax. How you folks doing today?" she asked.

Then somebody else came in and a group of four followed them. Stump glanced at his cell. Six o'clock, and four tables already buzzed with customers who'd seen the story on TV. He went to the kitchen to give Zax a high-five.

As the early morning unfolded, more people poured in and Stump did his best to answer the countless questions. *The little girl's name was Anita. She had polio. Yes, he was really disturbed when he saw the skeletons. No, you can't go downstairs and see the tomb.*

At 6:45 Xander walked in, scanned the dining area where half the tables already had paying customers. Stump grinned and rushed to greet him. "Dude. We're kicking ass. Six more parties and we'll have to make a waiting list."

"I can see that. Have you called Myles?"

"No. I've been too busy."

"I think he'd like to know. Should I ask Zax what to do?"

"Good idea," Stump said palming his phone to call Myles. "She needs help in the kitchen."

Then Michael rushed toward the door. "I'll be right back. I might be able to get a couple of the homeless guys to do dishes."

The pace remained intense throughout the morning and countless more questions arose. *Do you deliver? Is your menu on-line? What's upstairs? Are you taking applications?*

At just past eleven, Myles and Katherine arrived to get a late breakfast and check things out. Myles's beaming grin inspired Stump to snag a few pictures and savor the two hours that they hung around.

It wasn't until just after 3:00 that the chaos died down and the crew could gather their wits. "Wow. That was crazy," Stump said while he and Xander happily chomped down a waffle and eggs. "I've only slept a few hours in two days and I'm beat."

Xander smiled. "Be careful what you wish for."

"Yeah, no shit. And the college students aren't even back in town yet."

"Once word gets out, you should be in pretty good shape."

"You know something. Now that I know I'll have some reliable income out of this place, I've been rethinking about that fracking deal of yours again."

"We can discuss it with Myles, but I'm pretty sure we'll want to see you finish the upper floors on this building first."

70

"**I** needed this," Stump said while he and Michael drove to Mitzy's Massage Therapy Studio. "You'd think with Egg-Zaklee's under control, I could relax a bit, but—"

"What about going to classes?" she asked. "At one point you said you were going to get back into it. That must take a lot of time too."

"It does, and it's so damn boring I just do the bare minimum. I'd rather spend that time with Grandma Pauline and try to figure out how to keep her and Minnie Moore together."

There was something else he hadn't done: make a legitimate attempt to grow his relationship with Michael. Naturally, he'd thought of it a lot, especially when he was alone in bed at night. But their age difference made it awkward, which was one of the reasons he'd recommended they get professional massages together. Something like that had to have sensual overtones and might give him a better idea if she'd relate to him in a carnal way. When she agreed to go, he couldn't wait.

"I know what you mean," she said. "It's been two weeks since we found those bodies and I've only had one other day off. The next day I had to cover for Zax while she took a day off. If it weren't for these little adventures with you I'd probably go crazy."

"I hope you don't mind," he said, "but when I made our appointment, I booked us both in one room. The lady said they keep everything discreet."

"That's good, cause if you ever saw me naked you'd pluck out thine eyes."

Stump had already imagined that wonderful possibility and his mind's eyes were all for it. "Why's that?" he asked wanting to hear more about her naked body.

"Are you kidding me? Self-esteem. Women are notoriously worried about their bodies. In addition to our facial problems, we think we're too fat or our necks are too long or our thighs are too big. The daughter of one of my old girlfriends thought her vagina was horribly ugly, so when she was 13 she secretly took a selfie of it and sent the picture to a site run by medical experts who deal with young women who need that particular reassurance."

Appreciating Michael's openness, Stump snickered. "Don't tell James about that. He might want to start a site like that of his own."

"That wouldn't surprise me. Regarding our massage, I hope that one of our physical therapists is male."

"I got one of each, but I thought you'd prefer a woman."

"No way. The men have stronger hands."

"So, you've done this before?"

"A few times," she said tapping her gym bag. "That's why I brought my headphones. The combination of soft music, scented lotion and a therapist's magic fingers is absolutely heavenly."

Shortly thereafter, they made their way into the reception area where fresh-cut eucalyptus stems were packed in tall vases, and soft jazz drifted down from ceiling speakers. Behind a counter, a middle-aged woman in a flowery summer dress shook her head so her shoulder-length hair would fan away from her eyes. "Help you?" she asked.

"I'm Stump Randolph. We have an appointment for 10:00."

She glanced at a laptop. "Deep tissue massage?"

"Yeah. This is Michael McFadden."

"I have you down for our 30-minute service. For just a few dollars more you can upgrade to 45 minutes and get a free foot massage."

Stump glanced at Michael, who raised her eyebrows. "I'd love that. I'm on my feet a lot."

"Okay then," the receptionist said, handing them flip-flops. "The locker rooms are right over there. Hot robes and towels are provided."

"Am I supposed to take a shower first?" Stump asked.

"It's up to you. Some do. Some don't." She turned to Michael. "Bras are optional, but most of our clients don't wear them because they are always covered by a sheet."

Michael grinned. "I wouldn't want any unnecessary restrictions."

"Alright then. You can wear whatever you want under your robes."

"What do most guys do?" Stump quizzed.

"Varies. About half the people wear their undies. We have an elderly client who wears her pajamas. It doesn't really matter to any of us. You'll be covered all the time, anyway. When you're dressed the way you want, step into the relaxation lounge. From there your therapist will lead you to your treatment room."

In the spotless locker room, Stump stripped down to his boxers and wrapped a heated, blue terrycloth robe around his shoulders. He tied the belt and glanced at himself in a large dressing mirror. He couldn't help thinking that Michael was on the other side of that very mirror and stripping down too, which awakened his penis.

Seconds later, in the relaxation lounge, a 50ish woman, wrapped in a robe, sat in one of several couches. Low lighting, scented candles, nature sounds and two tables loaded with gourmet cheese, crackers, cookies, fruit and chocolates completed the mood. Stump took a cookie and sat across from the woman. Moments later Michael came in and sat next to him.

Almost instantly another door opened and a male, presumably a masseur, invited the other woman to follow him.

"That was weird," Stump said to Michael. "I couldn't look straight ahead because that woman might have thought I was trying to look up her robe."

Michael chuckled. "Well, I doubt if she would have let you see anything."

The door opened yet again and Stump and Michael were escorted to the *couple's room* where two therapy tables rested ten feet apart and toe-to-toe. "I'm Vernon. She's Naomi," a handsome tanned man with an accent said.

"We changed our mind," Stump said. "Michael wants the man cause he has stronger hands."

Michael nodded. "If that's okay?"

For the next forty minutes, Stump listened to nature sounds while Naomi moved the sheet around and rubbed lotion on the bulk of his body. She softly reminded him to relax and enjoy how good it should feel. Meanwhile, based on the non-stop "oohs" coming from Michael's table, it sounded as if she got a lot more out of it than Stump did.

"Okay," Vernon finally said in a soft voice. "Time for that foot massage. Lie on your backs and lift your knees."

After a cushion was placed under Stump's legs, Naomi took his left foot and slowly rubbed lotion deep between his toes and up to his ankles. Having ticklish feet, he had a difficult time concentrating.

Before long, at the other table, Michael's repeated whimpers of pleasure about drove Stump nuts. "Oh, that feels so good. Keep doing it," she groaned as if she were on the verge of having an orgasm.

All of it caught Stump off-guard. This place was supposed

to leave him feeling rejuvenated and relaxed, but the opposite happened. Relieved to be covered by a sheet, he hoped Naomi couldn't detect his untimely erection.

71

Two days later, in a class with James about the court system, Stump's mind wandered back to the massages and Michael's regrets about her body. He smiled. In the time he'd known her he had looked her over pretty well, and didn't see anything to complain about. He hoped that someday soon he could rub her back and, from there, find out for himself exactly what she meant.

"Mr. Randolph . . ."

James nudged Stump.

The professor's steely eyes looked right at him. "Are you paying attention, Mr. Randolph? Which court would best fit the case under discussion."

Uh oh. "Er . . . I guess I wasn't listening," Stump said, knowing his face was red.

"Your grades aren't very impressive, Mr. Randolph. If you want to pass this course, I suggest you come to class more often and pay attention when you're here." The professor turned to James. "How about you Mr. Nagel? Which court would be appropriate for the case in question?"

"The County Court."

"Correct. At least somebody is doing his work."

Later that afternoon Stump picked up Michael so they could visit her father. "I'm glad you're getting a lot of repeat business," he said, referring to Egg-Zaklee's.

"You were right about the publicity and the menu. The customers love it and come back. There are also plenty of referrals. Some people ask if they can go downstairs to see the *tomb*."

"Now you're making me think we should let them go look."

"I wouldn't. I think it's more mysterious with the *Do Not Enter* sign on the door. By the way, I want to thank you for coming with me to see Daddy. He likes you."

"I like him too – and most elderly people – I think their experiences are interesting."

A few minutes later, Michael reached for the brass knocker on her father's door. She smiled at Stump. "Daddy always tells me to come right on in, but I don't want to startle him. His heart isn't the greatest."

They waited to hear Catts's footsteps, but this time the foyer remained silent. Another knock proved equally fruitless. Michael drew her eyebrows together. "This isn't good. I'll have to use my key."

Her usually steady fingers trembled as she inserted the key and pushed the door open. Inside, the door leading into the main room where Catts performed his ceremonies had been closed tight. "Daddy? You okay? It's me and Stump," she said before sliding one of the doors into the wall pocket. Back in the corner Mr. McFadden sat in an armchair with elbows on his knees and his head shaking back and forth in his hands.

"Daddy? Are you okay?" Michael repeated. "What's wrong?"

Catts finally lifted his head revealing a folded piece of paper in one hand. "I guess I might as well tell you. They're going to throw me in jail."

"Who?"

"The court." He handed her the paper. "They say I can only have four pusses - but I can't get rid of my babies."

Michael scanned the paper. "Oh, my God. They're only giving him ten days."

Stump glanced at Catts, whose eyes were bloodshot.

"Not only that. They want me to have a veterinarian certify that the final four have been neutered."

"That shouldn't be a problem," Stump said. "You were a veterinarian, weren't you?"

Catts shook his head and sighed. "That's not good enough. I'm not licensed anymore."

"Well, I'd think they still have to give you more time than that. Nobody could find homes for that many animals in ten days."

"You guys don't understand," Catts whispered as he reached under his chair and pulled out a shoebox full of mail. "NOTICE" was in large print on the top letter. "They've been after me for months."

"Who has, Daddy?"

"Everybody. The neighbors. The government. I'm surprised you two don't hassle me."

"We wouldn't do that, Mr. McFadden. That would be like breaking up your family and we both know what that's like." Stump looked through the top few pages in the box and pulled one out. "This one says you had a court hearing a month ago. What happened then?"

"I don't know. I didn't go."

"But Daddy, you never said anything about any of this. Did you think the problem was going to go away on its own?"

Stump looked through more letters. Several were about animal hoarding. A private party said he had "at least a hundred" cats, but that person must not have known that many of them were *preserved*. Another letter simply called him *disgusting*. "Here's a notice from the Health Department dated last year," Stump said. "Didn't you call them to work something out?"

Catts sat motionless. "I knew what they wanted but the no-kill shelters kept calling me to take on more pusses and I couldn't say no. What would you two do if somebody told you that you couldn't see each other any longer?"

Good point. Stump knew exactly what that was like. That's why he fought so hard to keep Grandma Pauline and Minnie Moore together.

A complete examination of the papers exposed all the buzzwords—residential regulations, *Department of Environmental Protection, Health Department, nuisance, stiff fines and jail.* "This looks pretty bad, but I bet there's a good chance you could get an extension if you hire an attorney."

"What's the use? They're all in cahoots."

"What about your commercial building?" Stump asked. Could you keep your animals if you move them over there?"

"That won't work. I couldn't leave them alone at night and the neighbors would accuse me of negligence."

"We could put in surveillance cameras, Daddy. Then you could keep an eye on them when you're not over there."

"That's not the same. What if you were a mother and couldn't sleep in the same house as your kids? A surveillance camera wouldn't make you feel any better."

Stump raised a hand. "What if you moved over there too?"

"It's not set up for anything like that and I couldn't afford to make all the necessary changes."

"That's ridiculous, Daddy. I've seen your bank account. You've got enough money to put up a few walls and make a small apartment."

"That would wipe out all my reserves."

"Couldn't you sell this house, Mr. McFadden? You could use that money and still have some left over."

"I can't do that. I have too many memories here, and what if I had to move back? I'd be screwed. Besides, I've already looked into it. If I were to move into that building, it would become my residence and I'd have the exact same problem. You can't have that many pusses in your residence."

"I don't know much about this kind of thing, Mr. McFadden, but I have worked with some lawyers and some City Council members when I was in high school. They tried to find ways to help people. Some of them even worked for free. If you don't mind, Michael and I could see if we can find somebody who'd help you."

Michael nodded. "Stump's pretty smart, Daddy. It couldn't hurt."

"I don't want to lose my babies."

This time, the dampness in Catts McFadden's eyes blurred the redness.

72

"Edna Kline is gonna break my grandma's heart if she splits them up," Stump explained to Michael en route to Meadowlark Flats.

"At least that's one problem Daddy won't have if he would like to live in a place like that. He can definitely afford it."

"I've thought about paying Minnie's expenses so she wouldn't have to leave, but Myles said if I help every struggling person I meet, others will come out of the woodwork and I'll be broke, too. Then I can't help anybody."

"That makes sense, so what are you going to do?"

"Just enjoy my grandma as much as I can while she's still happy. I just wish that story about Minnie's gold coins would have proved true."

A little later they gathered in a meeting room with a staffer named Josie and discussed the possibility of Catts moving to Meadowlark Flats. After hearing about Catts's situation Josie said, "We'd be glad to have him, but we only allow two cats per apartment."

Michael sighed. "That would be a lot easier on everybody."

"I think he'd fit nicely in the Independent Living section. I don't have anything I can show you over there right now but we can see an apartment in the Canary building. They're almost identical."

"I just hope they're not too small," Michael said.

Moments later, Josie opened the door to the second-floor of the assisted living section where a chunky woman wearing nothing but baggy white granny panties spread her arms unashamedly and asked, "Do you guys know where I put my bathrobe?"

Stump covered his eyes and spun around.

"Hi there, Mrs. Duncan," Josie said, calmly. "Let's step back into your apartment; I'll help you find your bathrobe."

No more than a minute later, Josie returned. "Mystery solved. The robe was in her hamper."

"I'm impressed," Michael said. "You helped the woman without making her feel bad."

"Kindness is always the best option."

Both Stump and Michael nodded.

After checking out the vacant apartment, they wandered back toward the center of the complex when Michael pointed to a beautiful turn-of-the-century loveseat with a classy flowery material. "There are a lot of striking decorations in here," she said. "I can see why so many people like it."

"Well, thank you. Family members of the residents have donated most of the older pieces. Many of those pieces take on a museum-like quality and everybody likes museums."

"I sure do." Michael said, causing Stump to halt.

"You know something, you guys? You gave me an idea. I need to make an important call. I can catch up to you in a few minutes." After sitting on a loveseat, Stump checked with Google and made a call to a legal hot line. After registering as "The Stumpster," a chat chain began.

ATTY14: *Hello Stumpster. I'm Josh. How can I help you?*

The Stumpster: *A friend of mine has dozens of cats. He's even stuffed a lot of them after they died because he's an amateur taxidermist. He's not a pet hoarder or anything like that. He's just a man who likes his animals.*

ATTY14: *Okay I understand. What's the issue?*

The Stumpster: *The government says he has to get rid of most of the live ones because he's keeping them all in his own house.*

ATTY14: *Cities and counties usually have laws governing how many pets people can have in their homes.*

The Stumpster: *That's what my friend said, but he also owns a nice old building in downtown Carlsbad, where there are stores and office buildings and bars. Do you think he could keep all of his animals over there? I was thinking he might call it a museum, especially since some of them are mounted.*

ATTY14: *Wouldn't be any problem with the stuffed ones. What about the others? You'd probably have to have some legitimate commercial purpose to keep that many of them.*

The Stumpster: *Like a shelter? He gives some of them away. We could call that an adoption center or foster program.*

ATTY14: *That might work. A veterinarian's office might be another possibility. I suggest you call the zoning department. If you need an attorney, let us know. We can refer somebody.*

Moments later Stump rushed to find Michael to tell her the good news. "All we gotta do," he eventually said, "is call it a museum and adoption shelter. I got the idea when you and Josie were talking about museums. I can help him move. So can some of the homeless guys."

Michael looked him in the eyes. "Nobody else gets Daddy like you do." She took his hand and whispered. "I just love that about you."

Stump may not have been as bright as a trucker's high beams, but he was smart enough to recognize the affection in her eyes and the softness in her tone. He gently reached for her shoulders and pulled her to him. Their arms wrapped naturally around each other and their lips drew together. The tenderness and her subtle sigh confirmed that their relationship had reached a new level, something more than *just friends*. He thought about inviting her into Grandma Pauline's suite, but that would be too crass. He opted instead to wait for a more appropriate time and place, when they could savor a longer and deeper experience.

He pulled gently away and whispered, "You're a rad kisser. You know that?"

"Sometimes, it comes naturally."

He took her hand and slowly led her toward the peacock pictures and the Memory Care wing. Nearly there, the receptionist spoke through smiling lips. "Your grandmother is in the Community room. She's laughing it up with Tamara."

How could that be? "Laughing? My grandma doesn't have the capacity to know when something is funny."

"Oh yes she does. Go on in."

As suggested, off to the right, in the big room, Tamara, wearing a puffy multi-colored blouse, had a half-dozen residents, including Grandma Pauline and Minnie Moore, spread across two couches and literally laughing out loud.

"How sweet," Michael said. "Let's go see what's so funny."

As Stump and Michael closed in, Tamara pointed to one of the laughing ladies, at which point the others looked at that woman and giggled like schoolchildren, after which Tamara directed a finger toward Minnie Moore. Once again, heads turned and happy faces erupted.

Anxious to see what was going on, Michael and Stump joined the tribe where Tamara had painted up her face to look like the happiest clown at the circus. With a large foam nose, two-inch circles of white make-up around her eyes and enough bright red makeup on her lips and entire jaw area, she couldn't have looked any sillier. That, along with some goofy hand and body gestures, genuinely amused her couch audience. "Okay, everybody," she said upon seeing Stump and Michael, and removing her foam nose, "I've got to clean up and get back to work now." She tapped Grandma Pauline's arm. "Lucky you. Your grandson is here."

"Did he bring my Christmas cards?"

Since it was June, Stump had no idea what she meant.

"Glad to see you again," Tamara said to Stump while dragging a tissue across her jaw.

"Are you auditioning to become one of your own clients?" he asked with a grin of his own.

Tamara smiled. "When I act silly, somebody usually smiles, too. Then I point at that person and the other people see the happy faces and they follow suit. Before long they're all giggling just because everybody else is."

Stump nodded. "You got me, too."

"See what I mean?" she said, turning toward Michael. "Who's our guest?"

"I'm Michael McFadden. I came to see if your facilities would be a good fit for my father, but the suites are too small."

"I hope he finds something he likes. Why don't we gather Pauline and Minnie? We can all move over to the couch by the window and talk for a while – that is, if you'll give me a few minutes to clean up."

While everybody was shuffling across the room, Grandma Pauline glared at Michael. "Are you Ellen? Cause you don't get any of my money."

"No, Grandma," Stump said with a quick pause. Given the kiss of minutes earlier, he wondered if he should refer to Michael as his girlfriend. "This is my special friend, Michael. She wanted to meet you."

73

Tamara cleaned up, then returned and pulled Stump to the side. "I probably shouldn't say anything, but I think you ought to know that Edna snapped at Minnie Moore and your grandmother again, mostly Minnie Moore."

Stump scrunched his eyebrows. "About what? Why would she do that?"

"Same old thing. Minnie started talking about the farm and coins. I understand Edna's basic frustration. Many Memory Care residents get stuck on a particular topic but the staff members don't get shook up about it; except Edna when Minnie discusses her farm life, which Minnie does quite a bit."

Stump. "Did you tell Opal Clemens?"

"Minnie's sister-in-law? No. It just happened this morning and Minnie has forgotten all about it. This whole coin story is why I try to keep Minnie distracted with other things, such as the clown act."

He smiled at her as they moved toward Michael, Minnie Moore and Grandma Pauline. "I'm glad you're here. It's a lot harder to be a professional caregiver than I realized."

"Thanks," she said, as a delivery truck pulled to the curb

and cast a shadow through the window. "Not everybody understands that."

Minnie pointed to the new shadow and perked up. "Me-Ma will be here in a minute."

Tamara grinned. "Shadows from windows, like that always remind Minnie of her mornings in Kansas, when she was a little girl and a giant tree casted shadows on her bedroom window."

"I know exactly which tree she means. I stood on that stump." Suddenly something occurred to Stump: He looked at the window again. He was facing south, and would have been looking into the sun were it not for the truck on the other side. The same thing would have been true for Minnie's bedroom window. To get morning shade, it would have been on the west side of that tree. But when he was standing on that stump, Herbert pointed to the north and the crumbled house was behind them and off to the east. Either Mrs. Moore was wrong or—. He spoke to Minnie Moore. "Are you sure you got shade in the mornings?"

Minnie Moore nodded. "Just when I was little."

"That confirms it, Michael."

"Confirms what?"

The only way Minnie could have seen shadows on her bedroom window in the mornings was if her house had been on the west side of that tree. But I saw the window area in that old house. The window was to the east, not the west."

"So what?"

"It means that Herbert was mistaken when he speculated that P-Pa had built both houses on the same spot."

Tamara rose. "If you guys will excuse me I have some other chores I need to attend."

"Thanks for being so nice to my grandma," Stump said before excitedly returning his attention to Michael. "It all makes sense, now. P-Pa clearly constructed the latter home where it would get the benefit of the much-needed afternoon shade."

"Again. So what?"

"So the first house — the one that provided shade to Minnie's bedroom window — had to be on the other side of that tree. I think everybody has been looking in the wrong place for those coins. Furthermore, that opens up new possibilities regarding where the coins and the papers about the magic cows might have been hidden, especially since it's apparent that they never were in the well."

Michael tilted her head. "I guess shadows don't lie."

"They sure don't. If I can share all this with Edna Kline, which will be like walking on eggshells, she might allow Minnie Moore to hang around long enough for us to go get those coins. If they're worth enough we won't have to break up Minnie and my grandma."

"You go ahead," Michael said while smiling at Minnie Moore and Grandma Pauline. "I'd like to hang with these nice ladies a little bit."

"Are you my daughter?"

"No ma'am, I'm Stump's girlfriend. My name is Michael."

Minutes later Stump joined Edna Kline in her office. "Good news, Mrs. Kline. I know how we can pay Minnie Moore's bill."

"Unless you're paying it for her, I'm afraid the last few grains of sand have just about left her hourglass."

"But this is different. I realize you don't like us talking about those coins, but when a truck went by the window, Minnie mentioned morning shadows on her bedroom windows and I figured out that everybody has been looking in the wrong place for them."

Mrs. Kline must have been in a good mood because this time she didn't shut him down. Grateful to have a chance to explain, Stump elaborated on the things he'd learned when he and Xander went to the land, and how that related to the shadow in the hallway.

Finally Edna sat forward. "None of that makes any difference. If there ever was a bottle, it was in the well, so it doesn't matter whether there was another house or not."

338

"I've been thinking about that too. When Xander and I were out there we were invited into the neighbor's cabin. He went into a root cellar to get some cold beers. All the houses had root cellars in the old days."

"And you think Minnie's coins are in the root cellar of the first house?"

"Has to be. Root cellars are nearly indestructible and P-Pa had no reason to destroy or abandon the one under the original home following the first tornado. Then the second home was built on the other side of the tree and the second tornado killed P-Pa and Me-Ma and nobody knew to look for the coins, except Minnie, but she was very young and sworn to secrecy. After that, decades of heavy winds covered everything up. By the time Herbert moved out there, all signs of the oldest place had been hidden beneath new dirt. Now all I need is ten days or so to help somebody move; then I can go get those coins, which might be valuable enough to keep Mrs. Moore and my grandma together for a long time. And this time I know not to say anything to Minnie Moore and make her anxious."

Edna Kline paused a minute. Then, "You wait here, I have to attend something in another office. I'll be right back."

While she was gone, Stump crossed his fingers and hoped he'd finally figured out how to keep Minnie Moore and Grandma Pauline together. Several minutes later Edna returned and nodded. "I've thought it over. Call me tomorrow morning and I'll see if I can give you a little grace period."

Stump blew out a deep breath. "Thanks a lot, Mrs. Kline. I hope this proves I'm not a kook. I'm pretty sure I can find that bottle. Then we just have to hope those coins are valuable."

Pleased with himself, Stump hustled back to the couch where he and Michael and Grandma Pauline and Minnie Moore happily spent the better part of an hour trying to figure out if Michael was really Ellen and if Stump had seen the Christmas cards. Then when Stump and Michael piled into his Fiat and headed home they'd barely pulled into traffic when

Stump observed a vaguely familiar light-blue van approach from the opposite direction. He slowed dramatically and waited for the van to pass. As he expected it turned onto the driveway of Meadowlark Flats. "That diabolical bitch," he shouted as he smacked the top of his steering wheel.

"Who?" Michael asked.

"Edna Kline. That's who."

"Why? What did she do?"

"I'll tell you what she did. A while back she convinced me that she didn't want me stirring up the coin story because it was psychologically damning to Minnie Moore, but that was all bullshit."

"Huh? Why?"

"That van changes everything, Michael. I saw that exact same van when Xander and I were on the dirt road by Minnie's farm. Xander even waved at the driver. That guy has to be a partner."

"Partner for what?"

"No wonder she was being so nice to me in her office. She was baiting me for information and now I know why. Edna has believed Minnie's story all along and wants those coins for herself. Well she can't have them. What a lying bitch."

74

"Bro," Stump said the second James answered his phone. "Michael and I just left Grandma Pauline and I need your help."

"Okay. 'Sup?"

"I figured out where that bottle of coins is. We gotta get out there now and get it, asap."

"To Kansas? Can't, dude. That'd take three or four days, at least, and I promised Yana we'd go shopping for baby clothes after she gets off work. Let's do it in a couple weeks when—"

"This can't wait, bro. I screwed up big time. I told Edna Kline what I discovered, thinking she would let Minnie Moore hang around until I could go get the coins and pay Minnie's bill."

"I take it she didn't believe you?"

"It's the opposite."

"Great. So what's the panic?"

"I knew that woman was up to something and now I know what it is; turns out the righteous Edna Kline has believed Minnie all along and she wants those coins for herself. She's got a partner, too—some guy in a blue van. I saw that exact same van when Xander and I went on our trip. Michael and I just saw it again, pulling into Meadowlark Flats."

"There are a lot of blue vans, dude."

"Not like this one. It's an odd sky-blue shade, has a dent in the fender and big chrome rims. That's DNA-type odds. I'm telling you, it's the same van and Edna and her partner want to get those coins."

"Okay. So it's the same van, but what makes you so sure Edna and her partner aren't just trying to help Minnie too?"

"Think about it, bro. She's been discouraging me from going out there from day one. Then when she heard about my discovery, the van magically showed up an hour later and she gave me a bunch of time to go find Minnie's coins. Why would she do all that?"

"I see what you mean. She gives you plenty of time so you won't be in a rush and that allows her partner to get there first."

"You got it, dude. We gotta go to Kansas now. My grandma's life depends on it. We should take guns too."

"What?" Michael yelped in Stump's ear. "Are you nuts? That's the last thing you guys should do. Somebody could get hurt over a few coins. That's stupid."

"Just a minute, dude, I gotta talk with Michael." Stump turned to Michael. "We gotta take guns, just for self-defense. I can't let anybody steal money that would save my grandma's life."

"You're being overly dramatic, Stump. You don't even know if there's anything out there and I heard Minnie Moore talk. She's not exactly lucid."

"My grandma gets like that too, but there's usually some underlying truth to what they say and Minnie has been saying the same thing for years. It has to be true."

"No, it doesn't and I'm not going to let you run head-first into a gun fight. You don't know a damn thing about warfare."

After several more minutes of heated debate, Stump retuned to his primary point. "Well, I have to have the guns 'cause everybody else around there has them."

Michael sighed. "You guys don't know anything about using guns in real-life situations and I'm not going to let you two idiots get killed."

"I keep telling you the guns are just for self- defense."

"And I keep telling you; that's the way people get hurt. If you insist on taking weapons, then I have to go with you and I have a hell of a lot of other things I'd rather do."

"We'll be okay, Michael. Honest."

"You're not listening to me. Gun fights aren't video games. I could never forgive myself if one of you idiots gets hurt or killed. People who live in areas like that know of places they can hide bodies. How would that help your grandmother? Huh?"

"My grandma is the most important person in the world to me and I'm going if I have to go alone; and I'm going to take Pops, so I can take tools and a cot. If James goes, we can take turns driving. If we can get there before the van, there won't be any shooting."

Michael shook her head and sighed. "You're a couple of friggin' air heads, but I can't let you go alone."

"You still there, dude?" Stump asked James. "Michael's going, too."

"Yeah, I heard. I know how important this is to you. I'm in, too. I'll just have to make it up to Yana when we get back."

"Good, bro. If we take turns driving and sleeping we can probably get back in four days. I gotta talk with Minnie's sister-in-law and get some tools and gas, so let's meet at Egg-Zaklee's at 5:00 tomorrow morning."

"Okay. That'll give me some time to smooth things over with Yana."

Stump hung up and spoke to Michael. "When we get back I'll hire some guys to help get your father moved into his other building."

"All this for pocket change? This is friggin' nuts."

"It's not about coins, Michael. It's about the well-being of two elderly women who need us."

* * *

The next morning, Michael slipped into the under-sized bucket seat on the rider's side of Pops. "I still think this is ridiculous," she said. "I should be staying here, helping Zax and Daddy."

James stuck his head forward. "You got it easy. I'm the one sitting on the floor of a cargo area, between a bunch of shovels and all this other crap."

"You'd better hope we don't have to use those shovels to dig our own graves."

"As far as I'm concerned," Stump said, hitting a blinker, "this is one of the most important things I've done my entire life and you're both heroes for helping me save my grandma and Minnie Moore."

Michael turned in Stump's direction. "Now that we've got all the preliminary bitching out of the way, what do we do now?"

"It's obvious that Edna and her partner have already invested time and money into finding those gold coins so they won't give up now. Fortunately for us, she thinks I won't leave for ten days and I want her to keep thinking that. That way the van guy might not leave for a day or two. He'll also take at least two days to get there, maybe three. Meanwhile, we can drive straight through by taking shifts."

"Good thinking, bro, just like the old days."

"I called Minnie's relative, Opal Clemens, to verify if this trip was worth all the effort. Opal said her husband Ronnie always believed there were a couple dozen coins, some of them gold. Each one could be worth tens of thousands or more to coin collectors."

"I hope so," Michael said, showing a hint of softening.

344

"Your grandmother and Minnie need each other. If it weren't for that and the potential for you dingbats to get hurt—"

Stump grinned. "Did I tell you guys about the magic cows?"

"Not really," Michael said, after which the bullshit resumed for several hours until they came upon a road sign about Vegas, which prompted James to make a comment about classy prostitutes.

Michael clucked her tongue, "Your girlfriend is going to have your baby in a few months. Why the hell are you talking about prostitutes?"

"Yeah, dude," Stump said. "That kind of physical gratification is a sign of desperation."

"You gotta be shitting me," James said. "Some of those women are gorgeous and they know all the tricks."

"I hope you're just kidding, dude, but I don't think married people should talk like that."

"If a single person wants a quick outlet and somebody else can use the money," Michael said, "I don't really see a drawback, but I get Stump's point: Relationships are more fulfilling."

"More problems, too," James said before the conversation morphed into something else and something else after that until they made their first pit stop.

While James refueled Pops, Michael slipped off to the restroom and Stump called Meadowlark Flats. A brief conversation with the receptionist revealed that the man in the blue van was Edna Kline's son and had a full-time job. After that Stump left a message on Edna Kline's voicemail affirming it would be at least ten days before he could get back to Minnie's farm.

Back on the road, they'd switched drivers. Stump took the cot in the cargo area and just about fell to sleep when he got a call. "It's that attorney I talked with yesterday. Hello?"

A few minutes later, Stump hung up. "Good news, Michael.

Josh confirmed that the zoning does indeed allow your father to move all of his animals to his other building as long as he runs some sort of a business, like a hybrid museum and pet shelter. I asked him to see if he could get an extension for your dad to move."

"What did he say about that?"

"He's looking into to it, but he's going to have to charge us this time."

"Well, that's okay, especially if he can buy us a little more time. I don't know how to thank you, Stump."

Stump could have made a recommendation, but that would have been too much like something tactless James might have done.

75

Later, barely asleep, Stump was wondering if he'd ever have a good opportunity to sleep with Michael. Then he felt Pops sway through a long gradual curve, indicating they'd made it to I-70. With his headphones slightly off-kilter, he heard James and Michael talking from the front seats.

"She didn't want me to go on this trip," James said, obviously speaking of Yana. "She said a daddy should be near his family."

"She has a good point, James."

"I know, but other people have to leave home for their work from time to time. She should understand that. Instead, she said I was too compulsive and if I go, she'd be gone when I get back, but I think she was just being dramatic."

"Oh, my God, James. If it was that important to her I don't think you should've left her."

"You did the same thing. You left your dad behind without resolving his legal matters. What's the difference?"

"Simple. He's not carrying my baby and he just has to move his animals."

"Well, there was something else. We haven't been getting along in the bedroom lately. That's only supposed to happen in the first trimester."

"That's all the more reason to be with her, James. She needs you."

He sighed, "I guess you're right. I was just caught up in the excitement. Maybe I shouldn't have come. I gotta apologize," he said, tapping at his cell.

Stunned by James's comments, and feeling sorry for his buddy, Stump had a goofy idea that might get James's mind off his woes for a while. He sat up and removed his headphones. "I needed that nap. How's Pops running?"

"Welcome back, sleepy head," Michael said via her rearview mirror. "It's running fine, but we'll need gas soon."

James turned in Stump's direction. "While you were out we decided to get a metal detector. I checked. We can rent one in Denver."

"Good idea."

Michael lifted one hand off the wheel and exercised her fingers. "We used detectors in combat areas to find IEDs." She shook her head. "That was gruesome stuff."

Stump cringed at the thought of somebody stepping on an exploding canister. "Now that we're eight hours away from home," he said, "I can tell you guys about something else that crossed my mind."

"What's that?"

"Minnie's father could have hidden the coins in a hole we haven't talked about yet. Remember when I said that Xander and I helped Herbert, the neighbor, move his outhouse?"

"Whoa, there, brofriend," James said, checking his phone. "I hope you're not suggesting that the coins could be in the pit of an outhouse because—"

"It's not impossible."

Michael stretched the fingers on her other hand. "Ya gotta admit that would be one place nobody would want to look."

"Well, I can tell you this," James said, shaking his head.

"I ain't sticking my arm in somebody else's shit pot. Ain't happening. No way. Not me. No how!"

Michael grinned. "This coming from a daddy who'll be up to his elbows in itty bitty kiddy shitty before long."

James shot Michael a full nod. "That's a good one, dudette."

"Relax, bro. We're talking about 75 years ago. If P-Pa really did do that, the poop soup would have dried up by now. I doubt we can even find it."

"Especially since I ain't looking for it."

Having successfully shifted the subject away from James's relationship difficulties, Stump silently pumped his fist and the conversations reverted to more benign topics until they closed in on the Colorado state line.

James checked his cell another time before making a predictable remark. "Say, Michael. Weed is legal here, but I ain't 21. If I give you a hundred bucks—"

"No way. It's too much like alcohol and I've seen what substance abuse can do to people. I worked in a bar. Remember."

"But it's just for medicinal purposes."

"I call b.s." Stump said instantly.

"I've tried it," Michael said, "but it makes me sleepy and hungry and I don't need the extra calories. If I'm going to do that, I'd rather just enjoy a good bottle of wine."

Stump tapped James on the shoulder. "Besides, you've got a girlfriend and kid to think about. You shouldn't be burning your money on weed."

James grabbed his cell. "I gotta text Yana again and tell her I'm sorry."

"It looks like we're going to have to make a decision, fellows," Michael said. "That rental place we talked about is open from 7:00 a.m. to 7:00 p.m. There's no way we're going to make it before closing. If we really want a metal detector, we gotta get a room somewhere and be there at seven in the morning, when they open."

* * *

"That's the first time I've slept in the same bed with a dude since I was a little kid," Stump said the next morning as they drove to *Big Del's Rentals.*

Michael shook her head. "What are you complaining about? I had to use the cot."

"It's your own fault," James reminded her while examining his cell for the millionth time. "I told you to pay for two rooms instead of registering as a single."

"And I told you if I had to front the money for our rooms then I got to choose the rooms and I went for a single cause I didn't see any reason to throw the extra money away."

"Yeah, but Stump said he was going to reimburse you."

"Too late now. Besides, I've slept in worse places."

A little later, Stump piled a rental detector on top of their other gear in the cargo area and then slid into the rider's seat.

"I'm glad we did this," Michael said while knocking on the detector from the cargo area. "It could save us a ton of time."

James shook his cell phone and blew out a breath of frustration. "What do you think, Michael? Do you suppose Yana will accept my apology?"

Michael curled her lower lip. "Hard to say. She seems to be more domestic than a lot of women her age. She probably wants her baby-daddy to stay home, too."

"If we hurry," Stump said changing the topic, "we can get to the land by early afternoon. Might even find the coins before dark."

As they hustled down the highway they took turns making phone calls. Michael called her dad and Zax. Stump called Xander and Myles. And James continued to bombard Yana with unanswered text apologies and comments about how nice it would be to be married to her. But none of it worked.

Ultimately, they passed the Seifert truck stop where Stump and Xander stayed; then at Hays, Kansas, they headed north for the final stretch. A few minutes later, James got the call he'd been waiting for. "Hi, baby. Thank God you called. Are you okay?"

"How would you feel if somebody who supposedly loves you and your baby ran off?"

"I'd feel like crap, just like I feel right now. I won't ever do anything like this again. I miss you so much."

"Well, that's good to hear. I miss you too. Did you mean that part about getting married?"

"Yes. I don't want to be away from you like this ever again."

"It wasn't a very romantic proposal, but I guess that's understandable. If I were to marry you, there would be certain conditions, you know."

"I'll do anything. What do you want?"

"First, you have to control your compulsive behavior. Promise to never run out on me again."

"I promise. I promise."

"That's not all. You have to stop this detective stuff. It's too dangerous for a family man. I want you to do something else for a living. You can get a job or change schools and get a different major. Anything is okay, just so long as it doesn't involve guns."

James hesitated, but only for a moment. "Okay, I'll do it. Is that all?"

"No. There's one more thing; could you hurry back? I really do miss you — and love you."

"You're damn right I can. I love you, too." He hung up. "Yahoo," he screamed. "She's taking me back. You guys gotta take me to the KC airport to fly home."

76

After taking James to the KC airport and returning to Hays, there was not sufficient time for Stump and Michael to drive 35 miles north to Zurich and look for the coins. There was, however, plenty of time for Stump to imagine how that evening's sleeping arrangements would work out. "After losing my mother," he said at dinner and answering one of Michael's questions, "I used to have bad dreams, but it got better when I told myself that dreams are just vague, gray moments between the black and white of sleep and awake."

Michael grinned. "Sometimes you say profound things, like when you said you'd rather be with one woman many times than many women one time. Comments like that reveal a certain sensitivity that I love about you."

"Thanks, but I didn't come up with that comment. I heard somebody else say it and just thought it made sense. What do you want to do after dinner?" he asked, changing the topic, knowing full well what he'd like to do. "Catch a movie, or miniature golf or knock the hell out of some bowling pins?"

"Before we do any of those things, I think we should get to a motel before the cheap rooms are all taken."

"Okay. Same deal as before. You sign us in and I'll pay you back when I get my expense money."

Immediately after dinner, they pulled into an Econo Lodge on the edge of town. Stump drove Pops to the back of the lot and parked so he could easily watch his mirrors for her return and then sneak a cot into a room if it were necessary.

As he waited, he assumed the entire situation had to be awkward for her. After all, the only reason she came on the trip was to keep him and James from getting drawn into some stupid gun-moment. But now they were all alone. One boy, one girl, who'd shared a small amount of affection, but still hadn't been intimate; and now they had to fill their time somehow. He reminded himself that the mere fact that James was out of the picture didn't mean that Michael was obligated to do anything romantic. She might even be signing up for separate rooms, which would certainly signal that any intimacy was unlikely.

After a short time, he caught a glimpse of her coming his way. She appeared to be talking to herself. He slipped out of Pops to meet her at the cargo door where he could grab some of their gear and a cot if need be.

"Room 220," she said. "It's in the middle of the building."

Good. That meant she expected to share a room and they'd be away from the stairs and the foot traffic. Stump opened the cargo door and grabbed his backpack and then went for the cot to illustrate he wasn't taking anything for granted.

She put a hand on his arm. "You won't need that."

Stump paused and looked right at her. "If you're saying what I think you're saying, I've been wanting to do the same thing for a long time."

"I know. I'm not blind. I would have wondered why you didn't hit on me if you hadn't said you don't like one-nighters. That's when I knew if we hooked up too quickly, it would have felt cheap to you. I liked that."

"I don't hate one-nighters. It's just that—"

"Now we know each other better. I can't say I'm in love

with you, but there are things about you that I love and I can't say that about many people."

"I thought you'd be out of reach because of our ages."

"Are you kidding me? Don't you remember my background? I'm a female MP and a Marine. I don't adhere to other people's stereotypes—and neither do you, so . . . "

* * *

After dropping their gear off, Stump had a pretty clear idea where that evening was headed, but they'd just eaten and Michael wanted to go to a movie. There, they held hands, heightening Stump's anticipation. He could barely pay attention to the screen.

He imagined what it would be like to make love with the most complete and mature woman that he'd ever been with in that way. He wondered if they'd come together in a natural embrace or would it just happen more matter-of-factly. Would he see her naked or enjoy undressing her or would they explore each other's bodies in the dark?

The possibilities were more erotic than some of the real-life bedroom experiences he'd had, and some of those former occasions didn't last very long. Already aroused, he sure as hell didn't want little Stump to explode too quickly.

Then Michael squeezed his hand and rested her head on his shoulder. At some other time he would have simply savored the moment, but his mind had leapt forward to a couple hours into the future, when they would be alone. That was the experience he wanted to prolong, and there was only one way to assure that he would last long enough to please them both.

He excused himself, and marched out to the lobby where he slipped into the bathroom, and locked himself in a stall. Up until that moment, he'd always thought that perverts were the only ones who masturbated in public restrooms, but if he could get some relief now, he'd be able to last longer later, and that was what really mattered.

77

Stump lifted his head from the pillow and smiled. After the movie of the previous evening, he and Michael went to a small café for some ice cream. After they rehashed the events that led them to the midst of the country and what Edna Kline might do if they do indeed find the coins, they spoke admirably of the love that James and Yana held for each other. All of which served Stump like some kind of prolonged foreplay.

But finally, after returning to room 220 at the Econo Lodge, Stump turned off all the lights except for in the bathroom while Michael picked a song-list from her iPhone and placed it on the night table. The waiting was over. Stump kissed her and slowly backed her onto the bed where subdued moans of pleasure led to the removal of their clothes. For the better part of the next hour he and Michael entangled themselves in erotic pleasure and Stump was thankful that he'd made his earlier side-trip to the bathroom at the movie theater.

Now, following a decent night's sleep, the warmth that Stump felt for Michael had little to do with the physical world. He had no way to know where their relationship would go from there, but he knew he'd never forget Michael and that was all he needed. "I just thought I'd let you know," he said as they sat up and prepared to take a shower, "last night meant something special to me."

She tapped him on the nose with her forefinger. "Me, too."

A little later, when back in Pops and on the way to the land, Stump sent a text to James to find out how he any Yana were doing. "He can be obnoxious from time to time," Stump said to Michael, "but he's the most loyal friend I've ever had."

Michael nodded. "I get that. A lot of people never experience deep friendship."

The reply came back a few minutes later. "What do you know? He's happy and working tables at Egg-Zaklee's with Yana."

"Probably doing my job," Michael said. "I wouldn't blame Zax if she were upset with both of us."

"Me neither, but the way things worked out, it was fate. I had to do all I could to help Grandma Pauline and you wanted to make sure nothing bad happened to James and me; and then James went home. That's not a coincidence."

Michael shrugged and nodded.

They soon arrived at the barn in which Stump had helped deliver a foal. By the time he retold the story they'd made it to the area where he and Xander had killed one of the country's most notorious frying pans. "After that, we dragged that outhouse I told you about to a clean hole and drank some home brew."

"No wonder you and Xander bonded so well. Those are some pretty memorable events."

"It's just a little farther to Minnie's land," Stump said. "We better keep our eyes open for that blue van just in case."

They slowed slightly for the last couple miles, then uneventfully arrived at the land. A glance across the road to Herbert's cabin revealed no truck or dogs. Good. Stump would rather not draw attention to what they were doing. He pulled over, opened Pops's cargo area and retrieved the metal detector and a couple shovels. "The big tree stump is right over there."

"I see the rubble in the weeds."

"That's the second house. If I'm right, the first house was on the opposite side of the tree stump." He handed Michael the headphones for the detector. "Since you've used one of these before, why don't you scan the area, while I see if I can find the foundation."

She sighed and untucked her blouse from her shorts. "Too bad that tree isn't here now to give us some of that elusive shade."

For the next hour, Michael methodically waved her detector over dried-up Kansas earth, while Stump dug multiple exploratory holes in search of a foundation that nobody else knew existed. Finally, he hit something solid. He dug faster, deeper and wider until he unearthed a softball-sized stone. Excited, he scraped away more hard earth until his shovel clunked a similar stone a couple feet away, this one encased in a crumbly cement. His heart pounded as his lungs welcomed new air. "I think I've got it, Michael. Come see this. If we imagine a line between these two stones and dig a few more exploratory holes along that line, we should be able to find both corners of this foundation wall. From there we can figure out where the rest of the foundation is and then we'll have a good idea where a root cellar might have been."

"All right, but we gotta pace ourselves. This heat is dangerous."

A half-hour later, they'd found both corners to the first wall, approximately 25 feet apart. "This is totally awesome," Stump said, sweating like crazy.

"What are we going to do now?"

Stump pointed toward one end of the wall. "Based on the corners, we know which side of the wall was on the inside, which is where a root cellar, or a 'big hole' would have been."

"Okay, that makes sense."

"We can also assume that a foundation wall wouldn't go down much deeper than a couple feet and P-Pa probably hid the bottle behind one or two of the foundation rocks. So, all we gotta do is dig down, outside the frame, about a foot deep and wide enough for the detector to read below that. Since it can read down another 16 inches, it shouldn't take too long to check out this first wall. If we strike out, we'll work our way around one of these corners and check the outside of the adjoining wall. We may luck out and find it fairly soon."

Michael wiped her forehead. "I doubt it."

Another half-hour passed. Stump had removed his shirt and they'd dug the trench. "Let's hope this is it," he said. Michael donned her earphones, lowered the detector over the newly-made trench and swayed it back and forth from one end to the other. Finally, she shook her head and rested the machine.

"Anything?" Stump quizzed.

"Some minor blips and a grunt but no squeaks. That's what we want. What now?"

"Around the corner. Pick one of the adjoining walls."

Michael shrugged. "Fifty-fifty, I guess."

Another long, hot, sweaty hour passed before a second trench was born, outside the foundation, one foot deep and wide enough to accommodate a detector swaying back and forth. "If this doesn't work," Michael said while lowering the detector into place. "I think we should come back tomorrow."

Stump nodded and watched hopefully as Michael carefully scanned the trench all the way from one end to the other. "That's it. I say we call it a day," she said, lifting the detector up out of the hole.

"Holy crap," Stump said enthusiastically. "We might have been doing this wrong. When that machine is scanning, what kind of a radius does it read?"

"Same as the coil. About the size of a plate."

"When you just lifted it out of the trench it was like lifting a vacuum cleaner by the handle. The coil tilted quite a bit and for a split second the bottom of the scanner was aimed at the wall instead of down toward the dirt. The coins could easily be stashed in between a few stones. If we can turn the detector on its side we can scan the rock wall, too."

Michael shook her head and wiped her neck. "Alright. I guess it wouldn't take that long to check it out."

Stump gripped the coil while Michael held the handles. They tipped the detector on its side and lowered it to ground level, scanning the rocks instead of the dirt. As they moved the detector along the foundation wall, they carefully tilted it from side to side and up and down to scan the greatest possible area. Then, when they got back to the corner that they'd bypassed an hour earlier, Michael raised her head. "Wait a minute. I'm getting something."

Stump grinned as Michael chin-pointed to Stump's end of the detector. "Lift it up a little bit."

Stump followed her instructions.

"It's squeaking, all right," Michael said with a big smile of her own. Now we gotta rotate it 90 degrees, to get a different angle."

Stump carefully turned the coil as if he were driving a slow dump truck around a curve.

"That's it!" Michael said enthusiastically. "This thing's screaming like a cry baby. The readout says there is metal about five inches away. That's in the center of the wall, just like you guessed."

"Wicked!" Stump screamed. He grabbed the shovel.

78

Super-stoked, Stump attacked the dirt with his shovel. At 20 inches, Michael handed him a screwdriver. He lay on his belly and dangled his arm into the hole while Michael watched him work the screwdriver as a combination one-fingered claw and mini-jackhammer. Then one of the stones shifted under the pressure. Another shot of adrenalin encouraged Stump to work faster and harder until two rocks fell from their places.

"This could be it," he said, pumped up.

Michael rose as Stump carefully chipped out a few more clumps of dirt and then hit something that clinked. A jar. Strange grunting sounds escaped Stump's mouth as he clawed for several more anxious minutes.

Michael crossed her fingers and looked over her shoulders.

The last few clumps of dirt seemed to be put there to assure that the glass prisoner would never escape, but there was no way that Stump could give up. He kept chipping away and getting closer and closer to his goal. Then a slightly bigger lump of dirt gave way. "I can feel the jar," he said, impatiently. "It's lying on its side."

Michael stepped closer.

Suddenly Stump rolled over on his back. "I've got it, Michael," he said loud and proud, as he carefully rose up his hand to reveal a large Mason jar heavy and dusty.

He jumped to his feet. Inside the bottle, a couple rolled-up papers and about 30 full-sized coins, roughly half of them gold, caught their first glimpse of daylight in generations. Many of them looked as if they were bruised.

Dirty as the ground itself, Stump beamed and Michael wrapped her arms around him, "Congratulations, Stump," she said as they bobbed up and down in unison. "You were right. I'm so proud of you."

"Yeah, me too," a deeper voice said.

They turned to see two dogs and Herbert Happy, the neighbor, with his rifle pointed at them. "Congratulations."

Stump quickly hid the jar behind his back. "Hi, Herbert. You remember me, don't you? I'm Stump. The one who helped you move your outhouse."

"I know who ya are."

Stump shuffled his feet. "We would've dropped by to say hello, but your truck and dogs were gone."

"We was hunting. But I saw your silly vehicle. Decided to see what was going on. I've been watching you for hours. Thought you were nuts, but it appears you was smarter than I thought. It don't matter now, though. I need ya to set my bottle on the ground and step back so I don't have to shoot ya."

"No way," Stump said. "These coins belong to two elderly women."

"No, they don't. I got the rifle, not them. Those coins belong to me."

Stump glared at his former beer buddy. "That's not fair."

"Fair? I'll tell ya city people what's fair. You're gonna give me my coins, and I might just let you and your pretty girlfriend live to tell about it. That's what's fair. Now, set down my jar before one of you gets hurt."

"Give it to him, Stump," Michael said. "He means business."

Stump exhaled and then heard pebbles crumbling under the weight of an approaching vehicle. He pivoted to see the familiar blue van come into view.

"Looks like my partner's here," Herbert said. "Things just got worse for you two."

"Partner?" Stump said, while watching the van glide to the side of the road. "That explains a few things."

"Yep. My friend Franklin. He's the one what told me about the glass jar in the first place. Now do like I told ya and put the bottle of coins where I can see it."

Stump did as he was told and watched Franklin jump out of the van with a revolver in one hand and a cigarette in the other. Franklin hustled toward the others, scanned the situation and took a position off to the side, ten feet away from everybody else. "Looks like you found it," he said, waving his gun toward Michael and Stump.

"Yep, they dug it up for us," Herbert said, "and if they don't back away from that bottle, I jest might haveta kill the both of them."

Michael chin-pointed toward Franklin Kline. Why don't you take the money and get out of here? We won't turn you in. Honest."

"I ain't stupid, Bigfoot. Your good-doobie boyfriend would sing like a bird."

"But if you guys get caught," Stump said to Franklin, "everybody will know that you heard about the money from your mother and she could go to jail."

"Who cares? We both know my mother's a bitch."

"Don't tell me you'd double-cross your own mother."

"It don't matter. She's been skimming old folks for years. She can just go on doing that. But this bottle of coins belongs to Herbert and me."

Herbert swung his rifle back and forth between Michael and Stump. "That's right. And I'm getting tired of all this stalling."

"Oh really, Herbert?" Michael said. "I saw your bushy eyebrows rise up when your good buddy Franklin here drove up. You weren't expecting him. Worse, you still haven't figured out that if Franklin was a loyal partner, he would've called ahead and told you what was up. But he didn't say a word. Don't you get it, man? If Franklin is willing to dupe his own mother, he's planning to do the same thing to you."

Herbert cocked his head and turned toward Franklin just as Franklin's hand rose and his revolver went off skimming Herbert's right forearm, and causing Herbert to drop his rifle and grab for his wound.

Franklin quickly scooted toward the rifle and kicked it away, then turned to see both of Michael's hands wrapped around her Glock just three feet from his face. "You move an inch, you piece of manure," she said, "and I'll separate your head from your shoulders."

Stump jumped up and down. "Yahoo! You'd better listen to her, dude. She's an MP in the Marines and an expert."

"Not an expert, Stump. Just a 'sharpshooter,' but from this vantage point I can blow a hole through Franklin's ears and kill Herbert, too."

"Alright. Alright. I'm dropping my gun," Franklin said, bending and letting it slip to the ground.

"Good boy. Now slowly go stand next to your partner."

Herbert squeezed his forearm and shook his head. "Great job there, Franklin. You let a woman get the upper hand. Thank God you can't shoot fer shit."

"Shut up, you fucking hillbilly."

"Okay, Stump," Michael said. "Round up their weapons. The revolver first and don't get close to either one of these gentlemen."

"Gladly," Stump said, grateful to be on Michael's team. He carried out her instructions and returned to her side. "What now?"

"Before we call for help, go throw their weapons in the well. After that, get a clean rag from Pops so I can patch Herbert up. While you're at it, grab a rope if you have one. We'll all wait."

"Got it."

Stump grabbed the weapons, hustled over to the well and said bye-bye to both of them. Then he swung back near Michael and picked up the bottle of coins before hustling off to Pops. In the cargo area, he peeked at the bottle and its contents while Michael still had both hands on her Glock and two bad boys at her mercy.

Taking advantage of the moment, and remembering what Michael had just said, he dumped out the contents of the bottle, set the rolled-up papers aside and observed the bluish rings that encircled the outer edge of most of the coins. He smiled and returned the silver coins to the bottle, which left him with 16 large gold coins—the more valuable ones. He climbed farther into the cargo area and slid one gold coin after the other into a sliver of space between the built-in cooler and Pops's inside wall, as if he were loading a piggy bank. "I'm sorry there weren't many more, Minnie Moore," he said out loud as he dropped the last one in the slot, "but these babies ought to help."

79

After stashing Minnie's gold coins, Stump grabbed one of his T-shirts and his grandfather's .38, complete with its brand-new, overly-flashy holster. After wrapping the holstered pistol around his waist, he returned to Michael.

Still training her weapon on Herbert and Franklin, she smirked at his holster. "Any luck finding a rope?" she asked.

"No. But there's one at Herbert's cabin. I've seen it before."

"Okay, then, we're going to do one thing at a time. First off, Stump, I want you to stay 10 feet back from these guys. Draw your weapon and if one of them comes at you, blow a hole in him just like you've done hundreds of times at target practice."

Another bolt of adrenalin raced through Stump's body. Being careful not to reveal his excitement, he did as he was told and unlocked the safety. "Got it."

"Okay," she said, tossing the T-shirt to Franklin. "I want you to tie this thing around your partner's wound. Pull it tight, cause if he bleeds to death everything gets a lot worse for you."

Stump's heart pounded fiercely while he watched Franklin submit to Michael.

"Alright," Michael said to Stump, when Herbert's makeshift bandage was in place. "Holster your weapon again and call the County Sheriff's office. Tell them who we are and that we need two cars and an ambulance."

"Will do."

Minutes later, Stump's call reached the sheriff's office. "Hello, my name is Neal Randolph. I'm on a farm in Zurich with Sergeant Michael McFadden, a former MP in the Marines. I'm in law enforcement, too. I'm a student at Carlsbad College of Criminology in California." He proceeded to fill in the rest of the blanks for the deputy on the other end. When done, he returned his attention to Michael. "It'll take a half-hour to get everybody out here."

"Good enough," Michael said. "Now, we're all going to stroll up to Herbert's place to get that rope. The bad guys are going to walk right up the center of the road. The good guys will follow. Which side of the road do you want, Stump?"

"I guess I'll take the left."

"Okay, gentlemen, now we're going to take that walk. Remember, you each have a gun aimed directly at you."

"And I've been practicing," Stump said, proudly.

Fifteen minutes later, when Michael tied the final knot, Franklin scowled. "I'm going to have my lawyer charge you people with police brutality."

Stump snapped his .38 back into his holster. "We're not cops, dude. We're just a couple of people who knew how to wrap you two around an outhouse so you couldn't escape."

Michael tucked her pistol in a holster under her blouse. "Yep, standing on opposite sides, giving Herbert's 'little outhouse on the prairie' a big old bear hug."

"But it stinks, lady."

"Face it, Franklin," Herbert said from the other side of the outhouse, "after you realized you're gonna be charged with attempted murder you shit your pants anyway."

"Screw you, hillbilly."

Michael took another look at Herbert's temporary bandage

and adjusted it. "The EMTs can clean this up. You're lucky it wasn't a lot worse."

Herbert grinned. "I wish I could be there when Franklin tells his mommy that he messed up."

"C'mon," Franklin said to Michael. "You gotta have some sympathy. Just let us loose. You guys keep the jar and we'll all go our own way and have a good laugh. What do you say, ma'am?"

"Don't you mean *Bigfoot*? That's what you called me before."

"I'm sorry 'bout that. I didn't mean nothin'—"

"That'll teach you," Stump said. "You better make sure you know who you're dealing with before you start pushing people around." He gestured toward the area where they found the bottle and spoke to Michael. "I had no idea you were packing. Didn't even see you draw your weapon."

She shrugged. "I told you once before that the Glock is easy to hide. We were out in the open, looking for a legendary bottle of rare coins and our other weapons were hidden in the truck."

"I thought we'd have time to get to them if we needed to."

"I know you did and I was glad to leave them in your vehicle. While you were digging, I saw Herbert out by the road, circling behind us, but he had his rifle and it would've been too dangerous to confront him until he got closer."

"So you let him think he had the upper hand?"

"But I didn't know that Franklin was going to roll up and complicate everything."

Stump shook his head. "I don't know what I would've done if I was alone out here. I might have—"

"Now you know why I insisted on coming with you."

"You saved my life. You're amazing. You know that?"

"That's one thing you and I have in common. We think certain people are worth fighting for. But now I'm the one who has a problem."

"You do? What?"

"I gotta pee."

Stump grinned. "And we just tied off the only bathroom in the area. I guess that means you have to go behind Herbert's cabin. The last time you did that—"

"Don't remind me."

Shortly after Michael attended her business, the familiar crackle of tires on gravel indicated somebody was coming. "Two sheriff's cars and an ambulance," Stump said. "Just like you wanted." A moment later and still a fair distance back, all the approaching vehicles stopped.

Michael held her pistol in the air so the occupants could watch her lay it on the ground. "Okay, Stump. Slowly, take your holster off, and set it down."

Stump nodded and did as directed.

"Good. Now step back from the weapons and hold your hands a foot from your body so they can see your palms."

In an instant the sheriff and two deputies, all hatted and double-handing their weapons, emerged. The Sheriff's weathered face contrasted with those of his two younger subordinates, one of each gender.

"I'm Sergeant Michael McFadden, U.S. Marine Corps. I have another weapon in that Popsicle truck over there. This is my associate, Neal Randolph. There are two additional weapons in a well across the road." She pointed her thumb over her shoulder. "Behind us, two dangerous men are tied to that structure. One of them has a minor gunshot wound."

Taking Michaels lead Stump added, "I have another weapon in that truck too. It belongs to my friend, James."

"Where is he?" the Sheriff asked while his deputies scanned the area."

"In California."

"Don't listen to them, Officer," Franklin said. "These people stole my jar of money. That kid hid it in that Popsicle truck."

The sheriff looked at Stump.

"The coins are over there alright, but he's lying about who owns them. You can call Opal Clemens."

"Who's that?"

"Minnie Moore's sister-in-law. They both live in California."

"Who the hell's Minnie Moore?"

"The real owner of the land. She's eighty. Her father hid some valuable old coins over there a long, long time ago, but me and Michael found them for her."

"Don't listen to them, Sheriff. My mother and I have the right to those coins."

The sheriff shook his head. "I don't know what the hell is going on, but we'll figure that out in due time. I'm gonna need everybody's ID."

While one officer patted down Stump and Michael, the other checked the rope and knots that held Franklin and Herbert to the outhouse; then the female deputy cautiously scanned the area in and around Herbert's cabin. Satisfied, they motioned for the ambulance to come get Herbert. Moments later, Herbert and Franklin were cuffed and separated.

The sheriff nodded toward Pops and spoke to one of the deputies. "Get their guns, that bottle, their cell phones and anything else you think we might need for evidence."

80

"My name's Sheriff Boyd," the sheriff said sternly as he and a female deputy entered the interrogation room where Michael had been told to wait, alone. "This here's Deputy Leslie Campo," he added as both cops plopped their cowboy hats on the table.

The deputy slid a glass of water across the table.

"Thank you," Michael lipped. "Pleased to meet you both."

"I don't know how the Marines do things," he began, "but out here, away from the big city, we put a high value on shooting straight. So, we're gonna ask you a few questions and you're gonna give us the shortest answers without leaving out anything you think I'd want to know. If I have any follow-up questions, you'll answer them in the same way —brief and straight to the point. Got it?"

"Yes, sir. Wouldn't have it any other way."

"And, I don't need no editorializing, either. Now, if I find out you lied to me or left out anything that you shoulda told me, then we can find ways to keep you here for a long while. Do you understand me?"

"Yes, sir. Completely."

The sheriff nodded to his partner. "Go ahead, Deputy."

Campo leaned toward Michael. "Do you know why we're interviewing you first?"

"I'd guess ya'll have good manners and believe in ladies first."

"No. That ain't it. When we arrived on the scene, we could tell you were in charge. You appeared to be one of us and we wanted to give you the benefit of the doubt."

"Well. Thank you. I appreciate that. What do you want to know?"

"Start off by telling me your version of what went on out there."

"Sure. This all begins with Neal's grandmother," Michael said before filling in the blanks about Meadowlark Flats, Minnie Moore and a story of the hidden coins.

"What's your relationship with Neal?"

"He goes by *Stump*. We met a few months ago, hit it off pretty well and became friends. Now it's a little more than that, but nothing serious."

"Okay. Go on."

"Other people had looked for the coins before, but most of the interest died down; that is, until Neal found out that the land owner, Minnie Moore and his grandmother might get split up." Michael sipped down some water. "He's pretty smart. He figured out that everybody was looking for the coins in the wrong place. "He and James wanted to look in the new place so Stump got permission from the other owner of the land, Opal Clemens. Then Stump and I saw the same blue van that you saw by Herbert's place entering the parking lot at Meadowlark Flats."

"Why is that relevant?"

"Stump had seen the van near here before and got suspicious. He and James decided if they were going to look for the coins, they'd better bring guns—just in case, but neither of those guys had any experience with weapons in dangerous situations so I pretty much had to force myself into the equation—to make sure they didn't do anything stupid."

"So when you saw the van you knew you had competition for the coins and you all raced out here from California?"

"Not quite. At the time, we didn't know that Franklin was the son of Edna Kline, the woman who runs the seniors' community. But, we had a secret too: They didn't know that we were on to them, so we assumed they wouldn't be in a big hurry to get to Kansas. We also knew they didn't have the owner's permission to come get the coins so they planned to keep the coins for themselves."

The deputy and the sheriff traded glances. Then, "Go on."

Michael nodded and told them how the metal detector and James's relationship with Yana more or less wasted two days. "Stump and I still got there first and worked our asses off. Then when we found the coins Herbert came sneaking up behind us with his rifle pointed at us. That's when Franklin and the blue van rolled in. He drew a pistol and started throwing his weight around too.

"As it turned out, those two were partners, but Franklin was looking to double-cross Herbert. When Herbert understood what Franklin was up to, they had a flashy showdown, but Franklin shot first and hit Herbert's arm, causing the rifle to hit the ground. In the chaos I drew my Glock and ended the drama.

"I immediately had Neal dispose of their weapons and then we tied them to Herbert's outhouse until you guys got there. You know the rest."

"All of that for a jar of coins. Sounds a little far fetched."

"They could be valuable and Neal is a special young man. He'd do nearly anything for his grandmother's well-being. He's helped my father too and opened a restaurant for another friend of mine to run. He's big hearted. That's one of the reasons I like him."

"Alright," the sheriff said, "I'm gonna need contact information for this Meadowlark Flats place and Opal Clemens."

"I've never met her, but Neal has all of that in his phone and probably has it memorized."

"One last thing. Do you have a permit for your weapon?"
"Yes sir. I surely do."
"Okay, stay here. We'll get back to you as soon as we can."
"Got it."

81

"**O**kay Neal, follow me," Deputy Leslie Campo said to Stump as her keys clinked in the lock. Alone, Stump sprang to his feet. Getting out of that holding cell was the first not-bad thing to happen to him in hours.

After being searched at the land, everybody was split up. Herbert got cuffed to a bar in the ambulance and taken for medical treatment. The others were distributed in the squad cars. In one car, the sheriff and male deputy sat in the front while Michael was placed in a backseat, where a ceiling-to-floor heavy mesh fence-like barrier and the lack of door handles and window cranks made the area inescapable.

Deputy Campo drove the other car. Franklin was placed in the caged backseat. Stump got handcuffed to a bar on the shotgun door, and his feet were cuffed to a rod on the floorboard. No talking was allowed, not even to Deputy Campo.

During the ride, and fairly certain that everything was going to work out, Stump grew more and more grateful that Michael had insisted on coming. If it weren't for her, Stump would have been alone on that farm and there was no telling how the drama might have played out.

At the Sheriff's office, Stump was placed in a cold eight by ten pen that couldn't have been less hospitable: three walls of thick steel bars were tied together with a wall of a thick steel plate. Throw in a cement floor, one folding chair, no bed, no toilet, no window, no clock, and no internet and he was glad to get out; it seemed like he'd been in there forever.

Campo took hold of his arm and tugged him forward. "You'd best not give me a reason to tell the sheriff you've been a bad boy cause the sheriff won't tolerate that."

"No ma'am," he said shaking his head. "I won't give you any trouble."

Moved into a small conference room with a lone round table and three chairs the sheriff was already waiting; so was his hat, dead center on the table. "I'm Sheriff Boyd," he said pointing to a chair in the corner. "Sit down."

Stump looked to the chair and instantly remembered something he'd learned in one of his classes. They didn't seat him behind a table because it would be easier to read his body language this way. He sat and crossed his arms only to unfold them, not wanting to appear that he had a bad attitude or was hiding anything.

"First off," the sheriff said with his holstered pistol in plain sight, "I want you to know that once guns got involved, this charade jumped to a very serious level. I don't like people shooting guns at each other in my county."

"I didn't like it either," Stump said, "but those guys—"

The sheriff raised a hand, palm toward Stump's face. "Spare me the rant. I'm going to ask you some questions, and you're going to give me short answers without leaving out anything I'd want to know. If you lie to me, or leave out anything pertinent, you'll wish you hadn't. Got it?"

"Yes sir. I understand."

"Okay then. You said you're a student. That right?"

"Yes sir, at CCC, Carlsbad Criminology College. I'm studying to be a detective. When I was younger I solved some crimes so I was encouraged—"

"Stop. I didn't ask your life story. What's your relationship with the young lady?"

"Michael? We're boyfriend and girlfriend. I wouldn't have met her if she hadn't been arrested."

The sheriff and deputy traded glances. "Arrested? For what?"

Uh, oh. "Well sir, after she served her sentence the charges got dropped, so maybe I shouldn't have said anything about it."

"You're in no position to be pulling punches. We're investigating attempted murder here and your role in the matter, so you just answer my questions and I'll decide what's relevant or not. Now, I asked you about her arrest."

"Well, it's sorta funny, actually." Stump jumped into a brief version of the days before opening Egg-Zaklee's and how all of that led to meeting Michael. "When Zax found out that Michael got charged with obscenity for peeing in public, Zax said she'd had to do that kind of thing herself." Stump glanced at Campo, whose head bobbed as if she'd been there too.

"Anyway," he continued, "the judge eventually dismissed all the charges, so I probably shouldn't have brought it up."

"Any other charges for either of you?"

"No sir. I've solved some crimes but I don't commit them."

"What about your age differences? Has Michael bought alcohol for you while you've been in Kansas?"

"No sir, but Herbert gave me a homemade beer after we moved his outhouse."

"Outhouse? That one behind his place?"

"Yeah. That was the grossest thing I've ever done."

The sheriff made a couple notes. "Okay, tell me what happened out at the land."

After telling the bulk of his story, Stump said, "I didn't even know Michael had her weapon with her. But that's the kind of thing that makes us love each other."

The sheriff glanced at Campo and then back toward Stump. "Who is this Opal Clemens woman?"

"She's a half-owner of the land where Michael and I found the coins. The other owner lives with my grandmother in a memory care place. That's where I heard about the coins."

After Stump clarified the coin saga, he explained how he met Herbert and came to learn of the blue van. "That's when I figured out that Franklin and his mother also wanted those coins for themselves. Then when Michael and I found the bottle, we learned that Herbert and Franklin were partners. If it weren't for that, I sorta liked Herbert."

The sheriff nodded. "Okay then, I'm going to need contact information for Opal Clemens and this place where your grandma lives."

"Sure. In the meantime, can I ask you guys a favor? Please don't tell Michael that I told you about her record. She might be embarrassed."

"We don't make promises."

The deputy winked at Stump as if to say *don't worry about it.*

82

After a brief drive, Sheriff Boyd and Deputy Campo entered Herbert Happy's hospital room, where Herbert, wrapped arm and all, was cuffed to his bed.

"Don't get up on our account," the sheriff said, sarcastically. "We just want to ask you a few questions."

"Cut the humor, Sheriff. What do you want?"

"I'm getting to that."

Herbert sulked. "Yeah, alright, it's that Franklin Kline and his mommy who you want."

"I don't need coaching from you," the sheriff said, placing his hat on a chair. "Now, here's what's going to happen. I'm going to ask you some questions. You'll get the best treatment if you cooperate with me and make this easy on me."

"All I did was try to get something that was rightfully mine."

"And what would that be?"

"Those coins ya'll heard about. I've been looking for them for months. Hell, the folks what owned that land ain't been out this way in a decade. Then that lady and her young *boy-toy*—I'd met him before—wandered out here and in a matter of a few hours lucked out. Now I want ya to get my coins from those folks 'fore I gets a lawyer after ya'll."

"And just what makes you think those coins belong to you? You don't own that land."

"Don't matter no more. I heard that the owners quit paying their property taxes so that land's been abandoned. It don't belong to nobody. Since I've been working the hardest to find them coins, they belong to me."

"Who told you all that?"

"Franklin's mommy figured it out about six months ago. She sent him out here and we partnered up. But they never done any of the hard work, so I figured if I found it first—"

"You'd just keep it for yourself?"

"That's right. If there was big money, I could start all over someplace else. What's wrong wit that?"

"Well, I'm afraid you misunderstand a few things so let me tell you how the cow chews her cabbage. For starters, when somebody doesn't pay their property taxes they have years to catch up. Until then the county lets somebody else pay the taxes for them. After three more years, if the owner still hasn't caught up, that investor person gets a tax certificate and he's the new owner of the property. Do you have that tax certificate?"

"I got calluses on my damn hands," Herbert snapped. "That's what I got."

"I'll take that as a no. Secondly, I was talking with that Neal fellow. He told me that you gave him a bottle of home brew. Was he right?"

"What the hell you talking about? Him and his daddy dropped by and helped me with one of my chores. I was jest being neighborly. I don't recollect anybody complainin'."

"Not the point," the sheriff said, shaking his head. "You know that Kansas has the strictest liquor laws in the country. Hell, we still have a dozen dry counties. It was against the law to give a beer to a minor if you weren't his daddy."

Herbert grinned. "Well then, it looks like you got egg

on your face, Sheriff, 'cause I gave two bottles to that boy's daddy and that man was the one what gave over a beer to the boy. Why don't you have that pretty little lady cop of yours take me home now."

"Oh, that ain't gonna happen. I still have more charges to discuss with you. Our investigation revealed that after those city people found that jar, you snuck up on them."

"Yeah, so?"

"They say you had a gun aimed right at them and wanted to take those coins away. That's what we call attempted armed robbery and making death threats with a deadly weapon. People who get convicted of that crime go to prison, maybe for a long time. You ever been in prison?"

"I got in a couple a bar fights in my day and a truck race one time, but that don't make me no criminal. What else you got? So far it sounds like I'm gonna get off pretty light."

"Your toilet."

"My toilet? Now that's a good one, Sheriff. Don't tell me you and your team went fishin' in my urination station for evidence, cause that'd make my day."

"Nope. The county outlawed outhouses for personal residences some years back. Something tells me you knew that."

"What the hell difference does it make? There ain't nobody else within a mile of my place."

"The law is the law, Mr. Happy. You were supposed to put in a septic system and—"

"I ain't got no money for nothin like that, Sheriff."

"I guess that's another one of your problems. So far, we've got assault and conspiracy to commit robbery along with attempted armed robbery and making death threats with a deadly weapon, not to mention trespassing. Oh, and that septic system violation. The way I see it, you're looking at some serious jail time."

"C'mon, Sheriff. We both know that most of those charges don't amount to a hill of beans."

"I wouldn't be so sure of that. If you get convicted of half of those charges, you'll spend a few years behind bars even if this really is your first offense. But fortunately, for you, you never actually pulled a trigger, so we might be able to work together."

Herbert squared up, looked at the sheriff straight on. "I'm listenin'."

"I want to know more about this Franklin Kline fellow. He's probably going to the big house for attempted murder because he shot you. Your testimony would just about guarantee me a quick conviction and with elections coming up, that would guarantee me my job for another four years. What do you say?"

"What's in it for me?"

"I can't speak for the DA, but I could ask him to drop most of the charges and limit your jail time to three months and then give you some probation."

"What about my toilet?"

"We might be able to look the other way for a while."

"Herbert tapped his blanket. Then, "How long will it take to get out of here?"

"You'll have to spend the night, and post bail, but you might get out on your own recognizance. I might be able to get you home tomorrow afternoon."

"Alright, Sheriff. If you can get somebody out to my place tonight to feed my dogs, then you got yourself a deal."

"I'll see what I can do. Now I have a few questions about Mr. Kline."

83

"Just the man I wanted to see," a hatless Sheriff Boyd said to Franklin Kline as the first whiff of dinner chili filled the air of the jailhouse's interrogation room. "I hope you've found the accommodations to your liking?"

"I don't like chili and I don't like being caged like an animal."

"I'm sorry about that," the sheriff said. "I truly am, but we had some homework to do and you're not going to like what we found out."

"Oh?"

"That's right. We've been building an invisible box around you. A box from which you can't escape. You want to know what we found out?"

Franklin folded his arms. "Mostly lies, I suspect."

"The first thing my deputy did was look into the backgrounds of you and your friends—that makes up the bottom of the box."

"They're not my friends and you didn't find anything on me, did you?"

"Oh, I wouldn't say that. Then that box needed sidewalls—you know to hold everything together—so we had a little talk

382

with Mr. Happy along with that lady MP, Miss McFadden, and that college fellow—I believe his name is Neal. Turns out, most people don't like you very much."

"So what? I admit I'm not a choirboy. Let me make a phone call. My mother will post bail or get me an attorney or whatever I need to get out of here."

"I'll be coming to her in a minute, Mr. Kline, but I'm still telling you my box story."

Franklin rolled his eyes.

"No box is complete without a top; only this particular box is the kind that has flaps that fold in on each other. Then you can tape them up, nice and neat. You know the type."

"And your point?"

"As it turns out, the flaps of this particular box come from the college student. He led us to the ladies who own the land on which those missing coins were found. We checked that out too. The county seat is just down the road. Sure enough, that land is in their names."

"So what? I wasn't on their land."

"I know that. But the young man had their permission to get those coins, but you and Mr. Happy didn't."

Franklin shifted his feet.

"Now, you aren't going to like the next flap very much. It comes from your mother. I did indeed call her."

"Okay, then. What'd she say?"

"First I want to tell you, you've got yourself quite a cheerleader there. She even yelled at me."

Franklin smirked. "Welcome to the club."

"That was right after I told her I was about to charge you with attempted murder with a deadly weapon and I had evidence that she had conspired with you to commit robbery. But what really set her off was when I let something slip out about *abuse of the elderly* and, well, whooee, that woman has a loud and nasty tongue."

"You got that right," Franklin said with a smirk.

"But you know what, Mr. Kline? She didn't deny the

conspiracy issue." The sheriff leaned closer to Franklin. "You see how the flaps are folding in on you, Mr. Kline?"

The muscles in Franklin's jaw tightened.

"So all I needed to do after that was tape up the box. And that's where your partnership with Mr. Happy comes in. Before we knew it he told us all about your trips to the property and what all happened when those coins came out of the ground. That's when you rolled in and started waving your gun around. And every single one of the people said you shot your partner. Like I said before, that's what we call attempted murder around here."

"I didn't mean to shoot that old coot. He swung his rifle my way and I shot in self-defense. It was all just a mistake."

"That's for a jury to decide, but you're going to have a tough time overcoming those witnesses. The lady was an MP. The young man is in criminology school and has already solved a bunch of crimes. Pretty impressive, actually."

The sheriff leaned in and glared into Franklin's eyes. "Everybody folded on you, Kline, and the DA is going to like this case. In addition to attempted murder, we've got you for assault with a deadly weapon, conspiracy to commit robbery, attempted armed robbery, abuse of the elderly - we can probably come up with some more, like fraud and littering with your cigarette butts, but you get the point."

Franklin looked the sheriff in the eye and finally understood he was screwed. The color left his face. His fingers began to shake. "This is all my mother's fault. I didn't even want to look for those coins, but she had to push the matter, just like she always does."

"Well, I was pretty sure your mother put you up to the robbery but I don't know about the rest of what you're saying about her. All I know is, abusing seniors is very serious. Now, you and your box have already earned ten years of free storage in a cage. If you want to get out of that box and that cage a little earlier, this is your one and only chance to tell me what you've got on your mother. If you can give me something I can use, I just might be able to get the DA to remove the tape on your box a couple of years sooner. The more you give me, the more I give you."

Franklin rested his elbows on his knees and plopped his head in his hands. Finally, "She's been scamming old people and doing a whole bunch of heavy shit for a long time. Felonies, fraud, identity theft, forgery. Getting credit cards in their names. All of it. Lots of it."

"Alright then, I'll get us a cup of coffee. Then you can give me the specifics and how I can verify everything and I'll see what I can do for you."

Franklin sighed. "I can give you the number of her home office. That ought to help you."

"Now, That's a good fella."

"I wouldn't even be in this fucking mess if it weren't for my damn mother."

84

Stump held his hand over his eyes to block out the low-hanging sun. "How'd it go with Herbert and Franklin?" he asked Deputy Leslie Campo from the cage in her back seat.

"That's all being worked out now. I'm sorry it took so long to let you guys go, but even though your story was pretty credible we still had to verify that you had approval to be on that land. When Opal Clemens called us back and confirmed it we had all we needed."

"In a way it was sorta interesting." Stump said.

Michael shook her head. "I'm glad you think so."

"Regardless of all that," Campo continued, "I can tell you our DA doesn't like gun crimes and loves this case."

"I just hope everybody pleads out," Michael said, "so Stump and I don't have to return for a trial."

"You should get your wish. Happy already agreed to a deal the sheriff offered him, and once Kline found out he was in line for several felonies, he sang to cut his losses. Even pinched his mother, called her the ring leader and said she funded it all."

Stump lowered his eyebrows. "I can't imagine anybody squealing on his own mother—even Edna Kline."

"People don't like prison. Anyway, we'll have to see if

either of those guys gets an attorney who would rather fight it out in court."

"How likely is that," Stump asked.

"You never know, but they could get worse sentences if they go to trial."

"Thank God," Michael said. "That should mean we won't have to come back."

"Can I ask you something else?" Stump asked when they nearly reached Minnie's land. "My grandma's friend really needs her money. When do we get the rest of the coins back?"

"I imagine they'll hold them until everything is finalized. A month or so." Campo pulled up alongside of Pops, climbed out and opened the back door.

Stump slid out. "It was nice meeting you and the sheriff. I learned a lot," he said as the last few rays of daylight clung to the western horizon.

Michael rolled her eyes. "I coulda done without any of this."

The deputy opened the trunk and returned their cells and weapons sans the ammo. "I hope you don't need these again."

"Me too," Michael said, just before the deputy retuned to the driver's seat and drove off.

"What now?" Stump asked Michael. "We've got a 20-hour drive in front of us. You want to head for California, drive straight through?"

"I don't think I'm up for that, but I would like to clean up. Didn't you say that truck stop across the state line has public showers?"

"They did in the men's locker-room. I assume they'd have them for the women too. If not, we could always get a room and clean up in there."

"Okay, let's do that. After we clean up and catch some dinner we can head west until we want to stop for the night." She grabbed her cell phone, put it on speaker. Then, "Hi Daddy. I've been worried about you. Are you okay?"

"You're the one who's running around the country like a lost kitten."

"Stump and I are still in Kansas. We found the missing coins, which should help his grandmother. But we won't be able to get back to help you with your animals until late tomorrow."

"No problem. That attorney friend of Stump's said I can put up a few walls and stay over there on the same floor as the pusses. Once I do that, the new place will be more practical than my house. That'll teach the damn nosy neighbors to mind their own business."

Stump grinned and nodded.

"Another thing. I'm giving the house to you. It'd be yours sooner or later anyway. But you'll have to do your own decorating and remodeling — that is, if you want it."

Michael gasped and covered her mouth with her hand. "Oh my God, Daddy. I don't know what to say."

"Then just say 'good-bye' cause I got a lot of work to do."

"Wow! Okay, Daddy. Be careful. I love you. I'll see you when I get back. Bye." Michael hung up and turned to Stump. "Daddy hasn't been that pumped up in years." She scratched her head. "I don't know if I want his house."

"It's got a lot of character and there should be lot of contractors around, putting apartments in my building and the apartment for your dad's building. You could probably hire them and make it really nice."

"I guess I could get a loan. The payment could be cheaper than my rent is now."

"If you don't mind, I'd like to check in on Grandma Pauline."

"Yeah. It's too bad Minnie doesn't get her money for a while. I'd hate to see your grandma lose her sister."

Stump grinned. "No problem. After you said we were going to call the sheriff, I figured they'd want that jar for evidence, so when you sent me to Pops to get a rag, I took out the cow papers and the gold coins. All they got was the silver coins – the cheaper ones. Pretty clever, huh?"

"Oh, my God, Stump. I wondered what you meant while we were in the deputy's car and you said the 'rest' of the coins. If she would have put two and two together, you could have been charged with tampering with evidence."

"Well, it wasn't evidence yet."

"That's just a flimsy technicality, Stump."

"All that matters now," he said, punching speed dial, "is I want to check on Grandma Pauline."

After placing the call and getting reassurance that Grandma Pauline was doing well, Michael wanted to call Zax. "You want to listen in?" she asked.

"Yeah. Might as well."

Zax answered instantly. *"Hi Michael. What's going on? I'm very busy."*

"Stump's with me. We're on speaker."

"Hi, Zax. Sorry I took James and Michael away, but we found the coins. It's a long story."

"That's wonderful. I'm glad to hear that. James is helping out, so we're doing okay. I've got some other good news, too, but I don't have time to discuss it right now."

After they hung up, Michael addressed Stump. "That was weird. She had every right to be pissed off at us, but she actually sounded cheerful."

"Maybe she's got a new boyfriend."

"I guess we'll find out soon enough. It's your turn to make a call if you want."

"This is fun." He hit the speed dial, then speaker mode.

"Hey, Stump. What's going on?" Xander asked.

"Not very much. Me and Michael found Minnie Moore's coins. And we almost got shot and we spent the whole afternoon in the sheriff's office and I found out you can't use a cell phone in a real cell, which seems stupid. Oh, yeah, and James and Yana almost split up but they're back together. What's going on with you?"

"Wow! I hope everybody's okay now."

"Except for the bad guys. Me and Michael saw to that. One

more thing. I still want to invest a bunch of my trust money in that fracking deal."

"Oh. Myles and I talked about that. Neither one of us would want you to invest very much right now, Stump."

"But the commercial building is shaping up and the money I've set aside for Grandma Pauline, which is my safety net, hasn't really gone away. And you said this fracking investment is a good deal."

"It is. Otherwise I wouldn't have invested my own money in it."

"Okay, then, how much do you guys think I should invest?"

"Look, I'm all for this investment, but we can't go along with more than 50 grand until you finish what you've started."

"But that's not very much."

"That's the point, Stump. And we're going to want an update on how you're doing in school, too."

Ah, crap.

85

During the trip home, Stump made arrangements to meet Myles and Katherine at Meadowlark Flats so they could all be with Grandma Pauline at the same time.

Stump arrived at ten 'til nine, anxious to find out what had happened to Edna Kline. Inside, he checked in at the sign-in desk. "Can I ask you something?" he said to Wilma, the usual receptionist. "Is Mrs. Kline here today?"

"Yes, but she's been pretty busy lately. I don't think she'll have time to see you."

Hmm. Edna seemed unscathed by the goings-on in Kansas, but at the very least she should have found out that Franklin was in jail. Too bad Stump couldn't charge in and require her to catch him up.

"There you are," Myles said from behind Stump. "The man of the hour."

Stump quickly glanced over his shoulder then back. "Shh," he said to both Myles and Katherine, fingers to lips. He led them down the hall. "I know I told you that Franklin ratted out Mrs. Kline, but she's still here and nobody seems to know that she's in big trouble. I'm surprised the cops haven't picked her up."

Myles shrugged. "Sometimes the wheels grind slow."

"That might be your people there," Katherine whispered.

Stump spun around to see two men and three women, all formally dressed, marching up to the reception desk. "I'm Sara Shiller, from the home office," the shortest woman, with long straight hair said. "Is there anybody with Mrs. Kline in her office?"

"No. Not that I know of."

Myles whispered to Katherine and Stump, "I know that tall guy with the brown suit. We used to work together. His name is Danny Gregg. A good cop."

"You gonna talk to him?" Stump asked.

"Not right now. He's probably about to arrest your Mrs. Kline."

"This ought to be interesting," Stump said, as the cadre of suits and pantsuits with briefcases and file folders marched in unison toward Mrs. Kline's office.

Katherine watched for a moment, then pointed toward the community room. "I don't like this kind of thing. I think I'll wander into the big room and find Pauline."

"Good idea, K-Bear. We'll catch up to you pretty soon."

* * *

In her office, Edna got a ping indicating an internal call from the reception desk. "Yes, Wilma, what is it? I'm very busy."

"Sorry, ma'am, but I thought you should know that a Sara Shiller from the home office is going to be at your door in a few seconds with some other people."

Just then Edna's door opened. "Hello, Edna," Sara Shiller said, "I'm sorry to barge in on you, but these people have brought a few things to my attention and I wanted you to have a chance to respond."

Stunned, Edna scanned the group. "Respond to what?"

"First off, let me introduce you to everybody." Ms. Shiller pointed to the other woman wearing a blue skirt. "This is

Julie Meredith. She's our corporate attorney." Ms. Meredith nodded and laid her briefcase on Edna's desk. "The other three people are detectives," Sara added.

"Detectives? Does this have to do with my son, because I haven't heard from him in a couple days and I'm worried sick."

"No it doesn't, but the detectives know where he is. Let me introduce them." Shiller pointed first to the tall man. "This gentleman is Sergeant Daniel Gregg, This is Detective Francisco Lopez and Detective Kate Appleton."

The latter pointed at Edna's arm. "That's a lovely bracelet. Is it new?"

"I've had it for a while. Why?"

"We understand you have a lot of nice jewelry and clothes and such things."

"That's because I've worked hard and have to make a good impression on our residents."

"That's not how we hear it. Would you like to have an attorney before we ask you a few questions?"

"No. I don't need an attorney. What about my Franklin?"

"Alright, if that's what you want, I'll let Sergeant Gregg answer that."

The sergeant unbuttoned his suit jacket. "A few days ago, I got a call from a Sheriff Boyd in Kansas with some information he obtained from your son."

Edna's eyelids drew down. "What kind of information?"

"You can cut the theatrics, Mrs. Kline. We know that Sheriff Boyd told you about the charges facing your son: attempted armed robbery, attempted murder and more."

Edna backed into a chair and shook her head. "I don't know what's the matter with my baby."

"Right now this isn't about him, Mrs. Kline. I'm afraid you're not going to like what he had to say about you. He claimed that there's been a lot of fraud, embezzlement and elderly abuse coming out of this office – all done by you. What do you say to that?"

"No, no, no. There hasn't been anything like that. The sheriff must have misunderstood him."

"I don't think so. Franklin was very specific. He said he's gotten some money from ATMs and other items that you've gathered by various illegal means from residents' accounts."

Ms. Shiller leaned forward. "That's right, Edna. That's why we called in our attorneys."

Ms. Meredith tapped her briefcase. "We've all been working together. The detectives have spoken with several of the residents and verified your son's claims. There are additional residents we haven't gotten to yet."

"That's not all," the sergeant said, pointing to Detective Lopez, who opened a file he brought with him.

"Yes, ma'am," Lopez began. "I did a background check on you and had a bit of a rough time at first. I could track you back about 25 years but then I came upon something interesting, a newspaper clipping in Virginia. In it, a Mrs. Edna R. Kline – the real Edna R. Kline, a well-educated woman who had the same Social Security number that you use, died from a brain tumor."

The color went out of Edna's face as the detective continued. "That made me wonder who you really are, so I searched through old records in all the Virginia counties but when that didn't work, I widened my circle. An hour later I found what I wanted in Durham County, North Carolina."

Edna raised her hands to her ears.

"Your real name was Marjorie Sooth. Naturally, I wanted to learn why you changed your name, and I discovered that you got in some serious legal trouble about twelve years earlier - with your first husband. The two of you robbed a jewelry store where a guard got killed. You turned state's witness and your ex has been in prison ever since."

Edna's jaw visibly tightened.

"The bottom line is you found out about the dead Edna R. Kline and decided you'd rather be her than Marjorie Sooth, a failed jewelry store thief who ratted out her husband and never even graduated from high school."

"And you've been scamming people ever since," Sergeant Gregg said.

Edna went silent for a full ten seconds and then sighed. "Okay, I admit it, but what else was I going to do? I had a baby to feed."

The sergeant nodded to Detective Appleton, who reached for her cuffs and nudged Edna Kline's arm. "You're going to have to turn around, ma'am. You're under arrest."

"Please don't take me out in handcuffs. It'll shock the residents and they don't need the drama."

After a brief pause, the sergeant spoke to his deputies. "You guys read her rights, while I go out in the lobby and see if we can make a discreet exit."

"What about the cuffs?"

"Cuff her in front and cover her hands with a coat."

* * *

"There he is," Myles said before he and Stump hustled over to talk with his former colleague. "Hey, Gregg, you remember me? Myles Cooper."

Caught off-guard, the sergeant spun around and looked at Myles. "Of course I do, Cooper. What are you doing here? This isn't your district."

"My mother lives here. I take it you're arresting Edna Kline?"

"You got it, only that isn't her real name. How'd you know about her?"

"You got a tip from a sheriff in Kansas. That sheriff heard about the case from my son, here. This is Neal Randolph, but he goes by Stump."

"I'll be damned," Danny Gregg shook Stump's hand. "Are you the one in detective school?"

"Yes sir. I go to CCC."

"I saw your name in the file, but you guys have different last names."

"I'm adopted."

"Oh, yeah, I remember that now. Your dad is right. We never would have heard of this case were it not for you and that Marine." He glanced up the hall toward Edna Kline's door. "You guys are going to have to excuse me. My partners are ready to take Kline outside. Let's get caught up later. You won't believe Kline's backstory."

Just then, the woman everybody knew as Edna Kline and the others paraded out to the hallway with Edna's wrists hidden by a sweater. "I bet you're happy now," she angrily said to Stump as she walked by.

"No, ma'am. I feel sorry for you. Every mother deserves to have children who love her, but you don't even have that."

86

Later that day, and still buzzing from Edna Kline's arrest Stump followed up on his promise to help Catts McFadden. "Phew!" he said as he fanned his nose and entered Catts's home "It's me, Stump."

"I'm back here, Stump. Behind the shelving."

"Hi. Do you mind if I open a couple windows?"

"Please do. I keep thinking I'm going to get all the pusses moved and then clean up, but it's taking longer than I expected. Now I've got two places that need me." His tone was delightfully perky.

"I can clean out the litter boxes if you show me what to do."

"That's too much to ask. I'll tell you what. I'll clean up the litter boxes, while you break down these shelves into manageable sections. Then we can carry them up the street in a little bit."

"Gladly. We can use Pops to haul things. That'll save a little work."

"You know the best part of all this? The perverse justice. My smart-ass neighbors have always been threatening me, but now I get to stick it in their faces and there's nothing they can do about it."

"They should be careful what they wish for."

"I'll still have ceremonies and give the pusses away to anybody who'll provide safe homes, but they can stay with me forever if they need to."

"That's the best of all worlds. I'm surprised you didn't think of this earlier."

"It crossed my mind, but I wasn't ready to leave my house and I wouldn't dare leave the pusses alone at night. They need me."

And Catts clearly needed them.

After cleaning out the litter boxes and disassembling the shelves Catts and Stump moved several loads of shelving and furniture from his home to his commercial facility.

Then, in the late afternoon when the rush at Egg-Zaklee's calmed down, Stump traipsed over for a meeting that Zax had requested with him and Michael.

"She's probably pissed because the three of us left her shorthanded," Stump said to Michael while they waited at a table in the back of dining room.

"I dunno, Stump. She said it was a non-stop fire drill around here until James got back and lent her a hand, but she didn't really seem upset about it."

"Whew," Zax said from across the room. That was another hectic day. She glanced at Stump. "I bet you're still flying high."

"Yep. Edna's gone and I'm going to meet Minnie Moore's sister-in-law at a coin store. If the coins are worth enough money, Minnie won't have to leave Meadowlark Flats and that will ensure that my grandma is happy. That's all I really wanted."

"The reason I asked you guys to meet me is a few days ago I got a call from the home office of the Waffle House restaurant chain. Apparently, they heard about us from all the publicity."

"Really?" Stump said, cocking his head. "That's rad."

"Then while you were gone, two of their bigwigs came to

398

see our place. They want me to come to interview for them. Did you know they have 2,000 restaurants, mostly in the southeast?"

Shocked by Zax's comments, Stump widened his eyes. "But you already manage a restaurant and it's way better than those chain places."

"They want me to spend two months in their experimental kitchen, where they try out new recipes. Then I'll probably be an assistant quad manager over 20 stores in Pensacola or someplace else."

"Florida?" Stump said tilting his head. "But you've always been in California. This is where you belong."

"That doesn't mean I have to stay here forever, Stump. I'd have a good salary and benefits and a real vacation for a change. God knows I could use a break from all the stress."

"That's for true," Michael said.

"But you'd still have stress, Zax," Stump said in protest. "It would just be different."

"Maybe, but I could pay my bills and I'd work reasonable hours and be with Denise a lot more. My interview is Monday. I get to fly first class, like somebody important, for a change."

Stump slumped in his chair. "I suppose I should be glad for you."

"Michael can run this place while I'm gone. After that, if I get the job, she can replace me permanently. I'll sign anything you want to relinquish my rights to this place. I just wanted to tell you what was going on. Now, I need to get back to the kitchen. James is all alone and could use some help."

Michael and Stump traded glances. "I guess I should be pleased for Zax," Stump said, "but it's like trying to be happy for your girlfriend after learning she found a better lover."

Michael smiled and rested a hand on his forearm. "Well, she hasn't had an offer yet."

"She'll get one. She's really good at this business. That was why I tried to help her."

"I don't want to add fuel to the fire, but just so you know, I'm willing to fill in while she's out of town, but I don't want the responsibility for running this place on a full-time basis."

"Yeah. I get that. It's a big job. I don't want to run it either."

"I'm sure we can find somebody else. Maybe James will do it."

"I dunno. Maybe I shouldn't have bought this building."

"Then you wouldn't have met me."

"Yeah. That's the best thing to come out of all of this. You make it all worthwhile."

She smiled. "You have no idea how loveable you are."

"Loveable, huh? Sometimes love is painful. My mom. Grandma Pauline. Now Zax. They all leave holes."

"True, but holes can fill in. You've got me and Daddy and Xander and a new family."

"I was going to ask you to go with me tomorrow to meet Opal Clemens at the coin store and then to see Grandma Pauline, but now it looks like you'll be too busy."

"It's the weekend," she said nodding. "Zax will need all the help she can get and I promised to help Daddy. Maybe another time."

"I guess that makes sense. Have you decided if you're going to move into your father's house?"

"If I can get a loan to make improvements. They have some special loans for vets."

"That's one good thing. After we get both of our places put together, we'll live right across the alley from each other and can get together when we want to."

She tapped his nose. "I'm not that kind of girl, mister."

"Yeah, right," he said enjoying her playful nature once more. "Can I ask you something else, before you go back to work? Do you think you can help me with some of my homework? I still like solving crimes, and I was proud to tell that sheriff what I do, but classes and bookwork are dull. It'd be easier if you were close by."

"I think you ought to take me to dinner tonight so we can talk it over—only this time bring the Spider. It's a little classier than Pops."

87

"They're called double eagles," the gray-haired numismatist, named Bernard Fisk, said while examining Opal Clemens's gold coins. "You looking to sell them?"

"I wish I didn't have to. They meant a lot to my family, but we need the money now."

Stump used the rolled-up papers that he'd gotten from the jar of coins to point at his fave. "That one is over a hundred years old."

"Age isn't a huge factor when valuing coins like these. Rarity and condition, which involves a grading process, are usually more important. All of these have been circulated, with some of them very worn and scratched up, so there's not a lot of value beyond the gold price, unless you happen to catch somebody who's trying to complete a set. Even then, they wouldn't pay much of a premium."

"Why do they look bruised?"

"That's called toning. Some people look for that and these are nice."

"What are they worth?" Opal asked.

Bernard looked at one coin in particular. "This one, from

1905, is an AU-50. I could probably get $1,650 for it. The rest would sell for $1,450 each, but I couldn't pay more than $1,250 for them and still make a profit."

"Well that's $20,000," Stump said. "Still a lot of money."

"I might be able to give you a little more if you'll sell them on consignment," Bernard added. "That way I won't have to tie up my own funds in them. It just depends on whether you want your money all at once or if you're willing to be patient and get a little more over a few months."

"What happens if gold prices go up or down?" Stump asked.

"If I buy them from you, that's final, no matter what gold does; but if you put them on consignment and gold goes up, you'd get the difference, but—"

"If gold goes down," Stump interrupted, "our price would drop."

"Like I said, most of the value is in the metal."

"I don't want any risk," Opal said. "Twenty thousand dollars means Minnie could stay where she's comfortable for nearly another year. That's what matters."

Stump agreed, then spoke to Bernard. "We have a similar number of silver coins, but we don't get them for a while."

"Once again, if they're scratched up like these specimens they're not worth much more than the metal value, although the toning might help. You might be looking at an additional $600 for the lot, unless they're of low mintage, but I wouldn't count on it."

Opal rested a hand on Stump's shoulder. "I might give the silver ones to you as a reward, and to cover your expenses. You're the one who made all this possible."

Stump grimaced. "I might take one as a memento, Mrs. Clemens, but I'd rather use them to keep Grandma Pauline and Minnie Moore together as long as possible."

"We can cross that bridge later, but for now, I'd prefer to get all the money right away."

"Okay," Bernard said. "You can follow my wife down to the bank right now if you want to."

"What about these?" Stump asked, handing the man the rolled-up papers. They were in the bottle too. Do you know what they are? They're faded and we can't make them out."

"I doubt if they're important," Opal said with a smirk. "They're supposed to be about some silly *magic cows.*"

"Magic cows, huh?" Bernard said, grinning. "Now we're talking about something that really is rare."

Stump smiled too. "We heard that her relative did a favor for some guy who wanted to repay the favor with some fast-growing cows. It's a fun family story, and these papers could explain it all."

"I'm not an expert conservator, but I can take a look." He opened a drawer and grabbed an aluminum headband with a magnifying glass attached and pulled the glass in front of his eye. "This thin page looks like a handwritten note." He pinched the other paper. "This one is thicker. If you gently drag your fingers across it, you can feel that the printing was embedded in the paper, but I can't read any of it. A restoration expert might be able to make some sense out of it. I just don't know."

"I think it might be the deed to P-Pa's farm," Opal said.

"Could be. People don't usually use paper like this or embed the printing for day-to-day uses. Did anybody from your family get a law degree or a diploma from a big-time university?"

Opal scoffed. "No, they were just modest farmers."

"Well, I know a few document experts. One of them used to work at the Treasury Department and has some pretty good equipment. I could probably get him to take a look at it."

"That sounds good," Opal said, "but I don't want to do it if he charges anything."

Bernard hesitated a moment. Then, "Well, since you're a new customer now and you've triggered my curiosity, I might get him to take a quick look for free, as a professional courtesy."

"That should be okay," Stump said, mostly to Opal.

"If it's not going to cost anything—"

"Okay then, I'll let you know how that goes. In the meantime, I'll have to get your information for IRS purposes."

IRS? There was that dirty word again. "What do they have to do with anything?" Stump wondered out loud.

"Probably nothing, but they monitor large cash transactions, just in case you're a terrorist or laundering money. So I need you to fill out this info card and I'll tell my wife to start up the jalopy. I'll call you both when we have more information about your document."

88

"I don't know about you," Michael said as she served Stump his breakfast at Egg-Zaklee's, "but it just isn't the same around here without Zax."

"It's not what I envisioned when I bought this building. That's for sure," Stump said as his phone buzzed. "It's Opal Clemens. Must have something to do with the magic cows. Hi, Mrs. Clemens," he said. "Do you need something?"

"I got a call from Bernard at B and L Coins. He'd like me to meet him at his store this afternoon. He said it'll be worthwhile. You can come if you want to."

"Sure. He's not real far from Meadowlark Flats so I can get by both places while I'm up that way."

After hanging up, Stump spoke to Michael. "I gotta go to the coin store this afternoon. You want to go along?"

"I wish I could, but I told Daddy that I'd come help him design some brochures for his *one-man museum* after I get off here. You could take James though. Our new cook should be okay and I doubt if Yana will mind."

Several hours later, Stump and James arrived at the coin

store where a half-dozen people had gathered, including Opal Clemens, Mr. Fisk and his wife plus two men and a woman with a very nice camera. James patted Stump on the back. "I wish I coulda been with you when you found that jar dude."

"Me too bro. What's going on?" Stump asked one of the men. "Is this about the paper I left here?"

"We're doing a story."

"Media guys?" James asked. "Do you know Irv Wedlock? He's a friend of ours."

"He's TV. We're newspaper. My name's Hector Gonzalez. That's Stacy Prepper behind the camera."

After Stacy smiled, Bernard Fisk walked over with a bearded, studious-looking fellow. "Hi Neal. I'd like to introduce you to my document specialist, Shaffer Ryan. You're going to like what Shaffer has to say. I guarantee it."

Shaffer shook Stump's hand and nodded at Opal Clemens. "I've got bad news and good news for you folks. The bad news is I'm going to have to charge you $700 for looking at your papers. It took more work than I expected."

"But I thought you were going to look at them as a professional courtesy," Opal said.

"It depends on what I have to do. It took a long time to decipher what you had there. We determined that the thinner paper was a hand-written note from a famous person. Here's what it says."

"Dear Mr. Clemens. I know you said you don't want any compensation for saving my son's life, but maybe I can do something else for you and your family. The other night I helped my friend, Mr. Ernest Woodruff, put together an ad campaign to promote his product at the ballpark. As usual, Mr. Woodruff paid me for my services with some stock in his company and I am passing that certificate along to you. Please find enclosed 3 shares of the Coca-Cola Company. Someday it might help somebody in your family, like you helped mine. Sincerely, Ty Cobb."

"Ty Cobb?" Opal said instantly. "Wasn't he a famous baseball player?"

"One of the best of all times," Shaffer said. "His signature, in good shape, is worth thousands. This hand-written letter has value too, maybe enough to pay my fee, but it would have been worth more if it were more legible."

Stump looked toward Opal and puckered his lower lip to suggest he was sorry.

James nudged Stump. "That's still pretty rad."

"All of this leads us to the other paper," Shaffer continued. "Based on Cobb's note, I did a little more research. The original Coca-Cola stock came out in 1911. Then, in 1919, Ernest Woodruff, who we just heard about, bought the company and issued 25,000 new shares so they could expand. Your thick paper is a certificate from that group. Your shares aren't as valuable as the original group, but you're still going to be happy."

Opal shuffled her feet. "Well, I can sure use some good news."

"A guy like me doesn't see many documents like this so I dug a little deeper and found an old bulletin from the church that Mr. Cobb and his family attended in Atlanta, where all this took place. Apparently there was a colossal rainstorm and one of Cobb's sons took the family car, a Model A, for a ride but it rolled over and pinned the lad underneath the car, where he nearly drowned. Then two men showed up and lifted the car off the youngster, saving his life. The heroes were offered a cash reward but one of them said it wasn't right to be paid for doing the Lord's work. Obviously, that man was your ancestor. What did you call him?"

Opal smiled. "P-Pa or Pappy Med."

"Anyway," Shaffer resumed, "in those days Ty Cobb was notorious for taking stock in lieu of cash whenever he did promotions. He had an especially good relationship with Mr. Woodruff and accumulated several dozen Coca-Cola certificates just like yours.

"Intrigued by all this, I called the pastor of that congregation who has used the Good Samaritan message several times in his sermons. Apparently Mr. Cobb gave the note and your certificate to a trusted friend and sent him out to your P-Pa's farm, which would have taken a week to get out there."

"That's really rad," James said.

"We're just getting started. Now we come to the certificate. It is indeed three shares of stock in the Coca-Cola Company."

"Now it makes sense," Opal said with a hand to her cheek. "When Minnie was little and heard about *fast-growing stock* she wouldn't have known anything about stock certificates, so she must have assumed they meant livestock like some of the farmers had."

"I think your P-Pa might have thought that, too. At the time, the shares were worth $40 each. A full-sized cow was worth $70 and weighed a half-ton. Your P-Pa wouldn't have any way to get three head of livestock to his Kansas farm, and if he went to Atlanta to sell them, he'd lose a few weeks of work and have to pay expenses. So in addition to his unwillingness to accept a reward, it simply wasn't practical."

"And he died a few years later," Opal said.

"How much is the stock worth now?" James asked.

Stump had been wondering the same thing. "I hope it's enough to buy Mrs. Moore a few more months in the nursing home."

"That shouldn't be any problem," Shaffer said with a jack-o'-lantern grin. "Ever since Warren Buffet spent 600 million dollars on Coca-Cola stock in 1988, the price has been steadily rising."

"How much, dude?"

"According to a recent article–I can give you the link—with splits and reinvestment of dividends they've grown quite a bit."

"You're playing with us, dude. How much?"
Shaffer looked at Stacy. "Get ready."
She aimed her camera at Opal.

"How does twenty-two thousand sound?" Shaffer asked Opal.

She lifted both of her hands to her cheeks. "Twenty-two thousand dollars? That's fantastic."

Stump rose to his tiptoes. "That means she can pay for another year and Grandma Pauline—"

"I'm afraid you people don't understand. I'm not talking about twenty-two thousand dollars. I'm saying twenty-two thousand 'shares.' At $42 each, that's about nine point three million dollars, give or take."

Opal's jaw dropped and the camera flashed.

"I call b.s., dude," James said. "There's no way these three shares of stock are worth that much money. It ain't possible."

Shaffer nodded. "You're right and wrong, young man. These three shares aren't worth nine million."

"Oh, I knew it was too good to be true," Opal said softly.

"The truth is, each one of your shares is worth that much. The total reward for your P-Pa's good deed has grown to nearly twenty-eight million dollars." He turned to James. "And you can look it up, dude."

James slipped out his cell and began a search.

"Yes," Stump yelped while thrusting a tight fist as high as he could. "All I ever wanted was to make sure my grandma's last years were happy ones and now that's guaranteed."

"I don't know what to say," a smiling Opal said, obviously stunned.

Stump exhaled a very deep breath. "I can't believe I almost threw those papers away."

Stacy caught a few more pictures before Stump recalled one of his previous problems. "Wait a minute. I bet there's a lot of taxes?"

Bernard chuckled. "I'm afraid so. Federal and state taxes will add up to around 50%."

"Damn government," Stump said having a little more empathy for how Myles got caught off-guard over the previous tax matter. "But that still leaves 14 million for

Minnie and Opal to split up. They could buy Meadowlark Flats with that kind of money."

"All you have to do is take your certificate to a stock broker with my letter of explanation. They'll want to verify my findings, but you should have your money in 90 days. And that's why I'm charging you folks $700 for my services."

"I'll be damned," Stump said. "Minnie Moore must have heard something about Coca-Cola being important when she was a kid and subconsciously clung to that idea ever since."

"He's right," James said to Stump, holding up his cell. "Over nine mill for each of those shares."

"There really was some magic," Opal whispered, fanning her face with a piece of paper worth 28 million dollars - more or less.

"I'm surprised you came with me," Stump said to Michael. "Are you kidding me? In the brief time I've known you, you've bought an old building, put in an off-beat breakfast joint, plus found two bodies and a jar of gold and silver coins. Then yesterday, I missed seeing a woman discover that her family is worth millions. I don't want to miss seeing Minnie Moore's face when she finds out she was correct about her father's treasure."

"Don't forget handcuffing two bad guys to an outhouse. We both did that."

She chuckled. "That too."

"Shaffer Ryan said it's just a matter of time until the stock certificate is validated. Then Minnie Moore and Opal Clemens can pay the taxes and split up their money."

"How wonderful. Do you think Minnie will actually understand what all happened?"

"Hard to say. Sometimes the Memory Care people surprise me."

After congratulating Tamara on her promotion, to Edna Kline's former position, Stump and Michael soldiered into the community room and located Grandma Pauline holding hands with Minnie Moore, who had her ever-present Coke bottle in her lap. "Hello, Grandma. Hello, Mrs. Moore. It's me, Stump. This is Michael. You've met her before."

"Do you work here?" Grandma Pauline asked Michael.

"No, ma'am. I'm Stump's friend. We're here with some good news for Mrs. Moore."

"Have you seen my glasses?" Minnie Moore asked. "I think that man over there hid them."

Michael delicately rested her hand on Minnie Moore's forearm. "You're wearing them, honey."

"I am? I don't trust that man. He dances."

Stump grinned. "Do you remember what you told us about your P-Pa, Mrs. Moore?"

"He was here yesterday, you know."

"I mean about the secret jar he buried on your old farm. Do you remember the magic cows?"

Minnie turned her head from side to side. "That sounds familiar."

"Well, we found the information about the cows," Stump said, realizing it would have been impossible to explain the difference between three shares of fast-growing stock and three head of fast-growing livestock. "The important thing is you were right about that treasure. It was very valuable."

"Have you seen Ellen?" Grandma Pauline asked.

"No, Ellen's not here today, Grandma."

Minnie Moore looked closely at her Coke bottle. "What's this?"

"It's your Coke," Michael said. "It's probably warm. Would you like me to get you another one?"

Minnie Moore frowned and set the bottle on the end table. "Get that thing away from me."

Stump traded glances with Michael and shrugged. "Are you sure, Mrs. Moore? You've always liked Coke."

"I have not. That stuff is for children."

Michael grinned and placed the empty Coke bottle in

her purse, then spoke to Stump. "I'm going to put this in a shadow box so you can keep it forever."

Pleased, Stump hugged his grandmother. "Now, you and Mrs. Moore can stay together for a long time."

* * *

Late that Friday night after Stump and Michael had cleaned out nearly everything from Catts's home sans a few pieces of furniture, Stump plopped into a love seat and sighed. "Do you think things will ever get easier?"

"I dunno," Michael said, sitting on an armchair off to his side. "We've been through a lot lately, with Egg-Zaklee's and that trip to Kansas and Daddy."

"For a while there I was thinking about beginning an urban renewal project for the downtown area, but I have way too many other things to do first."

"Like meeting the rest of your family?"

"Yeah, that's a biggie. Xander's going to bring the core family out next week. I can hardly wait."

Michael paused a few seconds. Then, "I have something to tell you, Stump. I thought you ought to know that an old boyfriend showed up at work yesterday. He wanted me to go to Europe with him."

Stump's stomach tightened. "What did you say?"

"I said *not now*, and that I'm in a relationship, but I thought I should tell you just to keep the *wrinkles out of our pillows*, as Daddy says."

Stump grinned. "I'd be sad if you left."

"That won't be happening for a while. I've been thinking about turning this place into a B&B. Of course, we won't make breakfast for the guests. We'll simply give them a voucher to eat at Egg-Zaklee's."

"We?"

"Yeah. You can help me run it."

"Well, I might be willing to help on a part-time basis, but

since I met you I've learned a lot about guns and life outside California and that nearly anybody can be a bad guy, even women, and other things. I've also decided to take school more seriously."

"Oh, really? What makes you think they'll let you back in after all your attendance problems and flunked classes?"

"I'll just explain what I've been doing. It shows I have an interest in what they teach. Heck, I can offer to make a large donation if I have to. The money I got from selling the jet could help with that."

She moved next to him on the loveseat. "Now that we've got all that figured out, how would you like to move into this place? It's plenty big enough for both of us."

"Interesting. Where do you envision me sleeping?"

She grinned. "You can have your own room or I'm open to other suggestions."

"Ooh. I was hoping you'd say something like that. I gotta admit I like the idea of living with the most dynamic woman I've ever met. But it's intimidating to know what a bad-ass you can be. What if I misbehave?"

She scoffed. "You're the one who's dynamic. You change more lives than anybody I've ever met."

"Well, then I guess it's worth a try, but I have to tell you, I've never lived with anybody before. Except family and James and Yana."

A loud knock came from the front door. "It's almost dark, he said. "You expecting company?"

"No. Come with me," she said tugging him to the foyer and opening the door.

"Are you Stump or Michael?" the visitor asked while hosting a large insulated bag between his feet.

"Who wants to know?" Michael asked.

"I'm an Uber driver. I have something for you." He bent over, unwrapped his insulated package and produced a large pink box with a wide red ribbon and bow. "It's breakfast-in-bed."

Michael grinned at Stump. "How sweet of you."

"Not me. I had nothing to do with it." Maybe her old boyfriend had sent it.

Michael took the package while Stump slipped the driver three bucks and then followed her into the kitchen.

"Oh, my God," Michael said at first glance, "This is incredible. Here's a bottle of sparkling juice, plus a scented candle, and some pretty red napkins and a single oversized Hershey's chocolate kiss."

"What's in the Styrofoam containers?" Stump asked as he reached for both of them and flipped open the first lid. Michael smiled. "Two heart-shaped, pink pancakes. How lovely."

"They're still warm." Stump flipped the lid off the other foam container and pulled out a can of chilled whipped cream. "That's a lot more than we'll need for two pancakes."

Michael chuckled. "I think that's intentional. Here's a card."

"Who's it from?"

"How precious. Listen to this:

This Sweetheart Special is for two of my all-time favorite people. Love, Zax."

ABOUT THE AUTHOR

Like most Americans I liked my career of several decades but I have to admit that I didn't always approach the mornings with wild enthusiasm.

But then, I retired and discovered something I never would have guessed: When the day is mine, I love to get up even earlier. Now I'm the guy who wakes up the rooster. I still work as much as I ever did, only I now work on things that bring me a different form of compensation. Like writing books.

Some have asked me where I get my ideas, but it's no mystery. I had a storied youth with six sisters and a wild family. When I wasn't engulfed in that world, I spent a fair amount of my time wandering the alleys and streets of our neighborhood. A fellow learns a lot from all of those people even before he arrives for his first day of school. If he has the ability to recall the characters and the activities in which they engaged, and blend that with a dash of make-believe, there's a goldmine full of fodder from which to draw his inspiration.

BOOKS BY THIS AUTHOR

NON-FICTION

Instant Experience for Real Estate Agents
(Multiple Award Winner)

Stop Flushing Your Money Down the Drain
(Multiple Award Winner)

FICTION

Three Deadly Twins
(Available on Amazon)

Monday's Revenge
(Available on Amazon)

Grandma's BFF Does Coke
(Available on Amazon)

Zero Degree Murder
(to be released in 2019)

All books available in paperback or ebooks

**Books may be ordered from
Amazon or other online bookstores**